VOID'S VENGEANCE

DEATH'S DISCIPLE: BOOK FOUR

EMMA L. ADAMS

DEATH'S DISCIPLE:BOOK FOUR

VOID'S VENGEANCE

EMMA L. ADAMS

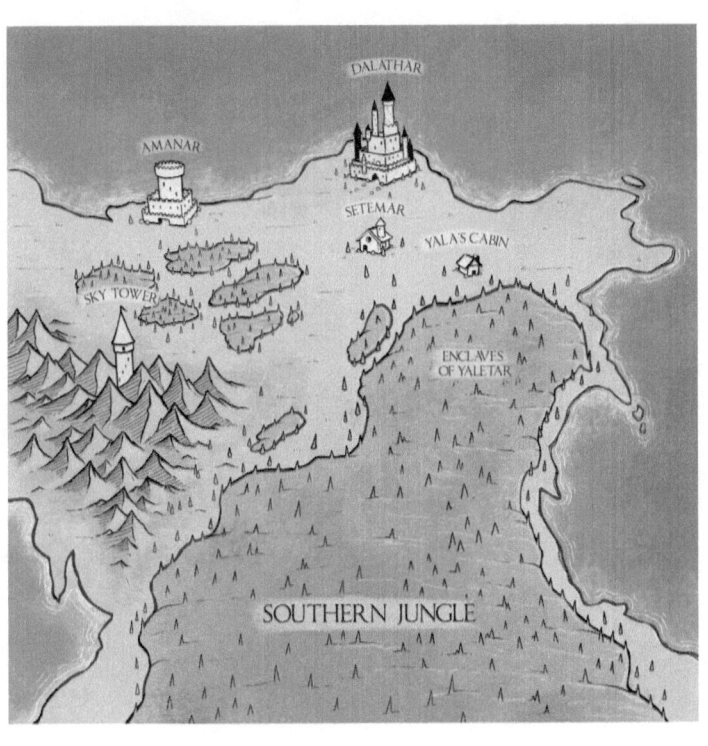

THE STORY SO FAR

Seven years ago, Captain Yala led a squad of six fellow soldiers and their armoured war drakes as part of Laria's army's flight division against the rival nation of Rafragoria. During a clash with Rafragoria over possession of an unmanned island between their nations, the monarch, King Tharen, called Yala's squad to take on a secret mission and claim the island before their rivals could gain a foothold there. Yala agreed to take on the mission before the watchful eyes of the king and his trusted allies the Disciples of the Flame, little suspecting that the island in question would contain an abandoned temple to the god of death, Mekan.

When Yala's squad landed on the island, they found Rafragoria's soldiers had already infiltrated the temple and had met their deaths at the claws and teeth of Mekan's monsters. Their actions ripped open an opening to Mekan's realm, otherwise known as the Void, and Yala and her squad found themselves fighting for their lives. Yala managed to slay the monstrous void drake and sustained a life-changing stab wound to her leg as a result, while her squad-mate Dalem begged the god of the flames to help them escape the island alive. As a former Disciple of the Flame, he was able to gain the god's attention, but he paid the price for the destruction of the island with his own life.

When they returned to the mainland, Yala and her surviving squad-mates learned that King Tharen was assassinated by Rafragorian soldiers during their absence and that he told nobody else of the mission he gave her squad. While she hoped that her squad-mate's sacrifice would help her gain the sympathy of the Disciples of the Flame, their leader Superior Datriem refused to believe Yala's reports and threatened her life if she ever shared the truth of what they saw on the island with anyone else. Shortly after, the new king disbanded the flight division of the army and Yala and her surviving squad members parted ways.

After years of living in seclusion in the deep jungle, Yala little expected anyone to disturb her early retirement, much less a war drake. The beast turned out to belong to a Disciple of Life called Niema who claimed to have been sent by her Superior to seek out Yala and to deliver a cryptic warning of danger. It emerged that Niema learned of her location from Vanat, Yala's former squad-mate with whom she'd had a brief romantic entanglement after the war, but Yala's refusal to leave her home came to an end with the arrival of a group of mercenaries vying to claim a price on her head.

Yala killed the mercenaries with the aid of a Disciple of the Sky, Kelan, who was pursuing the mercenaries for his own reasons. Distrusting his motives, Yala reluctantly joined forces with Niema instead to seek out Vanat, but found he was taken captive by a mysterious group called the Successors. Following Vanat's tail to the capital, Yala and Niema once again clashed with Kelan, who revealed that he was sent by his own Superior to investigate the rumours of someone meddling with death magic in the capital when he found the mercenaries. Niema, meanwhile, revealed that Yala appeared in a vision experienced by the Disciples of Life showing her to be a powerful ally against the rise of Mekan, the god of death.

Suspecting a connection with her experiences on the island, Yala firmly explained to Niema that she and her squad members survived through Dalem's sacrifice and not because Yala possessed any unique ability to resist Mekan. They then found Vanat's dead body on the road. Furious at the loss of her friend, Yala parted ways with her companions upon reaching the capital and went to track down her surviving squad members. While Machit was willing to listen to her, Saren refused, while Viam was safely working within the royal palace and Temik's whereabouts were unknown. Yala warned Machit of the mercenaries' seeming intention of eliminating all the survivors from their squad and he agreed to help her find the truth about the Successors' motives.

Yala and the others soon discovered that the Successors had indeed been meddling with death magic, and in the ensuing confrontation, the Successors' leader Melian revealed her face. Claiming to be a Disciple of Death, Melian attempted to sacrifice Yala and her friends to gain the favour of the god of death and overthrow the monarch. While Machit was killed in the struggle, Yala managed to fend Melian off with the help of Niema, who called upon the war drake using her abilities as a Disciple of Life and ordered it to attack the mercenaries.

In the ensuing chaos, Melian escaped, while Kelan went to rejoin his fellow Disciples of the Sky and met with the unwelcome news that some of them believed Yala to be in league with the Successors herself. It soon transpired that the source of the rumours was none other than the Temple of the Flame, which Melian had infiltrated with the help of Yala's former squad member Temik. When Yala tried to tell him the truth, Superior Datriem attempted to have Yala captured and sentenced to death.

With two groups of Disciples pursuing them and Melian's whereabouts unknown, Yala was forced to accept Kelan's offer to seek out shelter with the Disciples of the Sky. While Superior Sietra believed Yala's innocence, she also revealed that Melian was right. Anyone who glimpsed Mekan's realm had the potential to become a Disciple of Death, including Yala and her squad, whether they acted on that potential or not. As a result, Superior Sietra decided to imprison Yala as a risk factor and sent a team of her own people to the capital to deal with Melian.

Kelan disagreed with his Superior's choice, but Niema's horror at Yala's connection to Mekan led to her turning her back on both of them. With help of some of his fellow Disciples of the Sky, Kelan helped Yala her escape captivity and returned to the capital – but too late. Temik, seeking revenge on the Disciples of the Flame for their role in his squad-mate's death on the island, already killed Superior Datriem and drugged the other Disciples of the Flame, leaving the path wide open for Melian to enact her plan. With the dead swarming the city at her command, Melian had enough power to slay Yala's war drake and cut her throat.

Before Yala could bleed out, Niema had a change of heart and returned, using the power of the god of life to rescue Yala from the brink of death. During her recovery, Yala reunited with her surviving squad-mates – including Viam, now working at the royal palace, who admitted that she was the one who found the books King Tharen used to learn of the island's existence and handed them to Temik in the hopes of revealing the truth of what their squad experienced there. After Temik gave the books to Melian instead, Viam wanted to make amends by helping Yala.

Accepting that the only way to beat Melian was to call

upon Mekan herself, Yala followed Viam's instructions and raised the dead war drake that Melian slew, riding upon its back to interrupt Melian's attempt to break into the palace and assassinate the king. However, Melian had already opened Mekan's realm by slaughtering some of Kelan's fellow Disciples. While Yala managed to kill Melian, she was unable to close the Void. At the last moment, Temik reappeared and gave his own life to the god of the flame in the same way Dalem did, closing Mekan's realm and ending the slaughter.

As the city made its slow recovery from the devastation of Melian's attack, Yala decided to stay with her surviving squad-mates to make sure nobody else attempted to follow in Melian's footsteps. However, several weeks later, Yala's attempts to lie low were thwarted when she learned of someone trying to raise the dead in the capital again. She was then invited to meet the Disciples of the Flame's new leader, Superior Shralin, who informed her that the book that Melian used to learn how to use Corruption was missing. He then effectively blackmailed Yala into going to find it by threatening to reveal her status as a Disciple of Death to the world.

Kelan, confined to Skytower after the events in the capital, was then sent on a mission to Setemar to find out why the Disciples of the Earth mysteriously cut off all contact with the outside world. She assigned him to travel with Laima, and neither of them was thrilled at this arrangement. After several failed attempts, the pair were eventually able to meet with the Disciples of the Earth's leader, Superior Dovial. He revealed that the reason for their isolation was that the Disciples of the Earth were inexplicably losing the ability to contact their deity or use their powers – and that the dead were rising from their subterranean graves.

Niema, meanwhile, returned home to the jungle to find

one of her enclave members dying from an unknown illness. Niema came to the horrifying realisation that in saving Yala's life when Melian cut her throat, she borrowed the life force of her fellow enclave members through their bond and is now too late to undo the damage. Worse, Superior Kralia had already figured out the truth, and sentenced Niema to be imprisoned for aiding a Disciple of Death. She then ordered two powerful Disciples to hunt down Yala, too. After all, Corruption must be eradicated.

Back in the capital, Yala's search for the missing book led her to travel to Setemar. There, she joined forces with Kelan to search the tunnels underneath the city, where they unearthed a hidden Temple of Death set up by the person who took the book... Melian's younger brother Trienan. Their confrontation ended in a stalemate, but complications abounded when Yala unearthed apparent evidence that someone from among the Disciples of the Earth had been dabbling in Corruption, too, which led to its infiltration of their temple. Superior Dovial's refusal to believe her reports culminated in Yala's arrest, but she gained the support of a Disciple called Pehin who allied with Kelan and the others to help her escape.

A spate of disappearances in the village near Setemar prompted Yala and the others to return to the mines where they found the Temple of Death. There, they found that Melian's brother had already opened the void, and to avoid destruction, Yala was forced to call the undead war drake back to aid in her fight. Most of the Disciples of Death were killed in the process, including Trienan, while Yala finally got her hands on the missing book. The book turned out not to be a guide to Corruption, but a journal written by someone who visited Laria—and the island where she found the Temple of Death—long before her own people settled on the continent. And apparently the Disciples of Life and Death were both already present at the time.

Two Disciples of the Flame then showed up looking for the book, not trusting Yala not to keep it for herself. Having witnessed Yala's conjuring of the undead war drake, they figured out what she was, and their confrontation ended in Yala being forced to kill them both.

While imprisoned, Niema managed to send a warning to Yala and then went on the run from the Disciples of Life who the Superior sent to capture Yala. Having received her warning, Kelan helped her escape to Setemar, where they found that the Disciples of the Earth closed their doors again, their Superior believing that the safest way to keep out Corruption is to prevent anyone from leaving the temple at all.

Yala, knowing the rot lay within the temple itself, joined with the others to entice some of the Disciples of the Earth out into the open, where they were able to gain access to their deity again – but too late. The dead attacked the city, resulting in many casualties, including Laima.

While the city was under attack from the dead, the Disciples of Life arrived, led by Superior Kralia, who now used her abilities as a Superior to mind-control Niema into obeying her command to take Yala's life.

While the battle between the Disciples of Life and Death broke out, Yala was forced to fight a mind-controlled Niema, who managed to break free of Superior Kralia's orders. The two joined forces to close the void and defeat the dead, which led to Superior Kralia's reluctant acceptance that Yala was not on Mekan's side.

In the aftermath, Niema decided to leave her enclave for good, while Yala returned to the capital to return the stolen book to the Disciples of the Flame. However, Kelan showed up to claim it for his own Superior instead, much to Superior

Shralin's annoyance, believing a dangerous book like that would be safer in Skytower.

As *Traitor's Tome* ends, Superior Shralin tells Yala of a Rafragorian soldier whose body washed up on Laria's shore, carrying note emblazoned with the following words: REMEMBER THE ISLAND.

A few weeks later, Kelan was called back to Skytower and his Superior unexpectedly gave him a mission to go with a team to meet with a team of Rafragorian ambassadors in the hopes of resolving the tensions between the two nations and learning why they left the note. Their mission swiftly went sideways when they discovered the Rafragorian messengers had been murdered and showed signs of Mekan's touch on their bodies.

Niema, meanwhile, opted to leave the enclave for the good and returned to the capital, where she was reunited with Yala. She then went to seek out the Disciples of the Flame and discovered that Superior Shralin and the others were concealing the remnants of Mekan's beasts washing up in the harbour. When Kelan told them of the ambassadors' deaths, they suspected that similar beasts were responsible and that they were sent by someone who wanted to ignite a war between the two nations. Yala's theory was that the Successors were involved, if any survived. However, while Kelan was inclined to believe her, his fellow Disciples of the Sky were not, and neither were the Disciples of the Flame.

Meanwhile, the monarch continued to rebuild the army and Viam found herself growing closer to him while struggling to keep secret her knowledge of the Disciples of the Flame's role in his father's death. After helping him escape an assassination attempt from Mekan's followers, she was surprised when he asked her to help organise a parade as his father once held to reassure the people of the city that he was still strong enough to protect them.

Kelan and the other Disciples of the Sky returned to Skytower, where their Superior gave them another surprise mission, this time to seek out the Disciples of the Sea, who haven't been in Laria in decades, in order to find out if they were aware of Mekan's activity off Laria's shores.

Back in the capital, Niema started working as a healer, using her abilities as a Disciple of Life to help the people of the city. But she found her abilities ineffective against a new threat in the form of dying servants of Mekan whose bodies were rotting while they were still alive. Meanwhile the Disciples of the Flame took an interest in her new services, including an unfriendly Disciple called Danir who also appeared interested in Yala.

While on the way to meet the Disciples of the Sea, Kelan and his companions were unlucky enough to encounter a group of Rafragorian soldiers who believed them to be responsible for their ambassadors' deaths. They were then saved by some Disciples of the Sea, but they refuse to answer any questions. In the night, they were attacked by a different group of Disciples of the Sea and realised that some of them were working with the enemy. They escaped and immediately went to warn the king.

Back in the city, Yala and her allies decided to watch the king's parade in case of another attempt on his life and were able to intercept Mekan's followers. When Yala tried to question one of them before she died, the assassin claimed to have been sent by the king. This makes little sense to Yala, and when she tried to warn the Disciples of the Flame, Danir drove her away, and she realised that he was friends with Mieren and involved in King Tharen's death.

Without knowing any of this, the king decided to reward Yala for saving his life by offering her to restore her former position in the army again. Yala accepted the invitation and used her audience with the king as the chance to reveal to him the truth of his father's death. He didn't believe her and ordered his guards to throw her out of the palace, and when they threatened to report her to the Disciples of the Flame, she intentionally got into a fight with them so that she was locked up in the guards' jail instead. In the jail, she met an imprisoned ally of Mekan's who claimed that the person giving him the orders was actually the deceased monarch, King Tharen.

With her allies' help, Yala escaped death at the hands of the Disciples of the Flame. During her imprisonment, word spread throughout the palace of the accusation she made, which led Viam's friend Brenat to guess the truth about the Disciples' role in King Tharen's death. The king decided to clean up matters by inviting the Disciples directly to the palace to explain themselves, and they gave a confession... but revealed that King Tharen did indeed escape alive.

In the meantime, Niema received a visit from her Superior, who flew to the city to warn her of the same threat, as she knew of the former king's survival. She passed on the same message to Kelan, who went to warn his own Superior. Among themselves, they amassed their theories and concluded that the former king had been hiding on the island all along. Yala intended to hunt him down there, but Danit attacked her on the way out of the city and forced her to kill him in self-defence. They then encountered Mekan's army coming the other way, but heading towards Amanar and not the capital, and also ran into a couple of Disciples of the Sea. This time, the Disciples admitted that the reason they hadn't been to Laria in so long was because Superior Datriem exiled them alongside the former king, and they also knew of the island's survival and that the king was hiding there. After some arguing, they agreed to help fight against Mekan.

Having heard of the upcoming attack, the king sent the

newly reestablished flight division to intercept Mekan's army, but most were barely trained except for Viam and she had to lead the squad as a result. Brenat, having confessed her feelings toward Viam, also volunteered to join the squad. They soon ran into trouble and both were severely injured in the fight but Yala saved them from certain death.

Kelan, meanwhile, went ahead to Amanar in an attempt to outrun the army, and arrived in time to witness King Tharen return and pretend to banish Mekan's army. He and his newfound allies then travelled to the capital, with Kelan overtaking them to warn Yala and the others.

With the army seemingly defeated, Yala and Niema renewed their plan to return to the island and destroy Mekan's temple before the army could return. However, since they suspected they needed the help of the Disciples of the Flame to help, they had to free the ones from jail who'd tried to kill the former king. Superior Kralia also helped, to their surprise, creating a diversion, and the surviving Disciples of the Sea helped guide them towards the island even when the king's army's arrival caused more chaos.

Yala returned to the island and found the temple was indeed still active and full of the king's allies. Mekan tried to tempt her to join His side and revealed the next stage of His plan... to create allies by taking living creatures into His realm.

Niema then helped destroy the temple with the unexpected help of power loaned to her by Superior Kralia. But while the island was gone, they were attacked by Rafragorian soldiers on the way back who revealed that the army the king had sent away was actually sent to attack Rafragoria. They gravely injure Yala and Niema is forced to use her abilities to control them and send them away – violating the law of a Disciple of Life.

King Tharen returned to the capital to reclaim his throne

and Kelan and the others watched as he forced the remaining Disciples of the Flame to surrender and pledge themselves him for the attempt on his life. Realising that he intended to seek out any Disciples of Death, Kelan helped Viam and Saren escape the city and they reunited with Yala and Niema, who'd escaped the sea with Superior Kralia's help in time to save Yala's life.

Their group then escaped to the jungle enclave to recuperate and plan... how to take down King Tharen and Mekan for good.

PROLOGUE

Yala wiped sweat out of her eyes, shielding her face against the glare of the sun. The thin fabric of her tunic clung to her skin, and the humid air was as thick as leftover stew. Silence prevailed save for the squelch of booted feet in undergrowth swollen with rainwater, the scrape of metal chains against bark as the war drakes traipsed behind their weary riders, and the occasional slap as sweat-slick hands found bulbous bloodflies hunting for a feast.

"I swear," Machit said, swatting at the air, "if I see another *fucking* insect—"

"It means your eyes haven't been put out by a Rafragorian arrow," said Vanat. "Be glad of it."

Machit grunted at the larger man. "I don't see any arrows. Don't see any Rafragorians either."

"That's the intention," Hothen said with the infinite patience of a squad leader. "They assume we're approaching by flight. They won't be looking for us on land."

"Some of us joined the flight division to *fly*, not creep

1

through jungle," griped Sialen, their scout. "Also, it's been two days. Maybe they went home."

Yala had her doubts. The spear-shaped island lay at the halfway point between Laria's northern shore and the southern tip of the Rafragorian peninsula, making it a highly contested target, and this was the third mission they'd taken to defend its shores in as many years.

"Wish *I* could go home," Machit said. "I'd settle for the barracks. At least they're less damp."

"Nobody joins the Flight Division to experience the luxurious life of a noble," Yala pointed out. "If you wanted to sit on your arse in the shade, you should have joined the foot soldiers instead."

Not that she blamed her squad-mates for complaining. Even Hothen's morale was flagging after two days of trekking through the jungle, tipping sand out of their shoes every few hours and tying up their unruly war drakes each sunset with muzzles fastened over their sharp teeth to keep them from eating anyone in the night. The earlier rain had been a reprieve from the heat but had soaked Yala's already sweat-drenched clothes; their army-issued drakeskin trousers and gloves were designed to blunt most weapons, but they also soaked up sweat and stank to the hells.

Yala let out a relieved breath when the sunlight brightened, streaming through widening gaps in the tree cover. "We're near the edge of the jungle."

"About time." Vanat hefted a spear in his hand, the other steering his war drake by the chain. "Is anyone out there?"

Yala's war drake growled as they neared the strip of sand at the jungle's edge, its nostrils flaring. "Yes. Tread carefully."

Yala's blood thrummed in anticipation. Rafragoria might have forged a seafaring force as strong as Laria's flight division, but the beasts they rode couldn't survive outside of the water, which would leave them vulnerable as soon as they set foot on land. To retake the island, they were likely to have resorted to all manner of trickery to even the odds of a victory in ground combat.

While Sialen went to scout ahead, Hothen counted the squad members to ensure nobody had fallen behind. Vanat and Machit crept in behind Yala, while Dalem and Temik brought up the rear of the group, speaking little except to each other. The pair had been the last to join their squad, taking the place of two who'd died on the previous year's mission. Not an uncommon occurrence; Hothen had lost at least one squad member per year since he'd taken leadership five years prior, one of whom Yala had replaced.

"There are people on the beach," Sialen murmured. Ours, I think."

"It's the other squad." Hothen strode into the lead, leading his war drake by its chain. "What are they doing that close to the sea?"

Good question. Yala trod through the rain-softened mud, her spine stiffening when her war drake let out an eager growl. The coppery scent of blood reached her nostrils, mingling with the salty tang of the sea. Her gaze followed a trail of crimson droplets to a young woman sprawled on her back, a spear protruding from her throat. Next to her lay a boy of around the same age, a year into conscription at most, flies buzzing around his ruined eye socket.

"Shit," she murmured. "They must have been ambushed."

Grim silence descended as they picked their way along the jungle's edge, past the corpse of another soldier; Yala had to yank on her war drake's chain to prevent its jaws from closing around a severed limb.

"Where are their war drakes?" Dalem asked in a choked voice.

"Gone," answered Temik in tones as blunt as his compan-

3

ion's had been soft. "Bet they fled when the Rafragorians attacked."

None of their team displayed surprise nor anger at the news; everyone knew that the extent of their war drakes' loyalty began and ended with the chain.

"Did any of the squad survive?" Yala counted a fourth body to add to the other three, his face torn in two by a spear's sharp edge, exposing glistening strips of muscle to the punishing sun.

"That's their captain," Hothen said, his voice laced with restrained emotion. "Ralin. He must have tried to defend the others."

"Gods." Yala averted her eyes, a bitter taste in her mouth. "Why did he take them so close to the sea?"

Machit nudged the bushes with a foot, stirring a half-buried sleeping mat. "They were sleeping. Rafragoria must have crept up on them in the dark."

"You're right." The night's storm must have covered the noise of the slaughter on the beach and the war drakes fleeing. Their armoured scales were tougher than their riders' fragile flesh, but a well-placed arrow or spear could kill one as surely as any soldier, and the Rafragorians had ample practise in shedding Larian blood, human or otherwise.

"There are only five." Hothen pointed out a fifth body in the bushes a short distance away, marked by a quivering spear in its shoulder. "That leaves two missing."

Yala scanned the beach but saw no signs of any more dead. "Which two?"

"Saren," Machit answered. "And... what's her name? The noble."

"Viam." Yala's heart gave an unpleasant jolt. Viam was a newcomer to the army, and the pampered noble had been at an obvious disadvantage in military training. "Did they flee?"

"Must have." Hothen held out a burly arm to prevent

Sialen from leading his war drake out of the bushes. "Careful. The Rafragorian squad might have wanted to lure us out into the open."

"We're not going to hunt them down?" Sialen's hand flexed on his war drake's chain. "How do we know they didn't set foot on land?"

Yala cleared her throat. "I don't see any sea drakes, do you?"

A flush darkened Sialen's sunbaked skin. *Honestly.* The man was a decent scout, but his common sense was lacking. "I thought they might've sent someone to chase the survivors."

"Not worth the risk." The words tasted sour in her mouth, like milk left out in the sun. "They have no way off the island without their mounts."

"No." Temik spoke up, his gravelly voice as stoic as ever. "Sorry, Dalem. We can't do anything for them."

Yala caught Dalem's eye. His brief time as an acolyte of the Disciples of the Flame had left him with a self-sacrificing streak that even his longstanding friendship with Temik hadn't quelled, and while his soft heart was sometimes an annoyance, she saw the reflection of her distaste for the idea of abandoning two of their fellow soldiers in hostile territory. "We can at least keep an eye out."

Despite the deceptive quiet blanketing the beach, they soon found a mass of footprints extending from the sand into the undergrowth.

"I was right." Sialen's tone wavered between triumphant and wary. "These are Rafragorians. Must be."

"Where'd they leave their steeds?" asked Machit. "More to the point, *why* would they leave them?"

"Must've thought two lone soldiers weren't a threat." Yala's stomach turned as she imagined the pair fleeing into

5

the jungle at night, pursued by the enemy. "You'd think they'd have guessed we have more than one squad."

"If they did, they'll be searching for the rest of us," said Hothen. "We need to leave."

"Then we'll condemn the two survivors to death." Dalem sounded appalled. "Can't we at least *look* for them?"

"I'm sorry." Hothen let out a measured breath. "If the choice is between your lives and theirs, I have to pick you."

I know. A squad leader's role was to ensure the team's survival above all else, yet she didn't have to be as soft-hearted as Dalem to acknowledge that the notion of leaving her fellow soldiers to rot in the jungle repelled her. Yes, Yala knew that her life ranked far below the army's objective of securing the island, but offering herself in exchange was a world apart from making the decision for others.

And the question remained: Where *were* the Rafragorians, and where had they left their steeds? A squad of foot soldiers would have a far easier time concealing their movements in the jungle than the Larians and their war drakes, but parting ways with the beasts that gave them mastery over the ocean ran counter to their usual strategies.

"We outnumber them." Vanat cracked his knuckles. "I'd say we head north and take them by surprise before they do the same to us."

"They already know we're here," Temik said. "If you ask me, they're counting on us walking into their trap."

"Except they're the ones who left their steeds behind." Sialen's war drake's chain clanked as he leaned over to remove its muzzle, freeing its sharp teeth.

"What are you doing?" she hissed. "Did you forget that beast's as likely to take a bite out of you as the enemy?"

The proximity of the bodies on the beach would only heighten the war drakes' bloodlust, but Sialen merely shrugged. "I'll take the risk if it means avoiding an ambush."

"Agreed." Vanat reached for his war drake's scaly head, and Yala gave him a rap on the leg with her spear's edge.

"Don't be a fool." If Sialen wanted to endanger his own life, that was his prerogative, but Vanat should know better. "Hothen, what's the plan?"

Their squad leader's brow furrowed as he traced the path uphill from the beach. "They won't be out in the open. Let's see if we can find where they left those sea drakes. It'll tell us how many there are."

Nobody argued, and they fell in behind their leader as they followed the curve of the beach back into the jungle. Yala tugged on her war drake's chain and continued until the path steepened and the thinning trees afforded a view of high cliffs protruding over the water. A distinct snarl sounded beneath the crashing of waves. *Sea drake.*

Hothen indicated to the others to fall back and made his careful way uphill, behind Sialen. Waves lapped at the cliffs, almost masking the sight of several serpentine necks secured to the rocks by thick ropes. *So this is where they left their mounts.*

At the sight, the war drake strained to escape Sialen's hold, dragging him towards the edge in an attempt to reach its foes. Yala moved to help, but he swatted her hand away. "Why not kill their mounts while we're here?"

"And risk losing one of our own?" Yala said. "I doubt the soldiers went far. Stay hidden."

"The monsters are tied up," Vanat argued. "All we have to do is cut the ropes, and the enemy will have no way off the island."

A scream rang out somewhere deeper in the jungle. Yala tensed, her grip tightening on her war drake's chain as their beasts reacted to the noise with low growls of displeasure. Sialen's went one step further, dragging its rider perilously close to the cliff's edge.

7

A second scream followed the first, cut off in a wet gurgle. Vanat reached for his war drake, removing its muzzle and loosening its chain, and Hothen gave a nod signalling to the rest of the squad to do likewise. Yala's practised hands moved fast, her ears tracking the noise of Sialen swearing as he skidded in the wake of his panicking war drake.

A spear flew past, embedding itself in a nearby tree. There came a scuffle and a yelp, more of a sob than the war cry of an enraged Rafragorian.

Yala hurried over to the source and found a Rafragorian soldier lying sprawled in the undergrowth, a bloody spear protruding from his chest. Behind, a pair of frightened eyes watched hers from amid the bushes.

Yala dropped to a crouch, saw the Larian uniform, the drakeskin trousers. "Viam?"

"Yala?" The young soldier crept forward, her face smeared with dirt. "I thought you were one of them."

"Be glad I'm not." She prodded the Rafragorian with the end of her spear, confirming his deceased state. "He didn't come alone, I take it?"

Her face clouded. "They're dead. My squad."

"I know." Yala caught Vanat's eye on the other side of the tree and gave him a reassuring nod, confirming she spoke to a Larian soldier and not an enemy. "Is Saren in here somewhere? He wasn't with the dead."

"Saren?" Viam blinked. "I ran when the war drakes left us on the beach. Maybe he did the same."

"And the Rafragorians?" She tugged her war drake's chain to prevent it from sinking its sharp teeth into the corpse. "There's a whole squad of sea drakes chained there."

Viam shuddered. "I was on my way to untie the ropes, but he ambushed me."

Yala followed her line of sight to the soldier's limp body. Her first kill, presumably. "I'm glad you struck first."

There came a hoarse shout from further up the cliff. Yala pinpointed the source—Sialen, who'd lost his grip on the war drake's chain entirely and now lay headfirst in the bushes. The beast itself barrelled past, an arrow protruding from its open mouth, and the smell of drake blood sent Yala's steed into a fury. It lunged, claws swiping at the bushes in search of the attacker, and she struggled to regain her footing as its greater weight dragged her feet through thick mud.

Yala threw her weight against the chain as her war drake's claw swiped a swathe of undergrowth aside, revealing a slight figure pinning down a much larger one. The former was clad in a Larian uniform so filthy that he effortlessly blended in with the mud, and he rolled aside with a yelp when the war drake's claw came down, finding its mark in the larger soldier's throat.

"Sorry!" Yala gave another yank on the chain, stilling the unruly war drake. "Thought you were the enemy."

"Speak for yourself." The smaller soldier rolled upright, dark eyes watching Yala's from beneath hair matted with mud and blood. "My steed abandoned me, the bastard."

"Saren?" Viam wore an expression somewhere between wariness and relief. "You escaped."

"Not for long, given how loud you lot are being." Saren stepped away from the dead Rafragorian, pushing a wad of mud-soaked hair from his face with a shaking hand. "I was doing a great job of hiding until you came rampaging through."

"I'm glad one of us made it out." Viam wore a rather forced smile; the pair, Yala had gathered during training sessions, did not get along particularly well. She hadn't the faintest idea why; the one time she'd spoken to Saren had been when he'd treated an arrow wound that she'd sustained on her first mission. Most soldiers were trained in basic healing, but Saren was the only person she knew who carried a full medical kit in his pack.

"Stay with us." Yala scanned the bushes. "How many Rafragorians are left?"

"At least three." Viam threw her arms over her head as an arrow bounced off a nearby tree trunk. "They're coming!"

Yala was ready with her spear in hand, Vanat close at her side. A shout of warning ahead pointed her to Dalem, who ran downhill to avoid a second arrow. The sharp edge bounced off his steed's scaly back, and Vanat lifted his spear and hurled it in that direction. A choked cry told Yala he'd hit his mark, but not before another arrow buried itself in Dalem's arm.

"Dalem!" Temik ran to him and fell to his knees as a fourth arrow skimmed overhead, narrowly missing his shoulder.

Yala hurled her weapon in that direction. The enemy combatant collapsed, blood fountaining from his throat. The discordant sound of fighting continued elsewhere, unabated, and her war drake gave another frenzied lurch. This time, the movement took Yala off her feet, dragging her into a shower of blood and raindrops shed by falling leaves as her war drake's teeth made quick work of the unfortunate soldier hidden in the bushes. Her fellow squad members' shouts echoed amid discordant growls and the crunch of greenery trampled beneath clawed feet. She dug her heels in, to no avail, her war drake tearing into another Rafragorian soldier and spraying her with gore.

Vanat caught her elbow, slowing her desperate slide, and yelled something in her ear. He had to repeat himself twice before she understood. "They brought *two* squads?"

"At least," he shouted. "The bastards copied our strategy."

Hadn't there only been one group of sea drakes? She threw her weight against the war drake's chain, her feet skidding over the broken remnants of the Rafragorian soldier as she and Vanat hauled the beast to a halt.

Yala's mouth went dry. A second body lay near the first, this one wearing Larian uniform, his face caved in with the imprint of a war drake's claw.

"Sialen." Had his steed trampled its own rider? Spying a discarded spear, Yala picked up the weapon, her mind a riot of confusion. "Where's Hothen? The others?"

"Didn't see." Blood smeared one of Vanat's cheeks, but he didn't look to have had suffered any major injuries. "They were heading uphill."

Yala swore, turning her back on the ruin Sialen's war drake had left in its tracks, and spied someone crawling on hands and knees through the bushes. Yala's heart thudded, and then she released a breath when she recognised Machit's blood-streaked face.

He coughed. "Yala... I couldn't... stop them."

"Stop who?" She ran to him, having to restrain her beast from snapping at the easy prey. Vanat seized the chain from her; he'd lost his own war drake at some point in the conflict, and she let him take hers without argument.

Machit coughed, leaning on one elbow. An arrow jutted from his ribs, blood blossoming on his tunic. "They doubled up," he wheezed. "Two or three riders per sea drake."

"Pity the sea drakes didn't object." Hothen and the others succeeded in cutting the ropes? She scanned the cliffs above, visible through undergrowth torn away by sharp teeth, but the only person within sight was Saren.

He made his way to Machit's side, fumbling for his pack. "Let me get that arrow out. Careful..."

Machit slapped his hands away with another rattling cough. "Never mind me. Help him instead."

"Who?" His groan cut off in a whimper when Saren grabbed the arrow, snapping off the feathered end but leaving the tip inside his chest. To stop him bleeding out, Yala knew, and trusted that her squad-mate was in safe hands with Saren.

Where, though, were the others? Yala trod uphill, angling towards the cliffs where the sea drakes had been tied. An eerie silence pervaded, muffling the air and making her racing heartbeat sound unnaturally loud.

Not a single beast was left. Ropes hung loose from the cliffs, and several bodies floated in the water. Rafragorian soldiers. She counted five or six. Two or three squads, Machit had said, which, when put together with the bodies in the forest...

A splash had Yala at the cliff's edge, a spear in her hand. Another soldier lay sprawled across the high rocks protruding from the water, the lapping waves nudging at his booted feet. A limp hand trailed loose in the water, trailing crimson.

"Hothen." Before Yala could shout a warning, Vanat had clambered over the cliff to their squad leader.

Rustling sounded behind her. She swivelled, lifting her spear in a practised motion that gave no voice to the pit of horror opening inside her.

Dalem and Temik limped out of the bushes, supporting one another, while an ashen-faced Viam followed them, clutching a bloodied arm to her side. Mutely, Yala pointed to the cliffs, to Vanat clambering up with Hothen's body draped in his arms.

With a heave, he placed their squad leader on the ground. "He climbed down there to cut the war drakes free. Succeeded, too, and took half their squad with him."

"*Why?*" Desolation filled Dalem's voice. "Why didn't he ask for our help?"

"Because he's squad leader." *Was* squad leader. That single word opened a gulf as vast as the sea. There were other words to say, a refrain for the dead, and she forced them past her lips. "He can rest now."

The others echoed the familiar refrain, spoken countless times in tribute to those fallen on missions. A refrain that promised peace and relief awaited after death, a welcome reprieve from the burdens of life.

And we're left to pick up the pieces. Her mind remained unmoored while her body went through the motions of gathering her squad, of moving Sialen's body to rest along-side his leader's, of checking that no further ambushes lurked in the trees.

Three squads felled by a third of their number was a feat worthy of praise from the king himself, but would His Majesty spare a thought for those who'd been lost?

What are our lives worth? The thought echoed in the back of her head even when her guard relaxed enough to kneel beside Hothen and let the tears fall down her dirt-smudged cheeks like rain.

A chorus of war drakes' cries cut through the haze in her mind. Leaping to her feet, she spied a dark blot in the sky, swiftly drawing nearer. "Is that...?"

"Yes." Saren held up a hand to block out the glaring sun. "That's the rest of the Flight Division."

"Couldn't one of them have thrown a spear to help us?" Machit looked a little better, his chest bandaged by Saren's expert hands, though his face was as tear-streaked as Yala's. "Would have been nice."

"Yes." Yala wiped her eyes on her bloody sleeve and summoned up her scattered wits. "They'll land on the beach."

Vanat lifted their squad leader in his arms. Yala secured her war drake to a tree and then picked out the least injured —Dalem—to help her carry Sialen. His dead weight pulled on her shoulders, and she tried to avoid catching his vacant eyes as he swung between them, his mouth half open as if he might utter a complaint at any instant.

"Fuck me," Saren breathed. "That's the king."

Yala's gaze lifted. A larger beast than the rest flew behind the bulk of the army, its crowned head catching the sunlight in a gold halo.

Did you know? she thought. *Did you know we'd have to die to make the landing safe?*

Did it *matter?* She shoved the thought aside and helped Dalem lower Sialen's body onto the sand.

"Yala." Vanat pointed to another steed near the king's. "There's the commander. I'll put in a word for you if you like."

"What?" she said.

"He means you're the next squad leader." Machit leaned on Saren as they made their stumbling way along the blood-drenched sand. "The gods know the rest of us aren't qualified."

Neither am I.

"Hothen wanted you to," Vanat added. "You know he did."

"Exactly," Dalem said.

Temik nodded in agreement, while Yala fought to assemble arguments that seemed entirely inadequate.

"We're short a member," she said. "Two, in fact."

Saren cleared his throat. "You might have noticed we lost the rest of our squad, and I'd say I like my chances with the ones who took out their killers."

"Me too," Viam added after a moment's pause. "If that's all right."

Saren gave her a sarcastic look but fell silent when the wingbeats became louder, the first squad landing upon the sand.

Yala took a deep breath. "I'll talk to the commander and see what he says."

He's hardly going to say no. An unpleasant knot formed in her gut as she contemplated the idea of taking her vows as captain. How could she kneel before the monarch without wondering if he'd intended for her squad to be marked as acceptable losses, a fair exchange for a battle won?

Would Hothen have acted any differently if he'd known what awaited him? Or would he have done the same regardless, knowing that his sacrifice would enable his squad's survival?

He would, she told herself, *and you'll do the same. For them, I have to take on the title of squad leader.*

1

Bone crunched under Yala's feet. She stepped over the corpse of the dead kekin, her hands curling as a tingling sensation travelled up her fingertips and urged her to reach for the shadows creeping beneath its rotting flesh.

Her fingers clenched around her cane until the sensation faded, but the faint chill emanating from the pouch she carried at her waist lingered as a reminder that the god of death was never far away. Even here, in the domain of His immortal enemy.

This is no hiding place for a Disciple of Death.

The god of life's power permeated the forest, a constant thrum of energy pulsing everywhere from the tallest trees to the rain-soaked undergrowth. The dense greenery was a stark contrast to the grimy city she'd left behind, yet both held bittersweet memories from a simpler time. Though only a few short months had passed, the years she'd spent living in her jungle cabin seemed like a half-remembered dream.

"Yala."

She halted, her thoughts scattering like falling leaves. "Saren."

"There you are." Her former squad-mate half crawled under a low-hanging branch and straightened upright, pushing a handful of curly dark hair out of his eyes. "I've been looking for you all day. What're you doing?"

"Getting away from the noise."

"Ouch." He grinned. "You know, it's got to be worse for Niema, being bound to her enclave members the way she is. Being tuned into four other people's emotions all the time would drive me out of my mind."

Yala grunted. She would never have consented to such a violation of her privacy, but there must be a comfort in the unspoken trust shared between Niema and her fellow enclave members and in the knowledge that they would always be present in her darkest moments. A similar pact had once existed between Yala and her squad-mates, too, but that well-tended garden was now overgrown with thorns.

Yet another reason I'm more suited to serving the god of death. "Something you needed?"

"The others want to talk to you." Saren's gaze flickered to the dead kekin; his shoulders trembled, but he refrained from acknowledging the shadows that were as stark to his eyes as they were to hers.

Yala fell into step with him, her cane scraping the damp soil. "Has Superior Kralia finally had enough of us?"

While Yala's desire to leave the enclave had initially been stymied by her recovery from a life-threatening injury, weeks in the company of Yalet's rejuvenating power had left her with little more than a faint scar on her ribs. Superior Kralia had offered her a refuge, but if she expected Yala to have forgotten the infractions she'd committed against both Yala herself and Niema, she was sorely mistaken.

"Oh, she'd had enough of us on the first day," Saren said.

"She had no choice but to keep us here on account of how we're her last hope against utter destruction."

"Drakeshit." If anything, the opposite was true. "She must know that every day she offers us shelter, she's gambling the safety of her own people."

The light in his eyes dimmed as if a cloud passed overhead. "Not necessarily. I won't lie, I wouldn't object to staying long term. Jungle life agrees with me."

"I'd have thought you'd be sick of eating leaves by now." Disciples of Life swore vows against harming other living creatures, including consuming their flesh. Other practices were optional—such as the bond some forged with fellow Disciples that allowed them to share emotions—but Superior Kralia enforced Yalet's will with as firm a hand as an adherent of the god of the flames. "And what of their rule never to marry outside of the enclave?"

A grin chased the shadows out of his eyes. "I can live with that. Marriage didn't work out that well for Machit, did it?"

Yala grunted in agreement. She'd seen him crouched at one of Yalet's altars a couple of times over the past few weeks, head bent in prayer, but she hoped this was just a passing fancy on his part. "I wouldn't expect Yalet to have any desire to claim someone who's been as close to Mekan as we have."

"True." He gave a short laugh. "We're corrupted to the bone."

That's one way of putting it. The dark stains on her fingertips lingered no matter how long she spent in the god of life's domain, and she'd learned to ignore the occasional pulse of cold from the pouch that hung from her belt, in which she'd concealed the claw of one of Mekan's beasts. While its presence within Yalet's domain was a risk, the claw also functioned as a warning system should any of Mekan's creatures venture into the forest. *Not that I need warning about dead kekins,* she thought, her ears picking up the hum of voices that indicated they were nearing the wooden huts that housed the enclave members.

In contrast to the fences and high walls that encased the capital, the jungle held no such boundaries. The Disciples' huts were sprawled across a vast area interspersed with communal areas where Disciples pooled their resources and gathered around cookfires. Taking in outsiders was unusual but not an affront to their god's wishes, and for the most part, the other Disciples had been cordial towards the newcomers.

Some more than others. As they rounded a corner, she saw Kelan and Niema stood engaged in a heated argument in the middle of the leaf-strewn path. The former was dressed in his usual light-blue robe—inappropriate attire for the jungle but made bearable by his ability to call upon the god of the skies to fan away the humid air—while the latter wore the simple leaf-woven clothing of her fellow Disciples. Niema's hair was braided tightly against her skull, her neck imprinted with the leaf-shaped birthmark that signalled her as Yalet's chosen.

"What's he done this time?" Yala's pace quickened. "Kelan?"

"He was..." Niema spluttered, too outraged to get the words out. "I caught him trying to seduce Bitra into spending the night with him in the village."

"Isn't that better than seducing her in the cabin with five others present?" Kelan said. "Granted, that might make the experience more interesting. Would they be able to sense her arousal too?"

Niema's face reddened with anger. "That behaviour is inappropriate."

"According to whom?" Kelan enquired, a smile playing on

his lips. "I would have thought the god of life would support all pursuits of earthly pleasures."

"You're here as an ambassador," Niema snapped. "How do you hope to forge an alliance with our Superior when you insist upon behaving like a tree-raptor in heat?"

"I didn't try to seduce *her*, did I?" Kelan's amusement grew at her analogy. "She's had no complaints about my behaviour. I rather think she's enjoying the entertainment."

Yala snorted. It was true that the younger members of the enclave had developed an inexplicable attachment to Kelan and happily listened to his wild stories of his adventures as a sword-for-hire that were almost certainly fictionalised to some degree, but Superior Kralia would have been unmoved if Kelan had brought an entire theatre troupe to perform for her alone.

Moreover—as she had to remind him on a not-infrequent basis—they weren't here for fucking *entertainment*.

"And how's that alliance coming along?" she asked pointedly.

"Spectacularly despite our pious friend's dismal attitude," said Kelan. "Really, Niema, did we not thoroughly corrupt you during your time in the city?"

The word *corrupt* ignited Yala's irritation. "That's why you dragged me here?" she asked of Saren. "To break up a petty fight between fools who ought to know better? I'm not their fucking captain, thank the gods."

Kelan's smile faded. "Now, I think that's harsh."

"In case you've forgotten," Yala said through clenched teeth, "we're fugitives."

"We haven't forgotten." Saren glanced at a figure sitting on a nearby tree stump, dressed in a fine shirt that was now considerably wrinkled and yellowed with sweat stains. Viam, the only other survivor of her old squad aside from Yala.

The others—Vanat, Machit, Dalem, Temik—had died one

by one, doomed by their status as the only squad who knew the truth of the last mission King Tharen had ordered before his death. *Or rather, before he faked his death.*

Seeing her, Viam pushed off the tree stump and padded to meet them. "There you are, Yala. Did you find anything in the jungle?"

"Aside from bloodflies?" Yala knew she meant signs of Mekan's presence, but a dead kekin hardly qualified. "Nothing. What were you doing over there?"

"Brooding," Saren offered. "Really, you two could at least do so in the same place."

"I'm not brooding," Viam protested. "I was waiting for the Superior to get back from her meeting."

"Another one?" No wonder everyone was restless. "Do you think the other Superiors might have finally agreed to put together their forces?"

Unlike those who served the other deities, Yalet's followers were spread across a larger area and consequently required more than one Disciple to hold the rank of Superior. Each enclave within the forest that covered the southernmost portion of the continent held its own priorities and rituals, with the result that there had been no consensus thus far on how to deal with the current conflict.

"No," Saren answered. "They're pacifists, remember? They don't want a war."

"Even Superior Kralia knows it's impossible to avoid one." Yala dug the end of her cane into the soft earth, her back teeth grinding. "The others can't bury their heads in the mud for much longer."

"It's not their fault." Niema said. "They've never had to deal with a threat like this."

"You'd think one of them would have run afoul of a patrol by now." Kelan hovered a little above the ground, a faint breeze stirring his long, curly hair. "They're all over the northern forest."

Niema spun on him. "You weren't supposed to be there either. What if you were seen?"

"I was careful."

Yala had her doubts, but the presence of the king's army outside of the capital was an unwelcome sign. "How many soldiers?"

"Fifty? A hundred?" He shrugged. "More than I'd expect. The king's been expanding his forces."

Nothing we didn't expect. The Disciples were bound by old treaties against engaging in warfare, but the king had long violated that truce, and the Disciples were the only force who stood a chance of resisting King Tharen's new reign.

Not that Superior Kralia agreed, but for all her claims, she'd offered no actionable advice as to exactly *how* Yala was supposed to remove the king from his throne.

The colour drained from Niema's face. "We can't match those numbers."

"Can't you?" Yala had stark memories of Disciples of Life riding upon war drakes like soldiers and wielding Yalet's power as effectively as any weapon. Not every member of their order avoided violence, as Yala and Niema had experienced firsthand. "We might have no choice."

"I think she's hoping *we'll* fight for her." Viam had listened to their discussion in anxious silence; she'd been keen to hear any news of what might be occurring back in the capital. In accompanying Yala to the jungle, she'd been forced to leave behind her romantic companion, Brenat, a fellow member of the palace staff, who had been recovering from a wound suffered in the recent battle.

Saren glared at her. "No fucking chance."

"Don't you two start," Yala said sharply. "I'm not *your* captain anymore either."

Technically, Viam outranked her, in fact, having recently had a brief, disastrous stint in the Flight Division of the king's army. As if she, too, had recalled that, Viam's shoulders slumped. "I'm starting to think I was too hasty in leaving the capital."

"Hasty?" Saren echoed. "The king demanded the immediate surrender of all Disciples of Death. You'd be dead on an altar if you stayed."

"You can't know that," Viam said. "None of us can."

The restrained frustration in her voice echoed Yala's. "We can make some educated guesses. Tharen will almost certainly have reclaimed the throne from his son in addition to rebuilding the army. As to his intentions for the Disciples of Death, I can't say. Don't forget he made it look as though he *defeated* the army of the dead."

As opposed to his true strategy: sending the same army to attack their rival nation of Rafragoria to ensure nobody challenged his rule. Having dealt with the external threats, Yala expected him to turn his attention to the internal ones, but he had no idea that a rival Disciple of Death had survived in the southern forest. Three if she counted Viam and Saren.

"Yeah, he's a fucking hero," said Saren. "I bet he has his soldiers singing those old military songs as they march around sticking flags in everything that moves."

"They seemed more interested in signing up recruits from the local villages, from what Bitra heard."

"From—" Niema cut off. "You were questioning her. That's why you cornered her, not just to seduce her."

"I'm adept at multitasking."

Yala didn't hear Niema's reply. A sharp chill emanated from the pouch in which she carried the claw, sending a wave of shivers through her entire body, and her fingertips tingled with static. Shadows coiled beneath her palm, fanning out from her cane, and a whisper as cold and sharp as a steel blade crept into her ears.

"Yala."

The voice's echoes faded as a shrill scream rang out from the jungle, reverberating in the air. Yala broke into a run, her cane slapping the ground with each step. Her right leg gave its usual twinge of protest; even the god of life couldn't heal the old wound inflicted by one of Mekan's creatures. Kelan overtook her with ease, drawing his blade.

A man staggered into view, recognisable as a Disciple only by the leaf-shaped birthmark on his greying neck. His body reeked of decay, his lank hair clinging to his skeletal face. Withered tendons creaked, bare knucklebones gleaming, as he lifted a bloodied knife.

Yala's cane struck him in the chest with a wet thud and sent him sprawling onto his back. She then drove the blunt end into his throat, severing the rotting tendons. Satisfaction sang through her veins at the exertion. Nearby, Kelan duelled another dead Disciple of Life, who carried a knife slick with blood.

As the Disciple crumpled, Niema ran over, her face taut. "Where did they come from?"

"I'd ask, but..." Kelan gestured in the direction from which they'd heard the screaming and released a gust of wind from his palm. The tree branches were swept aside, revealing a hut that resembled Niema's dwelling.

The door opened on the corpse of a woman, newly felled. Already, Yala glimpsed shadows stirring around her body, creeping through muscle and bone. She dodged the hand that reached to grab her ankle and stamped down hard. As the woman's brittle wrist snapped, she brought the cane down upon her skull, the dead flesh giving way with ease. Shadows surged upward, her fingers grasping the phantom sensation of a thread connecting her to the woman's rotting corpse, reminding her of how she'd once manipulated the bones of the dead with a mere touch.

A faint whisper sounded, accompanying the chill surrounding the claw within her pocket. *"I'm here, Yala."*

None of that, Yala thought and brought the cane down upon the woman's skull again.

"Yala, *stop!*" Niema's shrill cry stilled her hand. Breathing hard, she stepped out of the hut, and another Disciple of Life ran past her, dropping to her knees beside the dead woman with a tortured wail.

Others gathered around, watching Yala with appalled expressions. She clenched her fist to conceal the shadows within, to no avail. Her secret was laid as bare as the woman's skull.

We have to move the bodies. Once the spread of Corruption started, each person felled would rise in turn, their corpse claimed by Mekan. The Disciples of Life alone held the ability to lay them to rest, but that would be a short-lived victory. As long as someone bound to Mekan was present in the forest, He would always find a way to come back.

I think, she thought, *it's time for me to leave.*

2

Kelan lifted the body of the fallen Disciple, doing his best to ignore its twitching limbs and the stench of decay. "Where do you want me to put them?"

Niema let out a faint whimper. "I don't know. My Superior..."

"Is inconveniently absent." The only Disciple who didn't avoid treading near their group was Hachim, one of Niema's close friends, who pointed Kelan to a clearing into which to carry the dead.

"She picked a great time to leave," Yala muttered, wiping the bloodstains from her cane onto the damp undergrowth. "Niema, we need to destroy those bodies before they attract more."

Hearing, Hachim made a faint noise of protest. "We can't lay them to rest without our Superior."

"Do you want more of Mekan's creatures rampaging through your enclave?" Yala said.

Hachim flinched, but Niema didn't. She'd warned the Superior enough times that the god of death would not ignore the presence of one of His Disciples—to say nothing of Niema herself. Blinking tears from her eyes, Niema took in a shaky breath and addressed her fellow Disciples. "I'm sorry, but Hachim and I have to give the dead to Yalet immediately to prevent any further corruption."

The Disciples of Life murmured amongst themselves, but none voiced an objection. Even Bitra, whose sister was among the dead. Guilt knotted inside him as he watched her sobbing, wrapped in the arms of another Disciple. When he'd questioned her about her recent excursion to the local village, he'd little expected such a terrible intrusion to follow her home.

And if there were others? They were unlikely to have walked through the forest alone, so the nearest community was the obvious source. Someone would need to check, and soon.

The Disciples pulled back from the clearing entrance as Hachim and Niema approached the bodies. Kelan retreated, too, conscious of his outsider status as they crouched and whispered a prayer to Yalet.

The god of life answered. A green glow ignited that banished every trace of shadow. Creeping vines burst out of the ground, intertwining above the bodies until the dead were entombed in thick greenery.

Nearby, plants shrivelled and died, their essence having been taken to fuel their request. The god of life was, as all deities, a being of equal exchange. Life was needed to bring life.

Niema remained crouched, her body shuddering with sobs. Kelan let Hachim offer her the comfort she needed, instead joining Yala and her two former squad-mates outside the clearing.

"We can't stay here," Yala murmured, her countenance grim. "We were complacent, and others paid the price for our error."

"Agreed." Viam's hands clasped in front of her knees. "When the Superior returns, we'll speak to her."

"You want to ask *her* what to do?" Saren asked. "I'd be surprised if she doesn't feed us to her war drake."

Yala's mouth flattened. "She's the one who offered us shelter. Granted, it was based on a ridiculous claim, but she hasn't retracted it yet."

There is that. Superior Kralia, for reasons Kelan couldn't fathom, believed Yala was capable of toppling King Tharen from his newly reclaimed throne. "I'd say we leave before she changes her mind. I can take you with me to Skytower."

"Would your Superior be amenable to that?" Viam asked. "Our presence might paint a target upon your fellow Disciples too."

"Oh, we already have one, I don't doubt." According to the last message his Superior had sent from Skytower, when Kelan had helped Yala's companions escape the capital, several other Disciples of the Sky had also sneaked out of the upper city in the confusion following the king's return. He'd been relieved to hear that his fellow Disciples had escaped the king's undoubted wrath following the loss of the island hosting the only known Temple of Death.

"It's not the worst idea I've heard." Yala's gaze panned between her fellow squad members. "Though travel by sky will be risky, given that the monarch will all but certainly have revived the Flight Division."

"What are you doing?" Niema approached, red-eyed with grief. "Are you leaving?"

"I think it's safe to say we've worn out our welcome," Kelan said. "I'm intending to return to Skytower. You're welcome to join me."

"No," she croaked. "Your people will be in jeopardy if any of us come with you."

"Skytower is in the most remote area of Laria there is,

aside from here," he reminded her. "Mekan will have a hard time gaining a foothold."

"It only takes one mistake." Her eyes glittered with tears. "Bitra told me her sister and the others went to the village to get supplies and must have been ambushed by the dead on the way back."

"Which suggests the dead were already in the region," Kelan added. "They weren't following you nor Yala either."

"It hardly matters if they were," Yala said. "They're here now."

"I can check the village," Kelan offered. "If there are more, someone needs to inform—"

"The Superior. If she ever comes back." Yala scowled. "Her meeting had better have been worth it."

Kelan agreed, though Superior Kralia had had considerable difficulty convincing her fellow Superiors of the imminent threat when Mekan's beasts had yet to be seen within view of the jungle. *Until now, at any rate.* "I'll be back in a minute."

Kelan rose upward until his head skimmed the canopy, a thick web of branches that offered both shelter and concealment to the people who lived within the jungle's boundaries.

"If anyone ambushes you, yell really loudly, and we'll know the coast isn't clear," Saren called up at him. "Or send up a distress signal."

"Now, I'm capable of handling a few dead on my own." He didn't quite manage a light tone. His survival thus far had been largely a matter of luck, and he had as many scars as the rest of their group now. "I'll let you know."

The breeze stirred up by his flight cooled his sweat-damp skin and rendered the heat-thickened air easier to breathe. He'd had precious few opportunities to fly since his arrival in the forest. He'd needed the rest at first, as he'd pushed himself far past his limits when he'd flown nonstop from

Amanar to the capital, but his heart lifted notably when he found a gap in the branches through which to leave the enclave's suffocating confines.

The jungle stretched in all directions, covering Laria's entire southeast. While each monarch pushed further south while cutting down trees for timber and to clear room for farmland at the jungle's edges, even Laria's war-hungry rulers had no desire to attract Yalet's wrath by expanding further. From here, Setemar lay more than a day's travel on foot, its cliffs hidden behind a thick swathe of trees, while the capital and the ocean beyond were little more than a thin ribbon on the horizon. The sea lay to the east, too, but nobody except for Niema's fellow Disciples lived within the forests that ran up to the coastline.

He'd planned to check the village first, but movement caught his attention above the tree line to the north. A winged shape hovered above the mass of trees, and another two flew in behind, each carrying a human rider.

Those aren't Disciples.

The king's army was coming for the enclave.

With Kelan's departure came a renewed solemnity amid Niema's companions. She'd left Hachim to offer comfort to those mourning the dead, guilt settling in her stomach like a heavy stone sinking into a pond. Death had followed her ever since she'd saved Yala's life, trespassing on the brink of Mekan's own realm, and would pursue her until her own last breath left her lungs.

"Don't." Yala cut her a sharp glance. "Don't blame yourself. This is on the Superior. She should have listened to us."

Niema said nothing. Her unwavering faith in Superior Kralia had long since evaporated into mist, but the Superior's claims of Yala's fitness to depose the monarch had been spoken with such conviction that Niema had been sure Yalet had shared some insight with her that none of the others were privy to.

A thread tugged on her heart, telling her of Hachim's approach. Sorrow pulsed through their bond, both bolstering her own pain and making it easier to bear. He alone had stood beside her while the other Disciples of Life had believed her a traitor, and for that reason alone, she wanted to be honest with him.

"I'm going to Skytower," she murmured. "Kelan claims his Superior can offer us shelter."

I'm coming with you. Hachim didn't speak, but his intentions travelled through their bond, as clear as a cloudless sky, and brought tears to her eyes. "I would not ask you to exile yourself with me."

"The enclave won't be safe as long as a follower of Mekan sits on the throne." His soft tone held a hint of steel. He would not be deterred by any objection she threw at him. "It's our duty as Yalet's followers to depose him."

"Steady on." Saren tapped a foot, his arms folded over his chest. "Some of us have no intention of *deposing* anyone. Least of all the most powerful man in the country."

Yala's hands curled into fists. "And some of us would prefer not to pay heed to ridiculous prophecies."

"It wasn't a prophecy." *Why* the Superior believed Yala capable of such a feat was as much a mystery as it had been the day she'd first uttered the words. "Hachim, we need to tell the others."

"The young ones won't understand." He glanced down the forest path, his expression torn. "You're right. We should tell them."

Fresh tears burned her eyes. Threl and Diaman, the youngest members of their group, had suffered greatly during Niema's prior absence, and their oldest enclave member, Ekim, was on permanent bed rest with failing health. She was in no kind of shape to evacuate; Niema had to leave before that ever became a possibility.

They returned to the wooden hut in which their bonded group resided. Darkness swathed the room, and two small figures crouched beside the sleeping mat upon which the oldest of their companions lay sleeping. New emotions battered at Niema's worn heart, confusion and anger mostly, but also a weary sadness beyond anything a ten-year-old should have experienced.

"You're leaving again, aren't you?" Diaman eyed her from beside Ekim's sleeping mat.

"I have to." The words stuck in her throat. "It's too dangerous for me to stay."

"You aren't coming back this time," Threl said, his voice thick with grief more befitting an adult than a Disciple too young to have advanced beyond their first vows. "Are you?"

"Of course I am." Regret choked her. "When this is over."

"When what is over?" Threl asked in the same quiet, sad voice. "When the god of death is gone?"

Niema flinched. "Who told you that?"

"We heard you two talking," Diaman accused. "Don't lie to us."

"It's not as easy as that." Hollow words, she knew, but neither child had the vocabulary to express the tide of emotions that were doubtless rushing forth from her and Hachim.

Niema turned to Ekim. The old woman hadn't stirred since they'd entered, and her breathing was audibly shallow. When Niema reached through their bond, seeking her familiar thread, Ekim felt... cold.

"Oh, Yalet, no," she whispered.

Hachim's eyes met hers, panic flashing through his gaze.

The old woman's breath was faint, and the temperature plummeted with each passing instant.

How did I not notice she was so close to death?

As Niema watched in mute horror, the shadows around her body darkened, creeping over her cold skin.

Mekan was trying to claim her.

"I won't let you." Niema said. "I won't let you take her."

She knelt, placed her hands on either side of the elderly Disciple, and whispered a prayer to Yalet. Hachim did likewise, his voice joining hers, but the children's sobbing smothered their words.

Niema spoke louder, a pleading refrain that ended in a scream as a horrible wrenching sensation rippled through their bond. Three screams mingled with her own as the thread connecting them to Ekim pulsed once then vanished.

"No!" she cried, reaching for the thread of life and finding only wisps of icy darkness. Hachim's hand closed around hers, his body shuddering with sobs.

"She's gone," he whispered. "She's gone."

Not gone.

Her sight blurred with tears, Niema saw Ekim sit up, saw her reach out a hand and wrap her spindly fingers around Threl's neck.

3

Yala heard screaming from the cabin and ran to the door. Shoved it open with her cane in time to see the elderly Disciple's hand lock around one of the young children's necks.

The old woman's face was blank, her gnarled fingers thick with shadow as they dug into the child's skin.

"Stop!" Niema tried to rise from her knees, trembling violently. "Stop, *please!*"

"Get off." Yala lifted her cane and struck the old woman in the kneecaps. She staggered, but her grip didn't break. The child gasped, shadows creeping around his throat, ready to rip him out of existence and into Mekan's domain.

With her free hand, Yala reached for the claw at her waist and pressed her fingertips to the cold surface.

The shadows' edges sharpened, and an icy rasp sounded in her ear. *"I told you... there is no escape, Disciple."*

Yala raised her voice and addressed the dead woman. "Cease your attack. Let him go."

Ekim's hand unclenched; the child fell, choking, from her

grip. Fixing sightless eyes upon her, she spoke, echoing Mekan's words. *"No escape, Disciple."*

Revulsion roiled through her, yet a perverse instinct arose, urging her to take the dark reins that presented themselves to her, to travel with Mekan beyond this realm and into one where death was not the end of existence.

"What's going on in—" Saren ran into the doorway and recoiled. "Gods!"

"She's dead." Yala's voice sounded surprisingly steady to her own ears. "Niema?"

No response came from Niema nor Hachim either. Both remained on their knees, bodies racked with tremors, while the young girl had crawled to a distant corner, knees drawn up to her forehead.

The boy lay gasping where Ekim had dropped him, and Saren swooped over, seeing the marks on his neck. "Did that old woman try to strangle him?"

"She did." Ekim hadn't moved: her body stood like a statue, shadows supporting her frail limbs. "We need to remove her."

A glance told her that Niema was beyond helping, so Yala beckoned to the old woman to follow her out of the cabin. When she took her first jerky step, Saren fled as if a war drake was snapping at his heels. Yala coaxed the old woman from the cabin, a soft gasp alerting her to Viam's arrival.

"No." Viam's eyes rounded. "That's—"

"Ekim. Niema's going to be insensible for a while." Yala took in a ragged breath. "We need to find someone else to deal with the body."

She *could* keep the body suspended indefinitely if she kept using her affinity with Mekan—and kept ignoring His seductive whisper in her ear. Though Mekan spoke not a word, He was always present where the dead lingered.

Rustling above prompted Yala to lift her head; a shadow

cast by wings spread wide told her of a war drake's arrival. "That had better be Superior Kralia."

A shower of leaves crashed upon her head as someone else descended in a flurry of cracked branches and broken vines. Kelan landed beside them, breathless. "Sorry—gods, what's wrong with her?" He'd caught sight of the old woman standing blank-faced at Yala's side.

"Mekan," she said. "Was that Superior Kralia?"

"Luckily, yes." Uncharacteristic grimness filled his voice. "You probably don't need more bad news, but the king's army is searching the forest. I saw a flight squad not a half day north of here."

Yala swore, swiping leaves out of her hair. "I hope they run into the dead."

The vast winged shadow vanished beyond the trees as the Superior descended into the wide clearing in which she spent most of her time. Green light flared from within, and a sound like birdsong rippled outward through the forest.

The cold remnants of Mekan's voice ceased. Every tree and plant swayed as if blown by a soft breeze, while Yala's body swayed, too, overcome with the urge to lie down. The song continued like a lullaby calling her to sleep, and one by one, the others succumbed, sitting down on fallen branches or merely sinking to the forest floor as their eyes slid shut. Yala's hands clenched, her mind fighting the impulse to surrender to the song's alluring rhythm.

When the sound faded, everyone startled as if woken from a deep slumber. Niema came stumbling out of the cabin, her face ashen and streaked with tears but her body no longer trembling as violently. "I'll talk to Superior Kralia."

"So will I." Yala cared little for the Superior's penchant for manipulation but admitted that her tactics might have been needed in this case. Freed from the blanket of grief, Niema didn't even react when she saw Ekim standing blank-faced near the cabin.

With a crook of her finger, Yala urged the vacant corpse to follow her to the clearing where the Superior had landed. A wide, grassy area dotted with wildflowers and circled by sturdy trees served as the enclave's beating heart, though not a temple in the traditional sense. The Superior, too, wore simple reed-woven clothing with little adornment save for the flowers entwined in her curly hair, forming a makeshift crown atop her head. Her unassuming air belied the power that simmered in her eyes and in the threads of green light blanketing the war drake at her side.

Yala halted, resting both hands upon her cane and keeping one eye on the deceptively placid beast. A flick of the Superior's wrist would be enough to command the creature to rip out her throat. When she did move, however, it was to coax a creeping vine to descend from a tree and wrap around Ekim's body, lowering the old woman's corpse gently to the ground. "She can rest now."

Yala was in no way fooled by the Superior's casual echo of the military's refrain for the dead. Ordering a war drake to tear her to shreds was far from the worst application of her considerable talents. Turning one's abilities against a fellow human was a violation of the enclave's law, yet the Superior herself had violated that boundary when she'd sent Niema to kill Yala in Setemar. No level of apology would be enough to earn Yala's forgiveness nor her trust, but Niema's own feelings on the matter were more complicated. In the depths of her grief, Yala hadn't the heart to condemn her for kneeling at Superior Kralia's feet and pressing her forehead to the ground.

"Rise, Niema," Superior Kralia intoned.

Niema did so, her eyes dull with pain, her voice tremulous. "The dead... they came."

"I know." The Superior spoke in surprisingly soft tones. "I sensed them."

"And the source?" Yala's fingers curled around her cane. "The first dead came from the village."

"I have dispatched the elite Disciples to ensure no more of Mekan's followers remain in the forest."

Have you now? Yala had not had a pleasant history with Yalet's elite, but she couldn't deny their efficiency. "Kelan said he saw the king's soldiers heading south too."

"Correct," said the Superior. "That is the reason for my delayed return. I did not wish to alert them to the enclave's location."

Niema made a choked noise. "They're looking for us?"

"For me." Yala knew she'd guessed right when The Superior's eyes gleamed. "That's why my intention is to leave. Kelan has offered us shelter at Skytower."

"That would be unwise." The Superior's words were directed more at Niema than Yala, but her shoulders tightened with renewed tension at the unspoken words festering between them like maggots.

Fuck it. "I thought you offered me shelter due to your belief that I can end the king's reign. That's why you endangered your enclave."

Niema flashed her an alarmed look, but her Superior remained unmoved. "I believed that we would be safer with you hiding among us than the alternative. That belief has now changed."

You don't say. Yala bit back a less pleasant reply and instead spoke with exaggerated patience. "Before I leave, would you enlighten me on how one might kill a man who has won the favour of the god of death? How would you proceed if you were in my place?"

"How?" Her calm demeanour shifted, and the glow in her

eyes gained the hint of a threat. "I would surpass the other Disciple's faith."

"Commit myself more strongly to the god of death, you mean?" A disbelieving laugh rose in Yala's throat. "I doubt I can outdo the faith of someone who lived inside Mekan's temple for more than a half decade. Besides, the only commitment Mekan accepts would render me incapable of completing the act."

To truly become Mekan's servant required one to travel into His realm and allow Him to take possession of their body. She'd seen similar unfortunates, rendered unrecognisable as human at all, when she and Niema had destroyed the island upon which Mekan's temple rested.

One would think that act would have also obliterated any chance of her gaining Mekan's favour, but the god of death's awareness of the human realm extended solely to sacrifices offered in His name. He'd known the temple had been destroyed, but it had been Yalet's power that had struck the decisive blow, and from Niema's hands, not Yala's.

"I merely state what I would do in your place."

Yes, and we both know how deep your commitment goes. Was *this* the Superior's grand strategy? Surrender?

"Now," the Superior continued, "I would speak to Niema alone."

Niema swallowed, her throat bobbing, and stepped forward. Superior Kralia had calmed her grief for the time being, but guilt must be devouring her from the inside. Niema's tendency for self-blame was matched only by a penchant for martyr-like actions that left her vulnerable to her Superior's influence, but the merest shake of her head told Yala not to linger. She'd have to trust Niema's ability to resist any manipulation.

Not that I'm entirely immune. Surrendering to Mekan's will was no strategy, but her words nudged at the back of Yala's mind, seeking the half-formed plans she'd conjured and discarded over the past few weeks.

Yala found the others where she'd left them outside the cabin, gathered in a huddle.

Saren waved her over. "Ready to leave? Kelan said we'd have to travel on the ground to avoid detection."

"It'll take too long." Reaching Skytower would be a weeks-long journey on foot that would all but certainly end in their arrest or worse.

"I can help you hide somewhere nearer," Kelan ventured. "Setemar, for instance. It'll take a couple of days at most by river."

The idea had merit—they had allies in Setemar, not to mention Vanat's old house as a potential base—but not for Yala. "Does the king know that Setemar once sat upon a Temple of Death?"

If he did, he might know Yala's role in its destruction.

"He might," Kelan acknowledged, "but none of the king's soldiers have been sighted there yet."

Yala grunted in annoyance—she'd known he'd have trouble staying confined to the enclave but couldn't help wondering if his tendency to wander had played a part in painting a target upon their backs—and shook her head. "The others can go there. I'll head the other way."

"What, as a diversion?" Viam glanced at Saren, and they shared one of those looks that roughly amounted to, *I knew she was going to say that.* "Absolutely not."

"I concur," Saren said. "What will that achieve? Even if you manage to kill them, the king will just send more."

"As soon as they find me, they'll stop searching. The enclave will be safe."

"The king wants the enclave too," Viam protested. "You'll have given yourself up for naught."

"He doesn't have the faintest idea where the enclave is,"

Yala said. "He wouldn't have sent a single patrol if waging war on the Disciples of Life was the purpose."

"So what, you're going to let his soldiers torture you to death?" Saren kicked at a loose rock. "Fuck, you're too valuable for that. He'll want to finish you himself."

"That's what you're counting on." Viam's gaze searched Yala's face. "Isn't it?"

Yala met her stare. "How else will I get close enough?"

"To do what?" Saren spoke into the hush that ensued. "Yala?"

"What else?" A smile ghosted her lips. "To wait for King Tharen to turn his back and then slit his throat from behind."

———

Niema knelt before her Superior, taking comfort in the forest's steady calm that she knew was as much a facade as the mask of concern on her Superior's face. Though Yalet's influence had lifted the suffocating grief enough for her to breathe, the emotions beat at the doors of her heart, and questions pounded inside her skull.

"What should I do?" She stood, wishing she didn't sound so fragile. Her Superior was not the trustworthy confidant she'd once thought, but she found herself yearning to hear her voice speak soothing words that would fix her fractured heart. "I can't stay, but my presence—is a danger."

"That is true." The simplicity of her statement burned like a brand. "Nevertheless, the king's forces are already extending their reach, and we need allies."

"Allies?" she echoed. "The other Disciples? You wish for me to go to Skytower?"

"The Disciples of the Sky have already offered to aid our cause, but we have yet to send contact to the Disciples of the Earth."

"You want me to go *there?*" She shuddered, remembering the Superior's casual command overtaking her will. Ordering her to kill Yala. "Are you sure they won't have surrendered to the king as the Disciples of the Sea and Flame did?"

"They have not."

Niema's mouth parted, words tumbling over one another in her head. "You want me to represent the Disciples of Life? What if they—they—heard—?"

I'm marked by Mekan.

"The other Disciples know nothing of you except for your devotion to the cause," she said. "You have a unique resistance to Mekan that others do not, which might prove advantageous."

I don't. I hear His voice whispering to me. Her nails bit into her palms, but she dipped her head. "I'll leave right away."

"No," said the Superior. "Yala will leave first. You will wait and ensure that the king's army is no longer near the forest, and then you will follow the river to Setemar."

An objection rose on her tongue and fizzled like a cook-fire extinguished by rain. Yala had made her decision, and she and Niema would part ways as planned. The others, too, had their own intentions.

As for her? Being marked by the god of death was usually a precursor to becoming one of His Disciples, but Niema had already sworn her vows and had received the honour of a direct vision from Yalet herself. More recently, she'd even accessed the higher levels of Yalet's power when she'd imposed her will upon another human to save her own life and Yala's.

That Superior Kralia had not expelled her from the enclave on the spot was surely due to her own violation of those same laws; though Niema had yet to tell another soul what she'd done, little slipped past her Superior's notice.

The thought of how easy it had been sickened her almost as much as the notion of being bound to the god of death.

4

Yala waited at the clearing's entrance for Niema, prepared to rescue her from her Superior's clutches if need be. She did not stay long, returning with a glassy-eyed expression that had Yala worried. "Are you all right?"

Niema took in a measured breath. "The Superior asked me to go to Setemar to ask the Disciples of the Earth if they might consider an alliance."

"That's not a terrible idea." Kelan glided to join them. "The king hasn't pushed them to surrender. I can't say he won't, mind. He does seem unpredictable since his return from the dead."

The king had not, in fact, returned from death, and while Yala was unclear on whether he'd truly visited Mekan's realm, he still *looked* like a living, breathing person. She had to believe he could be killed in the normal manner.

He's no immortal.

"I'd like to think the Disciples of the Earth won't allow themselves to be conquered as easily as the last time," Yala said. "You should wait until tomorrow to leave. I'll be gone by then, and with luck, so will the king's soldiers."

Saren's mouth turned down at the corners. "Are you certain they won't kill you on the spot?"

"No, but I'd like to believe they'll realise my value."

I'm a prize to them, she thought. *I'm a Disciple of Death, and they'll want to present me to the king before they take my life.*

If her suspicions turned out to be wrong, she'd have at least diverted the monarch's attention from the forest and offered the others a chance to escape.

"My Superior agreed," Niema said. "She offered to prepare your war drake."

"How generous of her."

Yala waited for the beating of wings indicating a war drake's descent and returned to the clearing. The Superior was no longer anywhere to be seen, and in her place sat the war drake whom Yala had helped raise in the capital, already fitted with a harness but lacking the weapons of a fully equipped war drake. Without prompting, the beast crossed to her, lowering its head.

"Is that all?" Kelan appeared at her shoulder. "Aren't you at least going to give a heartfelt goodbye? This might well be the last time we speak."

"You expect to die, do you?" she said. "Or you expect *me* to die?"

"I'd like to hope neither of us will, but given the forces we're up against, it's best to be realistic."

Her mouth twitched into a wry grin. "Better hope we don't end up in the same place when we die, then."

Generally, one fate was reserved for Disciples of Death: an eternity in in Mekan's realm.

"I'd drink to that if I had one," he replied. "Otherwise, I might see you in Dalathar."

"As close to hell as you can get if you ask me." Saren

moved to hug Yala. "I'll drag you out of Mekan's realm myself if I have to."

"Likewise." Yala hugged him back. "Stay safe."

She hugged Viam next and then Niema. The Disciple of Life felt more fragile than usual, her body trembling as though she might shake apart like a pillar of sand, and Yala wondered how deeply she depended upon her Superior to hold her together in the wake of Ekim's death.

You'd better not let her break, she thought as she climbed onto the war drake's back. Her leg gave its usual twinge of protest, but otherwise, her body settled into the motions naturally; the beast was placid enough that she wondered if Superior Kralia had uttered commands in its ear for weeks.

Turning to the others, she lifted a hand in farewell. "I'll see you all again."

Hopefully not in the afterlife.

In a beat, the war drake took flight, its huge wings carrying her above the clearing. A thrill sang through her blood, one she hadn't experienced since she'd arrived in the jungle. The wind lifted her hair with each beat of the war drake's wings and brought a familiar sense of rightness unmatched by any other.

Yala turned northward, flying low until she was far enough from the enclave to risk ascending higher. It didn't take her long to spot the winged beasts above the trees: seven of them, assembled in the formation she knew so well. A full squad of seven, with a captain at their head.

The captain, she didn't recognise from a distance, but they'd already seen Yala. Their war drake overtook their fellow riders, its wide, leathery wings carrying it over the canopy. The beast was outfitted for war, spears in a bag strapped to its side and armour protecting its vulnerable lower belly from attack, while its rider was a hard-faced young woman only a year or two older than Yala had been when she'd taken command of her own squad. Not old enough to have enlisted the first time but dangerous all the same. She carried no weapons save for the void drake's claw concealed at her waist, and no lone rider could hope to best a full flight squad in open combat.

Too late for second-guessing. Nudging her war drake to slow its flight, she lifted a hand in a gesture that would be taken as a greeting from a fellow flier. Not a sign of an attack but not a surrender either.

"You're Yala Palathar." The woman guided her war drake to a halt above the tree line. "You've led us on quite the chase."

"That's right." Yala kept her face carefully neutral. "You were looking for me?"

Out of the corner of her eye, the other six fliers closed in around their leader. One, a man with a long, whiskered face that reminded her of a skirrit, eyed her with open suspicion, one hand twitching towards his army-issued dagger. The others wore expressions of mingled wariness and what could only be described as awe.

"The king ordered us to find you," the captain said. "Where have you been?"

"I suffered a severe injury," Yala said. "I was recuperating. Might I ask why His Majesty sent an entire flight squad to find one retired captain?"

Does he want me dead? None of the fliers had drawn a weapon, but death was far from the worst fate they might have inflicted upon her.

"Few possess a reputation like yours," said the woman. "It's my understanding that he intends to offer you a position as squad leader."

Squad leader? She'd expected to hear *Disciple of Death*—but this woman was starkly human, untouched by Mekan. Did she not know of the king's intentions, or had his strategy changed? The dearth of news that reached the enclave made it hard to judge, but these soldiers undoubtedly weren't Disciples.

"Well?" the woman pressed. "Will you accept his offer?"

Her question left Yala's mind blank. Did she *want* to be a flight squad leader again? She'd never expected to be offered that chance.

Nor did she trust the king's offer came without a price as blood-drenched as any bargain with Mekan.

Declining, however, was out of the question, and her plan would be easier to accomplish from the back of a war drake than on the ground.

"Yes," she said. "I'll speak to him."

"Good," said the captain. "You'll come with us. To Dalathar."

———

Niema woke entangled in the arms of her fellow enclave members. Grief and sorrow pulsed through their bond even as the others slept on; she surveyed the sleeping children curled up together, blinking dampness from her eyes.

The younger ones will be fine, she told herself. They'd find a new group to bond with. And Hachim... she hadn't the heart to wake him. Quietly, she gathered the travel pack she'd prepared the night before, after they'd given Ekim her final rites and laid her to rest.

Dawn cast cold grey light between the dense web of branches above. The murmur of voices—many, at least ten—drew her to the Superior's clearing. Disciples gathered within. All of whom wore unusual garments formed of thick layers of reeds interwoven with leaves and tree bark to form an armour of sorts. The elite Disciples of Life: those who were trained, in opposition to Yalet's will, to take the lives of any who threatened the enclave.

At one time, Niema would have recoiled at their presence. Taking a life was against Yalet's nature, but Mekan was the antithesis of everything Yalet stood for. The opposition of life itself.

For that reason, Niema could do nothing but hope that Yala's plan to kill the king succeeded. After all, what was one man's death weighed up against Mekan's conquest of Laria? Upon Yalet's annihilation?

Doubtless these Disciples had gone through the same dilemma. She watched through the gaps in the branches but did not venture closer; though the two elites who'd been sent to capture her on Superior Kralia's orders had died in the ensuing fight, her mistrust lingered.

The feeling was mutual. Any conversation she'd had with the elites had been terse, as if they knew, on some level, that she was marked by Mekan.

A gasp escaped when she recognised a new face amid the elites: Bitra, whose sister had been one of the recent dead. Around her late thirties, she wore her hair in looping braids against her skull and carried twin birthmarks resembling leaves conjoined at the tip upon her neck. The sign, taken as a blessing from Yalet, had also signalled that her twin children would be Disciples too, and that had certainly been true of Diaman and Threl.

Typically, the children of Disciples were raised outside of the enclave until they were old enough to take their first vows and then taken care of communally, but Niema had an enduring affection for Diaman and Threl's biological mother, enough to shield her from Kelan's dalliances. In her new armour, Bitra was almost unrecognisable, and when she spied Niema watching, the distrust in her eyes cut her to the bone.

"Niema." Superior Kralia strode from the clearing, clad in armour to match the elite Disciples. "Did you wish to speak with me?"

"I was… walking," she said. "I heard voices. I didn't know Bitra had joined the elite Disciples."

"I agreed to give her the chance," said the Superior. "Elite Disciples would normally face an extended period of training, but the situation calls for urgency and for as many as possible to assemble to oppose Mekan's threat."

Niema swallowed hard. "I'll do what I can, but I'm not sure Hachim ought to come with me."

"I would agree, but there should be two of you present in case one of you should fail."

Or one of them should fall to Mekan's influence. The implication was another blow to Niema's bruised heart. "And Yala? Do you think she'll succeed in her plan?"

"I believe that it's time for her to act."

That's no answer. "Do you not worry she might fall to Mekan's influence?"

"That is a concern," she said, "but nobody possesses skills as unique as Yala's. Except, perhaps, for you."

A flinch trembled through Niema's bones. "I'm no soldier."

"You have an unusual affinity with Mekan's realm, Niema," said Superior Kralia. "One that might make a difference to our survival in the upcoming conflict."

Nausea twisted inside her. She didn't understand how, exactly, her bond with Yala had enabled her to force her will upon the beasts that rose from the Void. Nor did her Superior, though evidently, that had not dissuaded her from hoping Niema would use that ability to benefit her fellow Disciples.

Niema herself would never place any faith in a talent that

had its origins in Mekan's domain. No... for now, her faith rested with Yala.

5

Kelan was jerked out of sleep by something sharp and scaly prodding him in the ear. He turned on his sleeping mat and found a pair of round eyes watching him from the bushes. "What is it?"

The creature—known locally as a tree-raptor—resembled a war drake in miniature, its head on a level with Kelan's knee when it sat upright. They were a common sight in the jungle, but it was usually the kekins that disturbed his sleep, inquisitive creatures that rummaged through their campsite at first light and stole anything edible they could get their hands on.

He'd been offered a place in Niema's hut, but like Yala's companions, he'd opted to sleep out in the open with the trees providing ample cover in case of rain. Rubbing sleep from his eyes, he sat up and checked on the others. Saren and Viam were awake, their packs readied for the journey to Setemar. They'd decided to seek refuge there first while Niema and Hachim met with the Disciples of the Earth. Should the situation prove unsafe, his invitation to Skytower stood, but he'd have an easier time avoiding the king's soldiers on the road if he travelled alone.

The tree-raptor continued to follow Kelan as he joined the others for breakfast, settling beside a nearby tree and emitting a curious chirping noise. Kelan tossed it a piece of groundfruit, which it snapped up with pointy teeth.

"What's with that creature?" Saren asked. "Why does it seem so attached to you?"

"It's Superior Kralia's," Viam ventured, putting her food bowl aside. "I've seen her using it as a messenger."

"Really?" He tilted his head and laughed when the creature mimicked the movement. "We could use one if we're going to part ways."

"Depends what Niema's Superior tells her," Viam said. "It won't be safe to leave until the flight squad has left the forest."

"Assuming Mekan's monsters haven't taken their place." Saren clamped his mouth shut as Niema walked over and sat beside Kelan with no acknowledgement of their previous argument. Grief and shock had pushed away all other considerations.

"The road's clear," she told them. "According to my Superior, the war drakes have gone."

With Yala. Whether she lived or died was out of their hands.

They finished breakfast and gathered their belongings. Kelan carried the least, as he planned to arrive at Skytower within a day or two at most. Lifting a hand in farewell, he addressed Niema. "I feel compelled to ask you not to throw yourself in front of any rampaging void drakes while we're apart."

A flush crept over her cheeks despite the lingering sorrow in her eyes. "Don't be absurd."

"I'm serious." Niema possessed a distressing tendency to

sacrifice herself on behalf of others, and her current fragile emotional state left too much to chance.

"I'll be careful if you are." She didn't return his smile, but some grief lifted from her expression. "Send word with Molin when you reach Skytower.

"With whom?" A chirp sounded at his shoulder, and a reptilian head emerged from his pack. *Ah.* "I'll see you soon."

At least he'd have company on his journey. When he rose above the trees, he found the skies mercifully free of war drakes and gained confidence the longer he travelled without encountering anyone either living or dead. A day passed before the mountains in Laria's southwest appeared like the spine of a great beast jutting out of the ground, and he opted to stay at an inn on the road to avoid running into an ambush in the dark.

He saw a few soldiers outside and entertained the idea of asking a few questions, but he little desired to draw attention to himself. He picked up a few snippets of conversation—the king had sent out a conscription order to any towns and villages within the capital's orbit—but didn't linger. It did not sound like the king was roaming, but Kelan would never forget the chilling sight of Laria's monarch seated upon a void drake. His shoulder tingled, a reminder of a wound inflicted by a similar monster.

Within the hour, he spied the formidable shape of Skytower jutting from the mountains. Its five stories were edged with balconies offering the airborne Disciples easy access to any of its rooms save for the one at the very top. Kelan aimed for the fifth floor, where the Superior's rooms were located, and landed in front of the door.

Knocking, he called out, "It's me."

At her confirmation, he entered and knelt on the large prayer mat dominating the room. Terethik's face loomed overhead from a vast painting depicting a scene of revelry, but the woman who occupied the seat in front of him bore no traces of levity in her expression. The Superior did not stand—as a child, she'd faced an illness that had taken her ability to walk—but she still towered over Kelan from her chair. Her embroidered clothing gleamed with gemstones, and bright feathers fanned across her high cheekbones.

"I apologise for not sending word of my return," Kelan began. "The enclave was attacked, and I thought you'd want to hear word directly from me."

"You thought correctly," she said. "Attacked? By the dead?"

"That, and a group of soldiers was sighted near the forest." He skipped over Yala's surrender—he'd get to that later—and explained the brutal assault upon the enclave. When he'd finished, his Superior's eyes flickered towards Molin, crouched on the prayer mat beside him. "And your companion?"

"Superior Kralia's," he said. "At a guess, she wanted an easy way to convey messages between here and the enclave."

"Her position has not changed following the attack?" she asked. "That is, she has no intention of meeting the king's forces with her own?"

"Not to my knowledge, but she thinks that collectively, we stand a stronger chance of resisting Mekan."

"I agree," she said. "It would not surprise me if His Majesty believes the same and will act accordingly."

"What, recruit us like he did with the Disciples of the Flame?" Unfortunately, he'd had the same suspicion himself. "I hope he's left Setemar alone. That's where Niema and the others were going. To meet with the Disciples of the Earth."

"A worthy idea." She drummed her fingers on her chair's arm. "It might be that I worry for naught, but I suspect he's looking carefully at anyone who might have had a hand in Superior Datriem's attempt on his life."

"You don't think he'll come here?" She wouldn't bend

before the king, not like Superior Shralin had, but angering a monarch who held an allegiance with the god of death carried its own perils.

"If he does, I will state that my loyalty is to Terethik alone." She gestured to the deity whose smiling face overlooked the prayer mat. "Niema plans to meet with the Disciples of the Earth... and what of Yala Palathar?"

She'd seen through him as she always did. He'd skirted around the subject, unsure of the response she might give to the news of Yala's seeming surrender. At one time, he might have stated it straight out, but the consequences of not watching his tongue had rebounded upon him one too many times. Affecting a casual tone, he said, "The last I saw, she was travelling north to intercept the soldiers searching for her."

Her brows rose. "Searching for her?"

"That was her assumption," he added. "The soldiers knew nothing of the enclave's location. Yala has a plan, I've no doubt, but I'm not privy to the details."

"I see." The tension in her voice indicated that she, too, remembered how she'd once tried to imprison Yala here in Skytower to prevent the enemy from taking advantage of her status as a Disciple of Death. "What did Superior Kralia think of her strategy?"

"She agreed that surrender—real or feigned—was the best path forward."

"I doubt Yala Palathar has a word of surrender inside her."

Kelan's mouth parted in surprise. Did his own Superior believe Yala stood a chance of thwarting Mekan? It wouldn't be the first time she'd done so, but the odds had never been so thoroughly weighted against her.

"Exactly," he found himself saying. "I think that if anyone has a chance of pulling off an impossible plan, it's Yala."

"Then we find ourselves in accord." She met his eyes,

power simmering in her irises. "However, in this war, I suspect it is the gods alone who will decide the outcome."

————

Yala shifted on the war drake's back. Her hips ached from the long hours of flight, and her right leg was bothering her again. She wished she had some bitterleaf to chew, but she'd had little access to her pack. They'd stopped once or twice to allow their steeds to drink from the rivers but had otherwise flown throughout the day.

Now, night was falling, and as she'd hoped, the captain led them to set up camp near a village on the main road to the capital. The beasts were unused to flying for long stretches of time, so they'd opted to split their journey in two. Though the squad leader, Lisek, couldn't have had more than three weeks of training, she was a natural flier in a manner that reminded Yala of her younger self.

Her squad members were less confident. Yala spied one of them struggling to attach their war drake's chain to a tree and went to help; the rider, a gangly youth named Thekel, reminded her of Saren, back when he'd first taken on the role of scout.

And so the cycle begins anew, she thought. *We train new riders so that they can take wing when our end comes, and they pass on those same skills to their replacements.*

"You have remarkable control over that war drake," Lisek observed as Yala returned to her own beast. The captain released her hair from its tie, and the firelight softened her features and made her look younger. *Gods, we were children back then.*

Yala made a noncommittal noise. "I was its first rider."

That, and Superior Kralia had exerted her influence over the beast during Yala's recovery. In truth, she didn't entirely trust the Superior not to order the beast to pitch her off its back to her death if the mood took her, but she had to admit that would be preferable to slow torture at the hands of the king if he should become aware of her treachery.

Seizing the opening, she went on, "You haven't told me why the king sent a full flight squad after me. Did he expect you to be challenged on the way?"

"He told us to be prepared," Lisek said. "There are wild beasts in the forest."

She made no mention of the Disciples of Life. Nor had anyone alluded to the *other* Disciples, the ones with whom the king had found companionship in exile. Indeed, the army's current role was less than clear to her, but pushing too far with her questions risked one of her fellow fliers stabbing her in the night.

I came here half expecting to die, she reminded herself. *What's a question or two going to hurt?*

She tried for an obvious one. "Are we still at war with Rafragoria? Is that why he needs to rebuild the army?"

"No." Lisek's brow furrowed. "There's been no mention of Rafragoria for a while."

They're dead, then. The knowledge left a bitter taste in her mouth. Perhaps she was a hypocrite to distinguish between taking a life in battle and indiscriminate mass murder, but Rafragoria had never conspired with Mekan. That had always been a lie, concocted by King Tharen to cover his ambitions.

Out of the corner of her eye, she caught sight of the skir-rit-faced man—Hian, he was called—watching her. Her well-honed instincts told her to end her questions there; not every member of the squad had readily accepted her excuses for not returning to the capital.

They flew above the ring of cliffs marking Setemar, the mining city that housed the Temple of the Earth. Legend said Setem had carved the temple into the cliffs with His own hand, but those stories didn't mention that beneath the earth lay a dormant temple built to a different god altogether long before any Larians had ever settled on the continent. If the king had a hint of Yala's role in the fall of that second Temple of Death, he never would have ordered her to be brought in alive, but she had the growing suspicion that his knowledge of what had transpired in his seven-year absence had been conveyed from the mouths of any merchant or sailor unfortunate enough to find themselves stranded on the island together with the exiled monarch.

The outline of Dalathar appeared as a sprawl of thatched rooftops extending from a high wall encasing the central portion of the city. Two buildings dwarfed the inner walls: the large, tiered palace, partially hidden behind a second wall that encircled its grounds and the adjacent barracks, and the taller, narrower shape of the Temple of the Flame. That the latter remained standing indicated that the king had accepted the Disciples' surrender, but that might not have been enough to earn forgiveness for their former leader's crimes.

Orderliness replaced the chaos that had engulfed the capital during her last visit, with armed guards at the palace's front and back gates watching their descent into the paddock that ran parallel to the palace complex's eastern wall. The war drake voiced an objection to landing in the confined pen, but Yala silenced it with a slither of raptor meat taken from a bucket near the gate. The flight division was back in working order, a minor miracle given the extent to which the king's son had fucked up his last attempt.

Lisek waited for her at the paddock gate. "The king will want to see you immediately."

A shiver trailed down Yala's spine, part fear, part anticipation. "I'm sure he'll want me to make myself presentable first."

Most of her clothes had been left in the capital after her abrupt departure for the forest, and she was smeared with dirt and grime from the road. She followed Lisek past a pair of uniformed guards into the palace grounds, each step bringing the uncanny sense of treading in the footsteps of her past self, as if she were sliding back into a reality long since consigned to the abyss.

The familiarity vanished when she spied the winged beast hovering above the palace, its obsidian scales blotting out the sunlight and casting the tiered building in shadow. Her breath caught, and she made no effort to hide her reaction. The others, too, were visibly unsettled at the sight, closing ranks around their captain.

Yala affected a casual tone, her fingers tightening on her cane. "What is that beast?"

The cold burn of the void drake's claw against her thigh seemed to paint her as a liar, but the others showed no reaction to Mekan's presence. *Whatever happened to His Majesty recruiting Disciples of Death? Or did he kill them all?*

"It's the king's new security." Lisek led the others alongside the inner fence circling the training grounds outside the barracks. "His Majesty does not trust the Disciples."

"You mean the Disciples of the Flame?" she said. "I heard they pledged themselves to serve the monarch." Not everyone had done so; Yala recalled a group of rebels who'd defied their Superior, but they were surely dead by now.

"They did," she said. "The king is merciful, but he has no intention of being betrayed again."

"And where is the king's son?" Yala addressed another pressing question. "In the palace?"

"Where else would he be?" was Lisek's reply.

In jail? No, he'd committed no errors by taking a throne

that had been vacant at the time, but Yala doubted King Tharen would suffer any potential rivals. He'd have tucked Daliel out of the way, inside a cell or otherwise.

As they entered the barracks, a group of soldiers walked past. A bearded face snagged Yala's attention. *Nalen.* The burly man had last been seen guarding the Undercity, home of the city's most impoverished. She tried to catch his eye, but Nalen kept walking down the corridor and out of sight.

It had crossed her mind that the king might rebuild his forces by forcibly recruiting those who'd once served in the army, but she had not considered she might be blamed. That, or Nalen believed her to have joined the monarch's side willingly. She'd have to set him straight on that when she told him her plan.

Should the king's offer of employment be genuine, Yala would not strike him directly, not at first.

To start off with, she'd make herself indispensable.

6

The day after his return to Skytower, Kelan faced the prospect of interacting with the Disciples he'd left in the capital when he'd helped Yala's companions flee the city. When he entered the cafeteria at breakfast, he collected a plate and took it to the table in the corner where Lakiel and Brikel sat. The siblings shared the same lanky frames and long noses, though Lakiel was several years older. Brikel wore a pleased grin when Kelan sat down, and since neither told him to leave, he assumed he was forgiven for his unintentional abandonment.

"So you survived," Lakiel commented. "I wondered."

"I was in the forest with the Disciples of Life." Kelan took a bite of peeled groundfruit. "Did the Superior not tell you?"

"She did." Brikel poked her brother in the arm. "Have they agreed to help us in our fight against the king?"

Lakiel jerked away from her, scowling. "Don't be absurd. We aren't fighting anyone."

"Not yet," Kelan corrected. "I'm impressed that you managed to get away from the capital when no Disciples were allowed to leave the upper city."

"My brother can be surprisingly devious." Brikel gave him another nudge, this time in the shoulder. "The guards weren't attending to every part of the city wall, so he slipped past them and created a diversion to help the rest of us escape. The hard part was avoiding patrols outside of the city. I swear every mercenary soldier across Laria has flocked back to Dalathar in the past few weeks."

"To join the monarch." He picked up another groundfruit piece. "I apologise for leaving you there. I was helping—"

"Yala Palathar," Lakiel finished. "I know."

"I was helping some of her allies escape the capital," he clarified. "The king ordered the immediate surrender of all Disciples of Death, and Yala and Niema were both seriously injured."

"Did you say you took Yala to the Disciples of *Life?*" Brikel's eyes rounded. "Since when did they offer shelter to Mekan's followers?"

"Believe me, nobody was more surprised than Yala." Kelan glanced up at the sound of beating wings as the tree-raptor descended upon the table and promptly snapped up a piece of groundfruit from his plate. In response to Lakiel's look of bewilderment, he said, "This is Molin. Superior Kralia sent him to convey messages back and forth from the tower."

"So you weren't just slacking off in the forest, pretending to forge an allegiance?"

"Lakiel!" said his sister.

"Of course not." Kelan offered a sheepish grin. "I was making progress, but I was pressured into leaving sooner than I planned by an unfortunate attack from the dead."

"Did Yala leave too?"

"That…" He put down his fork. "I believe the Superior would not want me to discuss the subject openly."

"No, she wouldn't." Kriam, an older Disciple who'd also

witnessed the king's return to power, walked past their table. "She also wants to talk to all three of you."

She's giving us a mission? He finished his meal and ascended to the topmost floor of Skytower. A few others waited outside the Superior's office, including Ranit, a younger male Disciple who'd been in the capital with Lakiel when Kelan had left.

Together, they entered the office and knelt before their Superior.

"I assume that Kelan has told at least some of you of his recent visit to the Disciples of Life," she said to their group. "And Superior Kralia's intention to seek alliances with the other Disciples."

"He did." Lakiel glanced at him. "He refused, however, to share what Yala Palathar is doing."

"I thought the matter was between us," Kelan said, somewhat insulted at the incredulity that briefly crossed the Superior's face. "If I have permission to share...?"

"Yes," said Superior Sietra. "In brief, Yala Palathar went to confront a flight squad the king sent to search the forest."

Lakiel made a soft noise of disbelief. "She gave herself up?"

"Not exactly," he said. "She has her own agenda, one I assume involves taking advantage of her enemy's closeness to learn his weaknesses."

"I agree," said Superior Sietra, "which brings me to your next mission. I believe it's in our interests for several of you to return to Dalathar."

"You want us to go *back* to the capital?" Ranit gaped at her. "We nearly died. We're not allowed to even enter the upper city."

"Technically, we are," Brikel put in. "If the king kept the same rules as his son, we'll have to report to the guards whenever we leave or enter, but it isn't an outright ban."

"*You* aren't coming," Lakiel cut in. To the Superior, he added, "This is an unacceptable gamble. The king will almost certainly force us to surrender to him as the Disciples of the Flame did."

"He might," she acknowledged, "which is why you'll have to be discreet."

"Discreet?" Lakiel cast Kelan an incredulous look that he thought rather unfair. "This plan is doomed to failure. I apologise, Superior, but I won't put my sister in danger."

"Your sister can make her own choices," Brikel retaliated. "Besides, how are we supposed to know what the king is up to if nobody is brave enough to go near the city?"

That was true, and if he was honest with himself, he wouldn't mind having a front-row view of Yala's confrontation with the king.

Looks like we're both going back into the war drakes' den, Yala.

————

King Tharen had removed the flowers. That was the first thing Yala noticed when she approached the palace, dressed in a clean uniform and smarting with the pain of Nalen's rejection.

I deserved it, she told herself. *I left him to the king's mercy.* Never mind that she'd been a breath away from Mekan's grasp at the time.

In her weeks of absence, the king had removed every touch of his son's influence, and the palace's tiers were as austere as a tomb. Soon, she was sure, the old military banners and flags would replace the flower beds, but right now, all lay in darkness as though the winged beast cast a shadow large enough to swallow the world.

Months ago, when she'd witnessed Mekan's beasts

tearing their way into this realm not far from the palace, Yala would have never believed she'd soon see those same beasts armed in defence of Laria, and part of her expected a claw to take off her head as she climbed the palace stairs. Each step brought a stab of pain in her wounded leg, and her body ached from the prolonged hours of flight. Or the memory of being chased down these stairs by an irate guard, who'd wanted to put her to death for accusing the Disciples of the Flame of murdering the same man who now waited for her inside the palace.

How very wrong her assumptions had been.

Unlike the exterior, the inside of the palace had changed little since her last visit. A succession of doors led into a wide room decorated with portraits of past monarchs and dominated by a towering throne. Serpentine figures representing the god of the flames flanked each side of the chair, and Yala wondered at the irony of the king sitting between two representations of the deity whose followers had nearly brought about his end.

Then, she locked eyes with King Tharen, and her heart stilled. Though several years older, the monarch was comparatively unchanged from the last time she'd seen him alive. His bronze skin had darkened, and he was dressed in his regular attire and not outfitted for flight, but his clothing was layered with its usual beads and coloured threads, and his crown might never have left his head. As for his son? Daliel had been swept out of sight as if he'd never existed.

Yala knelt, her injured leg throbbing in protest, and silently prayed to any god that might be willing to spare her that King Tharen saw no trace of deceit on her face.

"Rise, Captain Yala Palathar," he intoned.

Captain. The word summoned her past self as surely as Mekan's touch might stir the dead into a semblance of life. A smile stretched her lips, false as thin paper, as she rose to her feet. "Your Majesty. I confess... I didn't believe, at first, that you lived."

"Many did not." He surveyed her, his gaze lingering on her cane. "I am glad to see another of my former captains survived too."

Are you? His words invited an explanation, so she pushed on with her cover story. "I was injured and went outside of the city to recuperate. It did not seem safe to stay, given the recent attacks." She avoided giving specifics, though from what she'd heard from Lisek, Rafragoria had been entirely blamed for Mekan's assault on the capital. Not the man who stood before her and lied through his teeth.

"One of my first acts upon my return was to apply myself to restoring Laria's army to its former extent," he said. "The Flight Division in particular was in need of reform, and I would be glad of your assistance in that endeavour."

"You want me to be captain again." Her face ached from keeping her false smile in place.

"Correct." His gaze went, again, to her right leg. "I'm told you were injured during your squad's final mission."

Yala's fingers tightened around her cane. *Not dancing around the subject, is he?* They'd last seen one another before Yala's squad had gone to the island, but it had been he who'd given the order.

He who'd made her a Disciple of Death.

"It won't impede my ability to fly." She released some of her caution: Condemning her to death had never been his intention. "I hope you'll permit me a question. What enemies do you expect the flight division to face in the near future? Captain Lisek told me Rafragoria is no longer a threat."

"That is true," he said. "Laria needs to present a strong front regardless, but I'm sorry to say that we have other potential threats much closer to home."

"The Disciples." A stab of panic hit her when his mouth tightened with what might have been anger.

"Yes," he said. "You, I understand, are the one who broke the news to my son. Is that correct?"

Panic continued to twist inside, but she pushed it down, willing her racing heart to calm. "He told you that?"

"He did," said the king. "I understand that you were unjustly arrested as a result, and I would offer an apology for that transgression."

A disbelieving laugh caught in her throat. She swallowed it. "I am grateful, Your Majesty. I only shared what I believed to be true. If I'd had any idea you were still alive…"

"You would have done the same, I hope. To be exiled from one's country is a terrible crime. I was complacent, I admit… my assumption that the Disciples would adhere to the agreements of my predecessors clouded me to their treachery. Now I understand that those capable of drawing upon the power of the gods need to be more carefully watched."

Including Disciples of Death? Perhaps he did not entirely trust her yet, but he had yet to allude to any skills she might have picked up on the island. Nor did he display any awareness of the void drake's claw concealed at her waist.

I could use it on him now, she thought, weighing the odds of drawing the weapon and hurling it through the king's exposed neck before the guards at the door were able to intervene. Of course, that was assuming King Tharen had obtained no defensive skills upon the island himself. He'd spent more than a half decade inside a Temple of Death. For all she knew, the face he wore was as much a mask as her own smile.

"I will give you time to return to the barracks," he said to her. "You'll receive a new squad to train tomorrow. If, that is, you accept my offer."

If she refused, would he let her walk out of this room alive? Doubtful. "I accept."

Yala knelt, bowed her head, and thought, *I'll slit your throat with my own hand while Mekan is there to watch.*

Somewhere close, she could have sworn she heard the god of death's laughter.

7

The day after her return to the capital, Yala met her new squad.

The flight division's new hopefuls gathered in neat lines under Commander Sranak's watchful eye. The man had changed little in the seven years that had elapsed since the end of the war except for a few more grey hairs and more lines on his face, and he'd reacted to Yala's return with surprisingly little shock. Of course, her reinstatement as captain was a minor consideration compared to a dead monarch returning to his throne.

Yala surveyed the group of novices and wondered how many would be alive by the season's end. Some were barely of age, their skin dotted with acne and their expressions by turns eager and apprehensive. "Have any of you flown before?"

Nobody responded. Yala suppressed a sigh, resting her palms atop her cane. "Have any of you been within a *handspan* of a war drake?"

Two hands lifted, one belonging to a female soldier who already had a few scars on her face and the other to a larger male who looked more suited to hauling heavy objects around than performing graceful aerial manoeuvres. Yala committed their faces to memory and then addressed the others. "The rest of you are to come with me."

They hastened to follow her to the back gate. The smell of rancid meat drifted over from the paddocks along with the usual chorus of muffled snarls from disgruntled war drakes.

"What are we doing?" asked a youth that Yala suspected had lied about his age to get into the army. "I didn't know we were allowed in the paddocks yet."

"I want to be sure none of you are going to piss yourselves or pass out long before you have to climb on a war drake's back." The commander had given her the key to the paddocks, so Yala walked straight to the gate with a line of increasingly nervous soldiers behind her. "This is the most effective test."

They'd all been through a basic level of army training, some having served as foot soldiers, but she'd have a matter of weeks at most to forge an effective squad, and she preferred not to lose any of them on the first flight.

Her instincts were swiftly proven right. When she unlocked the gate, three novices fled outright. Others huddled behind her, the stench of urine filling the air as the fearsome beasts growled restlessly behind their muzzles and dragged their heavy chains along the ground. Yala took note of who appeared the most composed and chose the four remaining squad members from among their number.

On their way to the barracks, Commander Sranak accosted her. "Yala Palathar, what in the gods' names are you doing?"

"Most of those sorry excuses for novices hadn't been within a handspan of a war drake before now," she told him. "I've likely saved several lives by sparing them."

His moustache drooped. "That's not the method I would have chosen. In future, please ask first."

"I will." Maybe she'd been too bold, but she'd committed to her role, and no self-respecting squad leader would knowingly let cowards take wing.

Perhaps it ought to have disturbed her how quickly her old instincts had taken over, as if part of her had been waiting for her inevitable return to the army.

She had the squad run through basic exercises while she took note of who would fly best in each position. Toreth, the youngest and smallest, would fit well into the role of scout, while a young man named Gorel had prior training as a healer. The scarred female soldier, Yurel, was the most adept at offering advice on handling the war drakes as if she'd had extensive experience with dangerous animals. Yala didn't ask, nor did she make anything more than cursory conversation with her recruits. She didn't need to grow attached; in fact, her safety and theirs might depend on her doing the opposite.

After she dismissed them at the day's end, she went to report to the commander. On the way to his office, a commotion outside drew her ear. Recognising the sound of punches being thrown, she ducked outside and spied a pair of guards dragging a struggling man past the barracks. Yala recognised his craggy, worn face as one she'd seen in the Undercity, among Nalen's followers.

The man's eyes bulged when he spotted Yala. "It's you!"

Yala's spine stiffened, but she managed a confused lift of her brow. "Do I know you?"

"Everyone's lost their fucking minds." He fought to break free of the guards' hold, his face reddened with exertion. "The king is going to kill us all!"

Her hand curled tight around her cane. "I have no idea what you're talking about."

"Nobody leaves the palace grounds without the king's permission," one of the guards grunted. "His Majesty was clear: Desertion is to be severely punished."

"I saw what he's building!" the man shrieked. "I saw it!"

Saw what? Yala's fingers tingled beneath her drakeskin gloves, and the claw—always concealed at her waist—turned ice-cold against her leg as a vast shadow fell overhead. The guards released the man so abruptly that he stumbled forward.

The void drake descended. The man tried to run, but he didn't make it more than a step before the beast's claw cleaved through his skull. Blood and brain matter sprayed the ground as he fell, head peeling away into two halves. The man's knees hit the ground as the void drake rose in flight, trailing gore as it did so.

Well, Yala thought, watching its flight path return to circling the palace. *I suppose now, I know what fate awaits me if I'm exposed.*

———

Hachim and the others had walked for less than an hour before they came upon the first bodies. The village adjacent to the enclave was marked by a wide sunfruit tree that now shadowed a row of corpses. The elite Disciples had worked their magic, burying the dead beneath a web of greenery, but horror choked him all the same.

"Gods." Niema's tone echoed his own despair. "So many dead."

Sensing that she worried for those they'd left behind, Hachim slid his hand into hers, taking comfort from the thrum of her pulse. "The Superior will ensure no more come close to the enclave."

"Really?" Saren spoke up from behind. "We're putting a

lot of faith in someone who tried to have Yala killed. Or did everyone forget that?"

No. Though Hachim hadn't been betrayed himself, he'd felt the Superior's actions tear Niema apart through their bond until he'd all but forgotten the debt he owed her. He vividly recalled the moment when he'd crouched tearfully at the altar to beg Yalet for a miracle, no longer able to deny that he wasn't the girl the rest of the enclave thought him to be. Superior Kralia had heard his desperate prayers and had saved him from despair, letting him retake his vows with a new name and informing the enclave of his decision. Niema, meanwhile, had helped him cut his hair and find herbs to take to stop his monthly bleeding, and he'd never forgotten that kindness either.

How was he to reconcile the two loyalties? The Superior might have ulterior motives, but they had little choice but to follow her plan.

"She won't turn on Yala now," Niema said. "Her goal is to protect the enclave."

Saren made a sceptical noise but didn't pursue his argument. Leaving the village, they made for the river. Travelling by boat would be the quickest way to reach Setemar without encountering trouble, and they'd brought enough rations that they wouldn't need to stop at any villages or towns.

Upon reaching the river, he and Niema took one canoe and Viam and Saren the other. The journey passed without incident unless one counted the delivery of a letter from Kelan claiming that his Superior had ordered him to go back to Dalathar.

"What the hell is she thinking?" Saren asked. "Does she *want* her Disciples to get arrested or worse?"

"She must think it's worth the gamble." Niema reached out to steady the canoe, which tilted when the tree-raptor Kelan had sent perched expectantly on the edge. "He also told us to seek out a Disciple of the Earth named Pehin who helped during the attack on the temple."

"Why did his Superior not send him to Setemar?" Viam asked from the boat behind theirs. "That's the obvious choice."

Niema turned the paper over and began to scratch out a reply. "Maybe she thinks he can find some Disciples of the Flame who managed to get away."

"I doubt it," said Saren. "They're good for nothing but kneeling before their god. Or the king, as it were."

She handed the reply to Molin and picked up the oars again. Hachim watched the tree-raptor's departure with apprehension, and they continued to row until the cliffs of Setemar loomed overhead.

When they reached the outskirts of the city, the four of them climbed out of the boats and left them in the bushes near the river. Niema took the lead, following a dirt track between houses of wood and clay that resembled those in the villages near the forest more than the stone constructions he'd seen in the capital. Setemar was a smaller city whose boundaries expanded with every passing year, and the central area was circled by a wall that merged with the reddish cliffs bordering its northern edge.

"We're going straight to the Disciples?" asked Viam as they neared the tall gates set into the city wall. "It's nearly evening."

"Kelan said we were more likely to find this Pehin outside of the temple," Niema said. "In a tavern."

"Are you sure she's an ally?" said Viam. "Kelan has a reputation for making bad choices about who to trust."

"So do the rest of us," said Saren. "Look at us walking in here when we know a massacre took place right beneath our feet."

Chills prickled Hachim's arms. Though this was his first

visit to the city, there was something eerie about being near an abundance of living beings that were so estranged from one another. He hadn't spent long enough in the capital to become accustomed to the onslaught on his senses as Niema had, but this city carried a fresh array of bad memories for her too.

He took Niema's hand and spoke up. "The Disciples of Life put their efforts together, including the Superior, to drive out Mekan. The Disciples of the Earth owe us a debt."

"Then we'd better hope they remember that," Saren muttered. "Let's get this over with."

8

Kelan and his companions arrived in the capital late in the evening, having been forced to take several detours to avoid soldiers on the road. When they made their way to the inn the Superior had picked out for them, dusk blanketed the streets and long shadows stretched between the stone dwellings. The inn was a dingy establishment far from their usual accommodations; evidently, few people had been willing to take in Disciples at a time when they were in such disfavour with the king.

"The Superior must have plied the owner with money," Kelan remarked to Lakiel as they approached the inn. "Few would agree to keep a group of Disciples hidden from the monarch unless compensated."

"We're not in hiding," Lakiel all but snapped at him. He'd been in a sour mood since they'd left Skytower, as Brikel had refused to be excluded from the mission. "Unless you expose us to the city guards, in which case I'll drive you from the city myself."

"Lakiel!" His sister hit him in the arm. "The city guards

have no reason to confront us. We're not the ones responsible for the attempt on His Majesty's life."

"We also fought on *his* side against the dead," Ranit added.

Kelan opted not to remind him that it had been King
Tharen who'd brought the army of the dead to Dalathar in
the first place; all the rumours suggested the monarch had
decided to maintain the fiction that Rafragoria had been
responsible.

How thoroughly he's spread his lies. He caught a glimpse of
the city wall, wondering how Yala had coped with being
within its confines. Even in the outer city, he had the sense of
tight streets hemming him in and a web of roofs blotting out
the sky. Not so different than the forest, save for the
unpleasant smell emanating from the river.

Kelan had entertained ideas of passing the evening in a
pleasure house, but Lakiel reacted with predictable disdain
to that suggestion.

"We're here to spy," Kelan pointed out. "Where's better for
gossip than the pleasure district?"

"The place will be swarming with off-duty guards," Lakiel
argued. "I won't let you compromise the mission."

"The Undercity, then." Not a place he wanted to venture
after dark, so he waited for morning and slipped out of the
inn when the others were asleep.

Kelan followed a winding route through the outer city to
avoid any potential guard patrols. There were few people
about at this early hour, and he reached the alley unchal-
lenged. A set of stairs led down to a passage lined with
shacks constructed by the Undercity's inhabitants, but the
former soldier who usually blocked his path was markedly
absent.

So were the people. No children played in the alleys
between the run-down houses, nor had anyone lit the few
lanterns the city's poorest had procured.

Did everyone leave?

Rustling sounded, along with frantic whispers. He glided towards one of the ramshackle dwellings and glimpsed movement through the gaping hole in place of a window.

Kelan used a blast of wind to knock open the doors, revealing a group of terrified youths dressed in the orange robes of low-ranked Disciples of the Flame.

"Don't hurt us!" one of them yelped.

"Novice Yachim, right?" He recognised a cowering figure in the distant corner. "How have you managed to not get caught?"

"Kelan?" The novice Disciple of the Flame straightened, relief flickering over his face. Despite the dingy surroundings, his pale-orange robes were impeccably arranged, if grimy at the edges. "You came back. I hoped you would."

"Have you been hiding here all along?" He counted at least ten Disciples crouched amid the squalor. "Why in the gods' names are you still wearing your robes?"

"We don't have any other clothing."

"Has nobody else come looking in here?" he asked.

"Not since everyone left," said Yachim. "The king ordered every able-bodied soldier to rejoin the army."

Yala's friends would have been less than pleased with that command, Kelan was willing to bet. "What of the other Disciples of the Flame?"

He knew. They'd sworn loyalty to the king and accepted any punishment he might inflict on them for their prior leader's attempt on his life."

"They can't leave the temple." Yachim swallowed. "It's not possible for us to return, but neither can we leave the city. The soldiers are everywhere."

"I can help you escape."

"Escape?" Disappointment filled the novice's voice. "I thought you came to fight."

"You thought wrong." The Disciples hadn't thought *Kelan* intended to fight the king, had they? "You'll have to choose. Even if you stay undiscovered, this place floods frequently, and it's a cesspool of disease."

"There's nowhere else to go." His voice cracked. "Please, Kelan. Help us."

Lakiel would never consent to them staying in the inn—and there weren't enough rooms, besides—but there was one house he knew was unoccupied. "I can think of somewhere. Yala's old house."

Not a safe haven by any means—the city guards were certainly aware of Yala's address—but they'd last a little longer with a proper roof over their heads, if nothing else.

"Thank you." Yachim's eyes brimmed with tears. "May the gods bless you."

Not sure the gods' blessings are what I need at the moment.

———

Niema approached the wall circling Setemar's inner city, her bones shuddering as she recalled the ground cracking open and Mekan's beasts crawling out to terrorise the city. Today, the only sign of anything amiss was the two heavily armed guards who met them at the gates.

"State your business." A male guard with a scar on one cheek barred their path.

"We're with the Disciples of Life." Niema opted for the honest approach. "We're on the orders of our Superior to meet with the Disciples of the Earth."

"Disciples." He grunted. "Heard some rumours from the capital that the king doesn't like your sort much."

The king? A spike of alarm hit her. "We didn't come from there."

"Who'd you hear that from?" Viam asked, and Saren trod on her foot.

"Some soldiers stopped by the other day." He gave them a glower but stepped aside. "If I hear a hint of trouble from you, you're out."

Niema hurried through the gate ahead of the others, and when the gates closed behind them with a metallic clunk, she suppressed a flinch. Ahead, the jagged crack in the main street had sealed, leaving a raised scar stretching from the gate all the way to the stairs at the temple's entrance.

Saren let out a low whistle. "This is where Mekan attacked?"

"My fellow Disciples healed the damage. There are no traces of Mekan left."

Yet the memories sharpened with each step she took. *That's where my Superior forced me to try to kill Yala. Where I controlled a void drake and proved that I carry part of Mekan within myself.*

"Where to now?" Hachim took her arm gently, bringing her back to the present. "Should we find this Disciple that Kelan mentioned?"

"We'll go to the temple first," she decided. "If we're lucky, we'll get an audience with the Superior tomorrow."

"The king's people have already been here," murmured Viam. "What if he's already got to the Disciples of the Earth?"

"He hasn't." They'd never have been let into the city if that had been the case, but climbing the temple stairs triggered another flurry of panicked memories. Forcing herself to take calming breaths, she knocked on the front door.

A male novice robed in light brown answered. "Can I help you?"

"We're representatives of the Disciples of Life," said Niema. "We would like to request a meeting with your new Superior at a time of your choosing."

"Disciples of Life?" The novice's eyes flickered nervously between them. "I'll ask."

As he closed the door, Niema's attention went to the towering statues flanking the temple doors and the face of Setem looking down at them, craggy and austere.

"I hope their new Superior is more accommodating than the last one," she murmured to Hachim.

The door nudged open again, and the novice's face appeared in the crack. "He said he'll talk to you tomorrow morning."

"That's promising," Hachim said as they retreated down-stairs. "It doesn't sound like the king's been here."

"I wouldn't trust a novice to know," said Saren. "The ones at the Temple of the Flame can't even tie their own shoelaces. What're we supposed to do now, wait it out?"

"We can go looking for this Pehin," said Niema. "Kelan said she frequents the taverns at night."

"Of course he did." Viam wore a frown. "I'm not sure we should trust his word."

"Dying in a tavern isn't a bad way to go." Saren's light tone didn't convince; Niema knew of his struggles to break his dependence upon alcohol as well as any of them. "Anyone know a place?"

Niema thought back to her previous visits to the city. "Yala was acquainted with the owner of a tavern near here, but I don't know if it's still around."

Nor did she recall the way, but the inner city covered a smaller area than Dalathar's centre, and it didn't take her long to get her bearings. The others followed her lead through the warren-like streets to a building that, like its neighbours, was hewn from the same reddish rock that formed the cliffs. The details of her last visit came back to her as they entered the dingy room; a shiver trailed down her spine at the memory of Yala casually demanding to borrow some sacks with which to dispose of the bodies of some dead mercenaries she'd killed.

When she approached the surly-faced man at the bar, his eyes widened in recognition. "You look familiar."

"I'm Yala's friend," Niema told him. "Do the Disciples of the Earth frequent this tavern?"

"Gods, no." He grunted. "I'm too low-class for the likes of them. Yala's not with you?"

"No." She glanced behind her and saw Viam and Saren engaged in a whispered argument near the door. "Have the king's soldiers been here recently?"

"Funny you should ask that." His hand tightened around the glass he was polishing. "A group of mercs came in not two days ago. Said the king was rounding up any freelancers and conscripting them into the army."

Niema's heart missed a beat. *Just as long as he hasn't come here...* "Where do the Disciples usually spend their nights?"

"You might try the inn." He put down the glass, his scowl back in place. "That's more on their level."

"I'll look for them there. Thank you."

She'd assumed the Disciples' Inn was chiefly used by visitors from outside, not locals, but there was an obvious lack of tourists and not a single Disciple of the Sky roaming the streets. The inn was a more polished establishment than the dingy tavern—paid for by the Disciples, she assumed—resembling its counterpart in the capital except built of the same reddish rock as the other buildings in Setemar.

Niema peered through the inn's downstairs window and spied a small group of individuals gathered at a table in the corner. Though they weren't dressed in their typical brown robes, they could only be Disciples.

A woman in her mid-twenties caught Niema's eye and sprang to her feet. She wore a dress of crimson silk instead of her formal robes, but Niema recognised her face.

Approaching the door, the woman tilted her head, taking in Niema's companions. "This is unexpected."

"You're Pehin, aren't you?" Niema asked.

"And you're a Disciple of Life," said Pehin. "Haven't seen one of those in a while."

"I was here—"

"When everything went to shit, I know." She grinned. "Come on in. This place serves excellent wine, and I guarantee we'll give you a better welcome than your last visit."

Niema hesitated, one foot on the threshold. "Aren't you going to ask why we're here?"

"Did the city guard interrogate you?" Pehin beckoned her into the room. "They're as joyless as King Tharen—and I expect *he's* the reason you're here. Am I right?"

"You know he's back?"

"Who doesn't?" She beckoned again, and this time, Niema followed her into the inn's main room. Hachim accompanied her, but Viam and Saren lingered behind, still engaged in their whispered argument.

Someone fetched extra chairs and the Disciples moved back to make room at their table, watching the newcomers.

"This is... Niema, right?" Pehin retook her seat, crossing one leg over the other. "She's a Disciple of Life."

"That's right." Niema introduced the others, though Viam and Saren had yet to take their seats and continued to argue in low voices. Perhaps they thought they'd get thrown out for being non-Disciples. "I'm here on the orders of my Superior, to meet with... your new Superior." She did not know his name yet.

"Superior Geren," Pehin filled in. "Let me guess, you want to know if he's more competent than dear old Superior Dovial?"

Niema looked uncertainly at the others, her skin prickling at the eyes on her. "We have a meeting with him tomorrow. I'm glad he's willing to talk to outsiders."

Pehin snorted. "He's not *bad* and certainly not as inclined to bury his head in the earth as Superior Dovial was, I'll grant you. He's been swift to reply to His Majesty's messengers, at any rate."

Niema's heart sank. "The king has already been in contact with him?"

"Yes. And no, I haven't managed to intercept one of their letters yet," she said. "All we have to go on is rumours, and even those're in short supply since His Majesty started hauling the local mercs to Dalathar for conscription."

"Rumours," Niema repeated. "Were there any rumours concerning the details of the king's return?"

"Did you see?" New understanding rippled across Pehin's face. "You *saw* him come back?"

"Some of us did." Out of the corner of her eye, she saw Saren approach their table with his arms folded over his chest and a twitch in his jaw.

Whispers sprang up among the Disciples; Pehin's brows rose, but her smile didn't waver. "Go on. You can't leave us hanging like that. The king was exiled because someone tried to assassinate him, we know, but there are a hundred stories of his return, and most of them are a pile of steaming drakeshit. Did he really ride into the city on the back of a monster?"

"More or less," Saren said before anyone else could speak. "He's a Disciple of Death. He brought Mekan's army into the capital."

A shocked silence blanketed the table.

"A Disciple of Death?" Pehin recovered first. "Fuck. That puts things in perspective, doesn't it?"

9

Two days of training passed before Yala managed to corner Nalen after breakfast one morning. She lurked in an alcove outside the mess hall and grabbed his wrist as he lumbered past, dragging him into an arm lock.

"What is your problem?" she hissed in his ear.

He wrenched his arm free with such force that she stumbled against the wall. Planting her cane in front of her, she met his searing gaze. "Well?"

"You left us to the king's mercy," he growled. "All the children in the Undercity were ripped away from their parents and dumped in an orphanage. Everyone who tried to desert was sentenced to death. That's my problem."

"That's the king's doing, not mine."

"You never came back to help us." Accusation layered his voice, and his fingers twitched towards the army-issued dagger at his waist. "I should carve a reminder into your skin for next time."

"I never came back because I had a Rafragorian spear sticking out of my ribs." Yala's hand snapped out, locking around his wrist. "As I would have told you if you'd fucking asked me instead of acting as if I personally slighted you by not coming to your rescue while bleeding out."

His mouth parted. "I—"

"Save it, Nalen," she said, releasing his arm. "I get it. You were fucked over, but so was I. And if you think I came back here to passively surrender, you're mistaken."

"Then what?" He glanced behind as if it had only just occurred to him that they might be overheard. Yala, of course, had already checked for eavesdroppers before she'd confronted him. "All I've seen so far is you training your riders like a good little captain."

"I don't see you raising a fuss either." Her fingers tingled as if Mekan was cheering on her argument, pushing her to draw blood. "I've already seen that beast of the king's skewer one person who crossed a line."

"That," he growled, "is what happens to deserters. And that's why I played along, but unlike you, I don't have the ear of the gods."

Yala laughed. "That's what you think?"

"What else am I supposed to believe?" he said. "You ran off with those fucking Disciples without looking back."

True, at least from his perspective, and he needed someone to blame who wouldn't skewer him for the mere suggestion. "I'm not sorry I left when I did, but I didn't know His Majesty intended to immediately target the Undercity."

"He needs soldiers," Nalen said. "I gather that's why he brought *you* back."

"Yes." He knew something of her talents—he'd witnessed the aftermath of Mekan's first assault upon the capital—but not their true extent. "The man the void drake killed was from the Undercity, right?"

A shadow fell over Nalen's face. "Ruen. He was fool

enough to respond to a call for volunteers for some job in the palace. Thought it'd get him out of service."

"He said…" She recalled the doomed man's words. *"I saw what he's building.* Know what he was referring to?"

Nalen's hands curled into fists. "No, but he's not the first to walk in there. There're plenty of rumours, but they're all drakeshit."

"Such as?"

"Mostly where His Majesty has been hiding for all those years and what he did to his son."

"What *did* he do to Daliel?" Yala asked. "Lock him up?"

"No clue, but he'd deserve it."

"Being an incompetent ruler isn't a crime." She might have added, *and I'd rather have him in charge than his father,* but that was a given. "Let me know if I can do anything for the others. I want to help."

"Don't bother." He shook his head. "Half the folk from the Undercity think we're better off here than we were on the street, and why wouldn't they?"

He might be right; for many, the risks associated with desertion didn't outweigh the benefits of a roof over one's head and a regular meal. Yes, the meals consisted of tasteless gruel formed of grain and other scraps mashed together into something vaguely nutritious, while their baths took the form of buckets of cold water, but Yala had to admit that there was something comforting in having those minor day-to-day decisions removed.

"If you find out what the king's doing in the palace, let me know." She was running late for the morning's training session and didn't want to push her luck with the commander. Though they hadn't clashed on methods since the first day, he'd made it clear that she had only a few short weeks to get both the squad and their steeds battle-ready.

The gruelling schedule left her with little time to venture

outside of the barracks, and it had taken more than a day for her to have a spare moment to check the infirmary, where Viam's friend Brenat had been recovering from a severe injury. She'd been discharged and had presumably gone back to work in administration. Viam would be pleased to know that if Yala had the faintest idea how to get a message to her.

The only time she had alone was when she fed the war drakes each morning and evening; strangely, nobody else had been willing to volunteer. As she was locking up the door to the paddocks that evening, a breeze disturbed the still air, lifting the hair from her scalp, and a voice spoke. "I assume you don't mind me calling you Captain any longer?"

A breath slipped between Yala's teeth, half exasperated, half relieved. "Kelan."

"I was starting to think I'd never manage to corner you alone." He glided out of the alcove between the palace wall and the back of the paddock. "I've been here for close to an hour."

"Are you out of your mind?" she said. "What the hell are you doing in the upper city?"

"Did you expect anything else of me?"

"You'll get us both killed."

"I'd prefer to avoid that eventuality." His eyes gleamed with amusement. "I'm enjoying seeing you training those novices. You have a surprising amount of patience."

"Which you're testing," she said pointedly. "What are you doing here, exactly?"

"Sightseeing." When she growled, he added, "Now, don't be like that. I was under the impression you intended to get close to the monarch, not train his soldiers."

"That monster is in the way." Though she couldn't see the void drake from this angle, its presence was a constant, like the claw that pressed against her leg even now. "I hope, for your sake, it didn't see you."

"It didn't." Kelan's eyes flickered towards the palace, the smile sliding from his face. "Have you spoken to His Majesty at all?"

"Not since I arrived," she said. "The void drake slaughtered the last man who crossed him, and it'll do the same to rogue Disciples, too, I'm betting."

Kelan's hand jumped reflexively towards his shoulder, the one that had once been injured by a void drake's claw. "I'd prefer to avoid that, but I'm under orders to monitor the situation in the capital."

"From your Superior." She must have had faith in him not to get caught. "I'm treading a dangerous enough line as it is. If you cost me what little freedom I have left, *I'll* skewer you."

"Fair." His smile returned. "I think having someone on the outside will benefit you."

She grunted. "You can do all the spying you like, provided you don't drag me into whatever pile of shit you end up mired in."

"One of us is up to their knees in shit, and it's not me." He eyed her boots, which were splattered with war drake dung. "Think of me as a useful ally who can help you escape if the guards decide to haul you to the gallows."

"As long as you aren't the reason someone slips a noose around my neck," she retaliated. "Be careful."

————

Niema knocked on the door to the Temple of the Earth the following morning with growing apprehension, glad of Hachim's presence at her side to dull the memory of when she'd tried to take Yala's life upon these very stairs. They were greeted by the brown-robed novice from the day before, who beckoned them into the temple. "The Superior is ready to meet with you."

Wiping sweat-dampened palms on her knees, Niema stepped into a vast chamber carved out of the cliffs. Its smooth walls were inset with sconces containing statues of past Superiors far taller than their real-life equivalents; Niema recalled those same statues coming to life to defend their temple against Mekan's forces. Would they do the same again should the king launch an attack? Or would the living Disciples surrender before they were ever given the chance?

They climbed a stairway to the Superior's quarters. The modestly sized room was made more impressive by the carvings of Setem's serpentine figure upon the covering adorning the walls, lit from behind by a vibrant blue glow that seemed to emanate from the stones. In the centre was an obsidian seat on which sat the Superior, a man considerably younger than his predecessor. His light-brown hair was topped with a beaded headdress, and his pointed face sported few lines. Niema dropped to her knees before him, as did Hachim.

"Greetings," he said. "I am Superior Geren."

"I'm Niema." She rose to her feet, conscious of her voice's echo within the cave-like room. "This is Hachim, another member of my enclave. We're here on behalf of Superior Kralia."

"Is this regarding the recent letter she sent to me?" he enquired. "In which she sought an offer of collaboration between our temples?"

"Yes." It didn't surprise her that Superior Kralia had already made contact in the time they'd taken to reach the city. "She believes that it is in our interests to put our efforts together in the face of an imminent threat from the god of death."

"Mekan."

Niema suppressed a flinch when he spoke the name.

"Yes, I'm aware of those developments, as I received correspondence from the monarch himself."

"King Tharen?" Had the monarch declared his allegiance openly?

"Correct," he said. "He explained that his son stepped down upon his return from exile and that he would ensure that Rafragoria would never again use the dead to attack Laria."

The king was still painting himself as a saviour—and it sounded as if the Superior believed the false story. Few wouldn't unless they'd witnessed the events in the capital with their own eyes. A monarch returning from the dead was unlikely enough without him also gaining the title of Disciple of Death, and Rafragoria was a ready-made threat upon which to place the blame.

"The king deceived you." She forced the words between her teeth. "I apologise, Superior, but I was in Dalathar during the attack. The king was the one who sent the army directly from Mekan's temple and framed Rafragoria for any damage they caused. He wanted to paint himself as the one responsible for defeating them, but he was in control all along."

The echoes of her words resounded, leaving silence in their wake. The Superior blinked a couple times, his jaw opening and then closing. "You accuse the monarch of being an agent of Mekan?"

"I don't know if Superior Kralia was comfortable sharing the details in her letter," she said. "But it's true. I also saw the Disciples of the Flame surrender to him out of fear he'd have them sentenced to death. We're here because we think he might do the same to you."

"As I understand it, the Disciples of the Flame were the reason for his exile," said Superior Geren. "We were not involved."

"You communicated with him," Hachim said. "Has he already asked for your allegiance?"

The response came a little too fast. "That is a matter between me and the monarch."

Gods. Hadn't his predecessor lost his life precisely because he'd made the wrong choice? What might she say to convince him to change his mind?

"The king only survived exile because he made a deal with Mekan," she said. "The same god who nearly destroyed the very temple in which you stand. Allying with him will endanger your Disciples and put the city at risk of another tragedy."

"What would you have us do instead?" His closed-off tone told her he had no interest in hearing her opinion. "We can ill afford to provoke a rift between ourselves and the crown."

"Would you rather Mekan's beasts came to attack the temple again?" The question surprised even her, as if someone else had taken control of her tongue. Someone like Yala. "It's your choice, but we helped you to defeat Corruption once before. We'll gladly do the same again."

Footsteps thumped on the stairs. A shout: "The king's soldiers are here!"

We're too late. Heart sinking, she backed towards the door. "Please, don't let them into the temple."

Hachim opened the door and grabbed her arm, pulling her after him. In the main cavern, Disciples ran around like a stirred-up bloodfly nest.

As they reached the foot of the stairs, the front door swung open, and a number of armed soldiers ran in, forming a line between them and the way out.

10

Kelan found Molin waiting on a rooftop near Ceremonial Square with a strip of meat hanging out of his mouth. As the other Disciples of the Sky had refused to come into the upper city, he'd had to employ the help of his useful reptilian companion to create a diversion to get in. The guards patrolled each handspan of the city wall, making it near-impossible for anyone to fly over without being seen, and more patrolled around the Temple of the Flame. He squinted at the two men who blocked the front entrance, something striking him as odd. Though they were dressed in typical guard uniform, they wore adornments in their hair made of what looked to be seashells, and the weapons they carried were the colour of bone.

The Disciples of the Sea. He'd forgotten that some of them had joined Mekan and helped the king's return. Evidently, they'd found new employment within the capital, but what had become of those they'd left behind? His Superior had not mentioned the Disciples of the Sea when she'd suggested making alliances, but now, he had to wonder if any who'd declined to join forces with the god of death had survived. Likely, they'd been caught in the backlash when the king's army of the dead had surged across the ocean, killing everyone in their path. But if some had lived, they'd certainly be willing to fight back against the king.

That might be a route worth pursuing, he thought. *If I can convince the others.*

———

As Niema watched the chaos unfold within the temple's main chamber, Pehin hurried over to her and Hachim. "Come on. We can get out this way."

Pehin led them around the chamber's edge, staying within the shadows cast by the towering statues at the back. She opened a door on one of the many tunnels that had been hewn into the rock and extended deep inside the cliff.

"Viam and Saren." Niema halted, her foot on the threshold. "They don't know the soldiers are here."

"We can't go back." Pehin beckoned, and Niema stepped into the narrow passage. "The soldiers are demanding the unconditional surrender of all Disciples, and if they find out you're here, you'll be interrogated at the very least."

Niema hurried after her down the tunnel. "Can you help our friends get out of the inner city? They aren't Disciples."

"Then they shouldn't have a problem."

Hoping Pehin was right, Niema continued through the tunnel with Hachim close behind. They reached a door that emerged from the wall outside of the upper city into an alleyway. The beat of heavy boots echoed from the main street, indicating a second group of soldiers heading for the inner city gates. A thrill of dread sang through Niema's nerves. *Does the king intend to force a surrender?*

"You're staying?" Hachim asked Pehin, who hadn't followed them.

"I've been through this before." She planted her feet in the tunnel entrance. "My allies and I are prepared. You should head back and warn your Superior."

I can't go back. The words stuck in her throat. "Thank you for the help."

"Go on." Pehin gestured impatiently, and they hurried down the alley, waiting for the distinct thud of the gate closing on the second group of soldiers before they risked going any further.

"Niema." Saren came rushing out of an adjacent alleyway, Viam fast on his heels. "Thank fuck you got out. We saw the soldiers and ran before the second lot arrived."

"We need to leave." She thought back to where they'd left the boats. "We can follow the river, but there might be more soldiers on the road."

"There will be." Saren's jaw tensed. "They'll have left someone with their transport."

"I have an idea." Not one she'd thought of herself, but she and Yala had stolen a wagon during her first visit here with Kelan's help, and if they employed a similar strategy here, they might be able to leave the city unscathed.

As she'd hoped, several wagons sat at the roadside near Setemar's entrance, watched by a single young soldier scarcely at conscription age.

"This is your plan?" Saren laughed under his breath. "We're going to chase him off?"

"No need." Niema led the way around the back of the wagons. "I'll handle it."

They climbed into one of the wagons from behind. Niema whistled, prompting the raptors to launch into a startled run. The young soldier ran after with a shout of alarm, but they gained speed rapidly, the beasts responding to her and Hachim's commands until the city's outskirts were left far in the dust.

"Perfect." Saren sat back against the wagon's side, snickering. "You've been holding out on us, Niema. I didn't know you were that devious."

"Kelan's influence, I assume." Viam hung onto the wagon's side. "Where are we going?"

"I don't know." She looked to Hachim, her heart twisting. "I can't go back to the enclave, but we need to warn our Superior that the Disciples of the Earth have been compromised."

"There's a village that way." Viam pointed to a cluster of buildings in the distance, near which several farmsteads were spaced along the roadside. "There might be someone there who can help."

"Doesn't look like there're many other people around," Saren muttered. "I don't like it."

Neither did Niema. Where were the merchants travelling from the capital or the farmers making the journey from the villages into Setemar to sell their produce at the markets? Even the fields were bereft of workers, and a chill raced down her arms as they neared the first farmstead. There was no thrum of life, human or otherwise, within her senses. Inhaling, she choked on the unmistakeable scent of death.

"Ah, shit," said Saren.

11

"A bsolutely not," Lakiel said at breakfast. "It's not worth the risk. Half the Disciples of the Sea work for the enemy, and the other half are probably dead."

"Charming," said Brikel. "What do you suggest, then? Would you rather spy on the palace?"

"You shouldn't be here."

Kelan cut through Brikel's indignant reply. "I'm sure the Superior will want us to seek out allies."

He'd sent Molin to her the previous night with a note explaining his suggestion, and while he had yet to receive a reply, he had no reason to believe they'd be refused. In the meantime, he addressed the others. "Anyone else in?"

Nobody looked enthused. Kelan hardly blamed them; their last attempt to ally with the Disciples of the Sea had been a fraught affair involving kidnappings, attacks by the dead, and finally, a frontmost view of the king's return to Laria.

Ranit fidgeted in his seat. "I don't like the idea, but I think you're right. We need allies, and who better than the Disciples who resisted the king longest?"

"How do we know the king's army of the dead aren't waiting to ambush us?" Lakiel said.

The colour drained from Ranit's face. "Right... good point."

So much for having at least one person's support. "I can go alone," he offered. "I'm less likely to be seen."

"And more likely to wash up as a corpse."

That was unusually bleak, coming from Lakiel, but they'd had a number of close calls with the city guards already, and the others were less than impressed with Kelan's decision to help the Disciples of the Flame hide in Yala's old house. He'd left them to fend for themselves after making sure they had the supplies they needed, but it was frankly a miracle they'd lasted so long without being arrested. Since he was the one who'd unintentionally provoked Yachim's rebellion in the first place, he felt a lingering sense of responsibility towards them.

He went to check on them out of habit and was greeted along the way by a chirping noise as Molin swooped down, clutching a note in his clawed foot. Kelan took the folded parchment and disentangled the words with difficulty—despite his Superior's neat script, he'd always struggled with reading—and discerned that she'd agreed with his intention to learn more of the surviving Disciples of the Sea. A satisfied smile crept onto his mouth. *There you have it.*

Reaching Yala's house, he pushed the door open. Panic erupted among the Disciples of the Flame, all of whom jumped to their feet from where they appeared to have been praying at a makeshift altar in the corner.

"It's just me." Kelan closed the door behind him. "I thought I should warn you that I'm going to search for the

Disciples of the Sea, and I might run into trouble on the way."

"What?" Yachim gasped. "Those... traitors?"

"Not the ones guarding your temple," he amended. "The others."

"There are no others," said Yachim, a tremor in his voice. "Have you been to our temple?"

"I didn't get very close," he told them. "Do you want me to try to get in? I can slip a message to your Superior or anyone else who wants to escape imprisonment."

"There's no point." Yachim sank to the floor near the handmade altar. "Dalathik isn't answering our prayers."

"He isn't?" Kelan frowned. "When did this start?"

"Not long after the king's return."

"Oh." At a guess, Mekan had infiltrated the temple in a similar manner to which He had poisoned the Temple of the Earth. "When the same happened to the Disciples of the Earth, they were able to call upon their deity when they left the city."

He'd hoped they might have changed their minds, but Yachim shook his head. "It's no safer out there."

He might be right, but guilt nagged at him as he left the house and began making his way northward to the docks. He took a roundabout route to avoid venturing too close to the palace, and when the wide warehouses marking the seafront appeared in his line of sight, he spied the glittering ocean in gaps between buildings. Boats of all sizes bobbed amid the waves, some smaller fishing vessels and others large enough that they could only belong to the military.

Given the beating the king's fleet had taken during the last battle, he was surprised to see any ships at all, but teams of uniformed individuals were at work on the docks, and a chorus of hammering punctuated the cries of sea birds. *They're rebuilding the fleet.* The thought conjured the image of a large vessel bearing down upon the docks, borne by a tidal wave conjured by the Disciples of the Sea and leaving a trail of destruction in its wake.

"So," said a voice at his shoulder. "How do we get past them?"

"Brikel." He started. "You shouldn't be here. Lakiel will skewer both of us."

"You think I don't know that?" She folded her arms over her chest. "I've had enough of my brother patronising me. He might not want to risk his neck, but some things are more important than my safety. You got a message from our Superior giving you permission, didn't you?"

"Yes." He had to admit it was nice to have company aside from Molin. The tree-raptor was a great help finding a route that didn't pass in front of the innumerable soldiers at work on the king's ships, though, and in a short time, Molin found a particularly large vessel which stood intact, suggesting it had already been repaired.

As they skirted the large wooden boat, a shimmer on the water's surface caught his eye. Then, a figure rose from the water, wearing sparse reed-woven clothing adorned with jewellery made from seashells and stones.

"Nanek?" He'd acquired several new scars on his face and arms since Kelan had last seen him, but he looked remarkably intact considering the dire threat that lurked in the waters off Laria's shore. "Why are you so close to land?"

Nanek pulled himself out of the water onto the pier, rivulets of water running down his scarred face. "I'm rendering His Majesty's new fleet useless."

"You're sabotaging the ships?" He couldn't help but be impressed. "If you get caught, you're dead."

"We were dead the instant the false king poisoned our waters." Defiance shone in his eyes, which glimmered with the blue haze of Amanat's power. "His beasts murdered our

Superior. Our temple was overrun, and most were forced to surrender to the king."

"Your Superior is dead?" Brikel swore. "How many of you survived?"

"Too few." Nanek's eyes shone, but determination won out over grief. "We will not submit."

"You can still access your deity?" Kelan queried. "The Disciples of the Flame can't."

Brikel swivelled to him. "You spoke to them?"

"There's a group of dissenters," he said for Nanek's benefit. "They're in hiding, not unlike yourselves. I'd like to help you both."

"I won't risk our location reaching the king's ears." He shook his head, the shells woven into his long hair clinking. "If your Superior has set herself against him, it's only a matter of time before your temple falls too."

"Not if I have anything to do with it." Kelan was surprised at the force in his own voice. "Some of my people are in the capital. We can bring supplies and reinforcements if you need them. And if the dead threaten you, we can fight."

"The army has returned to the Void."

"Wait, the dead have gone?" Kelan asked, disarmed.

"Once Rafragoria surrendered, there was little point in the false king allowing them to wander outside of Laria's shores," he said. "He feared, perhaps, that the dead would turn upon him, and he banished them to the Void shortly after their destruction of our temple."

He banished the army. "He must have figured he could summon them again when he needed to."

"Undoubtedly." Nanek swung his legs over the pier into the water again. "I admire your goal, but we're all aware that we're only postponing our fate by refusing to surrender. It won't do you any good to ally yourselves with us."

"Oh, I like low odds. They make life more interesting." He

nodded to Brikel, who offered a grin in return. "The king hasn't found you so far, has he?"

"Yet," he said. "We're hiding on an island to the north of Dalathar. I will entrust you with the location, but the directions will likely mean little to you."

Kelan indicated Molin. "My companion can go with you and memorise the route. He was trained by the Disciples of Life and is intelligent."

Molin chirped in agreement, while Nanek gave him a sceptical look. "The Disciples of Life have set themselves against the king too?"

"They're opposed to Mekan by their nature," he said. "Remember that it was they who destroyed the island and Mekan's temple. I'm in contact with them too. They might agree to help you."

Nanek's expression, for the first time, showed a hint of hope. "Then you have my thanks, Disciple. I pray that the gods will see fit to spare us after all."

***

Yala tossed the raw meat to the war drakes. They snapped it up eagerly, crowding around her in the paddock. She'd claimed their trust easily enough, but beasts were simple creatures. Humans were trickier.

Not that her squad had any reason to suspect she had ulterior motives in volunteering to feed the war drakes, and in the past days, they'd tested her resolve not to let herself learn more about them than strictly necessary for the job. She'd found out that Yurel's skill at handling the beasts was due to her parents having been raptor farmers—a past she and Yala shared—while Gorel was eager enough to help his new captain that she'd had to tell him to leave twice. When she was alone, she relaxed her guard, and soon enough, a flutter of wind announced Kelan's arrival.

His descent over the fence prompted the war drakes to panic and snap at him Instead of the food. Swearing, Yala backed out of range of their teeth and hissed at Kelan, "Do you ever look where you're going?"

"I had to move fast to avoid the guards." He skirted the back fence smoothly until the war drakes lost interest and returned to their meal. "I learned something interesting today. The Disciples of the Sea survived."

"Did they?" She secured the war drake's chain to its post. "How'd you manage to dodge the army of the dead?"

"The army has gone." A smile spread across his face as he took in her disbelief. "The king banished the dead when Rafragoria surrendered. They already overran the Temple of the Sea and killed their Superior."

"What?" She sucked in a sharp breath. "You learned all this in a day?"

"That, and Nanek has taken it upon himself to sabotage the king's attempts to rebuild his fleet."

Yala swore. "He has a death wish. Is he the only survivor?"

"No, a group of others are hiding on an island off Laria's coast," he told her. "And there are the ones who allied with Mekan, of course. They're guarding the Temple of the Flame."

"Figures." Yala tensed at the thud of footsteps outside the paddock. "Go. Someone's coming."

Kelan glided to the back of the paddock, setting the war drakes into a frenzy again. As he vanished over the fence, Yala tossed them another piece of meat to calm them and then opened the gate with a gloved hand.

The commander waited for her on the other side. Yala darted outside and closed the gate on the unruly war drakes. "Commander Sranak."

"Captain Yala." He eyed the gate. "You volunteered to feed the war drakes singlehandedly?"

"Few others were willing," she replied. "I've found I've missed this part of the job."

"I expect you have." He almost smiled. "And how are your squad faring?"

"Well," she said. "No major injuries so far. We'll try mounting the war drakes tomorrow."

"Good," he said. "We don't have much time. The king wants all the flight squads ready to fly by the end of the month."

"Is there a reason he's in such a hurry?" she queried. "There's no ongoing war with Rafragoria nor anyone else."

"For now." He lowered his voice. "Don't spread this around, but I've heard talk of dissenters, rogue Disciples who've escaped the king's notice. I gather that you'll be instrumental in hunting them down."

Ah, shit. "He doesn't need fliers to do that, does he? The foot soldiers will be enough."

"Not when the foe is outside of Laria's shores."

Her spine stiffened as the implication sank in. The king wanted them to hunt Disciples of the Sea... the very people Kelan had sworn to protect.

12

The stench of death sent the raptors into a panic. As the wagon tipped sideways, a large animal ran at them from the nearby farmhouse. A hog, its teeth slavering, its skull caved in to reveal the rotting flesh beneath.

"Stop!" Niema leapt clear of the wagon and whistled. Green light bloomed from her hands, and thorny stems sprouted from the rain-damp soil, forming a cage that entrapped the dead beast.

The hog struggled, jaws agape, hungry for flesh. Niema was unable to exert her will over the dead; they were no creatures of Mekan's but mere empty shells reduced to the simple urge to kill, to spread Mekan's influence further by taking more lives. She could do nothing but entrap them within Yalet's power until their fury stilled.

Niema spied a second beast hurling itself against the gate to the enclosed pen outside the farmhouse. Hachim ran towards it, green light spreading from his palms, as the fence gave a worrying creak.

"Watch out!" She joined Hachim as the fence gave way,

107

trampled beneath dead feet, and more hogs came lumbering out of the pen.

Thorny plants sprouted from the earth, fuelled by their shared command. Yalet's influence took hold and their struggles ceased, calmed to silence, but a warning shout prompted her to turn around. The farmhouse door lay open, and a man emerged, his gaping mouth expelling rotting teeth. He lifted a cleaver over his head with one hand and seized Niema's arm in a claw-like grip.

Niema thrust her hand outward, unthinking, and the man's chest parted like a rotting groundfruit. She pulled back, tried to remove her hand, but the putrefied flesh enclosed her to the wrist. The cleaver continued to swipe, skimming the top of her head.

Gagging, Niema implored Yalet to spare her. Green light streamed from her hands, engulfing the dead man and allowing her to pull her hand free. As a shower of thorns encased him, a second person came staggering out of the house, this one female. His wife, perhaps.

A shrill whistle from Hachim brought her to stillness, vines rising from the ground to ensnare her feet. Clutching a knife in her hand, she swiped at the air, driven by Mekan's urge to kill.

"Gods." A shudder racked his body. "This is unnatural."

"I know." Where had the dead come from? She and the others had been nowhere near this farmhouse on their journey to Setemar. "Where did it start?"

"Over there?" Saren pointed down the dirt track leading to the village, whereon more figures meandered.

All were blank-faced, armed, and undeniably dead.

***

Viam lifted her dagger, a laughable defence in the face of

the number of dead tottering towards them. They'd lost their wagon, the raptors having long since fled and abandoned the vehicle in the dirt.

"The village." Niema staggered forward, her hand dripping viscera from the man she'd pushed off her. "The villagers…"

"They're beyond help." Saren's mouth twisted. "I don't know about you, but I don't want to die out in the middle of fucking nowhere."

"There's nowhere to run." Hachim lifted his head to the sky. "I can't sense a living soul out here."

Except for us. Viam counted ten, fifteen dead, some clutching weapons or items that could be used as such like shovels and rakes. Their path veered inexorably towards the four of them, Mekan's will guiding them to destroy the only living creatures within range.

Viam drove the dagger's point towards her own arm. Pain spiked up her wrist as she sliced through the skin, carving a jagged cut deep enough that blood blossomed to the surface.

Within her pocket was a strip of scaly flesh taken from one of Mekan's beasts, and its chill burned sharp against her side as the god of death answered Viam's call.

"Stop!" she shouted at the oncoming dead, lifting her arm to display the rivulets of blood streaming down her hand.

The nearest dead ceased to move, suspended mid-step like stuffed straw dolls. One or two at a time, then more as the blood continued to drip down her palm and splatter the earthen track. Niema and Hachim ran in front of her, lifting their hands and speaking a prayer that brought a flash of vibrant green and a flurry of plant life bursting forth from the ground.

Viam lowered her bleeding hand as the dead were ensnared, unease trailing down her spine in tandem with a rush of satisfaction at her success. She pushed the latter aside, sickened at the part of her that revelled in exerting her will over the dead. *That's Mekan's will, not yours*, she reminded herself. *You aren't Him.*

"I can heal you." Niema hurried to her side and held out a palm. A soothing warmth caressed her stinging wrist, and the cut sealed, leaving nothing but a smear of crimson behind.

"Thank the gods for that." Saren shuddered. "It'd better not be like this everywhere."

"It isn't." Not that Viam could speak to that with any authority. "If we go back to the river, the boats will be where we left them."

"Where are we supposed to go?" said Saren. "Back to the forest? The only other way the river goes is to the capital, but I'd sooner take my chances out here than go back to *that* place."

Viam took in a breath. "It's the one place I can think of that almost certainly isn't infested with the dead."

"Except the one on the fucking throne." Saren uttered a disbelieving laugh. "You're joking, right?"

He kicked at the dead farmer then cursed when his foot went straight through the man's shin and embedded itself in the rotting flesh. Niema gagged, while Hachim had already fallen to his knees and started vomiting.

Viam swallowed hard and averted her gaze. "I think we can be of more use in the capital than anywhere else."

"To Yala, you mean." Saren extricated his foot, kicking gristle off his boot. "The king'll put us in a cell."

"He wanted Yala," she corrected. "He doesn't know we're…"

Disciples of Death. The words hovered between them, as potent as the stench of death in the air. He'd never openly used his own abilities or even acknowledged the pull he surely felt towards the dead, the same as she and Yala did.

"He'll know what *you* are." Saren spat at the corpse's feet. "He'll think you deserted."

"I was injured in the battle," Viam reminded him. "I can use that as an excuse. Brenat will cover for me."

"Brenat." Saren had heard her say the name, but she hadn't spelled out their connection, and only now did his eyes widen in understanding. "Gods, you have a lover. No wonder you want to go back."

Scarlet coated Viam's cheeks. "I wouldn't call us lovers. We... we never..."

"I thought that didn't matter to you." When she made a noise of protest, Saren added, "I'm not dense, Viam. We shared a room in the barracks for long enough for me to figure you out. I know you prefer women, and I know you'd rather read a book with your lover than fuck."

"*Saren.*" Viam spluttered. "Stop it."

"You're right, though." Saren walked back to the wagon, which had been thrown to the roadside when the raptors fled. "I'm beneath the king's notice, so Dalathar's the one place I might survive longer than a day. We'll also be there if Yala needs us, which I doubt."

She might. While Yala had been set on acting alone, Viam knew her squad leader's tendency to take on a disproportionate level of responsibility and that she needed support more than she thought she did.

With an accord reached, Viam joined Saren in retrieving her belongings from the wreckage of the wagon. Niema and Hachim did the same, both ashen-faced and shaking.

"You mean to travel to the capital?" Niema asked them. "Hachim and I will stay near the forest and send a warning to the other Disciples of Life. Our Superior needs to know how widespread Mekan's influence is."

"Good idea," she replied. "Tell her about what we found in Setemar too."

Dalathar would be more dangerous, but the thought of returning made Viam's heart race for another reason altogether. She'd been certain in her decision to leave, but the capital was her home, and she'd left Brenat trapped in that nest of snakes without a way out. While Brenat might not be a Disciple of Death herself, that wouldn't prevent her from becoming collateral damage in the king's war.

That, Viam could never allow.

***

Yala helped Roven climb onto the war drake's back, her knees settling on either side of its neck. The beast growled but didn't try to buck her off. The young woman held on one-handedly, miming drawing a spear.

"Are you sure you haven't done this before?" asked Yala.

"No, but I trained as a dancer during a stint in the pleasure district." She flashed a grin. "Mounting a war drake isn't *too* different than a person... you just need to know their weaknesses." She slapped a palm against the war drake's scaly back.

"Watch it," Yala warned, though she couldn't suppress a smile at the way the rest of the squad laughed at her comment. "Don't try mounting a war drake in mating season is my advice. It'd end badly for you."

Yala helped Roven climb down, impressed at how quickly the squad had adapted to what was usually the task that caused the most grief the first time around. Only Toreth, the smallest, had fallen off his war drake, and he hadn't suffered anything more than a few scrapes.

Their real test would come when they flew in battle, and it was hard, sometimes, to remember that she wasn't supposed to be invested in their success. She had another purpose, and entangling her goals with theirs would only make it harder to extricate herself when their upcoming mission inevitably went south.

A mission, if she believed the commander, in which they would be tasked with hunting down the remaining Disciples of the Sea.

She'd hoped Kelan would be waiting to meet her at the day's end, but instead, Commander Sranak hurried into the paddock shortly after she'd dismissed the other fliers.

"The king wants to talk to you in the palace," he told them. "To give you direct instruction on your upcoming mission."

Yala's spine straightened in anticipation. This would be the first time since her arrival that she'd see him face to face. Not alone, however; the rest of the flight squad's captains also waited inside the palace gates for the commander. Lisek gave Yala a nod of greeting, but nobody spoke. An air of tension hovered over their group as the commander led them away from the barracks and towards the towering construction that dwarfed the rest of the palace grounds.

The oppressive sense intensified when they neared the palace stairs and spied the void drake circling above. Save for its brutal attack upon the would-be deserter, Yala had never seen the beast anywhere other than above the palace, its pitted eyes scanning the grounds as if to pick up on treasonous intentions. A ridiculous thought, but Yala couldn't help wondering what the beast would do if someone struck against the king while within the palace's walls, beyond its reach.

I suppose the idea is that they'll never have that chance.

Yala gritted her teeth against the painful twinge in her leg as they climbed the stairs to the front door and then followed the familiar path to the king's receiving room. Inside, the captains assembled in two lines before the monarch's throne.

As before, not a trace of the god of death's presence was evident in the brightly lit room. *Where is Mekan hiding?*

"I've called you here to instruct you about your upcoming mission," he told them. "The flight division will play a vital role in the safety of Laria, which includes, regrettably, rooting out traitors who have hidden in our midst."

The word *traitor* coiled inside Yala's chest like a serpent. *He doesn't know. He can't know.*

"I have reason to believe there are dissenters lurking outside of Laria's shores," he went on. "From among the Disciples of the Sea."

Some of the other captains shifted on their feet as if surprised, but none otherwise reacted.

"Many of Amanat's worshippers have pledged their loyalty to the crown, but regrettably, some have resisted," King Tharen said. "All members of the flight division will be sent to find their hiding place. You will not stop until you have found each traitor and brought them to the palace."

His gaze travelled over their group, and Yala's heart shuddered when their eyes locked. She held his stare, conscious of the guards stationed at the doors, poised to intervene if anyone dared lift a hand against their king.

"Those of you whose squads are ready for battle will assist in the search," he went on. "The rest of you will wait for further instructions. That is all."

Her squad would be spared from the search efforts, at least until their training was complete... but why would the king want to spare the Disciples' lives? As the captains filed out of the receiving room, Yala watched their movements, her mind conjuring recognisable images of hurling her dagger at the king's exposed neck. If she moved fast enough...

"Yala Palathar," said the king. "I would speak with you alone."

Yes. Her fingers tingled beneath her drakeskin gloves, itching to close around his throat and choke the life from him. Her gaze tracked the movements of the other captains— also armed—and she waited until the last disappeared through the door.

Meeting his eyes, she smiled. "Yes, Your Majesty?"

"I hear you've made exemplary progress with your squad in the short time you've been captain," he began. "As I would have expected of you."

"I'm honoured." A scraping noise behind her prompted her to turn her head, glimpsing two guards approaching, as if her treacherous thoughts had somehow reached their ears. *He's just being careful, that's all.* "They've shown themselves to be quick learners, but they haven't flown further than the paddock yet. I worry that they won't be ready in time for the mission."

"Most of you learned in a similar manner, did you not?"

"We did," she allowed, "but we were never set against Disciples."

Does he know where they're hiding? Kelan had *told* her, the fool, but if she'd ever had any intention of using the information against the Disciples of the Sea, she wouldn't have had a hope of finding their location without a map.

"The Disciples of the Sea are largely ineffective out of the water," said the king. "Your concern for your squad is admirable, but they will be in little danger should the Disciples surrender."

"Why?" She hadn't planned to ask the question, but it escaped of its own accord. "Why spare their lives?"

"Traitors though they might be, they deserve to be given a proper trial before their king," he said. "They were tricked, I don't doubt, by the one who betrayed me."

"Superior Datriem." *Does he really think that?*

No. The lie in his voice wasn't obvious, but even the old

King Tharen would never have spared the life of any traitor, Disciple or not. There must be another reason he wanted the flight division to bring them in alive.

"Yes." He strode forward until he and Yala stood a handspan apart. The tingling in her fingertips intensified. She was so *fucking* close—

"Come with me." He strode past her, and she cursed herself for hesitating, for letting the guards overtake her and flank him on either side. Each wore unfamiliar bulky armoured clothing and a mask, an odd addition to their uniform. *New security?*

As they walked out of the receiving room through a door on the right-hand side, Yala looked more closely at his companions. A surge of recognition hit her. The masks weren't that at all but were part of their faces, and what she'd taken for uniform was a layer of armoured scales instead of skin.

The guards were not human any longer, though they had been at one time. The king himself might appear as a normal man, but these individuals had set foot in Mekan's domain, and the god of death had reshaped their flesh. *Fool,* she chided herself. She should never have assumed he'd left all his allies on the island. Who would be more qualified as bodyguards than the few who'd passed Mekan's unknown tests and walked out of His realm as more than mere humans?

She didn't know if he expected her to acknowledge the inhuman nature of his followers, but they walked for only a short time before they reached an opening into a courtyard. The same courtyard in which an empty pyre had burned the day of the king's funeral.

Now, a set of stone pillars rose from each corner, and in the centre stood a large slab of stone. *An altar.*

He was building a Temple of Death.

13

Niema found the boats where they'd left them at the riverside, concealed among the bushes on the bank. She and Hachim took one, and Saren and Viam claimed the other, readied to go their separate ways.

"Good luck," Niema called to the others. "I hope you get there safely."

"And I hope you manage to convince some of the other Disciples of Life to help." Saren picked up an oar and settled into the canoe with Viam. "Preferably before we're outnumbered by the dead."

Easier said than done. Niema had washed her hands repeatedly, but the rotting stench of the dead clung to her skin, and every rustle in the bushes made her tense in anticipation of another attack. When they'd passed Setemar, Niema brought the boat to a stop to write a reply to the Superior. Rowing towards the forest relaxed her a little, but the potent smell refused to fade, as if Mekan clung to her skin like a bloodfly.

Superior Kralia's response came the following morning,

inviting them to meet with her at a riverside village not far from where Yala had once lived in an isolated cabin.

"Why does she want to meet us in person?" Niema reread the note. "Does she not worry the enclave will be attacked again?"

Maybe she doesn't need to as long as I'm not there. Though the dead had found that village without Niema being present, no comforting word offered by Hachim would rid her of the sense of being tainted.

When they neared the village in which they were set to meet the Superior, Niema was surprised to see her war drake waited at the riverside. She and Hachim brought the canoe to a halt and climbed out onto the bank. Her arms ached from exertion, and she was conscious of the faint bloodstains on her clothes and the lingering smell of the dead.

Superior Kralia studied the pair of them for a long moment. "It grieves me that the Disciples of the Earth have surrendered."

"They were surrounded by the king's soldiers," Hachim said. "There was nothing we could do."

"Some of them were prepared to resist," Niema added, "but we didn't dare stay in case the soldiers cornered us too."

"You then encountered the dead."

She swallowed and nodded. "We laid them all to rest, but it wasn't possible to check if other villages were affected the same. With only two of us, we'd be overrun."

"I have a solution." She gestured, and her war drake padded away from the river into the thin layer of bushes separating them from the huts at the village's outskirts. "This way."

Confused, Niema and Hachim followed the path cleared by the war drake's wide feet. More growling came from ahead, where a number of similar beasts had gathered in front of the wooden huts that formed the village's centre.

Each bore a rider dressed not in a soldier's uniform but in the unadorned garb of the Disciples of Life forged into armour. Niema's breath caught. The beasts stood in rows, deceptively still and uncharacteristically docile, while their owners watched the newcomers' arrival. They carried *weapons*, mostly in the form of bows and arrows and branches sharpened to spears. Elite Disciples. A chill rose to Niema's skin.

She'd observed Yalet's elites from a distance while in the enclave, but being this close to those who belonged to the same order as the assassins Superior Kralia had once sent to punish her for daring to save a Disciple of Death filled her with the urge to flee before an arrow found its home in her skin.

Niema turned to the Superior, panic rising. "Why are they here?"

"These individuals are the chosen elites," she said. "Those who Yalet has selected to hunt down Mekan's beasts and undo the damage He has inflicted upon our realm."

"You mean like the village we found."

"Correct," said the Superior. "And I would like to invite you both to join them."

"You want *me* to join?" Surprise filled her voice. Wasn't she corrupted? The others might not know the extent, but surely, it was no secret that Niema had strayed too close to Mekan's path to ever be trusted, much less handed a weapon.

The Superior spoke to her in a low voice. "When you received your first vision from Yalet, it was a clear sign that you'd been chosen for a great honour. If not for the events that followed, you would have long ago been promoted to an elite Disciple. As it is, I do not know if this is the right choice, but I trust in Yalet's wisdom."

Hachim's hand found hers and squeezed. "So do I."

Niema's eyes brimmed, overcome with emotion. Then, another question hit her. "We'll have to carry weapons?"

"Yes."

This was the price one paid to be Yalet's chosen. They would let blood stain their hands so that others did not need to.

"Will you accept this offer?" the Superior asked of them. "It's your choice."

It is... and it's Yalet's. The god of life had chosen her and had kept choosing her, even when her Superior had lost all faith in Niema's path. In this, she would be able to make a difference, to combat Mekan's attempts to destroy her people despite His efforts to sway her to His side.

She would not fail.

"I accept," said Niema.

***

Shadows coiled around Mekan's altar, beckoning Yala to step closer. Instead, she turned to the king beside her. Though he displayed no outward emotion, a gleam in his eyes betrayed satisfaction and expectation in equal measures.

"This is a temple." A safe enough observation to make. Any fool could identify it as such.

"Yes," he said. "It will be."

"To..." Gods, did he want *her* to say the obvious? "Mekan."

"Yes," he repeated. "No doubt it looks familiar to you."

The island. Gods, the island. Whether he knew of its destruction or not was immaterial when he intended to replicate Mekan's domain inside the capital itself. How close was the temple to completion? Did those involved in its construction know what they were building?

That soldier did, she thought. *That's why he tried to run.*

"It does," she said, "but I didn't think anyone knew how

the temple on the island was constructed, given that it was abandoned long before Laria's founding."

"That's correct," he said. "However, the carvings we found inside provided plentiful information, as did the rituals we performed within its walls."

Which rituals? He didn't bear any obvious marks upon his person that indicated Mekan had claimed him; in fact, he struck a stark contrast to the masked guards who stood as upright as the newly built pillars. How fitting that he'd chosen this particular courtyard to house his temple, constructing proof of his might upon the same stones where he'd once been mourned. A statement, perhaps, that nobody would ever succeed in ripping him from his throne again. And as tempted as she might have been to strike while he was within reach, spilling blood near the altar would have precisely the outcome she wanted to avoid.

"Is it your intent to use the temple to train more Disciples?" She licked her dry lips. "Disciples of Death."

"It is," he confirmed. "Mekan chooses only the worthy, and you, Captain Yala Palathar, are one of them."

Yes. He'd known all along, as she'd suspected, but if he'd had a hint of her past transgressions against Mekan, she'd have bled out on that altar the day she returned to the palace.

"You are among the few who have looked directly into the Void itself," he went on. "You even slew one of Mekan's beasts to save your squad, an act that bestowed on you that claw that you now carry upon your person."

Cold burned Yala's leg as if the claw itself wanted to assert its presence, and she cursed herself for ever expecting the king not to notice she carried a piece of Mekan wherever she went.

"You were right to keep it," he added. "Any remnant of one of Mekan's beasts can be a danger in the wrong hands, and as it is, you have proven yourself worthy of trust. For

EMMA L. ADAMS

that reason, I have chosen to allow you to be one of the first."

His words travelled through her mind, their meaning slow to sink in. She might have expected his admission of trust to elicit a rush of triumph at her success, but the sensation was more akin to having evaded a war drake's bite only to step into range of its claws.

"The first... what, Your Majesty?" she managed to say.

"The first to serve me as a Disciple of Death," he said. "And the first, should you pass the tests, to ascend to Mekan's side."

"Tests?" Yala's hands, damp with sweat, slipped on her cane. If she was to be tested by Mekan, he meant for her to step into the Void. To lose control over her will in service to the god of death. "I thought Mekan accepted only the dead to serve at his side."

Her eyes went, unbidden, to one of the guards. The man —or woman, she wasn't sure—was encased from head to toe in scaly armour. Not a being of flesh and blood but one who'd transcended humanity and lost their mind and soul in the process.

"Usually, that is true," he confirmed. "There are exceptions. I have, for instance, travelled into His domain myself."

What bargain had he sworn to have retained control over his will where others had not? What other favours had Mekan bestowed?

"The temple isn't ready yet." She forced her attention to the large stone slab and the shadows creeping at the edges. To open the temple would require calling upon the Void by means of a sacrifice of some unlucky souls. But whose blood was to be spilled on the altar if not hers?

"When it is, I will hold a great ceremony," he said. "Only the worthy will attend to witness Mekan's ascension, and to take their first vows as Disciples of Death."

Then she would have to stop him. Somehow. Heart beating against her ribcage, she released a question that had been planted in her mind during Kelan's last visit. "I thought... forgive me, Your Majesty, but I thought Mekan's beasts answered to Him alone and not His Disciples. Is there not, ah, a risk that they might escape the palace into the city?"

Does he plan to call his army too?

"Yes." The merest hint of tension rippled along his jaw. "There is a risk. However, my void drake will keep them in check. The beast obeys me alone, as it ascended to Mekan's side at the same time as I did."

Gods. Of course that's where it came from. He'd been riding a war drake at the time he'd been forced into exile, and he must have taken the beast with him to the island. Into the Void.

Which confirmed a suspicion she'd had for a long while: The beasts were Mekan's answer to the war drakes, just as every other creature in His realm was a twisted reflection of their own. Moreover, the king's admission that he held no control over the rest of Mekan's army was information that would serve her well.

"In any case, I brought you here in part to demonstrate why you must bring in the dissenters alive," he told her. "The traitors will be sentenced to death and will be executed here in this very chamber."

Yala's heart shuddered like ground shaken by a quake.

The Disciples of the Sea, she thought. *They're the intended sacrifices, and their deaths will open the Void.*

14

S aren was sick of the fucking river.

Travelling by boat had seemed a good idea at the time and was undeniably the safest way to avoid the dead, but he soon became weary of the ceaseless rhythm of rowing. And being surrounded by water yet unable to quench his thirst.

Nights camping on the bank were worse. Dusk always brought the same dread, and closing his eyes invariably meant his mind choosing to revisit those old images, of the Void opening at the heart of the island like a gaping mouth ready to swallow him whole.

The nightmares worsened the closer they drew to the capital, as did the pervasive dread, like a spiked collar closing around his neck until its sharp points pierced to the bone.

Viam didn't understand. Unlike him, she was able to filter out those memories and remain in the present. Yala, too, though she was given to facing her nightmares with a weapon in hand. Saren had admitted the cowardice to himself a long time ago, but it was hard to trust his own judgement when that same instinct was urging him to bury himself in drink and forget.

Part of him wondered if the fault was with everyone else, not with him. Who wouldn't shrink away from the knowledge that even death wouldn't bring respite? That nothing waited on the other side but bitter oblivion?

He'd thought, when they'd been in the enclave, that he might find a reprieve at Yalet's altar. His hopes had been in vain. The god of life had no interest in recruiting someone who'd already been claimed, and he'd heard nothing in response to his prayers but silence. Perhaps Mekan was too deeply embedded inside his heart to excavate.

He and Viam arrived in Dalathar as the sun began its descent beyond the rooftops on the third day after leaving Setemar. The river's infamous stench had become evident, and they abandoned the boats outside of the city walls, making their way into Dalathar on foot.

As they left the outskirts behind and wove deeper into the warren of cobbled streets and bridges, a rush of memories came surging back as inexorably as the filthy river. He had to suppress the urge to duck into the first tavern they passed and seek refuge in a bottle of rice wine until the voices in his head fell silent.

Viam noticed nothing of his inner struggle, but she broke the silence the fourth time he changed directions to avoid the king's guards.

"They don't know us, Saren," she said. "If they've stepped up patrols, we'll be hard-pressed to avoid them."

"I guarantee they know Yala," he said. "I just hope they've stopped hovering near her house now she isn't there."

"That's where you're going to stay?"

"Not many other options," he said. "What's your plan? If you walk up to the gates and ask to be let in, the first thing they'll want to know is where you've been for the past few weeks."

"I'll tell them I was recovering from my injury. They can't punish me for that."

"Desertion might be illegal now that King Tharen's back on the throne." He snorted. "It still doesn't sound real. He's not supposed to be here. He's supposed to be fucking dead."

Here in Dalathar, the truth was inescapable. Gods, he wanted a drink.

"I'll go there in the morning," Viam decided. "And I'll look for Yala."

"I wouldn't," he said. "If she's alive, she'll be under close watch, playing her role. Can you do the same? Pretend to be on his side? Fight for him?"

Viam's steps faltered. He'd hit on a weak spot, but she was such a poor liar that he wondered if she'd convinced herself that she could get away with deceiving the king, let alone fight his battles should he demand she do so.

He didn't want her to die. As to Yala, there was nothing to be done to stop *her* from hurling herself into the path of danger, but what would she say if she knew he'd allowed Viam to take that same risk? That he hadn't tried to stop her?

"I doubt it," he went on, the words tasting like ash in his mouth. "You're a noble to the core. You've never had to beg for anything in your life."

"What?" Viam spun on him. "What does my upbringing have to do with anything?"

Nothing, was the answer. He'd revisited their oldest argument, even though he knew that most nobles didn't have an easy time in the army, and those who volunteered when their societal position might have otherwise exempted them from service usually had a good reason to avoid their blood relatives.

Viam huffed and strode ahead. "I'm going to the Undercity. Nalen will know of any major developments since we left."

"He will." Saren little desired to visit the Undercity at this late hour, but he followed Viam regardless. The streets were quiet, and they encountered nobody except a few mangy skirrits at the entrance to the Undercity.

"Where's Nalen?" Viam trod downstairs into a street bereft of human presence. The shacks on either side of them had an abandoned air, as if every living soul had turned to smoke and evaporated. "Where is everyone else, for that matter?"

Good question. Had they left? Or...?

A less pleasant explanation presented itself, as keen as a blade. "We need to leave."

A breeze stirred against the back of his neck. He spun around, reaching for a weapon that wasn't there. "Kelan."

Viam lowered her dagger; unlike him, she'd been willing to grab a few weapons from the dead they'd encountered back in that village. "I thought you'd be at Skytower."

"And I thought you'd be safely in Setemar," he said. "Looking for Yala, are you?"

"*I'm* not trying to get into the palace," Saren said, jerking his head at Viam. "She is, but not if His Majesty has been rounding up deserters and having them hanged."

Kelan's mouth parted. "He *might* have, but I suspect everyone who once lived here is currently in the barracks. More pleasant accommodations, I gather."

"That's where Nalen is?" said Saren. "He'll be pissed off. Have you spoken to Yala?"

"Once or twice," he responded. "She's training new riders."

She's alive. And she'd stepped into her role as captain exactly as Saren had expected.

Viam's shoulders straightened. "Good. I'll go to the palace

tomorrow morning. We can spend tonight at Yala's old house."

"Ah." Kelan paused for a heartbeat. "About that. There's something else I should tell you."

***

Yala's house, it turned out, was occupied by no fewer than ten robed Disciples of the Flame. When Kelan opened the door, a couple of them jumped to their feet in alarm, but the majority remained seated or kneeling in front of a cluster of battered candles. Viam stared in disbelief at the intruders, while Saren fumed at her side.

"Why," he said, 'is there a group of Disciples in my house?"

"I had to send them somewhere that wasn't the Undercity," Kelan said. "I didn't know any of you were going to come back to the capital."

"The guards all know this address, remember?" Saren snapped.

"But they also know Yala isn't living here any longer," said Kelan. "They won't expect anyone to be around."

"There's room in the house for all of us," Viam said. "With luck, I'll be in the upper city by the morning."

A muscle twitched in Saren's jaw. "If the guards come here before then, we'll *all* be sentenced to death."

"We'll leave." A thin-faced Disciple climbed nervously to his feet. "We can go back to the Undercity."

"No need." Viam took Saren's arm. "Come on. We can figure this out."

"Really." Saren turned his back on the Disciples and paced away from the house, his shoulders hunched with tension. "Even if keeping them in the house wasn't a crime, they're a liability."

"They aren't," Viam protested. "They're Disciples, remember? They have Dalathik's favour."

Kelan cleared his throat. "Mekan infiltrated their temple. They're unable to reach their god."

Saren threw up his hands. "There you have it. You know, it shouldn't be so fucking difficult to hold a roof over my head without the god of death snatching it away."

Viam briefly wondered what he was talking about before she recalled how his old lover, Giran, had kicked him out after his home had been attacked by Mekan's followers, and more recently, he'd been working as a healer before the king's hunt for Disciples of Death had forced him to leave the capital. *He might have a point there.*

As Saren began to walk away again, Viam hurried after him. "Wait. Don't go off alone."

"I'm not going to a tavern," he muttered. "Don't worry. I won't embarrass you."

"That's not what I'm worried about," she protested. "I know it's hard for you, being back here. I didn't want this."

"Neither did Yala." He halted, swivelling to her. "She'd want me to drag you away from that place with all my strength."

"She needs us, even if she won't admit it."

Saren rolled his eyes. "She doesn't need me. *You*, though… you're friends with the old king. I bet that'll help."

Daliel. Viam had hardly spared him a thought in recent days, but for all she knew, he might be as much a prisoner inside that palace as anyone else.

"I'm not sure about that," she murmured. "I don't know if I'm still part of the flight division or if I'll have to go back to my old position in administration, but neither of those is a guarantee of seeing the prince."

"And if the king asks you to train as a Disciple of Death?"

Saren's voice held a challenge but also a warning, one that

coiled around Viam's heart like a serpent. Wasn't that why she'd left the city in the first place, out of fear that her history with Mekan would be discovered?

"Never mind." He ground his heel into the cobbles, his mouth forming a bitter line. "At least you *can* call yourself a Disciple."

"I thought you didn't want to." They hadn't discussed the subject much, as Saren steered the conversation elsewhere if she so much as alluded to his history with Mekan. "Or do you?"

"Fuck that." A shudder travelled along his thin shoulders. "Mekan might want *me*, but the feeling isn't mutual."

"He does?"

"What do you think?" He lifted his head to the darkening sky. "I've heard His voice, same as you. He wants us all."

"You don't have to listen to him," she told Saren. "Besides, the king might not want to share his title with anyone else. In fact, I'd be surprised if he does."

Or he might want to turn me *into one of* them. Viam recalled Yala's account of her second visit to the island, where Mekan's most ardent cultists had surrounded her. Some of those who'd set foot in Mekan's domain had returned with their flesh rotting and their bodies crumbling, but Yala had encountered others, those who had been transformed into scaly entities no longer recognisable as human. They might have had the appearance of life, but their will was no longer their own. They'd answered only to Mekan.

Viam put the thought out of mind. Whatever fate awaited her inside the palace, her mind was made up. She'd ensure Brenat and Yala survived, first and foremost—and then, she'd look for the prince.

15

Viam reached the palace gates, wiping sweat from her forehead. She'd passed through the gates to the upper city with comparatively little challenge, her face familiar enough to the guards to be associated with the army and not with Yala.

Around her, Ceremonial Square was beginning to bustle with the early-morning market, merchants and city workers congregating around the stalls laden with produce, but an empty space gaped between King Larial's golden statue and the palace gates. A dark cloud hung over that area in the form of a shadow cast by the void drake, which flew in an endless circle that turned her insides to snakes and stifled the words in her throat.

"Well?" said the hard-faced female guard at the front gate. "What's your business?"

"I'm Viam Tiathar. I'm returning to the palace." Her frantic heartbeat, loud as a chorus of drums, made it hard to think clearly. "I work in administration, but I was recently part of the flight division. My entire squad died in the recent battle."

Her assumption had been that the king hadn't received an in-depth report on exactly which soldiers had been severely injured in that disastrous mission, since almost every member of the flight division had been reported dead or maimed, and the monarch's return would have upended the palace as efficiently as a rampaging raptor set loose in the market.

"Wait." The guard squinted at her. "You used to work with King—Prince—Daliel. Didn't you?"

Viam's mouth went dry. "Yes. Briefly."

Would that work in her favour or against her? Disgraced though he might be, the former king was still the heir to Laria's crown. They'd shared a friendship of sorts, and while that might not have endured beyond his father's return, it was something solid to grasp, a familiar element in a place otherwise so changed.

"I can't promise you have a job," she said. "King Tharen's been cutting back on unnecessary admin. He wants all able-bodied employees in the army." Nevertheless, she stepped aside, allowing her to pass.

On the other side of the gates, Viam exhaled shakily, pulling her disparate thoughts together.

Brenat. She walked fast, the tension in her chest loosening when she was beyond the sight of the monster lurking above the palace.

The barracks had returned to their typical state as a hive of purposeful activity, with packs of soldiers exercising in the grounds and commanders walking back and forth from meetings. As she made her way down the corridor to the infirmary, the thump of a cane caught her ear.

"Yala." Her heart lifted despite the sheer incongruity of seeing her former captain walking the corridors of the barracks again with all the authority of a squad leader.

Yala swivelled to Viam, her eyes widening a fraction. "What are you doing? Rejoining the army?"

"I'm looking for Brenat."

"She's not here," said Yala. "Must have returned to admin after being discharged."

"I didn't know she'd have a choice." Viam shrank away from Yala's accusing expression. Did she think Viam's presence might sabotage her chances of killing the monarch?

"You should go," was all Yala said. "Nobody's asked after you or Saren, but I can't guarantee you won't be pressed into signing up."

"What, as a soldier?" She moved closer, lowered her voice. "Or a Disciple—?"

Yala's cane jabbed her in the leg, silencing her. "Later. Will you be staying in the staff quarters?"

"Only if they didn't eliminate my job."

"I'll find you there." Then, quieter: "Please don't get killed for my sake."

And then she was gone, the thump of her cane fading as she rounded a corner.

What did I expect? Giving herself a mental shake, Viam left the barracks through the front entrance and retraced her steps through the palace grounds until she reached the cluster of buildings hosting the king's administrative staff.

She found the head of the division, Malat, in her own office on the first floor of the main building, a small room that smelled strongly of the smokeleaf cigar she always had protruding from her mouth. The windows lay wide open, but the air was thick and humid and did little to disperse the suffocating smoke.

"Viam." Malat looked up from her desk in surprise, exhaling a fresh cloud of smoke. "I thought you left the city. Weren't you injured in the battle?"

"I was." She stifled a cough, relieved that her cover story

had been taken as a given. "Is Brenat here? She's not in the barracks."

"Oh, she took a job in the palace," said Malat, sounding displeased. "The king ordered all nonessential staff to be reassigned to the army, but he wanted volunteers for some construction work inside the palace. I can't say I know what it is."

Despite the heat intensified by the thick smoke, shivers sprang to Viam's arms. "She went into the palace?"

"Every day for the past two weeks," Malat said. "I can't say I know what His Majesty has her doing, but you can ask if he needs anyone else. I'm afraid if you want your old position back, you're out of luck, sorry to say."

What did I expect? She gave herself a mental shake for even entertaining the idea of being able to walk in here and reclaim her prior station. Hadn't she left that job voluntarily when she'd agreed to take on the role of flight captain?

The army always needed volunteers, but the thought of taking to the air again brought her out in a cold sweat. Yala didn't want her there, and Brenat... *What is she doing in that palace?* Why had she volunteered to work directly under the king? Hadn't Viam told her what His Majesty was capable of?

Now, she had no choice but to confront the place she'd been trying to avoid looking at, a formidable construction now barren of flowers and draped instead in Larian military flags. Though desperation spurred her on, her nerve faltered when she neared the stairs. The void drake hovered above, its winged shadow blotting out the sunlight as it flew in a ceaseless path.

She climbed the staircase, sweat trickling down her spine, her shoulders braced for those sharp claws to grasp her at any instant. The beast continued to circle above without deviation, as if following a silent command. The question of how the king had tamed one of Mekan's monsters lay far beyond her other concerns, but she wondered how the guards managed to stand directly in its shadow without being distracted from their jobs.

One guard, a broad-faced man with deep-set eyes, stepped between her and the doors. "Who are you?"

"I'm Viam Tiathar." The words escaped in a breathless rush. "I used to be acquainted with King—Prince Daliel. I was injured in the battle a few weeks ago, so I only came back to the palace today—"

"You're a friend of the prince?" He made a disbelieving noise. "A likely story."

"Ask him." If Daliel didn't back her up—well, she'd have bigger problems than the loss of a friendship.

"I'll do that," growled the man. "Now, get out."

Viam didn't dare linger. She returned instead to the administration building and made for the one place that had always been her sanctuary.

The library, a large room beneath golden archways filled with texts the likes of which weren't to be found outside the palace complex, was a comforting haven amid unfamiliar seas. She picked out a few books to peruse, but her mind was too restless to focus, and the volume of texts reminded her of her past failures to glean information that might help in their fight against Mekan. She'd once hoped to find insight into Mekan's weaknesses through accounts of the gods' history, but all she'd found were countless diverging accounts on how the other gods had banished Mekan from their own realm. In fact, even the weeks she'd spent among the Disciples of Life had taught her only that Yalet did not share Her secrets with outsiders, much less with Disciples of Death.

When the bells rang for the end of the workday, Viam left the library, fear scraping at her insides. She spied a number of people climbing down the palace stairs, and her heart jolted when she recognised Brenat's broad frame among them.

"Brenat." The name escaped in a gasp as she ran over to the other woman and threw her arms tight around her. "Brenat!"

"Viam?" Brenat hugged Viam back, peering at her through her good eye. The other was covered with a patch, and a deep scar bisected that side of her face. But she was whole and breathing and not enslaved to Mekan. "Gods, it really is you."

"What do you think?" Viam bit her lip, her vision misting over. "You weren't in the barracks. I went looking for you, and you were gone."

"You're the one who vanished from the capital for weeks," Brenat retorted. "Where *were* you?"

"I was with, ah, the Disciples of Life."

"Now, I bet *that's* a story." Brenat's remaining eye gleamed. "Tell me."

"Not here." They walked around the administration building as Viam ran through the main events of the past few weeks, a tremor entering her voice when she recounted Mekan's brutal assault upon the village. "There was nowhere safe to go but here, and I wanted to come back and find you."

"Now, that was a silly thing to do, wasn't it?" she said. "Wasn't the king searching for you?"

"Not me. He wanted Yala. Gods, Brenat, *why* did you take a job inside the palace?" The words burst out of her like a war drake crashing through a fence. "You must have known he—the king—"

"Clearly, I'm fine." Brenat rested her hands on Viam's shoulders. "Calm down. I've only seen the king twice in the past few weeks. He keeps to himself."

Viam's heart jangled against her ribs. "But—what does he have you *doing* in there?"

Brenat shrugged. "Manual labour. We've been building some fancy construction in the courtyard with all these pillars and a massive slab of stone. Can't say I know what it is."

"A slab of stone." An image slid into her mind, one that turned her blood to ice. "Not... an altar?"

"For the gods, you mean?" One eyebrow lifted. "Might be, now you mention it."

"There's only one god that matters to him." Viam drew her arms close to her chest. "Has he summoned anything in there?"

"What? No. He hasn't even been there." Nevertheless, Brenat's expression sobered. "What's the issue?"

"Brenat." A pleading note entered Viam's voice, unbidden. "If I'm right, he's building a Temple of Death. Did you really not know?"

"Shit." Her mouth dropped open. "That would explain it."

"Explain what?" Her thoughts raced in tandem with her pounding heart. "If the king's not around, who's supervising you? Not the prince, surely."

"Guards." She shrugged one shoulder. "New ones. They wear masks all the time and never speak. Never seen their faces either. Kinda creepy."

Cold fingers trailed across Viam's shoulder blades. "Are you sure they're human?"

"Well, they're shaped like humans. One head, two legs, two arms, that kind of thing."

That's no guarantee. Yala had described, in chilling detail, the beings she'd encountered on the island. The ones who'd once been human, before they'd pledged themselves to Mekan and surrendered their humanity in the process.

"And Daliel?" She hesitated. "What did the king do with him after he took his throne?"

"No idea, but I doubt the king has locked his son in a cell, Viam."

He might have done worse, Viam thought. *He might have turned him into one of Mekan's servants.*

***

"He's building a Temple of Death." Yala's grim admission sent concerns flying from Kelan's head. "That's what the king is up to."

"You've seen it?"

Yala inclined her head. "There's worse. He knows the Disciples of the Sea survived, and it's their lives that will be given to open the Void and the temple both."

Shit. "Does the king know *where* they're hiding?"

"If he did, they'd already be dead." She spoke dispassionately, but her gloved fingers clenched around her cane. "They'd better have a good hiding place. You aren't here to bring any more strays to my doorstep, I hope?"

"Are you referring to Viam?" He'd opted to stay in the upper city after he and Viam had parted ways, waiting for Yala to be alone in the paddock. "It was her idea to come back, not mine, to be clear."

"And Saren?"

"He's in your house." He'd neglected to mention the Disciples of the Flame, but the thud of heavy boots warned him that someone else was on their way. He cleared the fence in a swift glide, landing in the passageway behind the paddock.

I'll have to tell her another time. She would be as displeased as Saren to have fugitives squatting in her house, but the Disciples of the Sea had a significantly more urgent predicament between the army hunting them down and the imminent creation of a Temple of Death.

The latter would kick off a cascade of new problems. If

the king succeeded in creating the temple, only a Disciple of Life would be able to stop him, and there were none present in the capital, nor had he heard from Niema since she'd parted ways with the others.

Upon returning to the inn, he relayed the bad news to his fellow Disciples while scratching out notes to both his Superior and to Superior Kralia. Molin would only be able to carry one message at a time, but when Kelan asked him to choose, the tree-raptor picked up both in one outstretched claw and swooped out of the open window.

"Can that beast actually understand you?" asked Brikel, raising her voice over the sound of her brother ranting at anyone who would listen that they'd made a mistake in coming to the capital at all. "Gods, Lakiel, be *quiet*. The Superior told us to report on anything we heard from the palace. We wouldn't have heard anything if we weren't here, would we?"

"The temple won't be complete until the king sacrifices the Disciples of the Sea," Kelan added. "Which gives us more of an incentive to help them, wouldn't you say?"

"No," said Lakiel, while several more voices chorused yes.

Bolstered, Kelan said, "I'm going to look for Nanek at the docks. Anyone with me?"

"Yes," Brikel answered, to a predictable sigh from Lakiel. Ranit volunteered, too, and after a marked pause, Lakiel offered another sigh, as though resigned to the knowledge that his sister would refuse to stay behind and that protecting her would be easier if he invited himself along.

As before, Kelan found Nanek in the act of loosening the wooden boards on the underside of one of the king's ships so that any unfortunate soul who sailed in that vessel would swiftly find themselves foundering.

Lakiel narrowed his eyes at him. "You're risking discovery for the sake of a petty act of vandalism?"

"An act that might save our lives." Nanek pulled himself out of the sea, accompanied by a splash that mostly hit Lakiel. Kelan hid a smile as his fellow Disciple spluttered and swore while Nanek wore an expression serious enough to almost fool him into believing he hadn't done it on purpose.

"I'm afraid we have bad news." Recounting Yala's warning dampened his mood as effectively as the water, and Nanek's expression darkened with each word he spoke.

"My instinct told me she was not to be trusted," the Disciple of the Sea said. "Her actions on the island suggested otherwise, but she's clearly chosen a side."

"I didn't get the impression she had a choice in the matter."

"She might have walked away." A growl entered Nanek's voice. "There are Disciples on that island who are not ready to fight."

"They're on an island?" Lakiel's tone turned suspicious. "Larian or Rafragorian?"

Kelan swivelled to him. "What?"

Nanek ground his back teeth. "Larian, currently."

"What the hell does it matter?" Brikel asked her brother. "They're being hunted by the king. Rafragoria's hardly in any position to drive them out of their territory. We're more of a threat than they are."

"I was implying that they must have had outside help to have escaped the king's notice," Lakiel said defiantly. "If he's sent flight squads to search the ocean and found nothing, they must be hiding outside of Larian waters."

Oh. He might be correct, but who in their right mind would judge the Disciples of the Sea for hiding on any strip of land that might be available to them?

"The last battle for that island was more than a decade ago, and Laria was the victor," Nanek ground out, his hands curling into fists as if he would have liked to wrap them around Lakiel's throat.

"There you have it," said Brikel. "Also, Rafragoria is in no state to attack undefended Disciples hunted by their own nation."

"Nor do they desire to," said Nanek. "The Disciples have never been part of Laria's wars."

Lakiel made a soft noise, working his jaw. "And you've spoken to them? Since the recent battle?"

Nanek offered a flat stare. "Would it offend you if we had?"

"It's treason." Lakiel's mouth shaped the word as if it tasted sour. "To even *speak* to Laria's enemies is an offence against—"

"Treason?" Disbelief bled into Kelan's voice. "That's a term used by monarchs and soldiers, not Disciples. By their definition, *we're* traitors."

A flush painted Lakiel's cheekbones. "If our fellow Disciples are spreading information to Rafragorian spies, our Superior will want to know."

"Our Superior wouldn't give two shits," Kelan retaliated. "They're a seafaring nation, and the Disciples of the Sea live outside of Laria's shores. They're not Rafragorian spies."

"Precisely." Nanek's knuckles cracked. "If you call us traitors, you call my ancestors the same. The ocean's boundaries have always been fluid, and Rafragorian ships are as common a sight in our territory as Larian ones. Moreover, if not for our neighbours, we might never have learned of the Larian king's survival."

"And didn't tell anyone." Accusation layered Lakiel's voice. "In refusing to share the truth until it was too late, you doomed yourselves. Why should we then endanger ourselves to save you from your mistakes?"

"Who do you think King Tharen will target when he's

rounded us up and had us sacrificed on the altar?" Water splashed against the pier as the ocean responded to Nanek's anger. "He desires the submission of *all* Laria's Disciples, and two Superiors have already surrendered. You will not be spared by virtue of your remote location, Disciples."

Two surrendered and another was killed, he mentally corrected. That left... gods, would *Superior Sietra* be the king's next target?

Regardless, he had no desire to see the surviving Disciples of the Sea rounded up like livestock and put to death. There was no question. They had to intervene.

"Exactly." Brikel pushed in front of her brother and addressed Nanek. "We'll help. Tell us what to do."

"He doesn't know." Lakiel turned his back on the Disciple of the Sea. "He's reduced to sabotaging the king's fleet because no other options are available to him. We don't need him to get us killed too."

"The king's fleet." An idea slid into Kelan's mind. "Do you think the king will notice if one of his ships goes missing?"

16

A young man greeted Viam at the doors to the administration building the morning after her return to the palace. "Viam Tiathar?"

"Yes." Her heart stuttered; Brenat surreptitiously reached and gave her arm a reassuring squeeze from behind. "Can I help you?".

"The prince wants to see you."

Daliel. Viam fought to keep her expression steady. "Now?"

"This way." The man, a pimply youth of conscription age at most, led her to the palace stairs. When he spied the void drake circling above, he gulped and began climbing at a steady jog that had Viam puffing to keep up.

She and Brenat parted ways with a hug, and the youth followed her, leaving Viam stranded in the entrance hall. With sudden unease, she wondered if the young man had volunteered to help with the king's recent construction project to avoid being forced into service.

Two guards came to escort Viam to the prince. Both were human, mercifully; her conversation with Brenat the previous day had left her primed to encounter a legion of masked monsters on the other side of the doors. As it was, the palace interior hadn't changed as much as the outside, though the corridors through which the guards led her were new. In the past, she'd only visited the parts of the palace that were open to the public, and it was rare that the king received casual visitors.

Her breath caught as they entered a large room lined with bookshelves. A library. Bigger than the one she was used to, bigger than any she'd imagined. For a moment, as she breathed in the smell of old tomes and took in the dizzying sight of an array of worn leather covers on carved wooden shelves, she forgot she was in the palace.

Then, she saw the prince. Daliel rose from one of the plush armchairs scattered amid the shelves; hastily, she knelt. "Your Highness."

"Rise." Daliel's eyes crinkled as he smiled, as if he was genuinely relieved to see her. "You don't need to defer to me, remember? Viam, when I didn't hear of you after the battle... I feared the worst."

"I'm sorry." She clambered to her feet, conscious of the guards hovering near the door at her back. "I had to leave the upper city for a while. To recover."

"I am sorry for the losses you suffered."

A lump rose in her throat. She hadn't known her squad well—they'd trained for only a day—but guilt had haunted her for weeks, together with worry for Brenat.

Now, she had another reason to worry. Did Daliel know what his father was building here in the palace? Did she dare to ask, with eavesdroppers at the door who might repeat every word she spoke to the king?

"I wasn't sure if your father would want me to stay with the army," she fumbled. "His arrival was sudden."

"Yes." Daliel averted his gaze, instead contemplating a stack of books on a nearby table. "However, my father has reorganised the capital considerably, and the army is stronger than it ever was."

The hint of self-recrimination in his voice tugged at Viam's heart. *Fool.* Hadn't their friendship nearly got her killed once already?

She pushed the voice aside and took his offer of a seat next to him at one of the plush armchairs grouped around the table. "Does your father know that I'm here?"

"He doesn't police whether I'm allowed visitors."

Doesn't... yet, said a cynical voice in the back of her mind. "I thought, since you haven't been outside the palace since before he came back…"

"For my own safety." He offered a smile. "I'll ask my guards to bring us refreshments."

The guards, she noticed belatedly, had retreated from the room. The prince might be confined to his quarters, but the staff hadn't taken to spying on his every move. Not overtly, at any rate.

How was she to reconcile his easy smile with the slaughter she'd seen during her last visit or the betrayal on his face when she'd told him the true perpetrators of his father's death, little knowing that their assassination attempt had failed after all?

"I know this must seem strange to you," he added. "But I've missed having someone to talk to who isn't paid to be here."

"I used to be paid to be here." Her employment ought to be the least of her concerns, but Malat would ask questions if she stayed in the staff quarters after her clear dismissal. "My position no longer exists."

"It doesn't?"

"No." That the question had never occurred to him would have made both Saren and Yala roll their eyes, but Viam pitied the prince, trapped in a cage not of his own making. "I have to join the army again or seek employment elsewhere."

"We can't have that." He rose from his armchair. "I'll speak to my father."

"No." She bit her tongue as if to suppress a reply that had already slipped out. It was too easy to forget who she was talking to. Daliel might be a king no longer, but his father could order her death in a blink. "No, it's fine. He needs the army to take precedence, I know."

"You should not be forced back into service after the sacrifices you made." Agitation stooped his shoulders as he paced the room, lifting his head to the shelves as if they might offer him the answer. "I'll see what I can do for you. My father is busy, but he'll agree with me, I'm sure."

Will he? What was the king's plan for his son? He had no other heirs; he'd never remarried after Daliel's mother's death and had barely given her or his son any level of attention, but Daliel's disastrous stint as monarch would surely have prompted him to make contingency plans. The king was no immortal, despite his pact with the god of death. Right?

"I don't want to be of any trouble," Viam told him. "The king has some soldiers working on a construction project inside the palace, doesn't he? Brenat told me."

Yala would want her to ask more questions, and her disapproving face appeared unbidden in Viam's mind, as if to remind her that the prince would give her insight into the monarch's movements that nobody else had access to.

"He does," said Daliel. "I can ask if they'll offer you a job, but I believe the work is close to completion."

The temple is nearly finished. Her skin went clammy, her hands digging into the plush armchair. *Does Yala know?*

His brow furrowed at her stricken expression. "I'm sure he'll have another position. I'm not certain *why* my father is set on refurbishing the inside of the palace, but it's markedly better than waging war."

The door creaked open behind her. Viam jerked forward, but it was only the guards, back with a tray of refreshments. She took a glass of freshly squeezed sunfruit juice in a trembling hand and willed her heart rate to calm. Daliel didn't know anything of his father's plans. Or he *thought* he didn't—which made him an unwilling player in the king's game, albeit one His Majesty wanted to keep alive.

I can use that. Yala's face reappeared in her mind's eye and lifted a brow as if to goad her onward. *I can use him. I'd be a fool not to.*

"Your father…" she began.

"Must we talk of him?" His tone lost some of its openness. "I wanted to talk to you, Viam, as we once did."

A sympathetic pang hit her despite the imaginary Yala's recriminating stare. "What have you been doing, then? Since you, ah, stepped aside from your role?"

"Reading, mostly." He gestured to the shelves lining the walls. "I thought this place might appeal to you too."

"This is the biggest library I've seen," she admitted.

His smile returned. "Is there anything you want to peruse? You're welcome to stay as long as you like."

He wanted her to sit with him… and *read*? While she'd been unable to stop herself from admiring the treasure trove of information, now was not the time for such an indulgence.

On the other hand, this library contained texts that were not present in the administration building. Ones, perhaps, that the king wanted to keep hidden.

Viam let her gaze travel along the row of leather-bound tomes. "Do you have anything on the history of Laria and the gods?"

EMMA L. ADAMS

***

Yala had not planned for Viam's return. She should have, in retrospect, but Saren accompanying her suggested the mission in Setemar had failed. That meant more lives for her to protect. More loved ones to be wielded against her like a blade. An unfair judgement, perhaps, given that she hadn't achieved a thing in the days that had elapsed since her arrival in the palace save for training a squad who might be the first to die in the king's campaign against the Disciples.

That knowledge was all the more painful given her squad continued to exceed her expectations. Kithal had proven a surprisingly elegant flier, while Roven's skill at manoeuvring her war drake was adept enough that Yala suspected she'd make her first kill before long. Yurel already had. After an altercation with another squad member who'd tried to proposition her, Yurel had confessed the source of her scars to Yala. The man who'd tried to assault her in one of Dalathar's alleyways had found a new permanent home in the river.

Yala hadn't started them on practising with weapons from their mounts yet, but Vilat had disregarded her instructions and managed to throw a spear across the paddock, where it wedged itself between two fence slats. Yala had had him muck out the paddock as punishment so the others wouldn't get ideas, but she'd congratulated him in private and then wondered what the fuck she was doing. He and the others had warmed to her fast enough that she'd found herself responding like a sunfruit emerging from its shell. Like a real squad leader, not an impostor who lied through her teeth with every word she spoke to her soldiers.

How fast their easy smiles would fade when the truth emerged.

The day after Viam's arrival in the palace brought the

news she'd dreaded. After the morning's training session, the commander delivered an invitation to Yala and her fellow captains to come to the palace at once. They gathered again in the receiving room, assembling in ordered rows that didn't entirely suppress the air of excitement and anticipation.

"I brought you here to deliver the news that my scouts discovered the rogue Disciples' hiding place," said the king. "Thanks to Lisek and her squad, who saw some activity in the waters surrounding an island in contested territory between our land and Rafragoria.

Shit. Out of the corner of her eye, Yala saw Lisek straighten, a smile tugging at her mouth.

"Given the nature of the dissenters' abilities, the entirety of the flight division will be dispatched to ensure nobody escapes capture," he went on. "To that end, the commanders and I are working on a strategy for the mission, which will take place one week from today."

A week. Her squad might be performing beyond her expectations, but a full-fledged seaborne mission would all but certainly result in casualties on both sides.

While the other captains filed out of the room, Yala lingered and was rewarded by the king's beckoning hand. "Captain Yala Palathar. I would speak with you alone."

His twin masked guards appeared like smoke given form and once again escorted the pair of them from the room. In the background, their steps were punctuated by the thud and scrape of stone against stone. In daylight, the temple's construction was in full swing, and Yala had to admire how thoroughly they'd transformed the courtyard in the space of a few short weeks. Pillars climbed to a sky deceptively free of clouds, while the dusty haze in the air drew a cough from her lungs.

"The work is almost completed," said King Tharen. "A few

more days will ensure that the temple is ready for the arrival of the captives."

Bile crept into the back of her throat. "Are you sure the flight division is ready? My squad will have had no practise in open combat."

"You did the same when you first took flight, did you not?"

We weren't set against Disciples. "What if the Disciples surrender without fighting back? Would they still be sentenced?" She almost said *sacrificed*, but some cautious part of her refrained, wanting to hear his reply first.

"They have resisted all prior attempts to convince them to listen to reason," he said. "I little expect them to change tactics. This will be a dangerous mission, but if you succeed, you will be granted the honour of being among the first to spill blood on Mekan's altar."

Honour. Her eyes went, unbidden, to the great slab of stone. Yes, gaining Mekan's favour would bring her closer to wielding the god of death's influence against the king, but hadn't that strategy been suggested by someone who would be more than happy to see Yala perish along with her enemy?

As for the king's promise? He would never let anyone else step near the altar without first drawing blood with his sword, to ensure Mekan served him above all. Despite having played no part in the mission, he—

An idea slammed into Yala's mind with the force of an air current catching a war drake's wings. Swivelling to the king, she asked, "And will you be participating in the mission, too, Your Majesty? Like you used to?"

No major mission had ever taken place without the king riding at the head of the army, seated upon his golden-crowned war drake. The elapsed years had cast many traditions into uncertainty, but the king's aggressive approach to the revival of the army would surely extend to a public appearance on the flight division's first major mission. It would have the twin benefits of boosting the soldiers' morale and restoring the public's faith in the crown.

She saw all those thoughts and more flicker through King Tharen's eyes in the moment of silence that passed, taut as a held breath. Then: "Yes. I will lead the army myself."

A triumphant smile threatened to creep onto Yala's face. She bowed her head as if in deference. "I'm glad to hear it."

***

Stealing a ship from under the king's nose proved a divisive strategy. While Nanek went to consult with his fellow Disciples, Kelan worked on convincing the others, and they were entering their second day of arguments when Molin returned from delivering Kelan's messages.

The reply, scrawled upon a strip of bark pulled from a tree, was undoubtedly penned by Niema. *I'm joining the elite Disciples of Life. I'm now one of Yalet's chosen.*

Elite Disciples? He cast his mind back to his time in the enclave and recalled that those higher-ranked Disciples were allowed to violate Yalet's law against taking a life. That Niema had taken the vows regardless pointed to her desperation, and her note ended with the desire to set up a meeting somewhere close to Dalathar.

She's near the city? He reread the note to check he hadn't misread; if he hadn't, Niema had a way to reach the capital far faster than taking a boat or wagon. *Got herself a war drake, has she?*

"You can meet her alone," Lakiel said to him. "I'm not responsible if she gets you killed."

"She's a Disciple of Life," Kelan said. "You know, the one person capable of destroying the temple the king is building."

"What Yala Palathar says he's building," Lakiel corrected. "And we know she's on the king's side."

"Drakeshit," said Brikel. "Kelan made it clear she's acting on her own, not for the king. She's working against him from within."

"And how far is she willing to go to keep up the ruse?"

That, Kelan didn't know. The question tailed him like a spectre while he waited for his next chance to meet with Yala after the day's training was done. As before, he slipped past the guards on the upper city wall with Molin's help and waited for her to be alone with the war drakes before he glided over the paddock fence.

"He's found them." Yala told him without turning around. "He knows where the Disciples of the Sea are hiding."

Shit. "Already?"

"I have less than a week to the mission." She swivelled, one hand wrapped around her cane, the other clutching a war drake's chain. "That island is one of the contested areas between Laria and Rafragoria. It's known to the flight division."

"You've been there before?"

"Yes." An unreadable series of emotions passed over Yala's face in the space of a heartbeat. "A long time ago. If memory serves, the island is covered in thick jungle that makes it easy for anyone hidden inside to stage an ambush. Perhaps you might use that in your favour."

"To fight back?" he said. "Not all the Disciples can fight. Unless you plan to help?"

"Not quite." A satisfied smile nudged onto her mouth. "But I did talk the king into coming with us on the mission. As a show of support to the soldiers."

"Shit, Yala." What better place to strike him down than in midair over the open sea?

If the king perished, it didn't matter if the Disciples of the

Sea were unable to find a safe hiding place. They might not even have to leave the island at all.

"That's right." Yala gave him a measured look. "The trouble is, I need the rest of the flight division to be looking the other way. That something you can arrange?"

He felt a rush of shame for ever doubting her. "I'll do it."

17

Niema and Hachim parted ways with the other Disciples of Life outside a village claimed by the dead. Their presence was a constant companion now, their foul stench clinging to Niema's skin and their blank faces haunting her dreams.

She'd found herself looking forward to the stretches of time when they flew on their war drakes across open fields and left Mekan's taint far behind. She'd never grown used to the unnatural sensation of being suspended in the air and the strange hollowness that came with no longer being close enough to the ground to sense the thrum of life all around that marked Yalet's presence, but anything was better than being encircled by the dead night and day.

We have to do this, she reminded herself every time they descended over a newly claimed village and faced the horrors within. *We have to remove Mekan's presence from Laria.*

Such was the price she paid for joining the elite Disciples. One she would willingly pay, though it grieved her to see Hachim suffer alongside her. Each night, they camped under the stars, curled together for comfort and protection, and she often wondered if he was the only tether keeping her grounded.

Now, they flew side by side, following Kelan's directions towards the coast. The words of his recent note rang in her mind like a gong.

The king was building a Temple of Death in the palace. Should he achieve his aims, he would summon his army directly onto Larian soil. And the Disciples of the Sea would shed their blood for his ambitions.

She cut across a field and landed behind a bank of trees to meet the robed figure descending from the sky, hands in his pockets and an unusual air of seriousness about him.

"It's true?" were the first words out of her mouth.

Kelan inclined his head. "Yes. I'm afraid so."

"Please tell me you have a plan to help the Disciples of the Sea." His note had implied he did, but Kelan's strategies tended to involve a certain element of unpredictability that was as likely to backfire upon himself as not.

"I'm going to steal one of the king's ships and help them escape," he said. "If I can find somewhere to hide a giant ship, that is. That part, I haven't figured out yet."

"That's a terrible idea." Or was it? Kelan's note had given the impression that the number of rogue Disciples numbered thirty or more, far too many to escape via any route other than the sea. "What did Yala think?"

"She doesn't know."

He didn't need to state why. Yala was at the head of one of the flight squads hunting down the Disciples of the Sea. For all intents and purposes, they stood on opposing sides.

"What did you want *me* to do, then?" asked Niema. "I don't know any hiding places. I don't even have a home of my own."

She felt Hachim's pain on her behalf like a vibration travelling down a plucked string, but she blinked the sting from her eyes. The Disciples of the Sea were in a worse plight than she. Many were injured and unable to fight, or too young, and even their deity had been unable to save them.

As for Niema? As an elite Disciple, she now held the highest honour possible for one of her people to attain. In Yalet's name, she was permitted to utilise her skills to any extent, provided she furthered the goal of eradicating Mekan. She might not have touched the weapons her Superior had given her, concealed in a bag strapped to the war drake's side, but they were present for this very purpose.

To protect others against Mekan's depravity.

"We'll figure something out." The sympathy in Kelan's voice made her cheeks flush with fresh shame at her self-pity. "If Yala succeeds in bringing King Tharen down from his steed, finding a hiding place will no longer be a concern."

A gasp escaped. "The king will be there in person?"

"At Yala's insistence." Kelan grinned. "I got the impression she appealed to his ego. I doubt he'll openly be participating, but she'll certainly be ready. Though she'll need your help."

"My help?" she echoed. "With what?"

"Distracting the king's army."

"The dead." Niema's heart beat unevenly. "I don't know that my abilities will work on so many at once."

"They don't have to," Kelan said. "We just need a distraction. If the army's eyes are elsewhere, Yala will have the chance to strike."

Hachim spoke. "You want Niema to take this burden upon herself?"

Guilt flashed across Kelan's face. "Not if she doesn't want to. I rather hoped you two wouldn't be alone."

"You know I'm the only person who can control the dead." Moreover, the other Disciples of Life would require convincing to confront the king's soldiers. They might have no fear of violence, but their mistrust of Niema was a far cry from the warmth of her enclave that had once been a constant in her life. She little blamed them, given that two of Yalet's elite had once been ordered to hunt her down and had lost their lives on that mission, and she had not yet sworn the vows that would fully establish her as a member of their sect.

"He won't summon the dead army until he opens the temple." Kelan surveyed her. "As to the living, we'll assist you in any way we can."

Right. The king had dismissed his dead army, sent them into the Void until he had need of them again. If King Tharen succeeded in creating a Temple of Death, he would summon that army into the capital.

Her choice was clear. It always was. "I'll help."

———

This wasn't one of my best ideas. Kelan ducked out of sight behind a large wooden boat. A few workers roamed the docks even at this late hour, and he'd intentionally left the inn after dusk in the hopes that their thievery would be less conspicuous by night. As he watched, Nanek's head broke the water's surface near the vessel they'd chosen. Several other Disciples of the Sea followed, visible only by the faint moonlight glinting off the shells woven into their hair and the bone daggers in their hands.

The ship's movement was subtle at first, the Disciples in the water manipulating the ocean's currents to push the vessel away from the pier. Kelan sent Molin to divert the attention of the dockworkers and he, and his fellow Disciples glided off the pier, conjuring a breeze behind the ship's rear. The combined power of both their deities ensured that they reached the open sea within minutes, without a sound from anyone on the docks.

Several hours into their flight, Nanek called them to a

halt. Kelan squinted into the unbroken darkness and made out the jagged outlines of cliffs jutting over the ocean. They'd reached the island.

After they'd secured the boat, Kelan spied an audience watching from down on the beach. The Disciples of the Sea ranged from children to the elderly, with most of their able fighters having accompanied Nanek to guide the boat to the shore.

"I see why nobody found you for so long," Kelan remarked as he landed on the beach in front of them. Dense jungle ran up to the sandy bank, vast and dark enough that a pack of war drakes might be hiding within, and nobody on the outside would be any the wiser.

"Did you steal the king's ship?" A boy of maybe thirteen eyed the vessel in awe.

"That's right." Nanek emerged from the ocean to join his fellow Disciples on the beach. "Anyone who can't fight will be able to escape to safety."

"What if we want to fight?" The boy exchanged encouraging nods with some of the other youngsters, the oldest of whom were almost of conscription age.

Nanek shook his head. "No. This is not a battle we can win."

Kelan helped guide the Disciples of the Sea up to the cliffs, where they boarded the vessel. With three days until the mission, they ought to be far from the capital long before the flight division left Laria's shore. Their temporary hiding place, chosen by Niema, was a cove on Laria's northernmost edge, east of Dalathar.

Some did refuse to board. Nanek organised an informal attack force to stay on the island and distract the king's soldiers, a group consisting of fifteen Disciples at most. Hardly enough to rival the flight division, but if Niema managed to bring some of her fellow Disciples of Life and

Kelan's allies offered their help, too, they might at least be able to divert the enemy's attention from Yala.

When the ship began to leave the island, a cry of panic shattered the night. The water churned with a warning that arrived too late; a serpentine head rose from the water, its jaws closing around Brikel's ankle. She let out a startled scream, twisting to left and right in a desperate attempt to free herself from a mouth too big to belong to a sea drake.

As the beast began to pull her down, Kelan drove his blade into its skull. The point bounced off hard scales as obsidian as the night sky.

With a splash, Nanek tackled the beast, his arms wrapping around its neck. Moonlight flickering on the water revealed its sheer size, several times longer than a war drake with its coils topped with vicious spikes. Nanek grunted, several of those spikes digging into his arms, but he held on until it twisted from side to side to dislodge him.

As its jaws opened, Brikel launched from its mouth. Kelan moved in, taking aim. His blade cleaved through its fleshy tongue and dug deeper until the beast's thrashing forced Nanek to release his grip. When he broke away, he was bleeding from both arms. *And I thought I had a penchant for risk-taking,* Kelan thought, driving his sword into the beast's mouth until its thrashing began to slow and its long coils sank deeper into the ocean.

Brikel caught her balance, sagging in mid-air, and her brother caught her arm. "Brikel!"

She groaned, lifting a foot bent at an odd angle. "Gods, that hurts."

"More of them!" Nanek shouted, gesturing at the black expanse of the water. Three more beasts had risen from the depths of the night-darkened sea, their spear-tipped coils glistening beneath the moon.

The Disciples of the Sea swam into a defensive line

between the beasts and the ship, baring weapons in the form of spears forged from the spines of captured sea drakes or daggers of gleaming bone. Kelan lifted his own blade, cursing the lack of visibility, and positioned himself in front of the hull alongside Ranit and Brikel. Behind, the escapees huddled on the deck, watching the water in horror.

Churning waves became a torrent that slammed into the oncoming beasts and pushed them away from the ship. Screams rang out when the boat tipped, but a second, softer current caught the vessel like a comforting arm. Amanat had not forsaken Her Disciples yet.

Trusting the god of the sea to keep the boat upright, Kelan joined the Disciples advancing on the three monstrosities in the water. The beasts were coated in dark scales, with few weaknesses aside from the eyes and mouths, and there might be any number of them hidden beneath the dark water.

"Who summoned these bastards?" He drove his blade into a bulbous eye, grimacing as a shower of gore splattered his cloak.

"You think I know?" Ranit said from beside him, his own sword gleaming crimson in the light of the moon. "Nanek said the king banished his army of the dead."

"He picked a great time to unbanish them." His stomach sank when he spied a body—human—floating face-down in the water, their severed leg floating several feet away. Spying the culprit, the Disciples of the Sea descended with a roar of violence, their daggers stabbing and the ocean itself lashing at the beast's flanks.

As the monster was caught in a whirlpool, unable to free itself, Kelan's fellow Disciples descended with weapons in hand. Two beasts were dead, and the third fell to Nanek's bone-daggers, one in each eye.

"This is the king's doing." He pulled out one dagger with a grim *squelch* then the other. "Foul creatures."

"I hope that's all there is." If more dead roamed outside of Laria's shore, the Disciples of the Sea might be sailing into their own doom. Whether that would be any worse than being marooned on an island with the dead circling its shores, however, he couldn't answer.

"I don't sense any others near the island." Nanek spat crimson into the water. "We cannot linger, but if these beasts are near our chosen hiding place too…"

"They won't be." Kelan spoke with more certainty than he possessed. "The Disciples of Life are waiting there. The dead won't go near."

And if they did, Niema's ability to repel them with a word would ensure no danger befell them.

"We can't come with you." Lakiel glided to Kelan's side, one arm supporting his sister. "We need to find a healer."

Kelan cast a concerned look at Brikel. It didn't look as if the beast's teeth had penetrated her boot, but her ankle was clearly broken with the severity that would lead to a permanent limp if left untreated. Ranit, too, had suffered a vicious scratch to the face that cut through the edge of his brow and ended at his chin. None looked enthused at the notion of flying through the night to reach the cove, and they would have little to contribute now that all the Disciples of the Sea were safely on the ship.

Unless the dead attacked again.

A chirp drew his attention to the ship's deck; Molin had emerged, having presumably hidden during the attack.

"What is it?" Kelan watched the tree-raptor approach at a glide and then gesture southward with an outstretched claw. "You think we should go back to the capital?"

He surely wasn't suggesting that they take the ship with them.

"I think that beast of yours is communicating that those monsters were sent from Dalathar," Nanek ground out. "At a guess, shortly after we left the docks."

Then the king knows we're here.

"Shit," said Ranit. "We left some of our people at the inn."

"We have to warn them." Lakiel was already retreating, one hand around his sister's shoulder. She didn't look happy at being manhandled, but her face was pinched with pain and concern. Kelan glanced between her and Nanek, torn.

"Go," Nanek growled at him. "We shall manage without you."

His tone suggested they had a lower chance of being caught without a group of airborne Disciples guiding the ship, which wasn't inaccurate. Kelan left Molin to help guide the Disciples of the Sea to Niema and Hachim's hiding place and then joined the retreat to the capital.

Their flight back passed in a grim, tense silence. Even Kelan didn't speak a word, splitting his attention between the sky and sea in case the king had sent more dead to intercept them. It was possible that his actions had been nothing more than a stealthy midnight summoning session, although *why* His Majesty would conduct a ritual to Mekan at the docks made little sense to Kelan.

No. The dead had been sent for them, and his heart sank when they neared the docks and spied a large number of city guards gathering on the pier's edge, crossbows and spears pointed in their direction.

Lakiel made to change directions, but Kelan shook his head. "They've seen us. We don't need more injuries."

"What's all this, then?" called out a muscular guard with an unfortunate haircut that made him look like a half-plucked fowl. "Disciples in the capital without the permission of the king, looks like."

Kelan glided in front of the others and addressed the

growing crowd. "I didn't know we had to ask permission to be here."

The guard stepped up to the pier's edge, levelling a crossbow at him. "It's common knowledge that all Disciples are to report their presence in the capital to the king, by the direct order of the crown."

"Doesn't His Majesty have more important matters to concern himself with?" He wasn't present himself—that much was clear—but who else had summoned the dead? "We were taking a walk."

"Across the ocean?" Scepticism dripped from the guard's voice. "You'd have to be living in a cave not to know that some of your fellow Disciples are designated as enemies as the crown and are to be killed on sight."

"Not me," he said. "I'm afraid we're here for nothing more threatening than perusing the fine offerings of Dalathar's pleasure district."

"And the recent theft of one of the king's ships has nothing to do with you?"

"Clearly not." He indicated his fellow robed figures hovering above the water. "Do any of us look like we're hiding a ship?"

"You look like you've been in a fight," growled a female guard who looked as if she'd been in several scuffles herself. Her nose was crooked, as if it had been broken several times, and one front tooth was notably chipped. "With a war drake."

"We didn't steal one of those either." Kelan heard a faint whimper from Brikel, who was leaning on her brother, her forehead slick with sweat. "Be reasonable. As you can see, some of us need a healer."

The guards knew they were lying, but there was no evidence to connect them with the Disciples of the Sea whatsoever, nor the ship's theft. They'd been careful.

Not careful enough, evidently.

"Then I'd advise you to get out of the city while you can," said another. "We'll be running a coordinated search of all known trouble spots in the outer city by the morning. In case you're hiding any *other* Disciples in your accommodations."

Kelan stared at him for a moment. He might have meant the Disciples of the Sea, but he'd never confirmed whether the king or the guards knew the escaped Disciples of the Flame were still at large in the city. Regardless, Yala's old house would almost certainly be counted as a "trouble spot," as would the Undercity.

Shit. I have to warn Saren.

———

A knock on the door woke Saren from sleep. He answered groggily and came to sharp wakefulness when he saw the uncharacteristic seriousness on Kelan's face and the crimson stains on his blue cloak.

"We've been ordered to leave the city by tomorrow," he said. "The kings' guards are going to run a search of known trouble spots, too, and I would assume Yala's house qualifies as such."

"Fuck." Saren ran a hand through his tangled curly hair. "Trouble. Yeah. That's me."

He'd brought this on himself by staying, he knew, but his attempt to reconcile with Giran had ended in the door being slammed in his face before he could begin to explain that he wasn't there to plead for a return of his stash of rice wine. And the rogue Disciples had been so fucking pathetic that he hadn't been able to bring himself to turn them in.

"I can help you get out of the city," Kelan added, "but you'll need to be ready fast."

"No." Novice Yachim appeared on the stairway behind him. "We can't abandon our Superior."

"Your Superior needs a good beating," Saren said. "Be sensible. We need to get the fuck out, and unlike some people, we can't fucking fly."

"Exactly." Kelan grimaced. "I am sorry about this. Meet me in an hour on the south bridge."

Saren opened his mouth to object and closed it. "We'll put it to a vote."

As Kelan left, Saren swore explosively, tugging at his hair. "Fucking *gods*. Right. Tell the others, Yachim."

"We're not leaving." The novice shook his head, his mouth trembling. "We said we'd stay and help the others."

"Help yourselves first." Saren ran to the corner and began gathering his belongings together. "Go *on*. Tell them."

As the novice ran upstairs, someone thumped loudly on the door. He swore and dropped his pack, running to the window. *Guards.*

The door crashed inward, and three guards entered, wielding shortswords. Saren's instinct told him to run like hell, but he held his ground, affecting a startled air. "What's going on?"

A beefy man with a flushed face looked askance at him. "This house is supposed to be unoccupied."

"According to whom?" Saren folded his arms to hide his shaking hands. "I'm in charge of taking care of this place since the owner joined the army."

It wasn't far from the truth, but expecting a room crammed with terrified Disciples to stay quiet was a futile endeavour. At a faint thud from overhead, the red-faced man looked up at the ceiling. "And who's upstairs?"

"Nobody." The answer came fast, given that a fair part of him resented the Disciples for endangering his life, but a second thud put an end to the ruse. "Nobody important. They're my tenants."

"Are they now?" The man loomed over him, and Saren

caught a whiff of stale rice wine that made him want to gag. He knew a drunk when he saw one, but the man was also armed, and Saren was not.

Moreover, his two companions were sober and just as dangerous. Elbowing past Saren, they made for the stairs, shouting, "Who's up there?"

"We're travellers," returned one of the Disciples, his voice trembling. "From Setemar."

Saren groaned. They were as bad a group of liars as Viam was, and that was saying a fucking lot.

He caught them up at the top of the stairs as the red-faced man held up a length of faded orange fabric. "This yours?"

"Disciples of the Flame," said another. "Thought so. Arrest them all."

18

Niema and Hachim found the other elite Disciples at another village that had fallen to the dead, where newly quietened bodies lay beneath a blanket of greenery.

Ragem, their leader under Superior Kralia's command, was in the process of leading a prayer. The Disciples' voices merged into a chorus that thrummed in the air like an invisible tapestry connecting each of them to one another and to their god. Niema and Hachim joined in as they came to land and dismounted, trying not to look too hard at the skeletal remains buried under the newly blooming flowers.

"You're back sooner than I expected," Ragem said in his gravelly voice. If not for his leaf-woven attire and the birthmark on his neck, Niema might not have taken him for a Disciple at all. His arms and face were laced with a web of scars, and a chunk was missing from one ear as if sharp teeth had torn at the flesh. His voice, which sounded as though his throat had been shredded from the inside, further added to the intimidating impression if the wooden bow and arrows strapped to his back weren't enough on their own.

EMMA L. ADAMS

"The king has planned a mission for three days from now," she told him. "The flight division intends to hunt down the surviving Disciples of the Sea and bring them back to the city to be sacrificed."

The word sent a ripple of anger and revulsion through the other Disciples, including Bitra. Niema's friend barely resembled her former self from the enclave; already, her eyes were harder, her soft features sharper.

"Their deaths will open a Temple of Death," Niema went on. "The Disciples of the Sky have decided to help them escape, but there aren't enough of them to challenge the army. Especially if the king summons the dead."

"And you wish for us to assist them." Ragem spoke in dispassionate tones. "We cannot expose ourselves in that manner. There aren't enough of us to take on an army."

"We don't have to," Niema said. "We only need to divert their attention from the Disciples of the Sea."

"Their battle is not ours."

Niema shrank from his cutting eyes, swallowing her fear. "It's all of ours."

"She's right," Hachim added. "Mekan is a threat to us all. If we help the Disciples of the Sea escape, the king won't have anyone to sacrifice." He, too, snagged on the word like a burr.

"Their lives are not the only ones of value to him." Ragem shook his head, exposing more scars clustered on the back of his neck in a manner that suggested claws had tried to rip out his spine. "He will try again with another."

"Does it not matter if we save them?" For a Disciple of Life to weigh up the fates of others struck her as against the very definition of what made them what they were. The elite Disciples' role was to make judgements that no other Disciple of Life would ever have to make, but appealing to logic felt as wrong as the corruption spreading across the land as Mekan extended His reach. "If he opens the Temple

168

of Death, his army will be called into the capital. Nobody but a Disciple of Life can destroy it, which will require us to risk our lives regardless of whether we act to defend our fellow Disciples or not. And—if we help them, they'll return the favour. It might mean all the difference in this war."

Ragem gave her a long, unreadable look, his scarred face impassive. "I will consult with our Superior first. If she agrees, then yes, we will unleash Yalet's wrath against the king's army."

Niema's skin prickled. His words ought to have elicited relief, but instead, dread rooted itself inside her chest, digging as deep as the thorns spreading over the village of the dead.

Daliel might not have spoken to his father, but he'd certainly had words with someone. Viam had woken the day after her visit to the palace to learn that her position had been reinstated and she was to start work immediately.

What should have been a kindness swiftly became frustrating. Her visit to the prince had afforded her little information, admittedly—she'd borrowed a stack of history books but had found no titles alluding to the Temple of Death on the shelves—but she found her time now overloaded with admin tasks heaped upon her by an irate Malat, who'd taken to prowling the administrative building in a haze of cigar smoke and muttering about the chaos resulting from the king's decision to divert most of the department to the army instead.

Two days before the mission, all palace staff were permitted to take the day off for All Gods' Day. Viam had hoped for another chance to question the prince, but when no invitation from the palace arrived that morning, she let Brenat drag her to the market instead. Both had hoped a change of scenery might cheer them up, but even outside the palace gates, the upper city felt oppressive, and Viam had the sense of countless unseen eyes watching her every move.

"Grim, isn't it?" Brenat scowled at a group of passing guards. "You'd think there were Rafragorian archers beating at the gates from the way they're acting."

"Someone's at the gates, but it's not Rafragoria." She spied a group of ragged individuals shuffling towards the square, flanked on each side by heavily armed soldiers. Their clothes were torn and stained with dirt and, in some cases, blood, while their hands were bound behind their backs. What had they done to earn that level of punishment?

Brenat watched them with interest. "Who're they?"

"I don't know, but—what are you doing?" Viam swore as Brenat began to tail the prisoners from a distance. "Stop that. They'll see you."

The guards, as Viam had suspected, led the group down a side street on the palace's right to the very same jail in which Yala had narrowly escaped being sentenced to death. Viam tugged on Brenat's sleeve in an attempt to pull her out of their line of sight and caught a few words of the guards' conversation.

"Disciples of the Flame," one muttered. "The ones His Majesty were searching for. They were found hiding in a civilian's house."

Disciples of the Flame. She hadn't recognised them without their robes. She lifted her head surreptitiously, and her attention caught on the man at the back of their group.

"Saren," she gasped. "It was his house they were hiding in —Yala's house."

"Shit." Brenat stood on tiptoe to see over the guards' heads. "He knew they were Disciples when he took them in?"

"It wasn't his idea to hide them in the house. I can't let them punish him for someone else's crime."

It had been Kelan's idea, but she saw no signs of him nor

of the other Disciples of the Sky waiting to leap to Saren's defence. Not a soul intervened as they were ushered into the jail behind the guards.

The door closed on the prisoners with a snap.

***

Yala had forgotten quite how much work went into preparing for a mission. When she wasn't training her squad, she was sitting in meetings with the commander as he outlined their strategy to ensure not a single Disciple of the Sea escaped by land or by sea. Even on All Gods' Day, when the rest of the palace staff were permitted to take the day off, they had a full schedule.

The result was that she didn't see Viam hovering near the fence while she had her squad running laps until Gorel came jogging over to her. "Captain—there's someone trying to get your attention over there."

Yala swore. "I'll deal with it."

She marched over to the gate and outside, hoping to hell that the other captains were too occupied preparing their own squads to notice her departure. "Viam, didn't I tell you not to speak to me in public?"

"I had to find you," Viam gasped. "It's urgent."

"Gods, what now?" She took in her former squad-mate's sweaty face and shaking hands.

"The Disciples of the Flame. They were arrested, and Saren is with them."

"Saren is what?" Why would Saren have anything to do with *them*? "Arrested where?"

"There." She jerked her head towards the back wall covering the upper city jail, in which Yala had spent an unpleasant stretch of time in the company of a dying man and had narrowly avoided being burned alive. "They were hiding in your house. Kelan's idea."

Gods. She was serious. "Where is he?"

"I don't know." Tears glistened on her lashes. "I haven't seen him, but Saren… they'll hang him for this. Or worse."

Or worse. The words rang through Yala's skull like a portent, accompanied by the image of a bare altar thirsty for blood. For *Disciples'* blood. And while the king had thought the Disciples of the Sea would be the next available sacrifices…

The thud of the gate closing brought her back to the present; another squad had returned from the paddocks and would walk right past her and Viam if they lingered here more than another minute.

"Talk to the prince," she found herself saying. "Tell him how urgent it is."

"I will," Viam whispered. "I'll do my best. I'm sorry."

"Don't be." Weariness crashed over her. "I'm squad leader. This is on me."

She'd been too focused on her mission to pay attention to anything else, including Kelan's propensity for putting others at risk with his absurd schemes.

"No, it isn't," Viam said. "You focus on the mission. It's tomorrow, right?"

"Yes." Would the king punish the transgressors before the mission, or would he wait until after? "Ask the prince to convince his father to delay the trial, assuming there is one."

There might not be, given what she'd seen of the king's approach towards punishment thus far. Leaving Viam at the fence, she ducked back into the paddock grounds.

Yala returned to her squad, trying to forget that if the king *did* decide to use the Disciples' deaths to open the temple, she would have no chance to strike him down before he achieved his aim and summoned his army to Dalathar.

***

Kelan watched the guards cross the square from his position hidden among the market stalls, stifling a yawn. He'd spent a sleepless night lurking outside the jailhouse where they'd locked up Saren and the Disciples of the Flame, unable to bring himself to leave the city with Lakiel and the others. Confronting the guards would earn him a place behind bars to match theirs, so he'd waited for daylight, leaving his cloak behind to lessen the chances of being recognisable.

One look at the jail told him that breaking in was out of the question. Guards prowled in front and behind and outmatched even the number stationed outside the Temple of the Flame. His position in the market afforded him a view of its tall windows that tempted him to move closer. He glimpsed a few cloaked figures lurking at the edges as if afraid to let the guards catch a glimpse of them even on the other side of the glass. There did not appear to be any on the inside, however.

An impulse seized him. When the guards departed together with their captives, he directed Molin to distract the attention of the guards atop the city wall. Then, taking careful aim, he sent a well-placed gust of wind amid the market stalls.

A box of groundfruit was the first to fall, sending ovoid fruits rolling in all directions, including the area behind the Temple of the Flame. As he'd hoped, some of the guards moved in to help the merchants stop the runaway produce. Kelan darted behind them and glided to the temple's rear stairs, and, with another well-applied prayer to the god of the sky, knocked the door in.

Shocked gasps greeted him inside, but no shout of warning followed as he closed the door behind him. He looked upon the bewildered Disciples, a smile forming on his face. "Sorry to interrupt. I'd like to talk to your Superior."

The Disciples watched him with a mixture of incredulity and fear, none moving to fetch their leader. They didn't need to; Kelan hadn't taken more than a few steps before he was rewarded with the sight of a robed man wearing an elaborate headdress hurrying into view.

"What," said Superior Shralin, "are *you* doing in here?"

19

Viam flew from the barracks to the palace and sprinted up the stairs to the front door. Breathless, she skidded to a halt in front of the guards and gasped, "Please. I need to see the prince. It's urgent."

Luck was with her, and one of the guards had been present during her last visit to the prince. He raised a brow at her dishevelled state but agreed to pass on word to Daliel. Viam gasped out a thanks and half collapsed against the door frame, sweat soaking into her shirt. Abruptly, she remembered the void drake circling above. She hadn't so much as glanced up during her frantic sprint. Worry for Saren had blanketed every other thought in her mind, and the void drake had paid no more attention to her than it might have acknowledged a bloodfly on its tail. She was no threat.

But what of Saren?

When the guard returned, she followed him into the palace with an increasing sense of unreality, unable to recognise herself in this wild, desperate creature on her way to beg a prince for a favour.

Daliel waited in the library, his brow furrowed in bewilderment. "Viam? What's wrong?"

Viam waited for the guards to retreat before she whispered, "I need your help."

"My help?" Worry flitted across his face. "With what?"

"A friend of mine was arrested because a group of Disciples of the Flame took shelter in his house," she blurted. "I fear he's to be sentenced to death."

His eyes rounded. "A friend of yours sheltered rogue Disciples of the Flame in his home?"

"Is there anything you can say to your father to convince him to spare his life?" she asked. "Please. You're the only one who can help."

"I'm sorry." A heavy slump pushed his shoulders downward. "I doubt my father will listen to me, especially where the Disciples are concerned."

"They weren't the ones who betrayed him," she said. "And Saren did nothing wrong but protect those who need his help."

"Gods." He pressed a hand to his forehead—a hand that was, inexplicably, shaking almost as much as hers. "The truth is, my father came to me not an hour ago. He was distracted, but he told me that there's to be a ceremony at the palace tonight and that he expects me to be there. He's inviting the captains too."

"A ceremony." Viam sucked in air, an unseen rope tightening around her neck. "Do you know what this ceremony will entail?"

"He mentioned making an example of Disciples who betray him." He spoke in a whisper. "I'm sorry."

"It's worse than a death sentence." The invisible rope blocked her throat, but she forced out the words. "He follows the god of corruption, and Mekan only accepts one payment. Their sacrifice will open a Temple of Death."

Shock slapped the fear from his face. "You must not speak of such things. If he were to hear—"

"You *know* I'm telling the truth." Tears leaked from her eyes. "Please."

"I'm sorry, but I have to ask you to leave, Viam." He turned away, not meeting her eyes. "It's better for you not to come back."

No. Gods, no.

"Daliel—"

A door opened. Footsteps, the guards returning to escort her from the room. She made one last attempt to catch the prince's eye, failed, and felt her last hope slip away like a dropped glass.

The ceremony is tonight. If the prince wouldn't challenge his father in private, he'd never do so in public. But hadn't he said that the captains would be present too? If Yala didn't already know, she would soon.

And now, it seemed that Saren's last hope of survival rested in her hands.

***

"What am I doing in here?" Kelan wished he'd prepared an adequate response, but the best he could come up with was, "I'm afraid I have bad news."

"I know," Superior Shralin said. "I know that Novice Yachim and the others who tried to run away were arrested."

"Then you'll know they're certain to be executed," Kelan said. "Given that the king is in the process of creating a new Temple of Death, their deaths might well serve a dual purpose."

Superior Shralin closed his eyes. "Do not speak to me of this."

"You don't care to even *try* to save them?" Kelan had

expected little, considering the Superior's instant compliance with the king's demands, but to see him express so little regard for his fellow Disciples made him want to seize the man's collar and give him a shake. Kelan understood his despair, being trapped like this, but not enough to have more sympathy for the Superior than for those who had been jailed. "You have no access to your deity?"

The Superior lifted an embroidered sleeve, Indicating the large, serpentine statue of Dalathik with its back to the door through which Kelan had entered. "See for yourself."

From the temple's rear, the statue obscured Kelan's view of the main chamber, and it wasn't until he circled its base that the subtle sense of wrongness struck him. The chamber should be warm, suffocatingly so, and the altar in front of the statue should be decorated with offerings to Dalathik. Instead, a chill permeated the air, and the altar was covered in a thick substance that resembled slime, albeit semitransparent and insubstantial as shadow. Creeping tendrils spread from the altar to Dalathik's feet, and the candles that usually burned at the statue's base had been extinguished entirely.

"How did this come about?" He dragged his attention back to Superior Shralin, who had closed his eyes, murmuring a prayer under his breath.

"Two of Mekan's servants entered the temple shortly after His Majesty returned to the city." The Superior spoke so quietly that Kelan had to strain his ears to catch the words. "They were sent here to despoil the altar. Anyone who intervened was put to death."

Mekan's servants. How could Dalathik have been brought low by the dead? "Isn't Dalathik one of the two only deities who can counter Mekan's abilities?"

Superior Shralin uttered a disparaging noise. "It's not my job to dispel your ignorance, Disciple."

"No, it's your job to protect *your* Disciples." Reckless

anger loosened his tongue. "As for my ignorance, you're well known for jealously guarding your secrets from anyone outside your ranks. No doubt that's exactly what enabled the king to subdue you so easily."

Angry red suffused the Superior's face, but Kelan cared not a bit. The Superior had already knelt before the monarch and surrendered his dignity, and the Disciples who'd been arrested in that house were more worthy of respect than he.

"You..." The Superior worked his jaw. "You should know this. Dalathik might have fire at His command, but He has the same limitations as the other three deities of Sky, Sea, and Earth."

"Not Life," Kelan surmised. "Is that why Yalet is Mekan's natural enemy? She's the only deity strong enough to challenge Him?"

"There are no forces stronger than Life and Death." The Superior spoke as if he was reciting from a text he'd memorised. "One cannot exist without the other. They cannot be separated."

"Which means...?" he prompted.

Superior Shralin shook his head. "It's an old saying and not one that will be of any comfort to those who have been condemned."

"I didn't know you planned to offer comfort at all." Not that Kelan was one to talk, given his failure to spare them.

The Superior didn't reprimand him for rudeness; rather, his attention was fixed on the corrupted altar. "Perhaps there is something I can do."

"What did you have in mind?" Kelan watched the Superior disappear into an alcove to the side of the altar and noticed belatedly that they'd drawn an audience. A few robed figures gathered on the balconies above or near the chamber's many doors, though they refrained from setting foot near the corrupted altar.

No doubt the other Disciples had overheard him berating their Superior, but since their leader's cowardice had facilitated their imprisonment, Kelan couldn't bring himself to care.

When the Superior emerged, he held a small candle in one hand, unimpressive but intact and not tainted by Mekan's touch.

"Take this." He pressed the candle into Kelan's palm. "Give it to the Disciples if you can and tell them to plead with Dalathik for aid. That is all I can do."

"I'll do that." Kelan tucked the candle into a pocket and skirted the statue to the back door, belatedly wishing he'd planned how to get *out* of the temple once he was inside. He spied Molin perched on the windowsill, and when Kelan caught his eye, the tree-raptor took flight.

Trusting Molin to distract the guards, he nudged the back door open and slipped out into the narrow passage between the temple and the city wall. A commotion of shouts greeted him, accompanied by the sound of seabirds shrieking. Molin, he noticed with bemusement, had brought a whole flock of gulls to circle the city wall and harass the guards atop its edge. Arrows clinked down into the passage from their failed attempts to hit a moving target, and the tree-raptor, for his part, held one of the guard's shortswords in his stubby claws and circled above while they jumped up in a vain effort to retrieve the weapon. With their attention elsewhere, Kelan whispered a prayer to his deity and conjured a gust of wind to carry him out from behind the temple and into the market.

Now, for the tricky bit... the jail. Getting in and out without being caught would be a stretch even with Molin's assistance, to say nothing of the danger he might bring to the prisoners should the guards realise he'd tried to help them. As the screech of gulls died down, he entered the side street that ran alongside the palace's right-hand wall and strode past the jail as casually as he dared. On his other side appeared the paddocks; Kelan strained his ears and heard the murmur of voices within, but none belonged to Yala.

The thump of heavy boots near the palace gates sounded. Kelan ducked into the narrow passageway between the paddock fence and the palace wall as someone strode out of the palace grounds and made for the paddock. The clink of a gate opening followed, and an authoritative voice spoke. "My apologies for disturbing you, Captain. I bring a message from the palace."

The palace? Kelan strained to hear, his heartbeat quickening.

"His Majesty has requested that all captains present themselves at the palace at dusk," continued the voice. "He has an announcement to make prior to tomorrow's mission."

An announcement. Kelan had an inkling he knew what that would be: the official opening of the Temple of Death.

***

Saren sat on the bench and reflected that his life had been easier when he'd only cared for his own fate. At least when he'd sought oblivion in drink and lost himself in warm bodies to stave off the ever-present chill of the dead, he hadn't ended up in a fucking cell.

Now, that chill was as inescapable as the darkness pressing against his skin and the smell of unwashed bodies crawling up his nostrils. He'd been shoved into a cell with three Disciples, and their hysterical sobs persistently battered at his attempts to pretend he was anywhere other than here.

Is this where I die? After years of expecting to meet his end in battle, being hanged as a traitor wasn't a fate he'd contemplated. He'd never wanted glory, unlike some of his comrades. He'd been fine as the scout, the healer who supported his squad-mates—but even in that, he'd failed them one by one.

And now, he faced his own end with nobody in his company except a group of irritating Disciples who wouldn't even let him have a fucking nap before he met his demise.

When one of them wailed, Saren turned on them with a snarl. "Stop snivelling. You're Disciples. You should have some dignity."

"They're going to kill us all," the Disciple whimpered, but his sobs quietened to a murmur, and Saren was able to doze off.

He woke to the rattle of keys and looked up in bemusement at a lantern bobbing in a guard's hand as he opened the cell door.

His sleepiness swiftly dispersed when the guard reached in and hauled him out into the damp corridor.

"Hey!" Saren yelped as the guard's bruising grip tightened around his wrist. "What's going on?"

"You're in luck." The guard leered at him. "You're to be taken into the palace, and the king plans to deal with you himself."

The palace. The seat of the king's domain… and, if Kelan's reports were to be believed, where the king was building a temple. *Fuck. Tell me he isn't—*

"I didn't commit any crimes." Saren squirmed away, and the guard backhanded him. He tasted blood, his ears ringing. "The king doesn't know me, but I'm—"

The guard's knuckles struck him on the other ear. Head spinning, he sagged against his captor as rough hands bound his wrists together with ropes and shoved him towards the exit.

The sun was setting outside, its rays bathing the rooftops

in bloody light. *Fitting*, he thought as he fell into line with the Disciples of the Flame filing out of the jail.

He'd expected to approach the palace via the back entrance, but instead, the guards steered the Disciples towards Ceremonial Square. King Larial's statue shone bright gold in the fading sunlight, and though the market stalls had mostly packed up for the night, they'd drawn an audience regardless. *That's why he brought us here.* The king wanted everyone to see the procession of traitors marching to their deaths, escorted by so many guards that one would think they were a group of angry war drakes rather than some defenceless novice Disciples who couldn't even access their god.

"I'm not a traitor." Saren's faint voice sounded as if it belonged to someone else. "I'm a Disciple of Death."

The guards ignored him. His nerves spiked the closer they drew to the palace gates, which opened to admit them.

A gust of air slammed into their group. Disciples and guards alike staggered under the impact, and as chaos broke out, someone pressed a cold, small object into his hands.

"Take this," Kelan muttered and then vanished in a second, equally subtle breeze.

It took a moment for Saren to realise that the bonds around his wrists had loosened, allowing him to examine the object Kelan had handed him. A small candle, unmarked and unremarkable.

One of the Disciples of the Flame gasped. "That's from the temple."

"Take it, then." Seeing that the Disciple's bonds were also loosened, he passed the candle to the novice. "Go on, hide it."

What's that candle for? It seemed futile to pin any hopes upon such a tiny flame, but he saw its effect upon the Disciples in the form of calmer faces even as the guards regained control of the situation, grabbing anyone who'd managed to break free and rebinding their wrists. Kelan must have managed to evade capture, as Saren saw no traces of him amid the reassembling procession.

The gates closed behind them, and their march continued to the palace stairs. A winged shadow hovered above, and the chill returned, blooming inside his chest like a malevolent flower. Mekan was present, watching his every move, and Saren reflected on the bitter irony of his wasted attempts to avoid the god of death. He'd been willing to use any means necessary to shut out Mekan's voice, but now, he had no choice but to hope the god of death would listen to him.

As their sorry group was ushered into the palace entrance hall, he called to the nearest guard, "I have something I want to say to the king. Something I think he'll want to hear."

The guard didn't so much as glance at him. "Stop talking."

"What's he want to say to the king?" A female guard with a chunk missing from her nose peered at Saren. "This one isn't a Disciple. What's he doing here?"

"I'm a Disciple of Death."

Someone laughed.

"I am." Saren took a step forward, and a fist slammed into his sternum. He choked, gasping out, "I can prove it."

"Can you now?" The female guard cracked her knuckles. "Take him through. Let's see if he stands by his lies when he's faced with the king."

He was dragged through a warren of corridors shrouded in the fading light of evening. At the end came a courtyard that stood out starkly in his memory, albeit changed somewhat from his last visit. Pillars encircled the edges, and the area in which an empty pyre had once burned was now dominated by what could only be described as an altar.

The king—very much alive—stood at the front, his eyes as dark as the shadows creeping in at the altar's edges. "What is this?"

The guard shoved Saren to his knees. "This one claims to be a Disciple of Death."

Saren shivered, pressing his forehead to the ground as he felt the king's stare rake over him from head to toe. A whisper rose in the background, caressing his skin, and it took all his effort not to flinch.

"Since he was sheltering Disciples of the Flame inside his house, I'd say he's lying," added the guard. "Want me to deal with him?"

"Leave," said King Tharen. "I'll talk to him myself."

Saren could hardly breathe. His bold words had been easy enough to speak when he wasn't in front of the fucking *monarch* and on his knees in front of an altar intended to open Mekan's realm and unleash its monsters upon the world.

"Is it true?" asked the king. "Are you in contact with Mekan?

"I am." If these words condemned him, so would any others he spoke. He was already a doomed man. "I'm part of the same squad who went to the island."

"Yala Palathar's squad." Another moment of tense silence. "Yes, I see."

Saren pressed his fingers into the hard stone and held his breath until his vision blurred and he fancied he could see the shadows lapping at his skin and creeping up his arms.

"In that case, Mekan Himself will judge you," said the king. "When everyone is present, the ceremony will begin."

20

Viam watched the guards escort the Disciples up the palace stairs with an increasing sense of hopelessness. Saren walked at the back, his head bowed, flanked by so many guards that any chance of escape would mean an immediate death.

"It's over," Viam whispered to Brenat. "He's going to die."

Unless he gave himself up as a Disciple of Death, and since he'd refused to so much as acknowledge his prior connection to Mekan... gods, she couldn't let him walk to his death without speaking a word in his own defence.

As she moved forward, Brenat caught her arm. "You aren't going in there. At least, not without me."

"You can't," Viam protested. "You already lost an eye trying to help me, and I *am* a Disciple of Death."

"You think the monarch will share the stage with anyone else?" Brenat's eyes widened, her gaze fixed somewhere over Viam's shoulder. "I stand corrected."

Soldiers marched towards the palace, less than twenty in total. Yala's cane drew Viam's eye like a beacon, and she recognised several others too.

"The captains of the flight division." Viam lowered her voice. "The king might not want to share power, but he'll want to train other Disciples of Death to fight under him."

"Isn't that why you left the city in the first place?" Brenat said. "I'm not complaining at you for coming back, but trust me, you need someone in there who's on your side. Who isn't Yala."

Or Daliel. The prince had turned her away, and Yala would do the same if she knew.

Viam waited for her and the others to leave her line of sight before she followed them upstairs.

The guards at the front door shook their heads when they saw Viam and Brenat's lack of uniform. "You aren't captains."

"I used to be." Suspecting that wouldn't be enough, Viam added, "The prince and I know one another. He said I could come and attend the ceremony."

The lie tasted sour in her mouth. The guards exchanged glances and then stepped aside, one of them muttering something that sounded like, "We'll see what His Majesty makes of that."

The entrance hall appeared vaster than it was in daylight, long shadows stretching beneath the soft light emitted by the myriad lanterns mounted on the walls. The sound of Brenat's muffled protests reached her through the closed door; at a guess, the guards had refused her entry.

At least she'll be far away from the temple.

Viam followed the echo of soldiers' boots through a side door, following them through a series of corridors and out into a courtyard dominated by high pillars reaching into the darkening sky.

The king stood in the spot where an empty pyre had once burned, dressed in his military gear as if he'd sprung from the funerary flames untouched. His embroidered clothing was free of its usual adornments, topped instead by a drakeskin coat, and his boots were polished to a shine. A golden crown gleamed atop his head, but not a speck of light disturbed the shadows crowding around the stone slab at his side.

In front of the altar knelt Saren, his head pressed to the ground. Viam took a half step towards him and caught herself when the king's gaze passed over the assembling soldiers. Viam shuffled to the end of a row, sweat trickling between her shoulder blades.

The king's attention slid past her, lingering on the door through which she'd entered. Out of the corner of her eye, she glimpsed guards filing into the courtyard, flanking the Disciples of the Flame. They walked in a subdued huddle, faces drawn, frightened.

The final person to enter the courtyard was Daliel, accompanied by two guards of his own. Shock flitted across his face when he caught sight of her, and she lowered her head, silently pleading with him not to give her away.

The prince positioned himself on the altar's other side, opposite his father. King Tharen spared him a brief look and then addressed the courtyard at large. "We shall begin."

The soldiers knelt, bowing before their king, and Viam joined them. Even Daliel sank to his knees near where Saren knelt. *What's he doing? Has the king singled him out?*

"As you are all no doubt aware, my return to Laria was not without complications," the king continued as they rose to their feet. "The Disciples of the Flame, who were responsible for my exile, remained a threat. When their Superior offered to pledge himself to the crown, I accepted his offer with the understanding that no other Disciple would walk freely in Laria without doing the same. These Disciples violated that contract."

All eyes turned towards the Disciples of the Flame. Without their robes, they appeared ordinary, young, and helpless, but the king's expression of raw hate was one she'd never seen on him before.

"To ensure that no Disciple betrays me again, I will call upon the deity who helped me survive during my exile," said the king. "A god whose name was forbidden to be spoken in Laria for many years yet who is embedded deeply into our history. I speak, of course, of Mekan."

His name had a more visible effect on some than others. A few people flinched, perhaps recalling the devastation of the battle with the dead, but otherwise, the reaction was uniform silence as potent as a collectively held breath.

"I called you here because I require your help," he told the assembled soldiers. "Mekan will protect me, but to do so, He needs the assistance of the living. As my most loyal captains, it is my hope that you will pledge yourself to Him too."

Nobody spoke nor moved. The king beckoned to the guards escorting the Disciples of the Flame to the altar. "Bring them here."

***

I'm to be judged by Mekan Himself, am I? A fitting end by anyone's measure except for Saren himself. Every moment since he'd escaped that island he'd spent running away from the whispers, but they'd chased him straight to Mekan's own doorstep.

When the rhythmic thud of heavy boots as the soldiers filed into the room petered out, he glanced up in search of familiar faces. It did not surprise him in the least to see Yala among those gathered, but he hadn't expected Viam to be present too. She hadn't come for *his* sake, had she? Who had let her in? The prince?

Ah, there he is. Saren might have laughed to see the finely dressed man standing near his more formidable father, cast into shadow by the pillar flanking Mekan's altar. As it was, he wondered with a feverish desperation if the friendship Viam had cultivated with the prince might spare him too.

The guards dragged the Disciples of the Flame to the altar. Shadows spread from its base, and the thrum of Mekan's presence hung in the air like miasma. The king drew a sword, a crude, curved instrument that Saren thought was covered in rust at first glance before realising it was not metal at all. Its dark surface called to mind a claw that Yala carried upon her, sharper than any manmade weapon and wreathed in shadows not unlike those clustering around the altar.

The king spoke. "Let us bathe the altar in the blood of traitors."

***

The king's words rang across the courtyard. Like the others, Yala stood rigid, the soldier in her obeying even as her instincts urged her to grab Saren and drag him away from that altar. Away from the king.

The monarch paid him no more attention than he did anyone but the Disciples of the Flame. The prisoners shivered beside the altar, faces ashen, expressions slack with fear. Some knelt, but others held upright, clinging to their remaining shreds of dignity. As if it mattered. They had no access to their god nor any hope of escape from the shadows coiling around the altar's base.

King Tharen stood over them wielding a blade as dark as the shadows and spoke words Yala didn't hear. A whisper rose from all around them, wordless yet laced with menace, and some of her fellow soldiers turned their heads, looking for the speaker. They did not realise the voice came from the shadows themselves, from the darkness extending from the altar like a dark tide lapping at their feet.

Goose bumps pimpled her skin, and her heart raced in a familiar blend of anticipation and dread as the king seized one of the kneeling Disciples by the scruff of the neck and pulled him closer to the altar. With his other hand, he brought the blade down upon his exposed throat.

Blood sprayed across the altar, merging with the shadows and glistening like oil. Someone screamed, the sound fading out when the whisper returned, this time forming clear words. *"Thank you for the sacrifice."*

The king beckoned. Two guards stepped in and dragged the body away, leaving a smear of crimson on the stone.

When the king reached for a second Disciple, the young man shouted, "Dalathik, help us!"

His cry broke the other Disciples from their stupor. Someone else echoed the plea, and the others picked up the shout until the chorus formed a prayer.

"Quiet!" the king shouted. "Stop them!"

A spark caught Yala's eye, a bright flash in the gloom— and the king's shout was lost in a roar of flame.

Blinding white fire surged from one of the Disciples, consuming him from head to toe until he resembled nothing more than a pillar of dazzling light.

"Your Majesty!" A guard ran to grab the Disciple and let out a hoarse scream as his hands burned too. The column of blazing fire burned higher, dwarfing the altar and hiding the king from sight.

Yala stood rooted to the spot as the courtyard broke apart in chaos. Guards and soldiers alike ran forward and recoiled from the flames; the whitish fire leapt from one Disciple to another as if given the command to burn flesh alone.

The first Disciple folded in on himself, his body dissolving into a pile of ash. A second followed suit, and a third ignited a heartbeat later. They were choosing to sacrifice themselves, to die by their own god's hand rather than Mekan's.

Averting her eyes from the flames, she caught a glimpse of Saren scurrying away, unseen in the darkness. Viam, too, had vanished, as had the prince. The king... gods, had the fire finished him off? She swivelled back to the altar, squinting through fractured vision, and the whitish flames dimmed for an instant, revealing the untouched monarch.

Fuck. He's alive. He'd taken a few steps back from the altar, but he displayed no fear of the raging fire consuming the Disciples one by one. Raising his voice over the crackle of flames, he shouted, "Enough!"

The whisper rose again, catching his voice and turning it into an echo that came from all directions. The soldiers stilled mid-retreat, and the guards, too, fell into line.

Two detached themselves from the rest, crossing the courtyard without any heed to the deadly flames. In the flickering light, Yala glimpsed masked faces and scaled hands holding curved weapons similar to the king's, their body language displaying no fear of Dalathik's wrath.

How can that be?

A hissing noise sounded; it took Yala a moment to realise they were speaking in rasping voices indistinguishable from Mekan's whispers.

Darkness spilled from the altar like a sudden downpour unleashed on a cookfire. The flames vanished, and the surviving Disciples leapt up with cries of dismay. Four remained, one of whom clutched something in his hands. A candle, its light now extinguished, held by a young Disciple who was vaguely familiar to Yala. Yala's instincts as squad leader rose unexpectedly, and she bit back the urge to shout a warning.

"Dalathik will triumph!" The young Disciple ran straight at the king, lifting the candle like a weapon.

The king lifted a hand. The shadows themselves moved as if he'd lifted them as he might a curtain; the Disciple let out a scream when they wrapped around his ankles, brought him to the ground—and devoured him.

The novice's screaming face vanished, his cries fading to empty silence. The thickening shadows spread, and the remaining Disciples vanished beneath, their screams extinguished like the flames that had so recently burned in their hands.

The king gave another careless gesture. The shadows retreated, coalescing above the altar, leaving no trace of the Disciples behind. A dark patch formed in midair, resembling a hole or a door, perhaps, formed of the darkness alone. Indistinct shapes moved within, clawed and sharp-toothed beings that belonged to Mekan alone.

The Void.

"So much for Dalathik's triumph." The king lowered the sword, his fine clothes splattered with blood, remnants of the shadows he'd wielded clinging to his fingertips. Yala's fingers tingled, and a surge of unwelcome jealousy rose in her like vomit.

"This is the Void, the domain of Mekan, and the home of my second army," the king intoned. "For those of you who wish, this is also the place where you will prove your loyalty to the crown and where you will be granted advantages in return."

Advantages. The guards' seeming imperviousness to Dalathik's flames drove home how much Yala had overestimated her own abilities. She'd seen Dalathik's flames devour the island from top to bottom, seen them consume the dead until naught remained but ash. Her scheme had not included the Disciples of the Flame, but she'd always thought, in the back of her mind, that one would easily outdo a Disciple of Death.

Not those Disciples. That they'd surrendered their humanity to obtain those powers didn't quell the churning envy swirling within her. She averted her eyes from the king, looking instead for her squad-mates. Saren had gone, but Viam lingered at the back; when her eyes briefly locked with Yala's, there was horror there and pain. She derived no pleasure from this experience.

Yala wished she could say the same and that a part of her did not wish she stood in the king's place.

"This is where we will honour Mekan," the king said. "To maintain a Temple of Death requires a cost, and daily sacrifices must be performed. That is why you must capture the surviving Disciples of the Sea, so that their lives may serve a purpose."

He lifted the sword again, displaying the rivulets of blood trickling along its edge and dripping onto the altar.

"Each life you take upon this altar will win you a higher rank in Mekan's favour," he went on. "And mine. Tomorrow, Mekan Himself will aid our victory against the betrayers, and nobody—Disciple or otherwise—shall ever challenge Larian supremacy again."

21

Viam stumbled from the palace in a dreamlike haze, the scent of burning in her nostrils. Blood was on her hands. She didn't know how it had got there.

"Viam!" Saren slid down the steps, his face as ashen as hers. "Get me out of here. Please."

"You can't leave the palace grounds." Her voice sounded like it belonged to a stranger. "Not tonight."

She wasn't sure how she'd found her way through the dark corridors to the exit. She didn't remember anything but the blood and fire and Daliel's stunned, horrified face as he watched his father take the lives of the Disciples of the Flame.

Brenat's arms folded around her, anchoring her back to the present. "Viam, is this your friend? The one you were trying to save?"

"Yes, and I need to get *out* of here," Saren said. "The king only spared me because he forgot I existed. You know, with all the slaughter and horror and shit."

"Slaughter?" Brenat echoed. "What—never mind. It's

dark. We can hide you in the staff dormitories, and nobody will notice if you don't make too much noise."

"Sure, I can do that." Saren released a low, humourless laugh. "The king's unhinged. Who's to say he won't have us all put to death during the night?"

"Did you speak to him?" Viam stepped out of Brenat's embrace. "The king, that is?"

"He didn't kill me, which is more than I can say for those Disciples." Another bitter laugh. "He said Mekan could judge me. And I suppose He saw fit to spare my life."

"We can get you out of the palace in the morning," Brenat said. "The king will be gone, remember?"

"Gone?"

"He'll be hunting Disciples of the Sea." She spoke through numb lips. "For the next sacrifices."

"Forget him." Brenat took her arm, and after a heartbeat, she grabbed Saren too. "Come on."

They helped Saren find his way to the administrative buildings. Thanks to the king's efforts to divert staff members into the army instead, half the dormitories were unoccupied, and Saren had little trouble finding a spare sleeping mat. While he traipsed off to find somewhere to wash the blood from his hands, Brenat steered Viam into one of the empty dormitories. "Now, tell me what happened in there."

Viam sagged against the wall, gasps tearing from her lungs. The world tunnelled; her vision blurred. Brenat reached for her, squeezed her hand. "Viam. Breathe."

"He killed the Disciples of the Flame," she mumbled to the floor. "Used their blood to open the temple while we all watched."

"Fuck." Brenat sucked in a breath. "Did he notice you?"

"No." He hadn't spared a glance for his son either; she

suspected Daliel had fled the courtyard before the ritual was even over. "It doesn't matter. He's won."

"Drakeshit," said Brenat. "He's leaving on that mission tomorrow, isn't he?"

"It doesn't matter." She pressed her fist to her mouth, fighting a scream. "Even the Disciples of the Flame didn't leave a mark on him. And the Disciples of the Sea will be next to die at the altar."

"Not if Yala kills him first."

"Yala is…" She didn't have words for the expression on Yala's face when she'd contemplated the Void as if she wanted nothing more than to take the king's place at Mekan's side. "Fuck Yala."

"I hope not." Brenat chuckled. "That is, I hope that isn't your intention, because I have plans for you."

Viam stiffened, unable to stifle her instinctive reaction to the promise beneath her words.

Brenat peered at her face. "All right, I know now's not a good time."

"No." Gods, she did not want to have this conversation now. Didn't want to lose the only source of comfort she had left. "It isn't."

"I won't rush you if that's what worries you," Brenat added. "Though I have to say that we have a *lot* more privacy in here now that most of the staff members have gone."

"It's…" Gods. She had to tell her. Squeezing her eyes shut, Viam whispered, "I don't feel… attraction. In the same way that most people do." She opened her eyes a fraction.

Brenat watched with one brow raised. "That answers a few questions."

"What?" Viam's heart missed a beat as if she'd slipped on the stairs. "What questions?"

"Such as whether you enjoy this." She leaned closer, her

fingers caressing the back of Viam's neck, until their lips touched.

"No, I don't mind this." Viam leaned into the kiss then pulled back, feeling her face flush. "I don't mind any of it, actually. I just... don't get the same enjoyment as most people I know."

"Got it," said Brenat. "Then we'll have to find what you do enjoy, won't we?"

Again, her heart skipped, and she felt tears sting her eyes. "I don't think I can be what you want me to be. I haven't been for anyone else. They always want more."

"I don't want you to be anything other than yourself," Brenat returned. "Never doubt that."

An unseen weight vanished from Viam's shoulders. "You mean it."

"If the god of death didn't put me off, nothing will."

"Anyone else would find that a cause for concern." Viam let out a weak laugh, tears leaking from her eyes. "Gods, we're a mess."

"Who isn't?" Brenat drew her into her arms, and Viam gladly lost herself to the companionship, to the bright spark in the horror of the night.

***

Kelan flew over the ocean, scanning the waters for the Disciples of the Sea. He'd been too occupied trying to help Yala's friend to check they'd safely evaded Mekan's creatures the previous night, and the sense that he'd failed both gnawed at his insides. *I hope that candle I gave those Disciples turns out to be worth something.*

He caught sight of a ripple on the water, and Nanek surfaced. "I thought you abandoned us, Disciple."

"Aren't the others around?" His fellow Disciples had,

sensibly, left the capital and spent the night at an inn some-where outside of the city. "I thought they were coming to find you."

"They did," said Nanek. "However, there has been some dispute over their willingness to fight the king's army."

I bet that was from Lakiel. He glimpsed the ship then, bobbing gently against the cliffs near which they'd set up camp. It was still too close to the capital for his liking, but Niema had vouched for its safety.

"I'll talk to them. Have you heard from the Disciples of Life yet?"

"No. I hoped *you* had."

"I've been in the capital, remember?" Near the boat, he glimpsed robed figures gathering on the cliffs overlooking the sea. An obvious absence leapt out at him. "Where's Lakiel?"

"He left." Ranit waved him over. "Took Brikel with him too."

"Shit." He shouldn't have been surprised, but given her injury, Brikel had also been in no shape for an arduous journey either. "How many of us are left?"

"Eight. And we're to go up against the entire flight division."

"The Disciples of Life will come with us." He'd thought Niema would already be back from consulting with her fellow Disciples; he would have sent Molin to check, but he'd needed the tree-raptor's help in the capital too much to risk separating from him.

"I hope you're right," Ranit murmured. "For their sakes."

Kelan followed his gaze to the ship and the youthful, frightened faces peering at him from the deck. Not many people aboard were old enough to be full-fledged Disciples of the Sea, but the king had designated them as traitors worthy of execution.

The sun was setting when he finally heard beating wings in the distance. Kelan glided above the ship, tension melting into relief when he recognised Niema seated atop the front-most war drake.

"You came." He flew to meet her, counting the other war drakes following her lead. They numbered fifteen or sixteen at most, but each carried an impressive array of weaponry considering their reputation as pacifists. The frontmost Disciple behind Niema had enough scars to make Kelan wonder if he'd ever served in the king's army.

"Sorry we're late," Niema said. "There have been more attacks from the dead. They're everywhere."

"Not the king's doing, I hope." Like those monstrous sea drakes—and if he did succeed in opening the Temple of Death, far worse might follow tomorrow.

"Has he—?" She stumbled over the words. "Has he finished building the temple?"

Kelan grimaced. "I think you'll want to be on the ground to hear this."

As he'd anticipated, his account was met with horror, at least on Niema's part. The other Disciples reacted more with the grim acceptance one might display when faced with a horde of rampaging dead.

"We're too late," Niema whispered.

"We aren't. We don't know if the ritual succeeded." The argument held little weight, as insubstantial as any of the lies he might have conjured up on a whim. "The king might not have time to call his entire army, regardless."

"We shall proceed as if he has." The scarred Disciple spoke in the tone of someone accustomed to giving orders. "This does not change our strategy."

"But…" Niema trailed off, seeming surprised that the others agreed with their stoic leader. So was Kelan, come to that, but their decisive action was a welcome change from Superior Shralin's desperate grovelling.

"There you have it." He summoned a smile. "If the king *did* succeed, Yala is going to have even more incentive to take off his head. The least we can do is help her along."

***

As dawn broke on the day of the mission, Yala and the other soldiers gathered under a sky streaked with crimson and grey bleeding into one another like the scenes Yala had witnessed in the palace the previous night. The altar had followed her into her dreams, beckoning her into its shadowy embrace, and her own desire seemed to stare at her from the eyes of the other captains. Now they, too, had seen into the heart of the Void. They'd faced Mekan's temptation, and they'd accepted the king's offer.

None of her plans had accounted for this. She'd laid everything out clearly enough that she'd been able to see each scene in her mind's eye.

The king opening the Void had shattered that vision, and the upcoming mission loomed like a blank page onto which any number of horrors might be etched.

From daybreak, Yala had been under such close scrutiny that she hadn't even had a moment to check whether Saren had made it out of the palace. She'd have to trust in Viam to keep him safe. Yala had a different group of people to protect today who'd placed their lives in her hands.

To avoid getting under one another's feet, one squad at a time entered the paddock to prepare their beasts for combat and then flew to a beach where they'd reconvene and separate into their assigned groups. When Yala's turn came, her squad mounted with the disciplined eagerness she'd come to expect of them in spite of their nerves. They possessed the youthful confidence that she'd once had herself, eager to enter the fray and prove themselves.

Two weeks of training was far too little, in her view, but she had to admit that experience would prove a finer teacher than she could ever hope to be.

Please let me bring them back alive.

"Fly." Six voices echoed her command, six pairs of wings beat, and they flew into formation as if they'd done so a hundred times before and not less than ten.

Yala took the lead, heading northeast to the beaches outside of the city's boundaries. There, they would divide into three groups formed of several squads to circle the Disciples' hiding place and ensure none escaped.

As they descended over the beach, Yala glimpsed the king's steed perched atop a sandy bank, outfitted in the crown-like helm designed more for show than for practicality. The king wore ceremonial armour designed to draw the eye. She hadn't seen him partake in any of the battles she'd flown in as squad leader, but the absence of his usual entourage of guards suggested he would not hide behind anyone else during this battle.

Yala would have no better chance to confront him.

As she and her squad landed on the pristine sand, she spied a group of individuals in the water, swimming against the current with ease. Disciples of the Sea. *Shit. How could I forget some were allied to the king? To Mekan?*

Another unwelcome element to a task already weighted heavily against her. She did not know whether the king had made use of the temple after the previous night's slaughter, but she no longer trusted that the man they fought behind resembled the person whose orders they'd once followed to the grave.

While they waited for the rest of the army, she dug her heels into the sand and tried not to think of the last time she'd stood upon a similar beach prior to a mission that would redefine her life and rewrite her future.

All missions did, in a way. Nobody ever returned the same person they were when they left Laria's shore. Even on her last mission to the island that was their current destination, she'd flown in the company of two people who hadn't survived to see the journey home to Laria, and the island's dense jungles and high cliffs were forever marked as the place she'd claimed the title of squad leader.

When the entire flight division was assembled on the beach, they separated into their assigned groups. The first group of fliers went east, the second headed west, and the third and largest group would fly north. The commander, who would fly near the back of their arrangement, should be with the king, but the monarch remained apart from the rest, no war drake willing to fly near his beast.

Somewhere in the depths of the ocean lay Yala's dead war drake steed, its bones scattered and the shadows that had once held it together long dissipated. She would ensure that the king and his steed both joined the beast in its watery grave.

At the commander's order, she and the squad took flight. The sound of beating wings soothed her nerves, and for a while, nothing else existed but the familiar rhythm and the endless haze of blue above and below.

Then, the outline of a large island appeared, solidifying into thick greenery edged by soft, sandy beaches tapering to a spear's point at high cliffs.

Memories crowded in. An ambush waiting in the jungle. Bodies strewn across the sand, floating face-down beneath high cliffs. Crimson streaks in the pristine water.

Yala blinked the images away and called to their scout. "Toreth, has the first squad reached the shore?"

"Yes, but they didn't land." He pointed to the island's eastern edge. "There's someone in the water."

Disciples? "Careful," she warned. "Don't forget they can control the ocean's currents. Make sure you fly high enough to avoid them."

As they closed in on the island, Yala spied a blot above the water's surface, too large to be a person. *Sea drake.*

"Ambush!" someone shouted as the frontmost squad scattered in a flurry of vast wingbeats and a swell of waves.

The sea churned as if stirred by an invisible hand, waves lashing at their heels. Yala pulled upward sharply and called to her fellow squad-mates to do the same as a serpentine head crested the surface of the water. A second followed then a third, all carrying spear-wielding riders. Not Disciples— nor Larians either.

These soldiers were Rafragorian.

22

"You're going to get us all killed," Kelan warned Nanek. *"Rafragoria? You requested help from them?"*

Ignoring him, Nanek swam towards the island's shore to join his fellow Disciples. Sea drakes circled at a distance, their long, scaly bodies below the water save for the portion of their spines upon which their riders sat. The Rafragorians paid little attention to Kelan and his allies, but the realisation that their enemies would be fighting on their side had stymied the others' desire to stay close to the island, and they'd instead flown east to join the Disciples of Life.

Kelan had been less inclined to abandon Nanek and the others, but there was little doubt that the king would take the Rafragorians' presence as proof of their treachery and would react accordingly.

"Nanek!" He tried again to catch the Disciple's attention. "This is a mistake. We can't trust them."

"It is not," Nanek said over his shoulder, his arms cutting through the waves like blades. "Those soldiers are allies."

"Yala's flown in the army for half her life," Kelan said. "How do you think she's going to react to see us fighting on the same side as the people who almost skewered her to death a few weeks ago?"

"I would sooner face an honourable death rather than one given in tribute to Mekan," he said. "My people have made our choice."

"You might have mentioned it to the rest of us." He hadn't thought that revealing the king's intention to sacrifice his fellow Disciples at the altar would have provoked this result. Nor had he known Rafragoria had anything resembling a defensive force. These soldiers must have escaped Mekan's initial assault and had stayed hidden until the king had banished the dead back to the Void, but if there were other monsters in the water, the sea drakes would fare no better than their riders.

Cursing under his breath, Kelan flew above Nanek, surveying the cloudless sky in search of the coming soldiers. At first, they appeared the size of a distant flock of seabirds, dividing into three groups as they flew. Two split apart from the main one, heading east and west respectively, with the largest group continuing towards them.

A second Disciple of the Sea surfaced near Nanek, spraying them both with water. "They're splitting up."

"I can see." Kelan pointed. "How many are we dealing with, do you think?"

"That's not the problem." The Disciple shook her head, the bright shells woven into her curly hair clanking against each other. "*He's* with the squad heading east."

"The king?" Kelan's heart gave an unpleasant lurch. "Are you sure?"

"There's no mistaking his monster."

Nanek swore. "The king knows we smuggled most of our people off the island. He won't be fooled by the ambush."

"If he's going east, he'll fly straight into the Disciples of Life."

Would they be a match for that void drake? If not, and if he found the hiding place where they'd left the most vulnerable Disciples… they'd be slaughtered.

***

"Captain!" Gorel shouted up at Yala. "What should we do?"

Yala dragged her gaze away from the Rafragorians. "Stick to the plan. We expected an ambush."

Not from them. With an unwelcome jolt, Yala recognised one of the Rafragorians as the man who'd stabbed her to near death and left her bleeding out in Niema's arms on their way back from destroying the island. Had he and the others been hiding out here the whole time? With their country in ruins, they were hardly to blame for their predicament, but the Disciples of the Sea must know that allying with Laria's enemies would have only one outcome.

The water around the Island raged as Disciples clashed, while spears flew between the riders in the sky and those in the ocean. No movement stirred upon the island yet, but weren't the Disciples of the Sky and Life supposed to be here? Perhaps they'd turned tail upon seeing who their allies had invited to fight on their side, even Kelan.

As for Yala? She'd never had any qualms about killing Rafragorians before, and the gods knew she'd rather spill their blood than that of their fellow Larians. *Maybe I'm as much of a hypocrite as anyone else here.*

She reached for a spear, calling to her squad, "Ready?"

"You!" The shout came from the Rafragorian soldier she'd recognised, spoken in clear Larian. "You are dead!"

"Not quite." Yala readied her spear, the blood rushing in her veins, and hurled the weapon at the Rafragorian's throat.

The sea drake rose from the water, and the spear glanced off its scaly hide. Yala held onto her steed one-handed and reached for another as a second beast closed in with two Rafragorian warriors clinging to its back. Part of her was grudgingly impressed that the Rafragorians managed to hold their balance in waters stirred by the Disciples of the Sea; their control over their steeds matched that of Laria and their war drakes.

Spears flew too fast for Yala to track, and the war drakes lost formation as they dodged the assault from the mismatched army. Yala flew left to avoid a Rafragorian spear, and the weapon instead struck the flier behind her. Toreth let out a raw cry, and the fresh tang of blood filled the air as he tumbled into the ocean.

"Toreth!" Gorel flew down, reaching out a hand, but the waves had already swallowed Toreth's body. He veered sideways, narrowly avoiding the serpent's biting teeth, screaming his squad-mate's name.

Yala stared at the bloodied waters for a moment. Then, her instincts kicked in. "Kill them," she snarled between her teeth. "No mercy!"

The squad took up her shout, echoed it back and forth. Yala readied her spear and urged her war drake to fly faster, taking aim at the Rafragorian who'd stabbed her.

"You." The Rafragorian repeated the same word in Larian, his eyes locking with Yala. "You fight for dead."

The spear left Yala's hand and sank into the man's shoulder. She reached for another, blood pounding in her ears.

"No," he gasped, his arm falling limp to his side. "We—not —with the dead."

"What the fuck does that mean?"

Another spear flew over Yala's shoulder, burying itself in

his throat. Her eyes tracked the source—Lisek, leading her squad, who were the sole group to have held formation when the chaos of battle had split their forces.

The sea drake rose upright to snap at Yala's heels. She dodged, steering her war drake around the beast's spiny back as she reached for another weapon. More spears flew from her squad-mates' hands, peppering the sea drake's scaly head. It screeched, weaving to left and right, the remaining soldier clinging on for dear life.

Yala's war drake snatched the soldier from their perch. Bone crunched between its teeth, and with the spray of blood came a familiar tingling sensation in her fingers and the stirring of shadows below the water's surface. Mekan, ever drawn to bloodshed, without any care for who shed it or how.

"Thank you for the sacrifice."

The cold whisper's effect was akin to a wave upended on Yala's head. She wasn't here to fight Rafragorians. Where was the fucking king? He usually flew at the back to avoid being drawn too deeply into the thick of the fighting, but she would have expected him to play a more active role given his recent ascension to Mekan's side. Aside from the voice, she saw no traces of the dead, but they didn't need to participate when the flight division already had the upper hand. The few Disciples of the Sea left in the water had been driven back to the beaches, and some had already scaled the cliffs and vanished amid the dense jungle. Only the king's allies remained, circling the island like the serpents that now lay dead amid the waves.

"They're retreating!" Lisek called. "The Rafragorians have gone!"

Yala's gaze panned across the water. The serpentine coils of dead sea drakes lay entwined with the fallen bodies of soldiers from both sides, and four or five Disciples of the Sea were among the dead too. She couldn't tell if they'd been among those fighting for the king or the ones trying to defend the island, but no Disciples of the Sky were present nor Disciples of Life either.

"Pull back!" shouted Commander Sranak's voice from above. "All fliers, to me!"

"What's going on?" Yala flew higher, calling to him. "What is it?"

"New orders from His Majesty."

Yala relayed the order to her squad, and word swiftly passed amid the other squad leaders. Many of the fliers were injured, but they'd suffered few losses. *Except Toreth.* Guilt sank its teeth into her; she tried to dislodge it, but the sense of responsibility clung like a burr. Several of her squad members had been crying, including Gorel, and his gaze lingered on the area where Toreth had fallen.

"What's happening over there?" Yurel's question yanked her attention back to the island. Below, the waves were rising around the island's edges, swamping the cliffs and devouring the beaches up to the jungle's boundary.

"There'll be no escaping now," Lisek said with satisfaction. "Look at them. They're doomed."

Oh. The Disciples of the Sea—those who'd allied with the king—had the island surrounded, their heads scarcely visible above the rising waves. Each surge pierced deeper into the jungle and consumed more of the island's shores. The flood wouldn't kill the Disciples hidden within, but they'd be exposed, easy for the soldiers to pick off.

The cruelty was no surprise, given where the orders had come from.

"Commander!" Yala called. "Where is the king?"

"He went with the squads who flew east of the capital," he replied. "When the dissenters on the island are dead, we're to follow them. He thinks some of the Disciples might have escaped on a ship."

They did. And if Yala's instincts were right, Kelan and Niema would be there too.

***

Niema hovered above the sea, watching the horizon for any sign of movement. She and Hachim had opted to stay behind while Ragem and the others spread across the ocean to wait for their adversaries. He hadn't been willing to stay with the ship nor to aid the Disciples on the island waiting to ambush the king's army; their purpose, he stated, was to fight the god of death in accordance with Yalet's will. Defending the others was a secondary purpose. In war, even Yalet could not protect all life.

And yet Niema couldn't escape the impression that she was in the wrong place. That she ought to be out there, helping Yala, or else fending off the soldiers sent east of the capital.

She'd known they were in trouble when one of the Disciples of the Sea had brought the warning that the army had split into groups, with one following the coastline on a route that would invariably bring them into contact with the Disciples' hiding place if they flew far enough. They'd had no time to change their strategy, and leaving the cove meant exposing the ship to any other threats that might lurk in the ocean.

"Niema." Hachim pointed across the water, the tip of his finger alighting on a speck above the surface. As Niema watched, that speck divided, becoming two, four, six. Seven war drakes. A flight squad.

"Where's Ragem?" Shouldn't he and the others have been waiting to intercept them? A lone squad might have slipped past his notice, but that they'd ventured this close to the Disciples' hiding place suggested that they'd been given orders to search the coast.

"We need to send them away." Hachim's words sank into her chest like stones; he, too, was conflicted on the ethics of using Yalet's gifts against other humans, but nothing less than a direct command would dissuade a soldier set on slaughtering them.

Or would it? Gods, she had to at least *try* another approach. Besides, what if Yala had come with them? As they drew closer to the oncoming war drakes, Niema squinted, trying to make out their riders. Not Yala. The captain at the head of the group was larger, more thickset, and he carried a spear in his hand.

A shout told her that one of the soldiers had spotted their approach. The captain shouted something to his squad members, brandishing his spear.

"Niema," Hachim hissed. "Slow down. If he throws that weapon—"

"He ought to know we aren't soldiers." Their lack of uniform would make that clear, but the other elite Disciples' absence concerned her. As far as she knew, she and Hachim were the only ones among their number who remained repulsed at the idea of taking a life.

The captain's voice drifted over the water. "Who are you?"

"We are Disciples of Life." Niema did her best to project her voice the way she'd seen Yala do countless times. "We're here to defend Laria from the forces of the dead."

"The dead?" He brought his war drake to a halt in midair, his squad forming a circle around her and Hachim.

"Yes, the dead." Niema's voice wavered, but she held her head high, meeting his eyes. "Mekan is our greatest foe, and we are here to defend Yalet in Her hour of need."

The captain didn't seem to know what to make of her. He blinked a couple of times, while his fellow soldiers exchanged uncertain looks. Out of the corner of her eye, she glimpsed another group of winged fliers approaching from the west, and she fervently hoped they were Disciples and not another flight squad.

"Are you aware that there is a group of fugitive rebels in this area?" asked the captain. "Rebels who defied the crown?"

"Our only concern is with Mekan," she replied. "He is our sworn enemy."

"The god of death?" Something flickered within his eyes, an emotion she couldn't read. "Do you lie to me, Disciple?"

"What is this?" Ragem's voice drifted over the water; the newcomers were indeed Disciples of Life, and they rallied around him as a squad might around their captain. "Who are you?"

"I might ask you the same," he retorted. "I am Captain Dienen of the flight division, and we're here to find a group of fugitives from the crown. If necessary, we will also mete out justice to any who defend the traitors."

"Justice is for the gods alone to deliver." Ragem halted behind the captain, and the other Disciples spread out on either side of him. "We are Yalet's hand, and we dispense justice on Her behalf. You serve no god."

"Don't we?" That flicker appeared in the captain's eyes again. "You are incorrect, Disciple, and our purpose is that of justice on behalf of another."

Mekan. Niema's stomach clenched when the Disciples of Life began reaching for their weapons.

"Please don't," she said. "There doesn't have to be bloodshed. Yalet wouldn't want—"

"Yalet's order is to eliminate any who serve Mekan." Ragem reached for the bow strapped to his back. "And we will not have mercy."

"Stop!" Her cry was lost beneath a chorus of voices joined in a sound too harsh to be called a song, a wordless unrecognisable yet layered with malice. A prayer, and not one she'd ever heard before.

Captain Dienen's eyes widened, then his face went slack. His hand lowered, no longer reaching for his weapon. His companions ceased to move, their faces losing all animation and even their war drakes stripped of their menacing air.

Ragem lifted his bow and fit an arrow to it, and a rustle of movement followed as his fellow fliers did the same.

"Stop," Niema repeated. "He can't even defend himself."

"He serves Mekan." The arrow flew, loosed from its bow, and struck the captain in the throat.

Niema's shout of despair became a scream as her war drake fell into a dive, a spear glancing off its side. The squad's formation shattered along with the silence that had followed the Disciples' prayer, and in the ensuing confusion, she saw Hachim beckoning to her from above the hail of arrows and spears.

An arrow skimmed her ear, the sting prompting her into flight. She caught up to Hachim, watching the soldiers fall beneath the Disciples' arrows with growing horror.

"We can't do anything." Hachim's voice broke; he felt her pain at their deaths alongside his own. "I can't let you get hurt too."

Her throat constricted. "Hachim, this is wrong."

They were dead. All seven, their bodies strewn in the water like discarded toys.

"More soldiers!" shouted one of the Disciples. "On your left!"

A second squad closed in, letting out cries of anger when they saw their fallen allies. This time, Ragem didn't even stop to talk before releasing an arrow from his bow. The point hit the frontmost flier and knocked him from his war drake. The others split apart, a couple fleeing the scene, but they hadn't a hope of outracing the elite Disciples. Even Bitra had drawn her weapon.

"Stop," Niema whispered. "This is what Mekan wants. You're playing directly into His hands."

"That's right," whispered the god of death.

23

Kelan flew, his cloak streaming behind him, cutting a diagonal path towards the cove where the Disciples of the Sea had concealed their ship. He'd taken as direct a route as possible, conscious that he risked drawing the soldiers on his tail himself, but it was plain to see they'd already been given instructions to scour the waters east of the capital. West, presumably, as the army had split into three parts.

Condemning the Disciples on the island to death didn't sit well with him either, but they'd made the decision to sacrifice themselves to slow down the army, and he would honour that, even if he disapproved of some of their allies. *Rafragoria, really.* Though if their intention had been to piss off the king so acutely that he forgot about hunting for the escapees, the idea held merit.

Yala, though... he hadn't had time to see if she'd joined the battle on the island before he'd left, but if she hadn't accompanied the squads following the king, she'd be stuck fighting Rafragorian soldiers instead of aiming her spear at her true foe.

Sounds of fighting came from ahead. He picked up speed and nearly fell out of the air at the sight of the Disciples of Life fighting their enemies with a brutality that he'd never have dreamed of associating with their kind. He gaped as the last soldier fell into the water, felled by one of their arrows. His surprise at their bloodlust was matched by the horror on Niema's face as she watched the carnage.

"The rest of the army is behind us." He glided up so that he hovered on a level with her and Hachim. "Along with the king."

"He knows where the Disciples of the Sea are hiding?"

"He'll certainly have some idea." Kelan surveyed the bodies strewn in the water, impressed at her companions' efficiency. They'd taken down two entire flight squads in minutes without suffering a single loss. "The other Disciples of the Sky are on their way too. They left the island after we found out Nanek invited Rafragorian soldiers to join the fight on the Disciples' side."

"Nanek did *what?*"

"More soldiers!" shouted the scarred Disciple of Life who appeared to be their leader. He carried a wooden bow, light-weight but strong, and the others were similarly armed. They'd trained as well as any soldiers if not better. "That way!"

Kelan squinted at the new winged monsters that had appeared on the horizon. "Those aren't war drakes."

He knew, as did Niema, that the larger beasts did not bear riders. Void drakes, four or five of them, vast wings beating like shadows given flesh.

"We can't let them get near the ship." Niema swivelled to Hachim. "If the king's figured out where they're hiding, they'll be slaughtered."

"They'll have to hide on land." Escaping the cove via the

water would take them right across the enemy's path. "Escape through the jungle. We'll help."

He didn't expect any help from the Disciples of Life. Already, they turned towards the enemy with their weapons readied as if they were mere humans rather than monsters born from Mekan's own realm.

Niema watched, her expression torn. "I can control the dead. The others can't."

"I think they're capable of taking care of themselves." The carnage in the water proved that if nothing else. "Come on."

He caught sight of the other Disciples of the Sky as they split apart from Niema's allies, heading for the cove. Ranit led the way, catching up to Kelan with a gasp of, "The king's coming this way."

"Fuck."

"He's already here." Niema spoke in a desolate whisper, pointing to the five monstrous void drakes gaining speed as they closed in on the Disciples of Life.

One flew apart from the others, a crown upon its scaly head and a figure seated on its back. As the void drakes closed in, Kelan almost missed the warning shout from the water below.

"The rest of the army is following the king!" Nanek bellowed. "We need to move the ship."

Kelan swore. "We can't. Your people will be exposed."

"We don't have a choice." His arms cut through the waves with swift strokes, gaining on the cove where the Disciples' most vulnerable people sheltered. "He's not going to stop until he's eliminated us."

Kelan's gaze snapped to the king's void drake. Already, he was close enough for Kelan to make out the smaller crown on its rider's head to match his steed, but the king's garish attire did not detract from the terror elicited by the shadows rippling around him.

Damn it, Yala, he thought. *Where are you?*

***

This is no honourable battle, Yala thought, watching the waters around the island turn crimson. *It's a slaughter.*

Severed limbs floated within a sea of viscera; heads surfaced with their skulls shattered to pulp. The Disciples of the Sea might have mastery over the ocean, but the dense jungle had conspired against them, preventing them from taking aim at their attackers until the enemy was already on them.

"I thought we were supposed to capture them alive." Her words fell like pebbles into the sea, inconsequential. Nobody heard her save, perhaps, for Mekan. With every drop of blood spilled, His whisper became louder, and darkness seeped out from beneath her drakeskin gloves.

With the island reduced to flooded remnants strewn with bodies, the squads fell into formation behind their commander and flew eastward, parallel to Laria's coast. Lisek's squad flew beside Yala's. Unlike hers, they'd suffered no losses.

"Ready to make sure these runaways don't escape?" Lisek's hair was matted with blood, and her eyes were bright, excited. "We'll make sure they're sorry they defied the crown."

Yala made a noncommittal noise. "Don't forget these are the people who didn't stay to fight. There was a reason for that. The king told us to bring them in alive."

A snort came from one of Lisek's soldiers. Hian, the rodent-faced individual who'd taken a dislike to Yala during their flight to the capital. *I knew that one would be trouble.*

Yala met his challenge with a calm stare. "I wouldn't go against His Majesty's command, would you?"

He didn't answer, but she felt his eyes boring into her back as they flew onward across the open sea. Close to an hour passed before they came within sight of the coast, an unbroken line of cliffs dotted with villages and seaside towns. The only vessels on the water were fishing boats, but the distant clamour of a fight carried across the air from somewhere close. Yala twisted around, trying to see where the noise was coming from.

"That way!" someone shouted.

Yala turned back to the front and made out the distinct outline of a ship following the coast eastward, pursued by the frontmost flight squad.

Inexplicably, there was no sign of the king or his void drake. *Where is he? I thought he went to hunt them down.*

"There they are." Lisek reached for a spear. "Let's do this."

As they closed in on the ship, she made out a few figures gathering on the deck. Most were too small to be adults, but all were armed, and even the ones who hardly looked older than twelve held spears and daggers of bone and wood, sharpened to kill. *They're going to get killed.*

"Remember, we need them alive," she called to her squadmates. "Don't aim to kill."

The other squads had already forgotten that order. Spears flew towards the deck, and she nudged her war drake's side with her knees, urging it to fly faster.

Nearing the ship, Yala leaned down to call to the Disciples. "Don't try to fight. You need not die today."

"No." The reply came not from the deck but from the water. *Nanek.* Their informal leader, Kelan's ally... and, apparently, now her enemy. "We will never surrender."

"Now is not the time to play the hero." Her heart sank when the other soldiers closed in and the Disciples on the deck lifted their own weapons in retaliation.

A tremor shook the air. The squad in front of hers scattered, and the boat rocked and tilted, knocked off-balance by a gust of wind. Behind, cloaked figures rose into the sky, voices joined in a collective prayer.

"Stop them!" Lisek shouted, gesturing to her squad to regroup. "Kill those traitors!"

Spears flew at the Disciples; the wind caught them, scattering the weapons into the water. Yala called to her own squad to fly higher, hoping that Kelan had warned his fellow Disciples not to attack her and secretly glad of the chaotic melee to give the ship the chance to overtake the army.

When Nanek passed below, she flew downward on the pretext of taking aim and leaned over the war drake's side, hissing, "I'm not your enemy. Where is the king?"

"Isn't he the one whose orders you're following?" Accusation lined his voice. "You were never our ally, Disciple of Death."

"I'm here to kill him, fool."

The waves drowned out his reply. Saltwater sprayed Yala from head to toe as another gust of air billowed, catching the rising waters driving them into the oncoming army. Her war drake growled its disapproval, shaking its head to dislodge droplets into the ocean as Yala struggled to get her bearings. When her vision cleared, she spied Nanek's lithe form swimming away from the ship, heading north.

Yala followed. She knew it was unwise, but if one person wanted the king dead as much as she, it was someone who'd seen half his fellow Disciples slaughtered at the monarch's hands. Her squad had scattered, and when she saw Gorel trying to follow, she shook her head, indicating to them to stay with the ship and pretending she was going to chase down Nanek alone.

A second war drake appeared In the corner of her eye.

Not one of her own squad members but Hian, rapidly gaining on her.

Yala cursed. "Shouldn't you be with your squad?"

"I might say the same of you." The edge of his war drake's wing clipped her steed's side. "I saw you talking to him. That Disciple. You know him?

"We fought earlier," she evaded. "I can handle him alone."

"I saw you talking to that Rafragorian too."

Yala growled under her breath. "Did you also see me skewer him? I was returning a favour I owed."

"He spoke to you in Larian," he said, undeterred. "Did you know they planned the ambush?"

"Don't be absurd." She focused on Nanek, who'd gained enough speed that she could barely see the crown of his head above the water. "I'd appreciate it if you didn't distract me."

Ahead, she saw several more winged reptilian beasts that appeared to be grappling in midair. Some were clearly war drakes, but others had no riders, and shadows trailed from their wings. *It must be the king.*

And he'd summoned some allies. Void drakes, at least five of them. The beasts with which they battled could only belong to the Disciples of Life.

"Who are they?" Hian swore as his war drake veered sideways, having noticed Mekan's beasts too.

Yala's did likewise, and she drove her knee into the war drake's side, urging it to snap out of its panic. The war drake whined, shying away from the melee. The void drakes had their smaller counterparts on the retreat despite being outnumbered.

Mekan's whisper brushed against the back of her neck as she finally spotted the king, his back to her, recognisable by his bright crown. The golden sheen stood out amid the darkness swathing both him and his steed like a cloak. *There he is.*

Nanek hadn't slowed, as if the notion of being caught in a

battle between the beasts of life and death didn't bother him in the least. That or he expected to die and welcomed his fate.

As Yala struggled to regain control over her war drake, something sharp jabbed her in the spine. She turned, saw Hian leaning over his rebelling war drake so that his spear brushed the base of her neck. "What the hell are you doing?"

"Stopping you." Hian leaned further, panting from the effort of holding his war drake steady. "I know what you're going to do. You're a traitor."

"You're the one pointing a spear at your fellow soldier."

"I heard." The spear wavered as his war drake bucked forward, and he narrowly avoided being pitched into the ocean. "You plan to betray our king."

"I plan to end this war." Yala's fingers inched towards her dagger. "If you can't see that His Majesty is on the wrong side, that his war will bring nothing but our own destruction, I have nothing more to say to you."

She whirled, whipping out her dagger, and hurled it at him. Hian toppled into the water with a gurgling cry.

Breathing hard, Yala looked for Nanek. Salt spray flecked her vision with each stroke he cut through the waves as he advanced towards the battle, unrelenting.

"What are you doing?" Yala shouted at him. "You'll get killed."

Nanek did not turn back. Unlike her, he didn't have a war drake to corral, and the beast refused to obey her commands to fly closer to the fray. She swore, kicking at its side, helpless to regain control as the king began to turn on his steed...

A sharp whistle cut through the air, keen as a knife's edge. The sound rippled through war drakes and void drakes both, and the king stilled, his beast hovering as if caught in a spell that rendered it to stone.

Niema.

———

"Stop!" Niema screamed, the sound turning into a shrill whistle that pierced through the battle like a hurled spear. The void drakes attacking the Disciples of Life ceased mid-strike, heedless of the weapons that battered them, and even the king's steed came to a halt.

She sucked in air, this time directing her command solely at the void drakes. *"Leave!"* she screamed.

The void drakes turned tail and fled, scattering across the ocean. Spine-tipped wings beat, trailing shadow, and the golden glint of a crown flitted past as the king's steed fled along with the rest.

"Niema." Hachim stared at her, his mouth slack. "How did you do that?"

"I…" *I don't know.* "Where's the ship?"

"That way." Nanek surfaced, pointing across the water. "Assuming those beasts didn't fly straight to it. What manner of Disciple are you?"

Niema shook her head, having no answer. To Hachim, she whispered, "We have to help them."

She didn't dare look behind her to see how the other Disciples of Life had reacted to what they'd witnessed. Not a trace of the void drakes was within range, and when she did set eyes on a lone war drake flying in a panicked zigzag, she recognised Yala as the rider struggling to regain control over its flight path.

"Yala." Had Niema's spell caught her too? She whistled, urging the war drake to calm down, and caught up to Yala from behind. "Yala, I'm sorry. I sent the king away."

"Probably for the best." Yala's expression, laden with fury, said otherwise. "He'd have killed your Disciples otherwise."

Would he? She didn't know. Hadn't stopped to think.

Now, the Disciples of Life had seen her control the Mekan's beasts, and thanks to her, Yala might have lost her only chance to bring down the monarch before he summoned the rest of his army.

24

Air gusted from Kelan's hands. He kept one eye on the ship and the other on the soldiers trying unsuccessfully to regroup and launch another attack. Between the Disciples of the Sky and Sea, nature itself was set against the king's army, with billowing gusts of wind combining with raging waves and making it impossible for them to get anywhere near the boat.

"They're leaving!" Ranit shouted. "The army is leaving!"

What? Kelan caught the sound of raised voices and saw one of the flight squads retreating, their captain shouting at everyone within hearing distance.

"Retreat!" The cry was taken up by the others and passed along as more squads peeled away from pursuing the ship. "King's orders!"

"Nanek!" He spied the Disciple of the Sea down in the water. "What's going on?"

"Your friend," he responded. "She stopped half the army with a whistle. Sent even the king away."

"Who?" He could hazard a guess. "Where's Yala?"

She was the one who'd wanted to kill the king, but he

saw no signs of her nor Niema amid the retreating soldiers. The other Disciples of the Sky continued to fly behind the ship, sending a strong air current to push it along.

The king is no longer hunting them. However much he might want to see if Yala had managed to get near the king, the Disciples of the Sea might not have another chance to escape the soldiers. When the last squad had vanished into the distance, he flew down to Nanek again. "Where do you want us to take them?"

"We would rather be at sea than on land, but we know the water is no longer safe." Bleakness spilled from his voice. "Our fellow Disciples died for our collective survival. We will not sully that sacrifice by remaining exposed, but I fear we have only earned a temporary reprieve either way. The king's soldiers will return to hunt us down within the week if not sooner."

"Not just you." Kelan gestured to the Disciples of the Sea and Sky. "I doubt you'll be his priority."

Not when Niema had taken control of his army. But that trick might not work twice.

And He has only one temple left to conquer now, whispered an unwelcome voice in the back of his mind. *Skytower.*

———

Yala kept both eyes open for any signs of the king, but Niema's command held true. Wherever she'd sent him was a long way from the battlefield.

"Yala." Niema called to her. "Yala, I'm sorry."

"I know." She said no more, unable to trust herself not to give voice to the sheer frustration that her plans had been snatched from her grasp.

Some of the harshness must have come through regardless, because Niema's face crumpled. "I didn't mean to ruin your plan."

"You didn't. The king did." When he'd captured the Disciples of the Flame and used their deaths to open the temple.

Niema let out a quiet, horrified noise. "Did the ritual succeed?"

"Yes, and I'm willing to bet that's where those monsters came from."

She didn't look back to see the devastation that was sure to be stark on Niema's face. The ritual's success ensured any future attempts she made to strike against the king were bound to be a hundred times more difficult, and the odds had been long from the start.

"Then we're too late," Niema murmured. "Gods. I have to tell the others, but they *saw* me control Mekan's creatures."

"Didn't they already know?"

A faint sob came in answer. "I didn't get a chance to tell them. Gods. They killed those soldiers."

"They probably deserved it." The king was going to be livid, perhaps enough to take it out on anyone who defied him no matter how minor the infraction.

Of course, her transgressions were hardly minor. Hian's death would require an explanation if Lisek or any of the others had seen him flying after her, and for all she knew, others had caught on to her intentions as well. She hadn't been nearly as careful as she thought, and an unwelcome question nudged at her mind, the question of how many comrades she might have to kill to conceal her true motives. She'd known she would have to weight her soul in blood to achieve her aim, but for all her efforts, the king breathed still, unconquered.

"Niema," Yala said, "I want to ask you a favour. If I die, promise you'll finish the job for me. Kill him."

Niema let out a choked noise. "I can't. You know I can't."

"You can." She twisted in her seat and gave Niema a level stare. "You're capable of killing. You're bound to me, to Mekan. It's in our nature."

Cruel words, she knew, but she needed to trust that someone would step in should the king discover her crimes. Who better than someone who'd exerted her will over the king's own void drake? Nobody else in the entirety of Laria could have done the same.

Niema's eyes brimmed with tears. Yala's heart twisted in a sick knot, but she held Niema's gaze until the first war drakes entered her line of sight.

The battle is over. The flight squads were assembling, rallying around the commander. He looked shaken, frightened even, his voice hoarse and a visible tremor in his gesticulating hands as he called the fliers into order. Yala caught sight of her squad waiting for her, assembled in formation, and guilt punched her in the chest at the sight of the gap where their lost member should be.

"Where were you?" Goren called to her. "Captain? We thought you were hurt, or..."

"I got blown off-course." She brought the war drake to a hover and scanned the other fliers. Most squads had lost at least one member, including hers, which made Hian's death less conspicuous. If Lisek asked, Yala would tell her that Nanek had killed him. "Did the ship—"

"The king ordered a retreat." Kithal eyed the commander and dropped his voice. "Or someone did. Don't tell anyone I said that, but I haven't seen the king."

I have. And if the order had indeed come from the commander instead, Yala could hardly fault him for panicking at the king's abrupt retreat from the battlefield. *Maybe he's scared about what the king might do if we don't come back to the barracks right away.*

If nothing else, Yala had proven that the king *would* show

himself in the open if he believed the occasion called for it, and while Niema's command over his monsters might prompt him to change strategies, she had a hard time believing his bloodlust would easily be sated. He'd try again, and this time, Yala would be prepared.

With the fading adrenaline from the battle, Yala was too exhausted to answer her squad's questions with more than grunts as they began their long flight back to Dalathar. Rumours flew back and forth amid the soldiers, and while nobody else knew the reasons for their retreat, word soon spread that two flight squads had been slaughtered at the hands of a group of Disciples of Life who held no qualms about killing in Yalet's name.

As of yet, nobody knew that one of them had bested the king. Yala might not have been tactful in her choice of words, but she had little doubt that if anyone had a chance at helping her finish the job next time, it was Niema.

They landed in the paddock, and her knees buckled when she climbed off her steed, all her aches returning as unwelcome reminders of her vulnerability, her mortality, her limited lifespan. She knew she was supposed to gather the squad to say a few words for their lost member, but a more pressing need intruded. She'd left her other squad neglected for too long, and she didn't trust the king not to round up more sacrifices for the temple out of fury at having his victory snatched from his grasp.

Yala dismissed her squad and sent them back to their bunks. Then she went looking for Saren.

———

After Yala left to catch up with the army, Niema and Hachim searched for the other Disciples of Life. She spied Ragem first, his war drake circling the ocean above the bodies of the slain soldiers. Her gut tightened at the memory of arrows hitting flesh, lives snuffed out as casually as one might extinguish a candle.

Closer, she saw Ragem's lips move in prayer, a soft murmur that she recognised as one spoken in supplication to Yalet's will. Not a lament for the dead, but he'd already designated these soldiers as Mekan's allies. Still, to hear a prayer spoken indicated some level of responsibility for the lives he'd taken in Yalet's defence. The other Disciples hovered some distance behind, a few of them bearing traces of injuries in the form of crimson streaks on their faces and arms. Luckily, Yalet's blessing could heal even the deepest lacerations, and mercifully, none looked to have suffered a wound from a void drake's teeth that would invariably be fatal.

"Niema." Ragem had seen her. "The battle is over. We must return to the Superior."

That's it? Nothing about what I did? His face was as impassive as ever. Perhaps he wanted to confront her later, back on land, but Niema couldn't leave until the Disciples of the Sea had reached safety. After witnessing so much loss that day, she wanted to ensure they at least found somewhere the king's soldiers couldn't hunt them down.

"We need to check on the ship," Hachim spoke up first. "The soldiers will have retreated, but there are still dangers in the water."

"And the Disciples of the Sky can't guide them forever." Kelan and the others would doubtless be tired from the confrontation and had a long journey to Skytower ahead of them too. "Hachim and I can take them somewhere further up the coast. Then, we'll come back to find the Superior."

Ragem's jaw tightened in annoyance. "She will be displeased. There are elements of our report that require your input."

A spasm shook Niema. "She knows what I can do."

A heartbeat passed then two then three. Ragem's expression changed not a bit, but Niema became conscious of the other Disciples watching her from a distance. Whispers passed between them, too quiet to hear. Niema's imagination filled in the gaps. *She used Mekan's power. She's bound to the god of death. She cannot be trusted.*

Hachim broke the silence. "The Superior chose to promote Niema with full confidence. She'll understand that her actions were necessary. The king might have killed you."

"It was our duty to stop him."

What? Niema stared at him. Was he more annoyed at her for ceasing the battle than for commanding Mekan's creatures as if she was bound to the Void itself?

"You were losing the battle," Hachim said quietly. "I saw."

Gratitude dispelled the chill elicited by his words. "I'll apologise to her in person. Just—please, let me help the Disciples of the Sea."

If she had not sent the king's void drakes away, the army wouldn't have stopped until every Disciple of the Sea was dead. She'd forgotten, in the rush of guilt over preventing Yala from reaching the king, that she'd made the choice for a reason.

Another moment passed, this one less tense. "The Disciples, you may take to a village on Laria's easternmost point. Any of our people who you encounter there will not attack you."

Niema blinked in surprise. "There's a village?"

"Near one of our enclaves," he responded. "There are several in the jungles along the coast. I believe our Superior will dispatch us there soon, in any case."

"Why?" To meet with the other enclave? They'd been so occupied with purging Mekan's influence from the villages and towns that Niema had scarcely spared a thought for the other enclaves. Yalet's elite Disciples came from all over the forest, not just from her own enclave.

"To induct our newest Disciples into our ranks."

That means us. A shiver trailed down her back. She and Hachim had formally accepted the promotion from the Superior, but they had not sworn all the vows the elite Disciples were required to offer to Yalet. The dead had been too urgent a threat to neglect.

"The Superior seems to think your unique talent won't be a barrier," he added. "We shall see."

Niema swallowed. "Did the Superior tell you how it came about?"

"She told me you healed a Disciple of Death and unknowingly forged a link to Mekan between you." His voice held no accusatory note, but the shiver intensified all the same. "Undoubtedly it is Yalet to whom you are loyal, given your actions in the battle. However, you will need to work on curbing your instinct to avoid causing harm. It will only cause you more pain."

Inexplicably, she felt *his* pain nudging against her like the blunt edge of a weapon, almost as if they shared a link similar to her bond with her enclave members. The feeling was gone a moment later, so rapid that she wondered if she might have imagined the shift.

Niema dipped her head. She didn't know what else to do. "I'll keep that in mind. I'll send a messenger to the Superior when we reach the village."

She couldn't look at him a moment longer. Curb her instinct against harm? She might as well cut off her own hand. That her fellow Disciples had escaped from the encounter with the king's void drakes without any deaths was testament to their fierce fighting skills, but it wasn't lack of skill that had made her hesitate. Whatever Yala believed—and Ragem too—she lacked the instinct of a killer.

How, then, could she swear to serve as Yalet's elite in truth? Was she doomed to deceive the god of life, even as she remained entwined with Her immortal enemy?

She and Hachim caught up to Kelan and the other Disciples of the Sky near the ship, where they appeared to be engaged in a midair argument.

"Oh, there you are." Kelan waved her over. "Come and resolve this dispute. I believe there's a village at Laria's northeast. Ranit insists otherwise."

"There is a village." She pushed on. "Hachim and I will fly with the Disciples of the Sea."

"Excellent." He gave his fellow Disciple a look that said *I told you so.* "The alternative was to bring them to Skytower, but Nanek didn't react well when I made that suggestion."

"You'll need to leave soon?" she guessed.

"Some of us already left," he admitted. "Lakiel did, but his sister was injured. I doubt they're at Skytower yet. I think my Superior would appreciate an update, though, since the last time she heard from me was before I went after those Disciples of the Flame."

Regret twisted inside Niema's chest. If she'd made it to the capital herself, might she have been able to save them? To prevent the Temple of Death from being opened at all?

"Don't," Kelan said. In response to her raised eyebrow, he added, "I know you're trying to blame yourself for this somehow, but you can't take on the whole world's responsibilities."

"Yala told me to finish the job if she couldn't." Her heart ached. "To kill him. Tharen."

"Someone has to." Kelan tried for a light tone. "I just witnessed you send several of Mekan's beasts fleeing at your command, so who's to say what you're really capable of?"

She flinched. "I don't *know* how I did it. Nobody else can, and I—I'm no true servant to Yalet."

"I would have thought not wanting to kill anyone makes you *more* worthy of Yalet's favour, not the opposite."

Once, Niema might have agreed with him. Now, she had the sickening sense of a great chasm opening between herself and the person she'd once thought she would be—and between the person who followed Yalet's values to her core and someone willing to do the unthinkable to ensure Mekan did not gain dominion over the world.

25

"The army." Saren faced Yala with his back to the fence circling the palace grounds, arms folded across his chest. "You want me to join the fucking army."

"It's that or return to the temple for a second round," she retaliated. "I don't have the energy for this, Saren. If you won't help yourself, there's nothing I can do."

She'd found Saren hiding in an empty room inside the administration staff quarters, ignoring Viam's attempts to convince him that he'd be safer outside the palace grounds than on the inside. Admittedly, that might not be true, and the guards at the gates might recognise his face and drag him straight back to the king. At least in the barracks, he'd be spared any punishment for the day's disastrous mission, or so she hoped.

Saren's shoulders slumped. "And what if they declare me unfit to serve?"

"You have four functioning limbs and both eyes," she retaliated, tapping her injured leg with a palm. "That's more than a good quarter of the current recruits can claim. The king wants anyone capable of holding a weapon to serve, regardless of physical capabilities."

Saren might not have touched alcohol for several weeks now, but he was woefully out of shape and would be breathless after less than a minute of running. In the air, that wouldn't necessarily matter, but entangling another former squad member in the king's web went far against her intentions. While the monarch had yet to show his face, Yala knew he was back at the palace as soon as she set eyes on the void drakes. All five had come back and circled above the palace in a menacing procession that banished any thoughts of her smuggling Saren out of here unseen.

"Yala." Viam ran up to her. "The commander—"

Yala had already spotted his approach out of the corner of her eye. Stepping away from Saren, she whispered, "If you want to join the flight division, he's the person to ask."

That he'd walked all the way here could have only one reason. The commander had regained his composure now he was back on the ground, but the shadows in his eyes betrayed horror, no doubt at what he'd witnessed upon his return to the palace.

"Captain," he said. "The king has requested for you to present yourselves in the receiving room at the next hour's bell. You'll need to tell your squad."

"He wants the whole flight division to come?" She glanced surreptitiously at Saren, who'd made a half-hearted attempt to slink out of sight. "I'll let them know."

What did the king plan to do, reveal the temple to the entire army? With her squad already reeling from losing a member, the last thing they needed was to witness a scene like the one the king had inflicted the previous night. While he'd chosen to address them in the receiving room and not the courtyard, there'd be retribution, she was sure, for their failure to capture or kill the rogue Disciples of the Sea.

As the commander began to walk away, Saren swore under his breath and then hurried after him. "Commander, I want to rejoin the flight division."

Suppressing a sigh, Yala called, "I can vouch for him. I also lost my scout in today's battle, so a swift replacement would be welcome."

"Right." The commander's weary eyes travelled between them. The battle had affected him, too, and the gods only knew what *he* thought the king's announcement might entail. "Come to the barracks, then. You'll start tomorrow."

Yala, too, returned to the barracks. Before she changed into clean clothes, she relayed the order to the others, hoping that they saw nothing but calmness in her face while her mind whirled like a tempest. She ensured everyone was presentable to walk to the palace and led the way.

When everyone had assembled in the receiving room, they knelt as one before the king. He'd changed outfits since the battle, but his clothing more resembled the military gear he'd worn the previous night than his usual embroidered layers and long sleeves. His face held no hint of anger, but it was present, subtly, like the change in the air that preceded a storm.

"Firstly, I would like to thank those of you who fought for me today," he said. "For many members of the flight division, this was the first time you fought as a squad, and I am sorry for the losses you suffered in defence of Laria. It is due to your efforts that many foes are no longer a threat to the crown, and for that, you have my gratitude."

A faint, voiceless whisper arose in the background as he spoke, and a chill draped over her body like a cloak. *Here it comes.*

"However," he said. "Today's events have also made it clear to me that I have enemies far greater and more devious than I ever could have conceived, and one of those enemies is Yalet Herself."

When the king spoke the god of life's name, the whisper became loud enough that some of the other soldiers shifted on their feet or glanced around in search of the speaker.

Mekan is watching. Did that mean He was present in the entire palace or merely wherever the king walked?

"Yalet's followers committed a grave sin when they opposed us," said King Tharen. "It is clear that the Disciples of Life have never seen themselves as part of this nation nor as my subjects. For that reason, they are enemies of the crown, and it is our duty to bring them to justice using all means at our disposal."

His attention travelled along the front row, briefly lingering on each individual who'd witnessed the temple opening. When their eyes met, an unspoken message passed between them that Yala heard loud and clear. Mekan was the means by which he would achieve his vengeance upon Yalet, and Yala would wield His blade in her hands.

"To that end," said the monarch, "I will keep you updated on our strategies to ensure the security of Laria and the end of the Disciples' threat. You are dismissed."

Yala expected—hoped—that he would take her aside as he had before, but he did not. She wasn't to be singled out. Perhaps she'd lost that chance now that he'd brought the other captains into the fold, but the odds of slaughtering him inside the palace had been weighted against her even before he'd opened Mekan's domain.

No, she'd have to wait for their next mission. Until then, Yala would hone her patience like a sharpened blade and hope that she wouldn't have to shed the blood of any more of her comrades before then.

———

With the Disciples of the Sea on their way to safety, Kelan and his allies parted ways with Niema and Hachim and began the long journey to Skytower. At Niema's suggestion, they took Molin so that they would have a means of reaching her at the location the elite Disciples next chose, and the tree-raptor's antics kept them entertained throughout the day. Watching him diving into the sea to grab fish and chasing birds lifted the general mood of solemnity that had persisted since the battle. They might have won, but the cost had been great, and the king doubtless had them marked as the enemy alongside the Disciples of Life.

After retracing their flight path along Laria's northern coast, they cut southward to avoid the roads out of the capital and used Molin's scouting to track Lakiel and Brikel to an inn at a crossroads.

Kelan's heart lifted when he heard Brikel's raised voice as he climbed the stairs to the upper floor. "Lakiel, can you get out of my personal space?"

"Brikel." Kelan glided to a halt at a half-open door, through which he could see Brikel propped up in a bed while her brother hovered over her like an anxious raptor over their young. "I'm glad you're all right."

Lakiel scowled. "You're still alive, then?"

"Apparently so." Kelan glided to the bed. Brikel looked better, her foot bandaged and in a proper splint now. "Did your brother carry you all the way here instead of taking you to a healer?"

"I *did* find a healer," Lakiel said. "We came this far because I was certain that you'd follow us with half the army on your tail and get my sister killed for real this time."

"Oh, fuck off," Brikel said. "Kelan was helping save people's lives, unlike some. Did the Disciples of the Sea get away?"

"All the refugees sheltering on the ship made it to safety."

Those who'd stayed to fight had not been so fortunate, but he didn't want to revisit the details, and mentioning Rafragoria's involvement would invite even more disapproval on Lakiel's part.

"And where will the army go next?" he enquired. "Because it seems that there are two options. Either they hunt down the surviving Disciples of the Sea and make your efforts pointless, or else they'll come after the one temple they haven't already conquered."

Skytower. Kelan feared the same, but he didn't believe that leaving the Disciples of the Sea to their doom would have done anything other than postpone their own fates. "Yes, and I'm starting to worry that you'll be first in line to kneel before the king when the army does show up."

Lakiel's fist shot out and struck Kelan on the jaw. Pain rang through his skull; he staggered, catching his balance against the wall.

"Lakiel!" Brikel said, appalled.

"He deserved it," said Lakiel, stalking out of the room.

"I probably did deserve that." Kelan rubbed his jaw and smiled at Brikel, who half-heartedly smiled back. "But capitulation will do us no favours. I saw firsthand how caving to the king's demands did nothing to help the Disciples of the Flame."

"Exactly. Sorry my brother was such a prick," she said, propping herself up on her elbows. "It's only a broken ankle. Doesn't stop me from flying."

"Yes, but I'm the one who got you into that situation." He lowered his voice. "And we both knew what your brother would say if you got hurt."

"He's too stubborn to admit you were right," she said. "I don't believe the king was ever going to stop with the Disciples of the Sea. We're the last holdouts except for the Disciples of Life."

Exactly. The question remained of which the king would target first, assuming he didn't know precisely which Disciple had thwarted him. If he did... well, Yala's request that Niema should finish off the king with her own hands might be put to the test. Though he couldn't help wondering what she'd been thinking. Yala must have known it was ridiculous to ask someone who'd never lifted a weapon in her own defence to commit murder, justified or not.

Lakiel's foul mood lingered like a heavy cloud as they left the inn the following morning. Between that and the more frequent detours they had to take to avoid soldiers on the road, Kelan was relieved when they finally came within view of Skytower. Despite its remote location, the stone construction stood out in a manner that seemed more exposed when he considered the new target on their backs, and he kept both eyes open for war drakes and their less pleasant cousins as they flew up to the topmost level.

Kelan rapped on the Superior's door, and they entered her office. In the late hour, Superior Sietra's clothing was plainer than her daily attire, and the gold paint usually daubed on her cheeks was no longer present.

"I am glad to see you all," she said. "Your last report was concerning enough that I readied a second team to send to the capital if necessary. Did you manage to aid the Disciples of the Sea?"

"Some of them." Kelan launched into an account of the mission, aided by the others who'd been present. Lakiel had not been there for most of it, but reaction to Rafragoria's involvement was as Kelan had expected.

"Does that not prove how ridiculous this endeavour was?" Lakiel said. "Did the Disciples of the Sea expect anything other than slaughter after allying with our enemies?"

"Rafragoria isn't responsible for opening a Temple of

Death in Laria's capital," Kelan retorted. "Our own monarch did that himself."

"Yes." The Superior's mouth pinched at the corners. "Given that, I cannot ask you to return to the city. We shall have to rely on guesswork to discern the king's next move."

In other words, there would be no more secret visits to Yala at the palace. Kelan had expected as much, and he already had a strong idea of what the king's intentions were. "The king desires the submission of all Disciples to the throne. Since we're the sole temple that isn't currently under the king's watch, there's a high chance we'll get a spate of unwelcome visitors, and soon."

"Yes." The Superior paused, and a current of tension rippled down his spine. They both knew from which direction those visitors would come. "Thank you for your report. You can all leave... aside from you, Kelan."

Doubtless she wanted to discuss Yala's involvement in the battle, as his account had barely alluded to her involvement, but it wasn't Yala whose secret he'd held back to avoid further complicating an already messy account. None of his fellow Disciples of the Sky knew of Niema's unique ability to command Mekan's creatures. He'd never had cause to mention it in his reports until now, and given the Superior's initial reaction to Yala's status as a Disciple of Death, he'd been reticent to share that Niema held a link to Mekan too.

"Yala Palathar was present at the battle," Superior Sietra said. "I would guess from your report that she did not succeed in confronting the king."

"Her plan fell apart when he opened the Temple of Death," he explained. "He summoned four more void drakes in addition to the monsters that attacked us at sea. She couldn't get close."

"I see." The moment of hesitation after her reply suggested she wondered if there was more to the story than he'd let on. "Should he send the entire flight division to Skytower, Yala will be set against us by necessity. We'd have to see her as the enemy or risk our own destruction."

Kelan's response was immediate. "If it comes to it, she'll fight against him."

"Can you be certain of that?" Her searching gaze saw through to the worry he'd been trying to suppress. Frankly, he *didn't* know how far Yala would go to keep up the ruse nor what lines she might cross to cover her tracks. "Whatever Yala decides, your orders are to defend Skytower and defend your Superior. That order supersedes all else. Do you understand that?"

In the end, there was only one answer. "I will," he said. "I'll defend Skytower first. With my life."

And he hoped, with the faith he'd invested in Terethik, that it wasn't a lie.

———

Niema and Hachim journeyed with the Disciples of the Sea to the village, following Ragem's directions. After the horrors they'd witnessed during the battle, interacting with the people they'd rescued brought a reminder that their actions hadn't been for naught.

She soon befriended Ornel, a friendly woman with two young children who reminded her of Threl and Diaman in a way that made Niema's chest ache. She told Ornel of the enclave, sharing memories of the world she'd left behind.

"It seems such a strange thing for you to be so fully connected to others," she remarked when Niema had explained the bond with her enclave members. "And terrible, I am sure, to be apart."

"It is." She felt their absence more acutely when she was in the company of the Disciples of the Sea, who might not be bound to one another in a similar manner but had nevertheless grown closer following the great hardships they'd suffered together. "But I do have Hachim with me."

"Of course." Ornel smiled, one brow quirking. "Are you lovers too?"

Heat seared Niema's neck. "No. That's not how it works. We aren't…"

"No matter." She smiled then, amused by Niema's embarrassment. It wasn't true that she'd never considered the matter. Disciples of Life had no restrictions when it came to relationships, and children were vital to the survival of the enclave, but they worked under the understanding that Yalet was their priority, and no mortal lover was ever ranked above either in the physical sense or in their emotional bond.

But seeing the other Disciples violate the command not to kill had loosened her grasp on her own certainty that Yalet's will was knowable to her at all.

Soon, she was to swear her vows fully. Word came from the Superior by way of a messenger with a note inviting them to meet with her near the village. An unusual choice, but perhaps she worried they might be pursued by the king's soldiers… or the dead.

An unwelcome thought nudged at her mind: that the Superior wanted to ensure that Niema had not unintentionally brought Mekan's followers upon another enclave in addition to the refugees.

It seemed the other elite Disciples of Life would be heading in that direction next after all, as they, too, gathered near Superior Kralia on a rocky outcrop further down the coast. Niema's chest ached with a familiar blend of emotions upon seeing her Superior, relief and sadness warring with dread and anticipation at what the next part of swearing her vows as an elite Disciple might entail.

When her war drake landed, she climbed from its back

and bowed her forehead to the ground. Next to her, Hachim did likewise.

"The mission, I'm given to understand, was a success," said Superior Kralia. "And you rescued the Disciples of the Sea."

"They're at the village," Niema said. "Are you here to visit the other enclave?"

"No." Superior Kralia gave Niema a searching look. "We are here to escort the newest members of Yalet's elite ranks to be fully inducted."

Was that doubt Niema heard in her voice, uncertainty that Niema would be able to swear the vows as needed? She could only assume that Ragem had given a full report of the events of the battle, including Niema's refusal to kill. Heart racing, she asked, "Where are we going?"

"Yalet's heart," said the Superior. "It is there that you will swear your vows to join Her elite."

"Yalet's heart?" she echoed.

"The island of Yaletar," said Superior Kralia. "The sole temple dedicated to the Disciples of Life."

Niema felt Hachim's shock reverberate through their bond, mingling with her own. Neither of them had thought Yalet had any need for temples at all, though if recent events had proved anything, it was that Niema had large gaps in her understanding of the deity to whom she'd pledged her life.

A rush of dread overcame her. She'd already seen Mekan's power infiltrate the forest, drawn by her connection to the god of death. If Niema travelled to Yalet's most sacred place, in the heart of Her domain, how could she trust that she wouldn't bring Mekan with her?

26

Saren stormed away from the infirmary, blood seeping from his wrist from under his bandaged hand. His first attempt to climb on a war drake had ended as well as he'd expected—namely, with its teeth embedded in his knuckles and all the other beasts stirred into a frenzy. That prick Gorel lecturing him about the right way to handle a war drake—as if a child had a fucking clue—pushed his temper over the edge. Under his breath, he cursed Yala, cursed the king, cursed the whole army and the fucking country along with it.

Someone snagged his arm as he stormed past. Nalen, wearing a scowl on his bearded face, hauled Saren into an alcove and hissed, "Quiet. The guards will hear you."

"I don't give a shit." Saren wrenched his arm free. "I bet you don't want to be here either."

"No," Nalen growled, "but since I *am* stuck here, I'm going to keep my mouth shut. I'd suggest you do the same."

"How's that worked out for you so far?"

Nalen's glare deepened. "You might notice that I'm still

breathing, and you won't be if you carry on as you are. Not least because Yala might feed you to the war drakes herself."

"Better than dying in service of the king." He waved his newly bandaged hand. "As for Yala, you can see how well her plan to handle *him* has worked out. He was supposed to be a bleeding corpse by now."

"Yes," Nalen ground out. "She never told me the details of her plan, mind, but I'm guessing those void drakes showing up wasn't part of it."

"Don't remind me." Did Nalen even know of the Temple of Death? Perhaps he didn't, given that the flight division's captains were the only soldiers who'd been invited to the opening ceremony. Saren was not in the mood to revisit that horrifying night, so he continued with a shrug. "Whatever her plan, Yala failed, and we all overestimated her."

"We?" Nalen echoed. "Some of us already knew when the king's soldiers showed up in the Undercity that there was never any saviour looking out for us."

"Saviour." Saren gave a bitter laugh. "You know, I fought under Yala for years. She has this way of making you think she can topple mountains and raise oceans, doesn't she? But it's a fucking joke. She's as powerless as the rest of us, and we're all going to die in a war we didn't choose."

"Wasn't that what we signed up for back then too?" said Nalen. "This isn't anything new."

Nalen's words struck Saren to the core. When he'd initially joined the army, he'd *thought* their king had good reason for any war he pursued. Yes, he'd had doubts, had occasionally wondered if the people they were killing were any more in the wrong than they were. But he'd trusted Yala and would have been glad to die fighting at her side.

The past few years—tormented with nightmares though they might have been—had shown him a tantalising glimpse of another life. The time he'd spent with Giran, he'd been just as fucked up, no lie, but now, without alcohol clouding his mind, he regretted that he hadn't truly appreciated the freedom.

"Maybe we did," Saren said, "but now we've seen what it looks like on the outside. I don't know about you, but I'm not keen on dying in service to someone who thinks he's Mekan's chosen."

He'd spoken carelessly, forgetting that Nalen hadn't been present at the king's address to the flight division the previous day. In fairness, neither had Saren himself, and he'd learned the details through the whispered accounts shared among the other squad members.

"No." A shudder passed through Nalen. "I heard about the drakeshit he was spewing yesterday. Fuck, maybe he *is* Mekan's chosen, but I'm starting to think the soldiers who tried to desert chose the easy way out."

The ones the monsters killed. A spasm of fear travelled up Saren's spine, and he was doubly glad of the walls between them and the king's terrifying new security guards. "Did anyone try to walk out while the king was away?"

"A few." A spark appeared in Nalen's eyes. "You know, I was thinking that it's a shame we didn't *all* try to walk out when the entire flight division was off fighting at sea. I bet the guards couldn't have held us back without him or those winged monsters around."

"I hope that's a joke." Admittedly, the flight division was the army's biggest asset, and with a fair proportion of the foot soldiers made up of reluctant recruits who'd been dragged here against their will—he cut the thought off there. "He has a Temple of Death inside the palace now, so it's probably for the best that you didn't."

"Hmm." Nalen wore a calculating expression. "The king'll have a hard time killing *all* of us without hobbling his own forces. Maybe next time, we'll do it."

"You've lost your mind." The trouble was, the idea was tempting and a lot more tangible than any plan Yala might have concocted since her last failure. "I'll be with the flight division. No way out for me."

"Right." Nalen's brow furrowed in thought. "That friend of yours. The one who hid you."

"Viam. What of her?"

"Wasn't she friends with the prince?" His calculating expression returned. "The king won't take him on the next mission. Maybe we can take him hostage. He won't dare use that temple against us if we do."

"Hostage?" Saren took a step back. "That won't work. The prince never wanted his father to return to power, and for all we know, he'd be happy to walk out of here with the rest of you."

"Will he?" Nalen tilted his head. "If we get the heir on our side, that might be even better. Your friend can talk to him?"

Saren groaned. "She'll kill me for suggesting it."

But if anyone might stand a chance of talking some sense into the monarch, the king's flesh and blood might.

"It's worth a try," Nalen pressed. "Better than surrender, wouldn't you say?"

"Yeah." He exhaled. "Fuck it. I'm in."

———

The Disciples of Life opted to set up camp on the cliffs and fly to Yalet's domain the next morning. When the others settled down for the night, Niema approached her Superior alone.

"Superior Kralia," she murmured. "I don't think it's a good idea for me to set foot in Yalet's temple."

"What would make you say that?"

"What if my presence brings Mekan into the heart of

Yalet's domain?" She'd hoped the fear would grow smaller in the speaking, not larger, but panic swelled inside her chest, and rational thoughts threatened to flee. "I already brought disaster upon the enclave, didn't I?"

"Mekan cannot venture within Yalet's home," said the Superior. "Did you not believe I would have considered the possible ramifications of your unique condition?"

Condition. More like a curse.

"Ragem tells me that you sent the king's dead beasts away, breaking his control over his own army," she added. "That factored into my decision too."

"I was only able to do that because of Mekan, not Yalet." The words tasted of copper with the memory of the blood shed on the battlefield in Yalet's name. "I'm not trying to argue, but I worry that Mekan will use our—our connection, whatever it is we have, against Yalet."

"Yalet *chose* you." Her sharp words pierced straight to Niema's core. "Even when I did not trust you myself. Have you forgotten so easily?"

No. She had not, and that knowledge calmed the turbulence in her mind. Trust aside, Yalet would never allow Mekan into Her temple. If She held any doubts, She would surely turn Niema away.

"No," she whispered. "I... thank you, Superior."

That the Superior had more faith in Niema than she did in herself only underscored how much recent events had changed them both. She returned to her sleeping mat, to Hachim's comforting arms.

Thanks to Ornel's curious questions, she couldn't help looking at Hachim in a new light, wondering if his gentle smile concealed something else. Of course, any outsider would misunderstand their closeness, and Niema had never had reason to think of Hachim as anything other than what he was: a friend and an enclave member bound to her, heart and soul. If he noticed anything different about her behaviour, he didn't say, though when she woke at dawn, she found him watching her, too, his eyes half lidded, his soft lips parted.

Warmth pooled inside her when their eyes met, and a frisson of heat travelled through their bond, swiftly dissipating when he spoke. "Couldn't sleep. Sorry I woke you."

"No need." She pushed into a sitting position, glad of the shady trees to hide her blush. "We should say goodbye to the Disciples of the Sea. Let them know we're leaving."

After breakfast, Niema flew to the ship docked against the cliffs near the village. She found Superior Kralia already there, to her surprise, conversing with Nanek from her perch atop the cliffs overlooking the sea.

"You would leave us here, vulnerable to attack, or force us to walk into a hostile forest?" said Nanek. "Is that what you state?"

"I merely offered you the option of hiding on land should you choose to do so," said the Superior. "I'm afraid you may follow us no longer. We are going to a sacred place reserved for Yalet's chosen alone."

Niema's heart sank. Nanek's mistrust was justified—he'd watched his people slaughtered not three days prior—but needless conflict was the last thing the others needed.

"The forest will not harm you," the Superior added. "And no enemies will find you here. This coast has always been untouched by the king's armies, past or present."

That did seem to be the case. Niema had sometimes wondered why no Larian monarch had ever conquered the forests on the country's eastern edge, but given the Superior's recent revelation that Yalet's heart lay somewhere nearby, it was entirely possible that her ancestors had got there first.

Nanek's mouth thinned. "I will choose to trust your word

for the sake of my people. You have my gratitude for your assistance in aiding our escape too." He nodded to Niema and Hachim, who flew lower to speak to the others on the ship.

Ornel was there, and her two children waved up at Niema with bright smiles that made her eyes sting with tears. *Please, keep them safe, Yalet.*

"Have a safe journey," Ornel called to Niema. "Both of you."

Niema smiled and lifted her hand in farewell.

Their journey continued down the coastline, following rugged cliffs topped with dense greenery and sandy beaches merging with pristine ocean. Not a soul disturbed their path, nor did any trace of Mekan stir. Niema sensed only Yalet, the unbroken forest bursting with life.

When they veered away from the shore, Niema's thoughts turned to their destination. Her limited knowledge of geography had told her nothing at all lay to the east or south of Laria save for uninhabited ocean. While everyone knew Rafragoria lay to the north and the Parvan Empire beyond that, no king or emperor had ever mapped out this region.

She thought the island a mirage at first, a shimmering above the ocean's surface. A sharp inhalation from Hachim indicated he'd seen it too, and each beat of their war drake's wings revealed more of its forested edges until she had no doubt as to what they approached.

Yalet's domain. Her temple.

The god of life's presence hit her like an inhalation of breath after near-drowning, filling her lungs, her blood, her soul. Her mind cleared like a cloud had been lifted from above her head that she hadn't even known was there, and for the first time in a long while, she found herself smiling. "We're home."

The Superior landed upon the beach at the island's edge.

The others followed suit, climbing off their mounts. Together, they climbed the sandy bank and ducked beneath the cover of the trees, and after a short walk, they came to a clearing.

Trees encircled them, their towering trunks emitting a glow that bathed everything in glimmering white. At the front, one vast tree stood apart from the others, its thick branches reaching up to the heavens. Carvings stood out upon its surface but not etched with the brutality she associated with manmade tools. Rather, the images appeared to have grown *out* of the tree, taking the form of a serpentine figure entwined with the bark.

Yalet. Niema had never seen her god depicted so, but there was no doubt as to whom the figure represented. *It's Her.*

The Superior leaned down beside the tree and spoke in a low murmur. "Yalet is listening to us."

"I never—" Niema choked off, overcome by emotion. "I never imagined such a place existed."

"Yes," said the Superior. "Unlike the other Disciples, we usually have no need of material structures to reach our god. However, it is this island that was settled by the first Disciples of Life who ever set foot on the continent we now call Laria."

Niema's heart quivered. How long ago had that been? Centuries, perhaps, before even King Larial's time. Her ancestors had no written records, or so she'd thought, but the clearing was heavy with memory, and when she looked more closely at the trees, she glimpsed more carvings upon the bark, images etched by human hands.

"The trees remembered even as humans forgot," the Superior went on. "While the details have been lost to time, we do know that our people were first to reach these shores, and our foes arrived shortly after."

"Mekan's followers." The name brought a flash of fear, a break in the awed calm that had settled inside her since they'd come within sight of the island. "They had temples too."

"With Yalet's aid, we won the war between our deities," said Superior Kralia. "However, the price we paid was steep. Our numbers were heavily reduced, and the result was that when King Larial and his companions arrived some centuries later, they easily outnumbered us. They brought their own Disciples to settle the continent, and the rest of his story is widely known, if vastly distorted by myth."

"The war." Niema's thoughts tumbled. "The Disciples of Death were destroyed? Including the ones who lived near their temple, on the island?"

"Yes," Superior Kralia murmured. "As I said, we forgot too much, and the temple was left abandoned but not destroyed. It is that error for which we now pay the price."

"Because the king found records from outside the continent." Movement in the corner of her eye reminded her the other Disciples of Life were present, some watching the Superior in shock as if this was news to them too.

"Correct." The Superior raised her voice to address their collective. "It is here that I received the initial vision from Yalet warning me of Mekan's return. She will guide us."

A murmur of agreement followed, and the Superior continued. "Here, the new elite Disciples will swear themselves to serve Yalet to the utmost."

Niema and Hachim both stepped forward. Their companions had spoken so little to her that it came as a surprise when five or more of them separated from the others, including Bitra. The light streaming from the trees brightened, bathing them in vibrancy.

"Niema, you will go first."

Niema's heart hammered against her ribs as she moved in

front of the tree, while the others withdrew, offering her space.

"Kneel," said the Superior. "Today, you swear your loyalty to Yalet."

Niema knelt before the great tree, pressed her forehead to the earth. She whispered to Yalet, repeating her Superior's words.

As white light filled her vision, blazing bright, Yalet answered her.

————

If you ask me, Kelan thought as he completed yet another circuit of Skytower to check for any gaps through which a soldier might enter, *We'd be better off hanging a banner of welcome from the rooftop when the king's army shows up rather than trying to repel them.*

Skytower was not a construction built with defence in mind, as its remote location ensured most potential enemies perished long before reaching its wide balconies and high windows. With only the novices' quarters connected by a staircase, all the full-fledged Disciples had to fly up and down the tower to access any of the rooms, with the result that most areas were entirely exposed.

With Disciples in the tower playing a part, spreading across every possible entry to watch for intruders, a rota was set up to shuffle everyone across different locations every few hours so that the same unlucky individuals weren't stuck guarding the latrine chutes for long stretches at a time. The Superior's office had gained a rotating security guard shift of its own. Kelan volunteered to join, but the third time he mistook a bird for an approaching war drake and came within a whisker of raising the alarm, his Superior beckoned to him from behind the large back window behind the desk where she worked.

"I would advise you to swap shifts with someone less distractable," she said when he entered the office. "It'll do no good if an enemy was to slip past while you're looking the other way."

He flushed. "My apologies."

"Go downstairs instead," she ordered. "Join the Disciples waiting to greet our visitors when they arrive."

"Are you sure?" She wanted him to talk to the king's soldiers? Aside from the chance that they'd recognise him from their last mission, his track record with diplomatic missions did not inspire confidence.

"Should the negotiations turn sour, you'll be needed."

Kelan might have been flattered at the compliment, but her seeming confidence that any interaction with the soldiers was likely to turn to violence disarmed him. "Will they?"

"They might." The merest twitch of her hand drew Kelan's eyes to a blade sheathed to the side of her chair. While it was by no means unusual for Superiors to arm themselves, even her clothing had changed to something more suited to combat. In addition to the absence of the paint she usually daubed on her face, she'd forsaken some of her more ostentatious outerwear, favouring lighter clothing without any heavy embroidery. "I will not allow Skytower to fall the same way the Temples of the Earth and Sea did."

"There's one thing we have that they didn't," he said. "To my knowledge, none of our people are actively working with Mekan from the inside."

Kelan had expected an unequivocal agreement on her part, but a moment lapsed before she spoke. "To my knowledge as well, that is the case. However, if the king sends his

257

entire flight division against us as he did the Disciples of the Sea, the losses will be catastrophic."

"Not if we take out their messengers first," said Kelan. "He won't send the whole army. We can ensure whoever he does send never makes it back to the palace."

"I would prefer to resolve this without violence, at least as a first measure."

"So would I, but we both know they're going to mount an all-out attack when we refuse the king's offer." He blamed the time he'd spent with Yala for how quickly he'd jumped to the most violent response, but the king had not shown any mercy to the Disciples of the Sea. The instant they'd tried to defend themselves, he'd withdrawn any attempt to coax them to surrender. And the Superior's implied admission that someone *might* betray them from within the tower had left him rattled.

"Now…" She gestured to the window. Molin sat on the ledge and hopped onto the desk when he saw Kelan. "I have another job for you."

"Does that involve sending a message to the Disciples of Life?" he guessed. "I imagine Superior Kralia will have already concluded that we're likely to be the next targets for a visit from the king's forces."

"Precisely," said the Superior. "I believe your friend Niema will be concerned too."

"You want me to appeal directly to her, not her Superior." While she might feel an obligation to help, her fellow Disciples would not necessarily agree. He'd gathered it had taken a great deal of persuasion to bring them into the fight to defend the Disciples of the Sea.

Of course, Niema possessed an advantage they didn't. Her ability to control Mekan's beasts was the one factor that the king hadn't been able to predict.

Guilt lanced through him. Keeping Niema's secret from

the other Disciples was one thing, but his Superior deserved the truth, and he had no good reason for his reticence to share that information save for wariness born of her previous attempt to imprison Yala as a Disciple of Death. His Superior didn't always make the right choices and was as fallible as anyone else, but the same could be said for himself. He had to tell her.

He opened his mouth to speak—and a shout came from outside. Prompted by a nod from his Superior, he opened the door and darted out onto the front platform. The other Disciples closed ranks around her office door as winged beasts bearing armed riders flew towards the tower in a familiar formation. Seven of them. A full flight squad.

Please, Terethik, don't let it be Yala's.

The squad angled their path towards the large platform at the foot of the tower, the only space wide enough to accommodate seven war drakes. Kelan stepped off the tower's edge and glided downward to join the other Disciples assigned to greet any incoming visitors. When he landed beside Lakiel, his fellow Disciple flashed a disgruntled look in his direction before turning back to face the flight squad.

Kelan was relieved to recognise none of their faces. The soldier upon the frontmost war drake was maybe in her mid-twenties, clad in the drakeskin armour common to soldiers, and she held a sharp spear in one gloved hand. Her companions also did not look to have come for a friendly overture, and their war drakes growled a warning at the gathering Disciples as they landed.

Since nobody else was inclined to break the awkward silence, Kelan offered her a smile. "Can we help you?"

"We are here to speak to your Superior," she said. "I am Captain Veshan, and I bring a message from the king."

"We'll gladly pass it on to her," he said. "Our Superior is not taking visitors."

"The message is for her ears only." Veshan lifted her chin. "You will lead us to her, Disciple."

The Disciples bristled at the disrespect, but Kelan found himself more amused by her than anything else. "I'm afraid there are no stairs, and we can't let that beast of yours anywhere near the Superior. Would you like me to carry you?"

Veshan's mouth twisted in annoyance.

He suppressed a grin, unable to resist needling someone so obviously in need of knocking from her pedestal.

Lakiel tutted under his breath but didn't otherwise react.

"I will not place my safety in your hands," said the captain. "Nor will I part ways with my steed."

"I can assure you that we intend no harm provided you can say the same." He looked pointedly at the spear in her hand. "You'll give one of us the message, or you will leave."

"Fine." Veshan's voice vibrated with suppressed rage. "His Majesty the King has asked for the cooperation of all Disciples in the nation of Laria. All Superiors are to pledge their support for him, or else they are to be declared enemies of the crown."

Not holding back, then, is he? "And what is his goal in this? To make enemies of those who carry the power of the gods at their disposal?"

Lakiel cleared his throat. "What Kelan means to say is that nothing we have done has provoked this intrusion."

"On the contrary," she said, "many of you were seen helping a group of known traitors escape the king's justice. He has generously offered you the chance to redeem yourselves if you agree to stand beside the throne against his enemies."

"Which enemies are those?" Kelan asked. "If you mean Rafragoria, I'm afraid there are some centuries-old peace agreements that we would be in violation of should we accept his offer."

"Kelan is correct." The voice came from above as a strong gust of wind swept down that sent the war drakes into panicked flight.

The soldiers exclaimed, struggling to regain control over their mounts, while even the Disciples stared openly at the figure descending together with an ornate chair that hovered beneath her like a throne.

"I believe I am the one you want to speak to," Superior Sietra said to the startled soldiers. "Well?"

Veshan gave her war drake a jab with her spear's blunt end and growled a command in its ear. When its feet touched down on the platform again, she lifted her head and spoke clearly. "Superior Sietra, it is an honour to meet you."

The polite words rang as false as the Superior's reply. "I am pleased to welcome you to Skytower. I hear you have a message for me?"

"Yes." Veshan waited for the rest of her squad to land, their formation knocked askew by their beasts' wariness of the new arrival. "King Tharen sent us with a request that your Disciples pledge themselves to the throne in alliance against his enemies."

"My Disciples have already told you why that isn't possible," she said. "We form no alliances except with each other, as is laid out in the laws established at the founding of our nation. Unless King Tharen intends to revoke those laws?"

A collective gasp travelled through the other soldiers, but Veshan was unfazed. "It is in the interests of his safety that the king offers his request. He was exiled from the nation by the Disciples and thus has reason to mistrust you, but he has generously chosen to offer the hand of forgiveness."

"There is naught to forgive, as myself and my fellow Disciples had no knowledge of Superior Datriem's schemes," said the Superior. "We did not participate in the monarch's exile, and we will not pledge ourselves to anyone but our god."

"You refuse?" The captain spoke haltingly as if only now grasping the magnitude of who she was speaking to. While she had the full backing of the throne, the Superior had proven she could dispose of the entire squad with little effort, long before they took word back to the king.

"Correct," said the Superior. "I would ask you to take my response to King Tharen and remind him that the Disciples have always been a force apart from the throne."

"Times are changing," Veshan said. "We will respect your choice, but in your refusal, you forfeit the right to protect those who already stood against us. Some of your people aided in the escape of traitors to the crown and inflicted violence upon the king's soldiers. I would request that those Disciples are surrendered to the king to punish as he sees fit."

"No." Ice dripped from the Superior's voice. "I will not surrender any of my Disciples, and I will utilise all my force against any who oppose them."

Veshan stared at her. Then, her mouth thinned into a line. "So be it. King Tharen will see to it that you regret your decision."

For a heartbeat, Kelan expected the tightly clutched spear to leave her hand and violence to break out, but the captain took flight in a beat of her war drake's wings. Her squad followed suit, departing as efficiently as they'd arrived.

"Well," he said. "The king doesn't waste any time, does he?"

Images exploded into Niema's mind. She saw a forest consumed by darkness, shadows spreading among the trees like flames and leaving death in their wake. Every tree the darkness touched withered and decayed, every plant turned to dust, and birds fell out of the sky, their song eternally stifled. The losses hit her like a series of blows to the chest, leaving her breathless and shaking.

"Stop," she whispered. "Yalet, how do I stop this?"

No reply. The terrible scenes continued to play out. As her vision expanded, she saw Disciples of Life fighting back with their hands aglow, but they were like candle flames in a vast, endless cave. Before her eyes, a young Disciple of Life fell apart. Her body decayed—desiccated skin peeling off, muscles withering from bone—but before she hit the ground, she began to rise, shadows crawling beneath her skin and moving her worn limbs...

"*STOP!*" Niema screamed.

The vision cracked like glass, and Niema came to herself on her knees before the great tree dominating the Temple of Life. Her breaths came quickly, her heart pounding, body slick with sweat. Green light bathed her skin, washing away the vision, but its taint lingered. Lifting her head, she saw Superior Kralia standing beside her.

"Did I see the future?" Niema staggered upright on unsteady feet. "That's not possible, is it?"

"No." Superior Kralia paused. "Anything you saw was either in the present or earlier, more likely the recent past."

"It was real?" She hadn't recognised the forest in its decaying state nor the Disciple who'd died, but knowing the truth of her death brought a renewed wave of horror crashing over her. She sagged, her knees bowed, and noticed belatedly that the other Disciples had departed the clearing. They'd left her alone with Yalet... and with the terrible vision she had imparted. "How do you know for certain?"

"Because I saw it too." Superior Kralia indicated another much smaller tree that stood perhaps a handspan taller than Niema herself and was blanketed by thick moss and greenery. Thick, stumpy vines dangled at its sides, and its trunk appeared split into two halves at the base. *Wait... that isn't a tree.*

Niema peered closer then recoiled. "Is that a *person?*"

She'd thought it might be a statue for a heartbeat—its overgrown state aside, it was too oddly shaped to be a natural creation—but the eyes gleaming within the greenery were too bright, too real.

"This is the individual who witnessed the scene we both saw." Superior Kralia lifted a palm aglow with soft green light that bathed the figure in vibrancy, banishing any lingering doubts that it had been a living and breathing woman. "A Superior who gave her life in service of her people and Yalet."

"She was a Superior?" Niema was reminded of the manner in which the Disciples of the Earth had rendered their prior leaders in stone so that part of them would always be preserved inside their temple. "She died here?"

"Yes," said Superior Kralia. "She was wounded when she arrived on the island, and her final act was the same as every other Superior's. All of us give our lives back to Yalet in the end."

Chills pricked at Niema's skin. While the sight of her body had been unnerving at first, the Superior had found peace when she'd become part of the forest, with Yalet Herself. Niema might not be that lucky.

She let her attention drift to Superior Kralia, questions bubbling up inside. "Did you know that I'd see that vision?"

"No," said the Superior. "I expected you might, and it is proof that Yalet accepted your vows."

The words should have filled Niema with relief, but the chill lingered beneath her skin despite the renewed warmth of Yalet's light. "Does everyone see a vision like that?"

"Some do," she said. "Some do not. I am not surprised that you did, as you were unusual in that you experienced your first vision so far away from here."

Her first vision, the Superior had taken as proof of her suitability to be tasked with finding the one whom Superior Kralia had believed would save them all. This one, however, brought only dread, and its spectre clung to her thoughts like miasma.

"The death of a Superior is a terrible crime," said Superior Kralia. "She is the third to be killed in recent weeks."

"Three?" Niema gasped. "How?"

"Two were taken by surprise," said Superior Kralia. "The third sought out a site where Mekan's forces had already attacked, believing that a direct assault would be their only hope of driving the enemy from the forest. All of her Disciples were slaughtered, and with three of our leaders gone, only four of us remain."

EMMA L. ADAMS

"Four Superiors." More than any other branch of Disciples, but the thought of someone who'd once held the same power as Superior Kralia so thwarted made her bones quake under her skin. "Including you."

"Unlike the other Disciples, we do not have restrictions on how many may serve as our leaders," she said. "The choice is with Yalet, but She has yet to choose replacements for any of the fallen. It is my belief that the god of life will not divide Her power if it means taking any from the rest of us."

Niema's mouth parted. "Is that how it works? You share power? Does that make you—?"

She couldn't finish that sentence with *weaker,* a word that hardly seemed fitting to describe the most powerful person Niema knew. Moreover, strength had never been the goal of a Superior, as Yalet's true power lay in fuelling new life rather than inflicting death.

"Yes," said the Superior, as if she'd heard the word Niema hadn't been able to bring herself to speak. "All of us have decided to prepare a successor to step in if need be."

The implication was clear. "You can't die."

"Death is no terrible thing," said Superior Kralia. "True death, not the abomination that Mekan would call by that name. True death is not oblivion but renewal, and the only way to become one with Yalet is to offer every part of oneself. It is our fate and our honour."

Honour or not, her death would leave her enclave without a leader, with nobody to protect them from Mekan's army. "You want to train a successor?"

Not me. She can't mean me. At one time, the thought would simply never have entered her mind, yet she'd seen into Yalet's heart in a way that few others had.

"It might have been you." Superior Kralia's words struck like glass shards, lodged into Niema's heart.

Tears pricked her eyes and then fell. "If not for my link to

266

Mekan," she whispered, tasting salt on her lips. "I don't know why Yalet showed me that vision. I wish She could talk to me, if just to tell me if there have been others."

In those long-ago days of Niema's ancestors, in which Mekan's followers had infected the continent for the first time, had no Disciple of Life ever saved the life of a Disciple of Death, even unintentionally?

The Superior's expression showed a peculiar stillness, and she did not reply.

"Superior..." Niema paused. "There *have* been others? When? How? Please, tell me."

Superior Kralia held up her hand to silence her. "It is impossible to know specifics. I have studied every trace left upon this island by our predecessors, and some carvings seem to indicate that there were once those whose fates were tied to those of the gods of life and Corruption both."

Niema reeled. *I'm not the only one... but I am in any way that matters.* Who was to say what had been the eventual fate of those who'd become entangled with both gods? No carving on an ancient tree could indicate which god claimed those individuals upon death, Mekan or Yalet.

"Put it out of your mind," said the Superior. "Your task now is to act according to your new rank. You will have authority over any other Disciple you encounter save for those of the elite rank or higher."

"To do what?" Niema's sense of purpose, briefly restored by Yalet's acceptance, began to fray like a piece of old clothing. "I can't return to the enclave."

"No," said the Superior. "Instead, you will help me gather any Disciples who would volunteer to fight in Yalet's name. It is time for us to amass an army of our own."

The first attack on Skytower came in the middle of the night. Kelan woke from a fitful doze to a war drake's roar, followed by shouting and the sound of weapons being drawn. He hadn't been on official night duty but had opted to leave his door open and sleep fully clothed, with the result that the war drake's cry had him on his feet before he was entirely conscious. He grabbed his blade, whispering a prayer to the sky god as he conjured a wind current to carry him out of the room.

Spying the glint of a spear flying out of the darkness, he sent it harmlessly spinning out of reach. Its owner bore down on the tower, their war drake swiping at a Disciple of the Sky. Teeth crunched through bone, and the Disciple screamed.

With an oath, Kelan leapt in, driving his blade across the war drake's nose. The beast bellowed, its teeth snapping a fingerspan from Kelan's ankle as he darted out of the way.

"Cowardly of you to attack while we're sleeping," Kelan said to the rider, lifting his blade. "Was that the king's orders?"

The soldier threw a second spear in answer. Kelan whistled a prayer to Terethik, and the wind caught the spear and the war drake's wings. The soldier let out a hoarse shout as both he and his mount were flung away into the dark.

Kelan crouched beside the injured Disciple—his gorge rose when he saw the war drake's teeth had severed her arm at the elbow—and carried her out of harm's way. All around Skytower, others were raising the alarm, and discordant shouts rang up and down the corridors as the Disciples mobilised. One soldier already lay sprawled on the floor, blood and brain matter leaking from his cracked skull. With two squad members down, that left five unless one of their number or more had flown to the capital to report back to the king.

Kelan spied a third rising from the bottom floor and flew down to meet them. "Think you can change our minds by force?"

The soldier came at him, her spear at the ready. Kelan dodged effortlessly and conjured a blast of air that knocked her off her mount. The soldier vanished, her scream torn away on the wind. The war drake gave a half-hearted swipe at Kelan's leg but was plainly uninterested in fighting a tower full of armed Disciples. In a beat of its vast wings, it flew away into the night.

That's three of them... make that four, he amended, seeing a figure topple from the upper floor.

Then: *Shit. The Superior.*

As he began to ascend, there came a violent blast of air that shook the entire tower. Although his feet weren't on the ground, the concussive blast threw him backwards in midair. Head ringing, he righted himself, caught his balance.

The Disciples guarding the Superior's office had also been knocked aside by the blast. Kelan glided past and knocked on her door. "Superior!"

Air gusted outward, less forceful this time but enough to push the door open. Kelan entered, and a gasp tore from his mouth. The Superior sat upright in her usual chair despite the late hour, and someone lay prone in front of her, arms and legs askew as if dropped from a great height. Someone who wore the blue cloak of a Disciple.

"We did have a traitor in our midst," said Superior Sietra.

"How can that be?" Kelan looked closer and recognised the man as Tremin, a former friend of Laima's. Horror washed over him. Tremin had always been a violent lout—Kelan had been on the receiving end of his fists on one unpleasant occasion—but throwing his lot in with the god of death was a move Kelan couldn't comprehend.

Other Disciples entered, including Ranit, whose nose was

bleeding. They, too, gasped at the sight of one of their supposed allies lying sprawled on the ground.

"Have all the soldiers left the tower?" asked the Superior.

"They've gone," someone said from near the door. "Five dead, and the other two are missing. We're guessing they went to report to their king."

"Fucking cowards, attacking us in the night." Ranit shuffled beside Kelan, dabbing at his bleeding nose with a sleeve. "They must have planned to slaughter us in our sleep."

"They couldn't possibly have won." No, the attack was a diversion so that their insider could strike at the Superior while her guards were distracted. Had the Superior suspected? She hadn't allowed them to assign guards inside her rooms, but it wouldn't have made a difference if one of her protectors turned out to be allied with the enemy too.

"At a guess, that was a test run," the Superior agreed. "To see what we're capable of and to gauge our defences."

"They'll send more people next time." They'd been lucky not to lose a single Disciple despite the spate of injuries the war drakes had inflicted, but the beasts hadn't been interested in fighting a losing battle.

The dead, by contrast, would fight as long as Mekan demanded.

"Dispose of him." She directed Kelan's companions to pick up Tremin's body and carry it out of the room.

Kelan stayed put, his mind roiling. "Are you concerned that there might be others?" he asked the Superior. "I can ask some questions. Find out if anyone has been in contact with the palace."

"I doubt they'd admit anything, Kelan. You're known to have fought against Corruption too many times to be a confidant."

That was true enough, but gods, he couldn't live with

himself if he did nothing while traitors might walk in their midst. "What if they let the enemy into the tower?"

"They did, and we handled it." She sounded and looked tired, and it struck him how much older she appeared without her usual vibrant clothing and headgear. He wasn't sure of her age, but she was as much a part of Skytower as the stone itself. That someone had tried to kill her—even inexpertly—left him shaken to the core.

Gods. He had to tell her the truth.

"Superior..." Kelan licked his lips. "There's something I may have omitted from my report of the battle at sea."

She raised an eyebrow. "Is there?"

"Superior Kralia might not be pleased with me for revealing this," he hastened to add. "If she hasn't told you, she must have her reasons. The truth is, Niema is able to exert control over Mekan's beasts as well as living beings."

Her other brow lifted too. "She can control the dead?"

"Not the dead, but the beasts from the Void," he amended. "I don't know how it works, and I don't think it's something that even *she* understands. Superior Kralia believes it to be a side effect of her saving Yala's life."

"And that is how she sent away the king's army. I see."

He inclined his head. "The king had only five void drakes present. I don't know if her skills have a limit."

He'd sent Molin out with a message following the attack, but it would likely take a day or more for the tree-raptor to locate Niema, depending on how far she'd travelled since they'd parted ways.

"Nevertheless, I see why their presence at the battle was so vital," she said. "And why it is more important that they aid us in the same manner."

"I know." Guilt knotted inside him. "Niema's first loyalty is to protect her people, but she and the others came to help defend the Disciples of the Sea, and I believe they'll do the same for us."

The Superior inclined her head. "For all our sakes, Kelan, I hope you are right."

———

"They're dead." Saren joined the rest of the squad at the table in the mess hall with unconcealed smugness. "The Disciples wiped out Veshan's entire squad, I bet. Did His Majesty expect any less when he picked a fight with Skytower?"

Yala kicked him under the table. The rest of their squad was more subdued, not least due to their grieving their lost member, and while Saren's sour mood the previous day had been an annoyance, this was hardly an improvement. Her initial relief at her squad being spared from the king's order to demand a surrender from Skytower had long since faded into irritation at the lack of news, and with Kelan no longer in the capital, she'd lost all information from the other side of the wall.

"If he sends out a search party, who do you think he'll send?" Yurel jabbed a spoon into her dish of the tasteless gruel that passed for breakfast. "Us, most likely."

"Scraping bodies off the mountainside isn't the worst task he might put us to."

Yala kicked him again with her good leg, harder. Whatever had him in such a good mood, she didn't need him upsetting the rest of the squad even further. She'd had her hands full dealing with the others as it was. Gorel had taken Yala's reticence to mention their deceased squad member as proof of her deep grief, and the previous night, he'd even produced a prayer-candle from somewhere and said they should light it in Toreth's memory. Yala, of course, had immediately confiscated it on the grounds that the mere connection with the Disciples of the Flame might see the entire squad put to death.

Not that she'd *told* them that. They might have witnessed the king's ominous address the previous day, but as of yet, they did not know of the blood he'd shed in Mekan's name.

When they went out into the grounds, Saren's sharp eyes spotted the returning soldiers and a pair of war drakes approaching over the city wall. "Does that mean only two survived?"

"I'd say yes." Yala did not share his jubilance. If the squad had come out of the encounter with yet more losses, the king's retaliation would be swift and brutal. "I'm going to see if they need help."

Saren followed her, and his smirk morphed into a wide grin when they entered the paddock and found a bloodied female soldier attempting to strip her war drake of its harness. Captain Veshan had been among the group who'd attended the opening ceremony at the Temple of Death, but evidently, the king had not provided her with any extra advantages prior to sending her squad to Skytower. Her male companion sat slumped on the ground, blood seeping from a leg wound deep enough to expose the bone.

"Mission didn't go well?" Yala moved in to help her with the harness, and Veshan accepted with a nod of thanks. Her blood-matted hair clung to an ear half severed at the tip.

"The entire squad went down save for the two of us," she rasped. "We flew through the night to get back."

"The Disciples of the Sky did that to you?" She gestured to the gouge in the man's leg.

"No, one of our war drakes panicked."

Serves you right, Yala thought as she removed the second war drake's harness and saddle. Saren was much less subtle in his reaction; when she heard him snicker, she elbowed him in the spine.

Veshan swivelled to him. "Think it's funny that my squad got killed, do you?"

"You picked an airborne fight with a few hundred people who have the god of the sky on their side," Saren said. "Seems like you'd have lost fewer members if you'd gone to bait a wild drake instead."

"How dare you?" She drew herself upright. "*We* have a god on our side, too, if you recall, and Mekan will guide us to victory."

Saren burst out laughing. "What, you think Mekan will bring your squad-mates back from the dead?"

"Saren." Yala cuffed him over the back of the head, hissing, "Apologise. Then, fetch the rest of the squad. *Now.*"

Saren obeyed, with reluctance, while Yala helped Veshan pick up the bag of spears that had fallen from the war drake's side. "My newest squad-mate is adjusting. Ignore him."

When Saren returned with the others, she had the two strongest carry the injured soldier to the infirmary and the others help clean up. After she dismissed them, Saren tried to slip away, too, but Yala cornered him.

"What did I tell you?" she hissed. "Would it kill you to fucking listen to me?"

"You told me not to start fights with the rest of the squad. You never told me not to laugh when people get what they deserve."

She tried to cuff him again, but he wriggled out of her grip. "Who do you think the king will send next?"

"You don't have to remind me." He glanced towards the paddock gate then spoke in a low voice. "You won't like this, but Nalen's coming up with a plan to walk out of here while we're gone."

"What?" Was this ridiculous scheme the cause of his recent change in mood? "Don't be a fool, Saren. If Nalen wants to get killed, stay out of it."

"Not like I have much of a choice, given that I'm one of your honoured fliers." Mockery dripped from his voice. "I'm not going to try and change his mind. He's set on it, and he also thinks Viam might be able to persuade the prince to help."

"The prince is a snivelling coward." Yala tensed, hearing heavy footsteps outside the gate. "That'll be the commander. Now, keep your fucking mouth shut and let me do the talking."

She didn't wait for a reply. Exiting the paddock, she greeted the commander. "You spoke to the survivors from the Skytower mission?"

"I did," he said. "It's unfortunate but not unexpected that they were resisted in such a manner. Regardless, His Majesty will be displeased."

"Has he given any orders?"

"Yes," he replied. "He requested that all flight captains are to present themselves to him this evening at the eighth bell."

At the temple, she surmised. "I'll be there."

———

Viam might have received no invitations to the palace, but the temple haunted both her dreams and her waking thoughts in the days following the mission. Yala's report had left her with more questions than answers regarding how Niema had seemingly bested the king, and while it might have been comforting to know that he *did* possess a weakness, she had little doubt that he would devote himself to ensuring that nobody would ever exploit it again.

She found more comfort in the notion that Brenat was no longer working in the palace every day directly under the king's eye. Although her position in administration had been eliminated, too, Viam had pleaded with Malat to let her stay, pointing out that the sheer volume of neglected paperwork from the past few weeks required more than one person's efforts to shift. Brenat's persuasive charm had tipped Malat into agreeing, since the office was undeniably awash in discarded documents, most of which bore Daliel's name and not Tharen's.

Dealing with the mess was also a distraction from dwelling on the horrors the king might be committing inside the palace to maintain his temple's presence by way of sacrifice. The thought of more innocent lives being taken upon the altar preyed on Viam, and even spending her nights entwined in Brenat's arms didn't keep the nightmares at bay.

When a palace guard showed up at Viam's desk with an invitation to meet with the prince, she was half inclined to refuse in case what she took for a friendly request lead to another horrifying demonstration inside the temple. Her hesitation prompted Brenat to directly ask if the king had sent the request himself, to which the guard replied with obvious bafflement that no, His Majesty was not receiving visitors.

Thus encouraged, Viam followed the guard to the palace, though her nerves were as taut as a bowstring until they reached the prince's rooms. The great library had not changed a bit, and the number of lanterns gleaming on the walls even in daylight seemed designed to banish any shadows that might intrude.

Daliel put the book he was reading aside and offered her a smile that didn't mask the shadows crouching beneath his eyes. "Viam. I'm glad to see you."

"As am I, Your Majesty." She was surprised to find she meant it, given her fears that he might have been recruited to his father's cause.

His smile slid from his face. "I'm afraid I can't offer you

refreshments. My father made some changes to our staff, and many of the palace's household members were dismissed."

Dismissed... or killed? She sank into an armchair, her dread returning threefold. "Why did he do that?"

"Recent events have urged him towards caution."

Did he refer to the temple or the failed mission against the Disciples of the Sea? "Have you seen much of him?"

"No." His hands fisted in his lap. "I confess, I thought my father would offer me an active role in running the nation upon his return, but he has shut me out."

That meant, she surmised, that he had not attended any more ceremonies in the Temple of Death.

"It must be frustrating for you." If she were to have any hope of convincing him to stand up to the king, she'd have to start by appealing to the part of him that had once ruled in his father's stead. "Did you speak to him? You're his heir, and you *did* rule the country for seven years."

"Poorly, according to most."

"Not at all. There were no wars. Some might say it was better."

She wondered if she'd been too bold, but he nodded. "I thought we were on the right path. Decades of war left the economy in a terrible state, to say nothing of the number of lives ruined in the process."

"Exactly." She gave him an encouraging smile. "We might even have made peace with Rafragoria."

"No." His guarded expression returned. "Their recent actions prove they cannot be trusted."

"Recent actions?" she echoed. "Do you mean the assassination attempts?"

"Not those," he said. "Rafragoria assisted the Disciples who refused to surrender to my father and attacked the flight division."

They helped the Disciples of the Sea? "I didn't know any of them survived after what the king did to them." She clamped her mouth shut. She'd spoken carelessly, having forgotten Daliel's father would never have told him the truth of his unprovoked assault on Rafragoria. Nor that it had been he who had held control of Mekan's army.

"My father?" His brow furrowed. "He did nothing but defend Laria against the dead. We might not have survived if not for the allies he brought."

Her heart began to beat faster. *He sees the cracks in the story. He must.* "Do you know who those allies were?"

His confusion deepened. "Is that relevant?"

"Yes." Gods, but she was wasting her time here if she didn't at least try to convince him of his father's treachery. "How many Disciples of the Sea did you suppose he had with him? Surely not more than twenty. Would so few have stood a chance against an army of the dead?"

"I'm afraid I do not understand, Viam." His expression clouded. "I hardly think it matters how many there were."

Viam closed her eyes. Then, regret churning inside her, she spoke. "The dead who attacked the city weren't sent by Rafragoria. It was all King Tharen."

When she opened her eyes again, she saw the horror stark on his face. "Who told you that?"

"Nobody. I saw it for myself." A lie but a necessary one; mentioning that most of her knowledge had come from Yala would do nothing but cut her argument off at the knees. "The dead didn't flee out of fear but because your father commanded them to attack Rafragoria instead."

"Viam..." He rose to his feet. "These words are treasonous."

"They're the truth." Fear tasted metallic. If she'd misjudged—if he told his father—she'd have her throat slit upon that altar by nightfall. "I haven't told another soul who didn't already know. Please don't—"

"Tell my father?" He ran a hand through his shoulder-length hair, his eyes wide. "I *should*, Viam. Do you have any idea of the position you've put me in?"

"Didn't you see me at the ceremony when he opened the temple?" She spoke quickly. "That's why I thought you knew. He openly declared himself allied with Mekan. Rafragoria never did."

"Enough." His shoulders slumped, but his tone was firm. "I will not tell my father, but I cannot let you into the palace again."

Relief swamped her fear, though it was swiftly replaced with regret. She'd blown any chance she might have had of gaining insight into the king's movements, but it didn't sound like he'd allowed Daliel access to the temple at all.

Viam let herself be escorted from the palace with the sense that she moved through a dream, watching her body move without being fully present. The dreamlike sensation lasted until she neared the administration building, when Saren stepped in front of her and caused her to jump violently. "Viam."

"Saren." She pressed a hand to her racing heart. "What are you doing here?"

"I need to talk to you."

"Now isn't a good time." She continued to walk, but he fell into step with her, affecting a casual air.

"Have fun with the prince?" He lowered his voice to a whisper. "His father might be a piece of shit, but the prince might be the only sane person left in that palace. What do you think?"

Viam's shoulders tensed. "What does it matter?"

"Nalen's been recruiting other foot soldiers to walk out of here the next time the king goes out into the field, and he was hoping the prince might lend a hand. Since you have free entry to the palace…"

"I don't." She had to squash this idea before Saren got himself killed. "The prince threw me out when I told him the truth about who sent the dead to attack the capital."

"You told him?" He stared at her and then laughed. "Why'd you do that?"

Defensiveness reared inside. "Because he deserved to know. His father doesn't tell him anything important, so if you think he's going to be on board with whatever ridiculous scheme Nalen comes up with, you're mistaken. He's not going to help deserters."

"Doesn't he want to get away from that fucking temple?" All levity fled his voice. "This isn't a joke, Viam. Every day that temple stays open is another chance for Mekan's army to show up and kill us all."

"Do you think I don't know that?" Despite herself, Viam found her anger evaporating. "I think that if he calms down and thinks about what I told him, he'll forgive me and let me back in. But I'm not promising anything, Saren. He knows how dangerous his father is."

"So do we," he said. "Yala's been invited to another ceremony tonight. I bet he has too."

Another ceremony. Another sacrifice. Viam swallowed hard. "Then I hope another reminder of his father's real nature is enough to change his mind."

28

"It is time to begin your induction into Mekan's ranks."

At the king's words, anticipation burned inside Yala's chest like an inextinguishable flame. The altar waited, swathed in shadow that masked the lanterns at the courtyard's edges and cast the faceless guards on either side of the king in near-total darkness. The prince too. Daliel's eyes were on the floor, not on his father, and Tharen did not acknowledge his son's presence.

Who will he sacrifice this time? she wondered.

"The god of death requires a gift from His followers." The king held up the sword he'd revealed during the last ceremony, the one forged from a void drake's claw. "Blood is the currency He deals in, and as apprentices, the first blood you offer will be your own. Take out your weapons."

The captains hastened to obey, and even Daliel lifted a short dagger, his hand shaking.

"Shed your blood upon the altar." The king held up his arm in demonstration and drew the blade across his palm, opening a shallow cut. He then extended his hand over the altar. A few droplets of blood fell, swiftly vanishing beneath the shadows.

Then, he beckoned to Daliel, who approached the altar in a manner more befitting a man walking to the gallows than a prince. Daliel lifted his hand and drew the blade across clumsily; his audible gasp brought a scowl to the king's face that deepened when no blood spilled. Evidently, Daliel hadn't cut deep enough.

Yala felt a stab of pity as she watched Daliel raise the knife in a hand shaking worse than before. His second attempt sliced deep across two fingers; with another gasp, the knife slid from his grip and clattered to the ground. Its blade gleamed crimson a heartbeat before the shadows closed in, sucking at the blood like a wild animal's tongue lapping up raindrops from the ground.

"Mekan accepts your offering." The king did not look Daliel in the eyes, instead addressing the soldiers. "You will each do the same, one at a time."

Yala lined up with the others. Lisek came to the altar first and extended an arm, angling her blade carefully so that it didn't cut through any vital tendons and hinder her ability to hold a weapon. Really, it would have made more sense to shed blood from some less vital part of the body, but that would take away from the performative aspect of the ceremony. She doubted Mekan would care either way.

When Yala's turn came, she extended her hand and sliced open the back of her forearm. Crimson droplets fell into the shadows; the urge gripped her to follow them, to let the darkness embrace her.

Mekan's whisper rasped against her ear. *"Thank you, Disciple."*

My pleasure, Yala replied, but she wanted to say more. She wanted to *ask* more. How had the king attained the ability to command Mekan's army without turning into one of those masked monsters?

She also wondered about the extent of Mekan's communication with the king and if He had in any way alluded to Yala's past involvement with the Void, though she doubted that was the case. She'd long concluded that Mekan was a being concerned solely with sacrifices offered in His name and otherwise uninterested in anything humans did, and that was why He had not struck her down for her prior betrayals. Nor had He exposed her treachery to the king.

The strange urge to laugh took hold of her. Naught mattered to Mekan but the sacrifice of blood and flesh, and for all she knew, if Yala slew the king on this very altar, Mekan would have no objection. She wasn't strong enough yet, but in becoming an apprentice Disciple of Death, Yala now held the king's utmost trust.

And Tharen would give her the means of ending his life.

———

"I believe you."

Daliel spoke quietly enough that Viam had to strain to hear, and his words took a moment to sink in. "What do you mean?"

She'd come straight to the palace when the guard had delivered the prince's invitation, which had been both surprising and not, given that part of her had been prepared for Daliel to change his mind after the ceremony the previous night. She'd entered his quarters to find him in an even deeper state of dishevelment than the last time, with his fine clothes in disarray and his eyes notably reddened around the edges.

"My father—" His voice broke. "I wanted to believe the

best of him, but I asked some questions and… and you were right."

"What did you ask?" Fear flooded her. "Did you tell him what I said to you yesterday?"

"No, but I asked why Rafragoria attacked the capital and why none of their soldiers accompanied the army of the dead."

"He told you the truth?"

"He didn't admit that he sent the army himself, but it's the only explanation that makes sense." Sinking into his seat, he dropped his head into his hand. "He destroyed them, didn't he? He set the dead upon them."

Viam sucked in a breath. "I'm sorry."

A muffled sound escaped him that might have been a sob. "If any survived, they'll never seek peace with Laria again. And he doesn't plan to stop with Rafragoria either."

"The Disciples are his next target, aren't they?"

"They must surrender or die." He lifted his head, his eyes bloodshot. "And there's nothing I can do. He speaks more to the god of death than he does to me. Gods, I can't believe I said that. Forgive me."

"I won't tell anyone, remember? I'm on your side." Guilt churned inside her at his obvious distress, however necessary it had been for him to know the truth. "You're the prince, remember? You have a duty to your country, even if it means opposing him."

Daliel's shoulders hunched. "No. Gods, Viam, I can't. My father holds the ultimate authority."

"The Disciples have authority too." Her heart pounded as if to reprimand her audacity, but he'd called her back after she'd spoken out of turn for a reason. He wanted her honesty. "They won't surrender, and I bet they'd support your claim too."

He made a choked noise. "If my father even *suspected* I want to communicate with them…"

"He wouldn't harm you."

He hunched even further. "How do you know they wouldn't think me as weak as he does? They have no cause to hold any confidence in me. My father thinks I'm unworthy of succeeding him, and he's right."

"He's wrong," she said. "There's more than one kind of strength, and compassion isn't a weakness."

"Despite all he's done, I don't want to hurt my father," he said. "I don't want him to die."

The god of death already has him. "There are other ways."

The door swung inward with a creak that cut through her words like a knife; Daliel bolted to his feet, horror flickering across his face, and then bowed his head. "Father."

King Tharen stood in the doorway. Watching Viam as she stared, transfixed, for a time that might have lasted an age or a heartbeat. Falling to her knees, she murmured, "Your Majesty."

How much did he hear? Her chest constricted with panic, and the breath squeezed from her lungs until spots danced in front of her vision.

"Come with me." The command prompted her to lurch to her feet. "Viam, is it?"

The lack of emotion in his voice and demeanour somehow frightened her more. "Yes."

Once they were outside the library, he faced her, towering over her in his military clothing. Though he carried no visible weapons, the image of him standing over an altar was never far from her thoughts. "I was not aware you were acquainted with my son."

"We were friends. When… before…" She trailed off, not daring to refer to the monarch's time in exile even in passing.

"Ah, I didn't realise there might be a problem with my coming here, Your Majesty. I apologise."

"There is no need." Despite his calm tone, the hairs lifted on the back of Viam's neck. "My son has had trouble remembering his place of late. Perhaps he needs the company of someone who might remind him of his responsibilities."

"Which responsibilities?" She knew. Gods, she knew.

"You attended the ceremony," he said. "You were present at the opening of my temple but not the most recent one."

Fear strangled any replies in her throat. She nodded instead, her nails biting into her palms.

"My son has proven resistant to embracing his new role." The king's eyes narrowed. "He is heir. It is his duty to follow in my footsteps without complaint. There will be another ceremony tonight, and you will attend along with my son. You will persuade him to participate."

It wasn't a request. Nor should she have expected otherwise. She was lucky, she knew, that he hadn't worked out the true nature of the discussion he'd interrupted. That he hadn't sentenced her to death on the spot regardless of his son's open invitation to the palace.

Now, she was sure, she would not be allowed in except as an accompaniment to the prince while he stood at his father's side and committed any depraved actions Mekan ordered him to. Her role being to convince him, against her own instincts, to become a Disciple of Death.

———

After each newly promoted elite Disciple of Life had taken turns swearing their vows to Yalet, they left for the mainland and set up camp on the beach.

That night, Niema dreamt of darkness rippling across the water and the dead rising to consume forest and ocean alike.

When her eyes opened, she instinctively rolled towards Hachim. His arms enfolded her, his steady heartbeat soothing, his emotions as steady as the thrum of their shared pulse. Hachim meant comfort, reassurance, yet again, Ornel's words came to mind, and she wondered what he might do if she were to touch him, to run her hand over his bare shoulder and draw his lips to hers.

His eyes flickered open. "Niema?"

"Bad dream," she murmured. "I wish we could have stayed on the island longer."

"Me too." He half sat up, shielding his eyes against the sun cutting through the branches. "It's so peaceful there. *You're* happier there, and that makes me happy too."

Her blush deepened, though there was no cause for embarrassment at the undeniable truth. The vision Yalet had imparted upon her had washed away her doubts that her god and Superior both trusted her, and moreover, her fellow elite Disciples had warmed notably towards her and Hachim after the ceremony. They knew that Yalet would never have permitted anyone whose loyalties She doubted to land upon the island at all, and they were also aware that She had shown Niema a vision that nobody else had experienced.

Niema had only shared the details with Hachim, but she wasn't surprised when the others invited her to join them for breakfast and then began peppering her with barely concealed questions.

"Stop bothering her," said Bitra from her perch on a rock nearby. "The vision is between her and Yalet."

The others desisted with mumbled apologies, while Bitra climbed down to join her and Hachim at the cookfire. Wariness gripped Niema's shoulders. Despite their prior friendship, Bitra had scarcely spoken a word to her after her sister had been killed by the dead, and the naked distrust on her face had fed Niema's own guilt.

"Thank you," Niema murmured, lowering her gaze. "It's appreciated."

"I'm sorry I treated you as I did." Bitra settled on a smaller rock and began sharpening an arrow. "I blamed you for the attack, and that was unfair of me. It's clear that Yalet has chosen you."

"She chose all of us." Niema's guilt didn't lessen, but she managed a smile. "The island... it's astonishing."

"Isn't it?" She continued to sharpen the arrow. Niema watched, feeling a twinge of discomfort that she pushed down. "Gods, I wish I could show the children."

The thought of Diaman and Threl brought a painful throb that reverberated across her bond with Hachim. "I miss them too."

"I miss everyone. Even Rielen, the arse." Bitra wore a wry smile. "I didn't realise how tough it must have been for you when you left for the city. Not being able to sense them. You're lucky you have Hachim with you."

"I am." She'd forgotten, foolishly, that most of the other elite Disciples would have also been bound to fellow members of their enclaves and that leaving would have dimmed those bonds if not outright destroyed them. Bitra had it doubly hard, as this would have been the longest she and her children had spent apart since they'd moved to the enclave.

In spite of Niema's reservations about accepting every aspect of her new role, Superior Kralia had done her a kindness by offering her a position that would not make her feel estranged. All the elite Disciples were outsiders in a way, though if the Superior's attempt to build their forces proved successful, they'd have more company soon enough.

At the Superior's order, they started with the enclave near the village near which the Disciples of the Sea had docked. They retraced their path up Laria's eastern coast, and Niema was surprised to see Nanek swimming some distance from the ship. When they neared, he waved her down, calling her name.

"Nanek." She flew lower and spied a small, winged reptile hovering over his shoulder. *Molin.* "What is it?"

"We received a message." Behind, Molin lifted a claw, displaying a bedraggled roll of parchment. "I believe it's for you."

"Kelan." She reached over the war drake's side and took the note, unfurling it one-handedly. Despite the misspelled words and crooked writing, the message hit her like a thunderclap. "The king demanded a surrender. They refused."

"It's started." Nanek's expression turned bleak. "I fear the same fate that claimed our temple approaches."

"No." She couldn't believe that Skytower would be so easily conquered, but the last part of Kelan's note was the most concerning.

I know it might be too much to ask, but if the king employs the dead against us, you might be the only one who can help, Niema.

He might not have told his Superior of Niema's unique influence over the dead, but nobody at Skytower had any such advantage. Whatever her thoughts on Yala's claim that Niema alone could fulfil her mission to bring King Tharen's rule to an end, Niema couldn't deny that her abilities might be the factor that determined Skytower's survival.

When they landed on the cliffs near the ship, she approached her Superior and held out the note. "The king sent an envoy to the Disciples of the Sky. They attacked in the night, with the help of one of their own."

"I see." She read over the note, a knot appearing in her brow. "I cannot accept their request for help. Our current mission is imperative."

"But—" Niema took the note back, objections rising in

her throat, each less convincing than the last. "If we don't help, we're next."

"He will not find the island."

How do you know that? The notion of Mekan disturbing Yalet's heart didn't bear thinking about, but if Skytower fell, there was no doubt where the king would turn his attention next.

She dropped the argument for the time being, reasoning that the Superior's stance might improve when they recruited a few more elite Disciples from the enclave near the coast. They left their war drakes on the beach and walked to the pristine jungle that trimmed Laria's eastern coast.

The Superior was the first to stiffen, her hand falling to the weapon at her side. "Something is wrong."

The wrongness hit Niema an instant later, a subtle shift in the air and a faint breeze that should not be present in the humid jungle. A shiver crawled across her shoulder blades, and the damp, earthy smell that permeated the forested path became tainted with decay that worsened with each step. The sunlight streaming through the trees lost its warmth, the shadows thickening.

When they reached the enclave, the dead were there to greet them. Skeletal figures draped in decaying flesh staggered through a mass of rotting greenery, their sightless eyes watching the newcomers, their hands clutching improvised weapons.

Niema's gorge rose at the foul sight. Then, a wave of anger rose within her such as she'd never experienced before, penetrating deep into her bones. Green light sprang to her hands, unbidden, as if she carried the fury of the god of life herself.

One of the other Disciples began to hum, a wordless sound that grew louder as more Disciples joined in. Niema, too, found herself joining a vocalisation that came from somewhere deep within her soul.

Green light exploded across her vision. The light came both from the Disciples and from the forest itself as fresh life bloomed from the rotting trees and new greenery rose in abundance at a speed faster than she would have ever believed possible.

The prayer went on, and within moments, the dead were buried beneath greenery thick enough that no human might ever have set foot in the forest at all.

Only then did the prayer cease, leaving Niema's chest like a long, exhaled breath. She reeled, steadying herself against Hachim. He, too, wore an expression of shock. They'd both been driven by a force beyond comprehension, as if another entity had taken possession of their bodies and driven them towards a joined purpose.

This is what it means to be Yalet's chosen. She'd sensed the god of life's presence within her when she'd destroyed the temple on the island, but that had been temporary and shared with nobody else. This time, she'd been part of something larger, a shared experience that had brought her closer to the god of life than any other save perhaps for her vision inside Yalet's temple.

Her awe faded when Superior Kralia began to walk, treading carefully amid the newly restored trees. Niema followed, her grief returning at the sight of bodies cloaked in greenery. *So many dead.*

"Did any survive?" she whispered to the Superior. "How can this be possible?"

"I do not know," said the Superior without turning around, "but it must have been fast for Superior Tiela not to have sent warning."

Niema's heart lurched. Another Superior had died? How many were left now—three?

I can't ask them to come to Skytower. That much was clear. *If I'm to help Kelan, I have to go on my own.*

29

"This is your next test," the king said.

A pair of guards entered the courtyard, escorting a group of dishevelled figures with their hands bound behind their backs. "Those of you who volunteer will spill the blood of one individual upon Mekan's altar. All are criminals bound for the noose and will not be missed."

So these were the night's sacrifices. The performance turned Yala's stomach.

As before, the king made the first sacrifice, using his claw-blade to cut the throat of an elderly man who sobbed as he knelt to die.

Lisek volunteered next, her expression eager as she drew her blade and slit the throat of the next person the king's guards shoved in front of her. Then followed Veshan. She knelt before the altar and murmured a prayer both before and after slitting her victim's throat. Yala didn't hear the words, but Mekan must have been pleased, because the shadows darkened around the slain criminal and pursued Veshan as she walked back to her place in line.

Not everyone was so eager. Daliel hovered beside his father, his eyes averted from the bloody altar. Hoping he'd be spared. There weren't enough criminals for everyone to have a turn, and while Yala had intended to gain Mekan's favour, hadn't she shed enough blood for Him already? Killing in battle was one thing, but this ceremony was distasteful to say the least.

With one prisoner left, the king spoke. "My son will take the last sacrifice."

All eyes went to Daliel. The prince's face was ashen, as if he might faint or throw up, but he stumbled towards the altar as if he was walking along the deck of a rocking ship.

Daliel lifted his dagger. Paused. "I—can't."

"No?" The king's tone was as sharp as the claw-blade in his hand.

"No." Daliel turned away. "I'm sorry, Father, but I can't take another innocent life."

"You are heir to the Larian throne." A hint of anger crept into the king's voice. "You *will* honour Mekan."

Yala's heart twisted with disgust and sympathy in equal measure and then sank into her shoes when Viam's voice spoke up from the back. "I'll do it instead."

Shit. When did she get in here? Had the prince invited her? As Viam began to move forward, Yala stepped out of line, blocking the route to the altar.

"I will." Yala's voice rang out louder. "It would be my honour." She gripped her dagger hard until the ever-present tingling sensation in her fingertips turned sharp, painful.

The king swivelled to her. "Captain Yala Palathar. Yes… Mekan favours you."

Shit. What does he mean? He *might* only be referring to her experiences on the island as having offered her an advantage, but a murmur of interest travelled among the other captains, dissipating when the king continued to speak. "My son shall watch, and he shall apply the lesson next time."

Now, she had to follow through. Yala reached the altar, and regret tightened her throat when she set eyes on the trembling prisoner waiting for death.

If not her, someone else would have to wield the knife. She would not let Viam take that burden if she could avoid it.

Lifting her dagger, she leaned over and whispered, "I'll make it quick."

Yala cut the man's throat in one smooth motion and let Mekan's shadows wash over her hands like rain.

———

Scenes from the temple haunted Viam's dreams. Even encircled in Brenat's arms, she couldn't escape the memory of Yala's blank greed as she slit the man's throat. Daliel's horror. The king's rage. The prince had refused to kill, to take part in the ceremony as his father had wanted, and she feared the consequences would fall upon her own head.

Brenat insisted otherwise. "You didn't have time to talk to him before the ceremony, did you? The king knows that. And the upside is that he'll almost certainly ask you to visit him tomorrow."

"How is that an upside?" Every time she saw Daliel was an opportunity for King Tharen to blame her for his son's failures. He might not want to inflict harm on his only heir, but Viam herself had little value. She might well have had higher survival chances if she'd rejoined the army.

Brenat prodded her in the arm. "Because you have access to the prince without having to sneak around behind the king's back. You can work on convincing him to turn on his father."

Viam groaned. "Not this again. I told you, he's too afraid, and who can blame him?"

The rebellion brewing among the foot soldiers had proven more widespread than Viam had expected, and Nalen had been recruiting from every possible avenue, even amid the depleted ranks of the administrative staff. Brenat was naturally enthusiastic, and Viam had already caught her trying to smuggle a pile of documents out of the office to take to the barracks earlier that day.

"The prince is the only person who can talk some sense into his father," Brenat said. "Or at least work against him."

"He's terrified. So am I. If I don't convince him to take part in the next ceremony…" She couldn't finish the thought. Daliel couldn't escape the inevitable, not if the king intended to train him as a Disciple of Death, but Viam wasn't willing to find out how far the prince could push his father before he took out his rage upon Daliel's friend and companion.

Brenat's guess that the prince would invite her into the palace the next day proved correct, but Viam was half of a mind to decline. Every move she made inside the palace now had the potential to rebound upon her like a trap set for a wild animal, but refusal was almost as fraught if the invitation turned out to have come from the king and not his son.

The knot in her stomach loosened when the guard took her to Daliel's rooms as if nothing had changed. The prince greeted her with a wan smile, the shadows under his eyes even more pronounced than the previous day. "It's good to see you, Viam. I apologise… I am distracted. I did not sleep well last night."

"Me neither." They had that much in common. "I… your father…"

"He isn't here." He cleared his throat, glanced at the door. "He rarely visits me during the day. Yesterday was an exception."

"What he said to me yesterday." She stumbled over the words. "I have to convince you to—"

"I know." His hands fisted in his lap, grabbing handfuls of fine material. "My father was right to call me a coward."

"Not killing someone at his command isn't a cowardly act," she said. "You refused him. That was brave of you."

"Instead, Yala Palathar stepped into my place." His eyes burned with sudden intensity. "She is the one person who might stand a chance at stopping him."

Viam's mouth parted. "Stopping him?"

The prince made a noise halfway between a groan and a whimper. "I am a traitor to my crown to even entertain the thought, I know, but I sometimes wonder if it is he who speaks through his mouth, or..."

"Mekan." She pushed on. "If the king *is* acting on Mekan's orders and not according to his own will, you aren't a traitor. It's the opposite of treachery for you to oppose him, in fact."

"There's nothing I can do either way." He ran a hand through his hair, tugging at the roots. "I wondered if I might find support among the palace staff, but my father ensured that isn't possible."

"There are people who support you," she said. "In the army. The staff too. I can help—"

"I am not so naïve, Viam. I know you are more at risk than me." He took in a ragged breath. "My father will hold another ceremony tonight, and I will participate as he intends. I will not allow you to suffer on my part. Whatever it is I need to do, I will."

"You shouldn't have to." Her pulse raced, but she pushed on. "I really can help. There are some soldiers who plan to act when the king is at Skytower with most of the army. To walk out. They want you to help them."

"They do?" His mouth went slack. "Was this your plan?

Did you always intend to—to recruit me to help with this scheme?"

"No!" she said. "I'm not sure if *they* have a solid plan. I wasn't going to get involved." Not a lie, but it sounded like one. What had she been thinking mentioning Nalen's plan at all? "Never mind. I thought—"

"I will think on it." His expression shuttered. "And I will see you at the ceremony tonight."

———

After Niema and the others had finished searching for survivors, they went to the village to ensure Mekan's taint had not reached the enclave's neighbours too. The attack had spared the non-Disciples, but that Corruption had struck a community this remote was a reminder that no corner of Laria was safe.

Leaving the Disciples of the Sea so close to the site of Mekan's latest strike made her uneasy, too, but Nanek refused to move his people again, and hiding on a ship at least made it easier to leave at a moment's notice.

Back at the campsite, Superior Kralia announced that their next stop would be her enclave before they travelled south to the more remote areas of the forest to find new recruits.

I can't go back. The Superior knew that, and that surely meant she would offer permission for Niema to leave. Still, apprehension tailed behind Niema when she approached the Superior after the others had dispersed throughout the camp.

"I know the timing isn't ideal," she began, "but I can't return to the enclave, and the Disciples of the Sky don't have any influence over the dead."

"I am aware." The Superior gave her a searching look. "Does Superior Sietra know of your talents?"

"I didn't tell her." Had Kelan? Gods, she hoped not. "But the flight division is still recovering from the battle, which suggests the king will employ the beasts of the Void instead."

"Yes," said Superior Kralia. "All Disciples are vulnerable to Mekan's temptations."

Niema blinked, not understanding her meaning. "I don't..."

Hachim sucked in a sharp breath. "You mean, someone might attack from within? One of the Disciples might open the Void?"

Might they? The thought had not crossed her mind, but wasn't that how Mekan had entered the Temple of the Earth the first time around? If a Disciple of the Sky turned upon their allies, the dead would be able to get directly into Skytower without the king needing to lift a finger.

Fear clawed at her. "If the Void opens, the Disciples can't close it without help. They need a Disciple of Life."

"More than one." Hachim gave their Superior a beseeching look. "Niema can't take the burden on herself. We can spare a few people, can't we?"

Superior Kralia nodded to the other Disciples assembling at their camp. "I am not the one you need to convince. They are angered greatly by the losses we found in the forest."

I know. Guilt stabbed at Niema, but the Superior's warning burned away all doubt that she had to at least try to convince Ragem. He held the authority over the others and had been responsible for rallying them to help the Disciples of the Sea, but one look at his face told her he was not in a negotiating mood this time.

Yalet preserve me.

She halted in front of him and dipped her head. "Skytower has requested our aid," she said. "They were recently attacked by the king's soldiers and fear he will send the dead next. Hachim and I are going to help them, and we would appreciate anyone who might come with us."

Ragem gave her a cold, flat stare. "I will not permit the others to abandon their posts."

"They fought for the Disciples of the Sea." But that had been before the assault upon the forest. "If Skytower falls to Mekan, the king's attention will be fixed on us."

"It already is," he said. "It's our duty to bolster our ranks and protect the surviving Superiors."

"It is, but can we not spare a handful of people?" Niema glanced around the campsite. A few looked to have been eavesdropping, including Bitra, who offered an apologetic look but did not intervene.

"If we help the Disciples of the Sky, they will do the same for us," said Hachim. "We might need that in the future."

"Exactly." Niema pushed on. "Remember when we fought in Setemar to aid the Disciples of the Earth? They owe us for that, and Skytower will owe us a debt too."

"Our priorities have changed. Mekan would see us destroyed, and I will not risk our forces being split."

"But…" She'd lost the argument. Hachim knew, too, and as they turned away, she whispered to him, "Skytower is the last remaining temple."

Except for ours. The king didn't know it existed, but how long would that last?

How long before the king, having conquered all other temples, came for the one that belonged to Mekan's most hated enemy?

———

The problem with waiting for an attack was that one eventually reached the point where the anticipation seemed worse than the event. Or so Kelan thought after two days without any further visits from the king's soldiers or attempts on the Superior's life. When someone raised the alarm at sunset on the third day, he had to resist the urge to cry out in jubilance.

"War drakes!" The shout echoed up and down the tower, and the Disciples of the Sky launched into action. Kelan, too, hovered in front of the platform he'd been assigned to, peering at the two war drakes approaching the tower.

"That's not a full squad." He flew forward, squinting against the glare cast by the sinking sun. "They aren't soldiers. That's Niema and Hachim. The Disciples of Life."

The other Disciples were slower to retreat, but soon, the two war drakes drew close enough to the tower for everyone to realise they weren't part of the flight division. No others accompanied the pair, and their woven clothes, though sturdy enough to protect them from a stray arrow, were not made of the drakeskin typically used by the army.

When Kelan flew to greet the new arrivals, he found the lower platform crowded enough that he and Ranit had to herd the others back to make room for them to land.

"You didn't fly all the way from the coast, did you?" he asked when Niema's war drake touched down on the platform. "I have to admit, I hoped there'd be more than two of you."

Niema's mouth tightened. "I tried to convince the others, but we're under attack too. Mekan is targeting the enclaves."

His brow lifted. "Not on the king's orders?"

"I don't think so." She wouldn't say more with an audience, so he led the war drakes to the topmost level of the tower. After they dismounted, Niema and Hachim dismissed their steeds.

"Are you sure that's wise?" he asked. "What if they don't come back?"

"They're loyal," Niema replied. "They won't attack anyone in the tower either."

Kelan was more concerned that one of his fellow Disciples would assume the beasts belonged to the enemy, but presumably, the war drakes would stay away unless called by their riders.

Upon entering the Superior's office, the two newcomers surveyed the Superior and her office with some surprise, at least on Hachim's part. He'd never been to Skytower before, and the elaborate paintings on the walls and the Superior's finely styled hair and embroidered clothing would make their own Superior's clothing and décor seem austere by comparison. The newcomers knelt on the prayer mat before rising to their feet.

"Superior Sietra," said Niema. "Thank you for inviting me here despite the terrible circumstances."

"I am glad to see you too, Niema," said Superior Sietra. "And you must be Hachim?"

"It is an honour to meet you," said her companion. "We'll be glad to assist you in any way in which you need us."

"I'm sorry we came alone," Niema said. "The enemy is targeting our Superiors. The others couldn't be spared."

"Yes, Superior Kralia told me," said Superior Sietra. "A concerning development but perhaps unsurprising, given that the Superiors are living representations of Yalet."

Niema swallowed, her throat bobbing. "Another was killed the day we received the note. Three remain, including mine."

But they have more than one. Kelan didn't know why the Disciples of Life were an exception to the usual rule of having only one ruler, except that they were widespread enough for it to be impractical for a single Superior to give orders to every small enclave within Laria's forest. That Mekan was targeting them directly explained why only two

Disciples had shown up. *Are two enough to handle an entire army of the dead?*

"We are grateful," said Superior Sietra. "Take Hachim to the spare rooms, Kelan. Niema, I will have a word with you in private."

Oh, shit.

"Alone," she added, seeing Kelan's hesitation. "We won't be long."

Kelan flashed a guilty look in Niema's direction but obeyed. He hadn't had the chance to admit to Niema that his Superior was aware of her ability to control Mekan's monsters, but there was little doubt that was what she wanted to discuss and that Niema would not be thrilled with him for sharing her secret.

30

"Yala." Viam's whisper brought Yala to a halt partway up the palace stairs.

"Now isn't a good time," Yala said out of the corner of her mouth. "Talk to me later."

After the ceremony. Most of the other soldiers had already entered the palace; Yala typically lagged behind, slowed by her bad leg, but that did not mean someone wouldn't overhear her speaking to her former squad-mate. Nor could she ignore the void drakes, half hidden by the darkening sky.

"It's Daliel," Viam whispered. "His father isn't happy with him for not being willing to participate in the ceremony at the temple. I've been asked to convince him."

Yala's blood went cold. "The king asked you to? And you accepted?"

"I didn't have a choice!" Viam said. "He caught me visiting Daliel, and I already failed once. I can't fail tonight too."

Shit. When the king had demanded that Daliel slaughter that man, Yala had been the one to step into his place. The king had made no secret of his disdain for his son's weakness, but his status as heir likely spared him facing punishment.

Viam would not be that lucky.

"You can't force someone to serve Mekan," Yala added. "If Daliel has any conscience, remind him that he won't be the one to pay for his reluctance."

"He knows," she whispered. "And he is on our side. He thinks the king is being guided by Mekan. Controlled by him, even."

"He's finally on the same page as the rest of us, then."

Not strictly true, and if Daliel's words were taken in a literal sense, it raised the worrying question of exactly how much control the king had over his own mind and actions. He might not wear the masked armour of one of his guards, but maybe Mekan *had* taken more than blood sacrifices as payment for the power He had loaned to the monarch.

"I know you can't step in again," Viam murmured. "But I thought you should know in case tonight goes badly."

"It had better not." If Daliel got Viam killed due to his own cowardice, Yala would be more than happy to offer him to Mekan herself. "Tell Daliel that if he doesn't play his role, he'll have reason to fear me more than the god of death."

With that, Yala continued upstairs and caught up with the other captains in the palace entrance hall. That Viam had pursued her friendship with Daliel had been her own risk to take, but gods, she didn't need another reminder of the number of lives that would be forfeited if her treachery were exposed.

At the courtyard, they assembled in front of the altar. Behind, the jagged slash of the Void gaped like a festering wound. Yala's hands tingled, shadows seeping out from beneath her gloves. She made no effort to hide them. The king's public recognition of her status in Mekan's esteem might win her some enemies amid the other captains, but she couldn't bring herself to care. When Daliel joined his father at the altar, she levelled him with a piercing stare. *Don't you dare fuck up this time.*

The king paid no heed to his son, instead beckoning to the guards stationed at the edge of the courtyard. "Now that everyone is present, I have some criminals and traitors for you to enact punishment on."

The performance mirrored the previous day's, with a number of huddled figures assembling near the altar. One would think the king would run out of criminals to execute at some point unless he simply had his guards snatching people off the street.

This time, the king chose the first victim. When he beckoned a dishevelled man out of line, someone gasped.

Yala's gaze went back to Daliel, who stared in horror at the man kneeling in front of his father. Ignoring his son, the king lifted his sword.

"Stop!" Daliel's cry echoed across the courtyard. "There must be a mistake. This man is not a criminal."

"This man is a traitor." The king's voice boomed out, silencing his son in an instant. "He was caught trying to enter the Temple of the Flame."

Utter silence fell over the courtyard as all eyes turned to the prince. Daliel's face had drained of colour. His eyes were wide, and try as he might, he could not hide the emotions fighting for dominance. Shock, distress... and guilt.

It was him. For reasons Yala couldn't fathom, he'd sent an appeal to the people who were possibly the *least* likely to be able to help. The Disciples of the Flame were all but useless and craven and committed to the crown. If any dissenters existed, they'd have been long since executed or beaten into submission.

The king brought the sword down in a sweeping motion that took off the man's head. As it hit the ground, shadows spread from the altar like grasping fingers, encircling the guard's headless body.

King Tharen had not finished yet. Lifting a hand, he beckoned to the shadows stirring around the dead man and drew them up as one might haul water from a well. The headless body lurched upright on shaky legs and moved jerkily forward to his master's side.

Nobody uttered a sound, not even Daliel, though he looked sick.

"This is the next stage of your devotion to Mekan: the ability to exert control over the dead." The king gave another careless flick of his wrist, and the shadows dissipated, the dead man crumpling again. "You will be able to do the same in time."

As the masked guards stepped in to take away the body, Yala watched the flickering shadows. She'd never seen Mekan's control broken; usually, the dead kept walking until they were taken apart. *How did he do that?*

Once again, the king had demonstrated the limits of her knowledge concerning Mekan and the Void, though it seemed that the rest of them would not be able to exert that level of control over the dead. While Lisek all but shoved her way to the front of the line to slit the throat of another criminal, the body merely twitched a few times when she tried beckoning to the shadows the way the king had.

The guards took the body away, and the performance continued. When Yala's turn came, she slit the person's throat quickly without looking at their face and without giving into the temptation to lift them from death and urge them to take up a weapon against the king. Rather, she let the shadows guide the body into a standing position, long enough to hold the king's attention, and let it fall.

Daliel had not taken Viam's warning to heart. When one prisoner remained, the king called out before anyone could step forward. "That concludes tonight's ceremony. I will have words with my son before we deal with the last of those foolish enough to turn traitor to the throne."

He did not look at Daliel, but the prince looked as if he wished the darkness would swallow him whole.

"I hope this is clear enough to all of you: Nobody is ever to make contact with *any* Disciple. Anyone who does so will be executed without trial." His gaze landed on Viam. "You may all leave, except for my son… and Viam Tiathar."

———

Viam waited at Daliel's side, her mind roiling. *Gods, did he really send someone to talk to the Disciples of the Flame? Or was it a setup?* Whatever the case, Daliel was hardly to blame for his continued refusal to partake in the ceremony after witnessing someone he knew slaughtered at his father's hand.

"I am disappointed," said the king after the last of the soldiers had left the courtyard. "In both of you."

"It wasn't Viam's fault," Daliel blurted. "Toren was innocent. He was—"

"Did you seek to make peace with the Disciples of the Flame in the hopes that they might induct you into their ranks?" The king cut through his son's objections, and Viam looked at Daliel in surprise. *He thinks his son wanted to* join *the Disciples?* "Or were you and Viam Tiathar planning this all along?"

"The decision was mine." Daliel's voice was strained, panicked, but clear. "Viam had no idea. I planned this myself."

"I see." He beckoned to the guards standing behind the last prisoner trembling near the altar. "Nevertheless, you cannot shirk your duty any longer, Daliel."

This prisoner was cuffed like the others, their face covered with a sack.

"I have decided to be generous," said the king. "I will allow you to conduct your first sacrifice without my soldiers watching you."

Daliel advanced, lifting the dagger in a stance that made it clear that he'd been trained, but his shaky hands betrayed him. For a terrifying heartbeat, Viam expected him to refuse and to feel the bite of the king's claw-blade against her throat.

The dagger sliced into its target. Blood poured, at first a trickle and then a deluge. It seemed to take the man an age to die; his body spasmed, blood gushing over the prince's hands and splashing to the floor, into the waiting shadows.

Tears glistened on Daliel's cheeks as the dagger slid from his hands. Viam watched, sickened, mesmerised by the shadows swathing the fallen weapon and the dead prisoner both.

"You have proven yourself to Mekan," said the king. "There is no need for you to despair, son. This man was a criminal of no consequence. I would not be so cruel as to force you to slaughter someone you called a friend."

Killing a friend in front of his son apparently didn't count. And while Viam had been spared, she wished it had been she who'd been forced to take on that burden.

"It's wrong," Daliel whispered. "This is all wrong. Mekan is a being who understands nothing but terror and destruction. Embracing Him will ruin us."

"You are lucky that the god of death cares nothing for your treasonous words," the king said. "Mekan is generous. He forgives all, provided you offer Him the sacrifices necessary to maintain His favour. That you will do, and from this point onward, your friend Viam Tiathar will attend each ceremony alongside you. She will act as your incentive should you fail to perform adequately."

The implication was clear. Viam wasn't being spared. Not at all. Rather, she was to serve as a constant reminder that others would suffer if the prince refused to obey his father's command.

She was, in effect, a hostage of the crown.

———

"How long," said Superior Sietra, "have you been able to control the dead?"

Niema stared, not expecting the accusatory note beneath the Superior's question. "I can't—that is, not in the way you're thinking. Only the creatures directly from Mekan's realm, and I don't know that they *are* dead, since they can be killed."

"They can," she agreed, "but it was my understanding that none could control those beasts save for Mekan Himself."

"The king can. I think. Some of them." She stumbled over the words. "As for me, I think it's because I healed Yala and forged a link between us. Between me and—"

"Mekan," the Superior finished. "And that is how you defeated the king's army."

Niema inclined her head, a sinking sensation in the pit of her stomach. Yalet had undeniably accepted her into the elite ranks, but away from the temple, her certainty was as fragile as a feather caught in a wind current and just as likely to blow away. "I'm here to help in the same way if I can."

"That is why I invited you here," the Superior said. "However, I'd advise you not to share your abilities with anyone else. Some might believe you a threat to our safety."

I'm not the one who told you. Kelan had, and the warning left her wrong-footed, shaken. "I won't tell anyone."

"I expect not." The Superior's lips pursed. "You may leave. I hope you'll find the accommodations to your liking."

She found Kelan waiting outside the office for her. He offered a smile, which she countered with a blistering glare. "Thanks for telling tales on me to your Superior. Did you not stop to consider that it wasn't a secret I wanted spread around?"

"I didn't tell anyone else," Kelan protested. "And it's hardly irrelevant. You sent the king's army away, didn't you?"

"She thought the others would believe me to be a threat to their safety." What had she expected, though? Her mere presence invited the dead, no matter how much faith Yalet had placed in her when She had imparted that vision. Gods, for all she knew, it might have been Niema's presence that had drawn them to the other enclave.

"For what it's worth, I'm sorry," Kelan said. "I take it your promotion went well? Is that the right word?"

Niema shrugged. Justified though he had been when he'd shared her secret with the Superior, he hadn't earned the right to hear of her experiences on the island nor of the vision she'd experienced. The details were not necessary to help Skytower.

Yet the sense that she'd made a mistake in coming here lodged into her skin like a barb. If the king dispatched the dead to attack the forest instead of Skytower, she might not arrive in time to stop them.

And what if the dead followed me here too?

———

Niema didn't speak to Kelan as he carried her up to the guest rooms. He had to admit that he hadn't expected Niema to be *this* annoyed at him for sharing her abilities with the Superior, and her companion shared in her mistrust. Kelan tried to make peace by offering to take Hachim on a tour of the tower, but both declined and retired to their rooms.

He made one last attempt before Niema closed the door. "Now, you can at least tell me if the Disciples of the Sea are safe, can't you?"

"I'd have told you if they weren't," was her terse reply. "They're on their ship near the village where we left them, but they're prepared to leave if there is another attack."

"You said your Superiors were being targeted…?" he began. "It's not the king?"

"No." Weariness filled her voice. "It's not the king. It's Mekan. Can your questions wait until morning?"

"It's not an interrogation. What did my Superior say to you?"

"Aside from insinuating that my abilities make me untrustworthy to some?" Her mouth pinched. "Nothing. It's nothing."

"It definitely isn't." He frowned. "Did your Superior try to play mind games with you again? What did she do, fill your head with warnings about our upcoming demise?"

"This isn't a joke, Kelan!" she snapped. "She didn't say a thing. I came to my own conclusions."

A shout echoed up from somewhere below the tower. Kelan strained his ears, hearing the repeated cry:

"War drakes!"

This time, there was no doubt that the enemy was here.

31

B y day, Yala trained her flight squad. By night, she offered sacrifices to the god of death. Before long, all the others were accomplished at raising a body they'd slain, but the king stopped short of letting them give more complex commands. Perhaps due to the risk of injury, though the threat presented by a war drake was significantly higher. In the days since the mission, one flier had lost a few fingers during a training session in the paddocks, and another had almost been gored to death by their steed.

Keeping her squad safe during the day was a sufficient distraction from dwelling on the nightly horrors they witnessed in the temple. Of course, Yala's fellow captains had long overcome any initial hesitation, and any doubts they might have harboured had been extinguished by the promises Mekan whispered in their ears. Each night, she saw the greed in the others' eyes when they slit the throats of the unlucky souls the king had gathered for the purpose, the hunger for blood.

Yala longed to kill every single one of them.

The two exceptions, Viam and Daliel, were also the least

enthusiastic about their nightly proceedings, though it seemed that the threat of punishment inflicted on Viam had coaxed the prince to obey his father's orders. Yala had scarcely spoken to her former squad-mate since the grisly death of the man unfortunate enough to attempt to visit the Temple of the Flame on the prince's behalf. Precisely what Daliel had been thinking in sending him there, she couldn't have said.

Daliel might be a true Disciple of Death now, but the king showed him no special favour. Nor did Mekan, though he progressed at the same rate as the others, and Yala told herself that her growing irritation was rooted more in her desire to thwart the king than in jealousy that so many shared in the god of death's glory. Despite the blood she'd shed, she'd been offered no insight into the nature of the king's agreement with Mekan. Nor how much control the god of death held over the monarch's actions.

Not as much as the masked guards, certainly. The pair were present at every ceremony, stationed on either side of the monarch, and were as unmoving and emotionless as the stone pillars flanking the altar. Yala suspected that if the entire palace caught fire, they'd stay put, obedient to the last breath.

Of course, fire holds no power here, she thought while waiting for her turn at the altar one night. When she stood over the prisoner offered as a sacrifice, she surreptitiously brushed her hand against the claw concealed at her waist. She had yet to reveal her secret weapon to the king, though he surely knew it was there.

"Have I not served you well, Mekan?" she whispered. "Do I not deserve more than this?"

She spoke too softly for the king to hear, but shadows stirred at her words, coiling around her feet and rising to embrace the prisoner as she slit open their throat. Darkness trailed from her fingertips, too, manipulating the body as one might a puppet.

Now, how do I prevent the dead from moving, as the king did?

"Stop." She curled her fingers inward, beckoning to the shadows too. Demanding they release the body from their grasp.

Slowly, like a rope uncoiling, the body fell. It hit the ground, as inert as if untouched by Mekan.

Yala suppressed the smile that threatened to creep onto her face. As the guards removed the body, she turned away from the altar and found the king watching her with careful eyes. *Shit. Did I overstep?*

"Mekan favours you," he said. "The god of death's mark lies upon you."

Yala's hand twitched towards the scar on her face. That was true, but she should have known better than to draw attention to herself. Affecting surprise, she said, "Does it?"

"That will be an asset to you," said the king. "When you enter the Void, you will be rewarded."

When will that be? She suppressed the impatience building inside. Entering the Void too soon would result in losing her will, becoming one of those emotionless beings guarding the temple—or worse, rotting from the inside out as Corruption ate away at her earthly body while she still breathed.

Becoming a vessel for the god of death was out of the question, but whatever Daliel might think, the king did not appear to be entirely subject to Mekan's will. He spoke with his own voice, and however warped his priorities might be, he wasn't acting as someone driven by the urge only to kill without considering the consequences.

That might not last, but the question of how much Yala might need to give up in order to surpass him haunted her long after they left the temple behind.

And if that would happen before he took Skytower—or after.

———

Niema ran straight to Hachim's room as the warning shout echoed up and down the tower and the Disciples of the Sky who weren't already assigned to guard duty gathered near the balconies overlooking the lower levels.

"Niema." Hachim opened the door before she reached it, and together, they approached the nearest balcony, peering out into the darkened sky. "Where are they? The soldiers?"

"It's not the soldiers." Kelan glided past, reaching for his sword. "It's one war drake."

"Alone? It's not one of ours?"

A familiar chill seized hold of Niema as a breeze swept over them, too cold, too malevolent to have come from the Disciples. Her eyes picked out the dark, winged shape rising from the night, a steed without a rider. *A void drake.*

A scream cut through the air from above. Kelan tensed. "My Superior."

He rose into the air on a gust of wind that sent both her and Hachim staggering across the platform. Catching her balance, she whistled, calling to her war drake. The beasts had flown far enough from the tower not to be taken for the enemy but not too distant to hear their riders' commands.

More screaming, this time from below. Niema leaned over the balcony, trying to make sense of the confused melee of cloaked figures wielding swords against smaller winged shapes that she might have taken for tree-raptors if not for the viciousness with which they attacked the Disciples.

More attacked the floor above, while screams from elsewhere on their level prompted Niema to run in that direction. A lantern someone had left out revealed the monstrous bird-like creatures that Mekan had set against them. All were cloaked in dark scales as hard as stone and wielded claws sharp enough to cut to the bone.

"What kind of monsters are those?" The question came from a young Disciple who leaned against the wall, one arm gripping the other, blood seeping down to his wrist.

"Mekan's beasts." Many of the Disciples of the Sky hadn't been present at any of the prior battles against the dead, and while all would have been trained in combat, few would willingly volunteer to fight when the Disciples weren't subject to conscription laws. "You weren't bitten, were you? Those wounds can be lethal."

"No." He sank to the floor with a groan. "Mekan's beasts? Really?"

"Let me help with that." She leaned over and whispered a prayer to Yalet. His eyes rounded when green light spread up his arm, stemming the bleeding. He held up his hand in wonderment.

"Don't overdo it," Hachim warned. "They're all over the tower."

The Disciples had slain all the beasts on this level, so Niema ran to the balcony to see what was happening above and below. As she did, the war drakes finally came soaring to meet their riders. Niema clambered onto a balcony and helped Hachim do the same, mounting their war drakes as a familiar screech rang out and a body fell, tumbling head over heels into the empty night.

There's the void drake.

Niema and Hachim flew upward as the void drake appeared in a blur of claws and blood. Three Disciples were flung back, one striking the tower wall and leaving a smear of crimson as they slid down and out of sight.

Niema drew in air to whistle, but the void drake struck first. Its claws flashed, catching her steed in a vicious swipe

EMMA L. ADAMS

that sent her spinning away. Nausea swept over her, and as she struggled to catch her breath, Hachim's war drake tackled the monster.

The two clawed beasts slammed into one another, claws interlocking, teeth ripping. Niema found her voice and screamed, the sound turning into a sharp whistle.

Stop!

The void drake ceased its attack. Hachim's steed did not. Its claws dug in deep, ripping off scales to penetrate the flesh beneath. The void drake broke away, trailing blood, and another sharp whistle sent it fleeing into the darkness.

The Disciples flew in pursuit, air gusting from their hands and swords at the ready. Niema flew to Hachim, her heart in her mouth. "Are you all right?"

"I am." Blood speckled his face, and his war drake's claws were caked in gore. "Make sure there aren't any others."

Most of the attackers were smaller creatures, mockeries of birds or raptors, but big enough to overwhelm in larger numbers.

When she spied two younger Disciples—novices—trying to fend off a large raptor-sized beast with leathery wings, she pushed her war drake into a dive and whistled a command directed at all the dead, all the monsters attacking the Disciples' home, demanding that they flee.

As her dive slowed, she saw the dead retreating with the Disciples in pursuit, striking with steel and air. The wind currents were as cutting as their weapons as the Disciples unleashed the sky god's might against their assailants. When she looked for the void drake, she saw a distant winged shape falling gracelessly out of the sky into the valley below.

The battle was over as swiftly as it had begun.

Niema flew up to the topmost level of the tower, where Kelan and some others had formed ranks to protect their Superior's office.

Upon seeing Niema, he glided over to her. "They didn't come for the Superior. They weren't sent by the king."

No. They came for me. "Were any killed?"

"I don't know." Comprehension crept over his face. "Oh. You think Mekan might infect them?"

"I hope not." Her teeth chattered. The wounds those monsters inflicted might easily be fatal, and who was to say how long Mekan's taint would linger? "I can help the injured."

"You've done more than enough already." His cloak was torn and stained with gore, but he appeared to be unhurt. As he rapped on the Superior's office door, Niema climbed off the war drake's back and helped Hachim climb down too.

As she'd expected, the Superior wanted to talk to them both. At this late hour, her face was stripped of paint, and her countenance was strangely plain without her embroidered clothing and jewels, but she presented a formidable figure all the same. *Does she know it was my fault? That I brought the dead with me?*

"You saved lives with your intervention," the Superior said. "Thank you for defending us."

Niema drew her arms around herself as if she might fold up into a smaller shape and disappear. "I'm sorry for your losses."

"That is a remarkable ability you possess," said the Superior. "I see now why Kelan was keen to request your help."

"I drew them here." She couldn't hold that information to herself. "The dead—are drawn to me. I think it's another effect of—"

"Your bond to Mekan." The Superior's stare stripped her to the bone. "I see now why you didn't return to the enclave."

Her words lodged in Niema's chest like arrows. "I'll leave. I'm sorry."

"No." The Superior raised a hand. "You volunteered your

talents to protect Skytower, and it is undeniable that we shall have need of your help. We will willingly shoulder the burden."

"You shouldn't have to."

"The fault is mine," Kelan ventured. "I knew the risks when I invited Niema here, but I reasoned that her abilities aren't something we can afford to do without."

"You are quite correct, but I would caution against spreading word to the others," said the Superior. "There are many who would be opposed to inviting any element of Mekan's influence into the tower."

"That's why I should leave. I can come back if you're attacked again." The argument was hollow, she knew; she'd have to travel far from the tower to ensure Mekan's influence departed, and if the king's army materialised in the interim, she might not arrive in time to prevent Skytower from falling.

"There is no need," said the Superior. "We shall take precautions. However, I would like to know the extent to which the monarch is aware of this ability."

"He knows." Her heart pitched downward. "He knows I can control Mekan's beasts but not that they're drawn to me."

"Then I pray that he does not learn any more, and so should your fellow Disciples."

"What are you implying?" Hachim spoke up for the first time. "That the king might try to use Niema against the Disciples of Life?"

"If I were in his position, that is what I would do."

And with that chilling proclamation, Niema's hopes of sparing her fellow Disciples expired. She'd come here to avoid causing harm to the enclave, but if the Superior spoke true, if King Tharen acted out her worst fears...

Niema might be the blade Mekan drove into Yalet's heart.

———

After the king's warning, Viam received no more invitations from the palace during daylight hours. Nor did she dare venture close to the barracks to speak to Nalen for fear that the king's spies might be watching both her and Daliel. Brenat kept her updated; according to her, Nalen had even succeeded in convincing one of the commanders to join their cause, though quite what they hoped to attain was less than clear to Viam. She hardly blamed anyone who wanted to walk away from the king's army, but a cynical voice at the back of her mind told her that even if his entire army walked out of the palace grounds, the king would not be deterred from his mission.

Not when he had another force waiting deep inside the Void, ready to answer his summons.

Every time she saw the prince, he looked more subdued, his features lined with exhaustion. His hand shook whenever he had to wield the dagger, to take a life, but he always obeyed. Her own life was an axe held over his head, and though she hated herself for getting into this situation, that hatred was nothing to that she held towards the man responsible.

It had taken a few days for Viam to find her anger, but when she did, she wondered how Yala could stand that close to the king without betraying her desire to slit his throat. Her former captain had always been better at hiding her emotions, while Viam's face was as transparent as glass, and it was fortunate that the king held her too far beneath his notice to pay much attention. She was a hostage, not a Disciple in truth like the others were. The others had long outpaced her in Mekan's favour, and none more so than Yala. She was always first in line, the first to volunteer to shed blood upon the altar.

EMMA L. ADAMS

It was part of her plan, Viam knew, and she reminded herself of that every time those worries surfaced like roots sprouting inside her. Worry that Yala wanted to win Mekan's favour for her own advancement rather than any desire to use that power against the king.

After three nightly ceremonies had passed without a word between them, she'd had enough. The soldiers always left the temple first after each ceremony, and Daliel was always last, so she waited for him outside the door.

When the prince walked past, she caught his arm. "Daliel."

He pulled out of her reach, his frightened eyes darting to the courtyard entrance. "Viam. You can't."

"The guards aren't here." The masked creatures rarely ventured far from the king, and he always stayed in the temple long after everyone else had left. "Please, *please* come with me. Just for a moment."

"Why?" He walked, shoulders hunched, a short way down the corridor from the courtyard.

"I don't want to be distant from one another," she murmured, keeping pace with him. "Not when we're both caught in this trap together."

"You are the one who will suffer for any mistake I make."

"He didn't *say* I wasn't allowed to talk to you anymore," she said. "He encouraged it, actually."

"Only in the event that you persuade me to participate."

"For all he and the guards know, that's exactly what we're talking about now." She looked into his eyes, willing him to dredge up some resistance. "I haven't changed my mind. I have friends, people who can help."

"I already got someone killed through my carelessness."

"The people involved know the risks, Daliel," she said. "And you're still the prince. You won't be put to death for speaking out of line."

322

"He can punish me in other ways. The first time I refused to kill, he locked me in the temple overnight."

"Oh, Daliel." She laid a reassuring hand on his arm.

He flinched. "He did me a favour. He said that if I'm too weak when I enter the Void, Mekan will take over my physical body, and my mind will no longer be my own."

"Is that what happened to those guards?" she asked. "The masked ones?"

He dipped his head. "For all his power, he's mortal, and I'm his heir. He can't afford to lose me, at least not yet. But he did say that if I step too far out of line, he'll have me married to another noble, and our child will become the heir instead. Then, I shall be offered to Mekan as penance."

Viam gasped. "What?"

"So you see." His voice was low, tortured. "I am nothing to him in the end."

Why did that never cross my mind? Daliel was young, and he'd spent the years of his rule too busy dealing with ongoing crises to marry or produce an heir of his own. Viam had never imagined that his father might use that against him, but the king's comments also offered up a question.

"That implies it's possible to step into the Void *without* losing control over one's body or mind," she said. "Like the king did. He wants you to do the same. Right?"

"He wants me to be strong enough to resist control."

"How, though?" she pressed. "How was he able to travel into the Void without losing himself?"

"I dare not ask." His voice quietened. "I know that he and Mekan made a bargain."

"What does the god of death get out of this bargain?" Aside from the sacrifice of flesh and blood, which anyone might have offered. No, the king must have promised far more than that. "Can you try to find out?"

"I can try." He exhaled in a sigh. "That's all I can do."

"Thank you." She touched his arm again. "I don't fault you for anything you've done, Daliel. It's on him, not you."

"I see their faces every night," he whispered. "In my dreams. I can't escape them."

"I wish I could say it gets easier." The way in which the prince had been compelled to take up the knife was uniquely traumatic, and she suspected that he would be haunted by those he'd killed for the rest of his life.

As to how long that life would last? That might depend on whether he was able to forge his own bargain with Mekan, and one that did not involve surrendering his mind, body, and soul to the Void.

32

The Void's cold whisper scraped against Yala's ear like metal on stone. Shadows coiled outward from the altar, creeping around her feet and those of her fellow Disciples of Death, but the king was nowhere to be seen.

"Is he in the Void?" Veshan's voice strained with eagerness. "Does he wish for us to follow him?"

"Go ahead," said another captain. "I bet he's testing our obedience, and if we follow, the Void will eat us alive."

Fools, the lot of them. Yala dug the tip of her cane into hard stone, fighting the urge to investigate for herself. The king might well be testing their patience, and it was hard to say whether the person who cracked first would be rewarded or slaughtered. Yala held still, listening to the faint whisper within the Void and watching the shadows coil around her companions like a manifestation of her hatred.

Hatred, whispered a voice in the back of her mind, *or jealousy? Because Mekan's attention should be yours alone?*

Dangerous thoughts. The god of death did not share. He

did not care who occupied His attention. He wanted nothing but flesh and blood.

But whose flesh and blood will it be this time? The king must have run out of prisoners, surely, and it was one step from there to forcing his own allies to stand in their place. Would their next test be to take the life of another Disciple of Death?

Yala sensed the void drake before she saw it. The claw in her pocket stirred in recognition as the monstrous shape formed within the darkness shrouding the altar. Wings extended from shadow that became solid scale as the void drake put down a clawed foot then another. As its pitted eyes raked over them, the soldiers exclaimed, some reaching for their daggers, others backing away.

The king appeared like a spirit manifested and brought down the claw-blade in a sweep that sliced between the hard scales on the void drake's neck. As the beast writhed, blood leaking from the wound, he lifted the weapon again and drove the tip into its exposed eye.

"This is your next test." He raised his voice over the void drake's guttural death cries. "You will face the Void's beasts, and any who triumph will be able to claim a piece of Mekan as a trophy. As you can see, their claws and teeth are as potent as any manmade sword, if not more so."

We don't even have *swords.* Each soldier carried an army-issued dagger and nothing more, and while Yala also held her cane, the wooden edge would leave no impact on scales impervious even to the edge of a sharpened blade.

As if he'd detected her thoughts, the king indicated the altar's side, where a pile of spears, swords and other weapons had been left for them to claim. The offer hardly restored Yala's confidence. Most fliers' training would have been focused on dagger and spear, and many of them wouldn't have held a sword in years, if at all. Even drawing a bow was difficult when seated upon an unpredictable winged steed, though the Disciples of Life seemed to have made it work.

"Not every beast within the Void is as formidable as a void drake," the king said as the soldiers moved in on the weapons pile. "That said, their bites are invariably fatal and a terribly painful way to die."

A sharp cry resounded within the Void, and a raptor-sized beast leapt over the altar, its long tail sweeping across the floor. Emitting another earsplitting screech, it sprang at Lisek, the closest target.

Grabbing a sword from within the pile, she flung it at the raptor-like beast, an inexpert throw that nevertheless knocked off her target's momentum. Lisek leapt after, brandishing her dagger. A reckless move, but it paid off. Tackling the beast from the side, she brought her dagger up into its exposed throat, cutting into the gap between scale and flesh.

The beast fell, bleeding its last, and Lisek straightened with a grin. Yala suppressed a twinge of irritation that trod entirely too close to envy. *I could do that, once, when I had no regard for my own life.*

A laugh rose in her throat when she saw Lisek's gaze dart towards the king, as if hoping for praise. None came, but an ominous growl issued from the Void, and the stench of decay rolled over them.

Then came the dead. Winged beasts, some the size of giens or freks, others resembling larger featherdrakes or tree-raptors. Some were wingless, equipped instead with talons and tails lined with spikes. A flat-nosed imitation of a riverdrake came barrelling towards her, and Yala lifted her cane, struck it across the face. Its mouth gaped open, revealing two rows of pointed teeth, and Yala wedged her cane between them. Sharp incisors came down on the wood, which groaned but didn't break. Swiftly, she drove her dagger into its exposed eye then the other.

Around her, the Void continued to spew out more horrors. Nearby, one of the raptor-like beasts had sunk sharp teeth into a soldier's arm. He swore, trying to shake it off, using his other hand to drive a dagger into its face. The beast's grip broke, but the damage was done. As the monster breathed its last, the soldier slumped to his knees, his face slick with sweat. The image of a similar wound in Machit's arm entered Yala's mind, festering, killing him from the inside. He'd chosen to allow himself to be sacrificed instead, to die on his terms.

Revulsion seized her. Nobody had spared so much as a glance at the injured man. Most fought their adversaries alone, with two stark exceptions. Viam stood side by side with Daliel, each holding a shortsword defensively. The king had taken a major gamble in exposing his only heir to danger when the prince's reticence towards violence was well known, but Daliel knew how to defend himself as well as the rest of them did. Two smaller raptor-like beasts lay dead at his feet.

A shrill cry rang out, cutting through the general clamour, and the void drake's claw stirred at her side. From the darkness, a large claw emerged, swiping the smaller beasts aside and sending two soldiers crashing onto their backs. There followed a void drake's monstrous reptilian form, its spine-tipped wings extending to brush the pillars flanking the altar.

This time, the king was nowhere to be seen. He wanted them to fight this beast alone.

Lisek ran forward as its claw lashed out. She caught the blow upon the edge of her spear but staggered, losing her grip on the weapon. As she threw herself to the ground to avoid being impaled, more spears flew from the other soldiers, bouncing off the armour encasing its body.

Yala lifted her dagger, gauging the odds of reaching one of its weak points. From the sky, she would have a clear shot at its eyes, but not from here on the ground. Not only was it taller than a war drake, but its wings spread wide enough to blot out the moonlight streaming into the courtyard and hindered their visibility. Yala had fought in near darkness before, but she was willing to bet the void drake's pitted eyes could easily pierce the gloom to seek out its prey. Surviving in the Void would make night vision essential.

Yala took a step back, then another, using her cane to feel her way across the courtyard. The clatter of spears being thrown pursued her, and when the beast shifted, a thin stream of moonlight revealed the corpse of the first void drake sprawled next to the altar.

Grabbing a discarded spear, she tucked it under her arm and kept her attention trained on the altar as she made her way around the beast's side. Though her night vision was nothing compared to someone who'd entered the Void, even her weaker human eyes could tell the difference between the shadows brought on by the absence of sunlight and the blot of oblivion behind the altar.

Careful. She slowed her pace and extended her cane until she met the solid edge of a pillar. A few steps took her feet up to the altar. Slippery shadows tugged at her, creeping up her legs, but they did not prevent her from climbing onto the large slab of stone.

Yala let the cane fall from her hand. The clatter brought the beast's head swinging around—and in a lunge, Yala brought the spear up into the void drake's oncoming mouth. Burying the edge to its hilt.

The beast let out a sharp cry, piercing enough to make her

329

lose her balance. She slid from the altar, her leg screaming in protest, and crawled through a fractured web of moonlight and shadow to reach her cane. Shielding herself from the beast's thrashing tail, she pushed herself to her feet as the other soldiers moved upon the injured void drake, eagerly stabbing its exposed flesh.

Yala let them. Her leg throbbed with each step, her breath escaped in quick gasps, yet triumph surged through her veins. When the beast's death throes stilled to silence, the king once again stepped out of the shadows.

"That is the end of the test," he proclaimed. "You will take your prizes, as promised."

At his prompting, they helped themselves to remnants of the beast, using their daggers to sever its sharp claws and remove the spined claw-shaped tips from its wings. Some took several, glancing warily at the king as if worried he might stop them, but he did not. There were plenty to go around, and Yala too stepped in to claim another claw to join the one concealed at her waist.

A few braver soldiers climbed over the void drake's mouth to slice at its teeth, careful not to let the deadly edges penetrate their skin. The reminder prompted Yala to glance over at the injured soldier. He lay prone on the ground, his breathing shallow, ignored by all. Yala's stomach turned over. *He's going to die, and nobody here cares.*

When the last claw was severed from the monster's foot, the king called them to attention. "As you may have gathered, we are almost ready to take on Skytower. With those weapons in your hands, you now have the capacity to open the Void yourselves, and that is how you will achieve victory over your foes."

"We can open the Void?" Lisek looked down at the bloodied claw in her hand, an awed smile forming on her face. "Truly?"

"Any life you take while holding those weapons will be considered a sacrifice to Mekan," he told them. "Take enough lives, and the Void will open, and Mekan's beasts will come to aid you in your fight against the rogue Disciples of Skytower."

Is he implying he won't come with us? He would, surely, but the possibility of the king staying behind did not trouble her as much as the other disadvantage to their strategy, one that nobody else would be aware of.

"Your Majesty," Yala said, "if we open the Void, Mekan's beasts are likely to attack us as well as the enemy, are they not?"

The king swivelled to her. The other soldiers did too. Tension rippled across her shoulders, but she held firm, reasoning that anyone present might have guessed the same if they hadn't been too focused on revelling in their victory to remember that the monsters they'd triumphed over were the same ones the king wanted them to unleash against their fellow humans.

"It is a strategy that requires caution," the king agreed. "Should events proceed as planned, Skytower will swiftly fall. I will be present myself to ensure that there are no mistakes."

Despite the temporary thrill at the confirmation that he would indeed be accompanying them to Skytower, his proclamation brought a chilling weight to her shoulders.

No mistakes. Not this time.

———

Viam stumbled from the courtyard. Dark blood slicked her arm, and her leg stung from a shallow wound inflicted by one of the smaller monsters. At least the wound had been dealt by its claws and not its teeth, unlike the soldier who staggered out of the room last, hardly able to keep his feet.

We could have died. It was far from the first time the king's actions would have led to unnecessary deaths, but she could hardly believe he'd brought the soldiers this far in their training only to throw them at the mercy of the Void's most fearsome monsters.

Not that the other soldiers seemed to agree. They brandished their newly acquired trophies with pride as they made their way out of the palace, loudly boasting of their achievements. Their gloating turned Niema's stomach. Yes, a void drake was a wild animal driven only to kill, but didn't the king ride a similar steed of his own? His actions suggested he cared nothing if any of his allies were killed, whether they belonged to the dead or the living, and Yala had been right to remind him of the dangers of setting the soldiers directly in the path of the Void.

Yala walked at the rear of the group, leaning on her cane hard as if she'd injured her leg during the fight. Like the rest of them, her clothes and hands were smeared with blood. Viam kept pace with her, and they descended the palace stairs in silence.

Once they'd left the watchful eyes of the void drakes behind, Yala tilted her head at Viam. "How many pieces of that beast did you get?"

The question baffled her. "One. Why?"

"You had an opportunity." Yala tapped the pouch at her waist, from which several gleaming claws protruded. "These are stronger than steel. Useful weapons to arm a rebellion, wouldn't you say?"

"You know I'm not part of that." Days had passed since her last interaction with Daliel, but the king watched him too closely, and Viam had lost her nerve. Even now, she kept a close eye on the shadows in case of eavesdroppers, either the king's guards or merely curious soldiers. "I told Daliel. He didn't seem enthused."

"You told him."

"I didn't give names." Viam hadn't told Yala of their interaction either; her former captain had appeared reticent to publicly speak to her at all until tonight. "His father's holding the threat of the Void over him. He said that he might even be removed from the succession line if he fails to convince Mekan to spare him as his father did."

"How?" Yala's eyes gleamed in the darkness. "That useless prince must have *some* idea of how the king managed to win over the god of death."

"Daliel said that if his father and Mekan made a deal, the god of death must get something out of it."

"Yes, I can see that." Yala's brow furrowed as if she was thinking hard. "He must have promised something more valuable than his life."

Many lives. A nation. Chills crawled up Viam's spine. "Whatever it is, the mission will be soon, won't it? Daliel will be alone in the palace. I can go to him."

"Why, so he can make another pitiful appeal for help from the Disciples of the Flame?"

Viam took a step back, startled at the venom in her voice. "Didn't they almost destroy the Temple of Death?"

"Yes, at the cost of their lives." Yala snorted. "They likely thought it an honour, but unless the Superior has more of those candles, they won't be able to make another attempt."

"He might." Would the Disciples be willing to risk death for freedom? To destroy the temple or, at the very least, slow the advance of the Void?

A sigh escaped Yala. "Do as you will, but remember the likely fate of anyone who sets foot in the palace uninvited."

"Not like I can forget." Viam's hands clenched and unclenched as she watched Yala walk away. Strange how easy it was to grow accustomed to living under the shadow of a constant threat to one's life.

Of course, she'd lived with the same as a soldier; some were able to turn off that part of their mind when they weren't on missions, but Viam had always had trouble detaching from the crushing dread, the paranoia. In the years that had elapsed since, she had become accustomed to avoiding danger, to keeping her head down... but for all that, the fear had not gone away. And now, she'd found herself right back where she'd started.

If I waited until the fear lifted to act, I'd be waiting forever.

With that thought in mind, Viam made her decision.

————

Saren lay awake while the others slept, waiting for Yala to return to the barracks. He alone knew the details of her nighttime excursions, but the others had suspicions formed from the rumours dropped by less careful squad leaders, and he had to tell Gorel to go back to bed when he tried to tail Saren outside.

Tonight's ceremony must have run late. He waited outside the dormitory for at least twenty minutes, shivering in the cold air drifting through an open window. When at last the squad captains began to return, he ducked outside, anticipating that Yala would lag behind the others.

When Yala did appear, she was leaning heavily on her cane, her mouth pinched in pain. Her eyes narrowed when she saw him. "I told you not to wait for me, Saren."

"Nobody's out here. I checked." He affected a casual tone. "So, who did he have you kill this time?"

"A void drake."

His mouth fell open. "You're joking."

Yala grunted. "We outnumbered it. It was hardly a fair contest."

"Fair." Disdain underlined the word. "And there I was thinking you'd parted ways with your conscience outright."

Yala's fingers tightened around her cane. "Were you only waiting here to berate me?"

"No, I worried when you didn't come back." He studied her blood-streaked face. "A *void drake*? Why'd His Majesty want to risk skewering his own soldiers?"

"Because of these." She lifted the hem of her shirt, displaying the open pouch at her belt.

Saren eyed the gleaming claws. "Couldn't he get his own damn weapons? Those beasts would lie on their backs like wild hogs if he asked them to."

"It was a test," she said. "We're close to the mission, I'm sure."

"Did His Majesty let anything slip about his strategy?"

Yala's lips pursed. "He wants us to open the Void as soon as we enter Skytower and let Mekan's army swarm the place."

"Did he forget the dead don't tend to distinguish between friend and foe?" At a guess, the answer was *no*. "Shit. I guess our deaths don't matter as long as enough blood is spilled."

"Precisely." She displayed the claws again. "I doubt the king will let me give these to the squad, but anyone can use them, Disciple or not."

His thoughts went to Nalen, to his half-conceived thoughts of rebellion. "I'll ask Nalen, but you know what he thinks of Corruption."

Saren would play no part in anything that might unfold at the palace during their mission. Instead, he'd be bound for Skytower himself, as doomed as a bloodfly caught in a web.

Anger coursed through him as he followed Yala back into the dormitory, her clothes bearing the fresh markings of the monsters' claws. He hadn't asked if any soldiers had been injured or killed, but when they passed the infirmary, he glimpsed two people carrying in a wounded man, his arm ripped open to the bone. A few others occupied sleeping mats, recovering from minor wounds they'd suffered during training. The man who'd lost an arm to a war drake's bite certainly would not be fighting.

I wonder...

33

A s Yala had anticipated, the commanders called everyone into the grounds the morning after to announce their intention to begin the assault on Skytower in two days' time.

Some people laughed, the sound petering out when they realised he was serious. They'd barely recovered from the last mission, after all, and as reality sank in, panic spread amid the squad members like a contagious virus. Scuffles broke out intermittently throughout the day, and despite Yala's attempts to keep her own squad disciplined, Vilat and Roven had a full-blown fistfight on the way to the paddocks after the latter claimed that the former had been peeking at her as she was changing into her uniform.

Yala had barely broken up that fight when a commotion broke out inside the paddock. She ran that way and heard Saren cursing at the top of his voice. "Saren, what—?"

As she opened the paddock gate, the coppery tang of blood hit her nostrils, and Saren staggered forward, bleeding heavily from one arm. A war drake had sunk its teeth deep into the meat, and blood fountained from the wound, causing the other beasts to stir restlessly, straining at their chains.

"Fuck." She grabbed the war drake's discarded muzzle and roughly strapped it back into place. "What did you do, stick your hand in its mouth?"

He groaned in response. Yala took his uninjured arm and steered him out of the paddock, ordering one of the others to lock the gate. As they walked, she examined the injury. Deep though the gouges might be, the beast's teeth hadn't hit any major arteries, nor had they pierced through the bone. The wound would take a few weeks to heal, but he wouldn't lose the arm.

Coincidence, is it?

Yala took him to the infirmary and waited for the healers to finish patching him up before she confronted him.

"Was this planned?" she asked out of the corner of her mouth as the healer walked away with his arms full of bloodied bandages. "Or an impulse?"

"What the hell are you talking about?" Saren tweaked the edge of the bandage with his uninjured hand. "Why would I do this on purpose?"

"Why indeed." Her tone was flat. "I suppose it's a coincidence that the war drake bit you at such an angle that it'll get you out of missions for a few weeks but won't result in permanent injury."

He kept fiddling with the bandage, not meeting her eyes. "And how would I know that?"

"Because you're a fucking healer," she retaliated. "Don't treat me like a fool. You can at least tell me the truth about why you took yourself out of the action right before our most important mission."

A sigh rattled from his chest. "You wouldn't have let me be spared otherwise."

"Yes, and now, I have to find a replacement. If they die, it's on you."

Fuming, she left the infirmary. Her rage was disproportionate, she knew; Saren was less likely to get hurt if he stayed behind, but now, she had to worry about finding another flier on top of everything else.

In a rare stroke of luck, the commander had some volunteers in reserve, a necessary move after the last mission had depleted their ranks. While they walked through the barracks to fetch someone, she seized the chance to ask if he knew more of the king's strategy for the mission.

"He'll give you the specifics later," the commander said, "but your orders are to approach the Superior, capture her, and force a surrender, as I understand it."

"Capture the most powerful Disciple inside her own temple?" She couldn't keep the scepticism from her voice. "We'll be slaughtered, and we'd deserve it."

Bold words on her part, perhaps, but even a force of Disciples of Death would have trouble taking down a Superior in her natural habitat.

"The king plans to address all the captains later today," he told her. "He will give you the details of the mission then."

I thought so.

The order came when Yala was in the middle of escorting Surel, the new recruit, to meet the others. She put Gorel in charge of getting the newcomer up to speed on their routines before she joined her fellow captains on their way to the palace. Her leg ached from the previous day, and climbing the stairs was an exercise in torture, but her attention was soon diverted to an obvious absence. All the winged monsters above the palace save one were nowhere to be seen.

The thought crossed Yala's mind that the king had decided to offer the captains another test, but their meeting was designated for the receiving room and not the courtyard.

After she'd become accustomed to their nightly ceremonies, the room's splendour was a stark contrast to the temple's austere pillars and shadow-soaked corners, but the king wore the same drakeskin coat and military uniform. He also carried his claw-blade strapped to his waist out of either paranoia of an attack or the desire to remind everyone of what he was capable of.

"I have asked you here to outline my plans for the battle with Skytower," he told the assembled captains. "First, you will request a peaceful surrender. The Superior will have one chance to earn our mercy. Should she refuse, we shall strike immediately."

The Superior would be safely ensconced away and would not appear directly, Yala was sure, but Skytower was no fortress. Its remoteness alone was usually enough to repel invaders. They'd never had to deal with a full-blown assault.

"As I told you last night, your first goal will be to open the Void," he went on. "When the Disciples are occupied with the dead, you will seek out the Superior and pressure her to surrender. Should this prove untenable, you will kill her. Without their Superior, the other Disciples are unlikely to continue fighting, and we shall be able to occupy the tower ourselves."

A nod of assent travelled among the captains. He hadn't revealed any surprises thus far, but if the plan was that simple, why invite only the captains here? What did he have to share with them that he didn't want the rest of the army to know?

"There is one unpredictable factor," said King Tharen. "The Disciples of Life."

A pit of dread opened inside Yala's stomach. *Shit.*

"When we attempted to capture the Disciples of the Sea, the Disciples of Life intervened," he said. "One particular Disciple of Life caught my attention. A young woman, in her late teenage years, who rides a war drake. My scouts are currently determining if she is present at Skytower, but my instincts say she is. She may be alone or she may have companions, but she is dangerous. If you see her, you will capture her and bring her straight to me. Alive."

The pit deepened. The king hadn't overlooked Niema, not at all. He knew she'd exerted control over his void drake, but rather than ordering her death, he wanted her alive.

He wanted her for his own.

———

Viam wasn't invited to the king's address to the captains, but as it turned out, neither was Saren. While she and Brenat hovered outside the administration building during their lunch break, waiting for news, he came sidling over, his hand and wrist wrapped in thick bandages.

A gasp escaped her. "What happened to you?"

His mouth split in a grin. "As you can see, I'm on temporary leave from training."

"What did you do, provoke a war drake?" She caught the flash of guilt in his eyes. "Shit, you did it on purpose, didn't you? I bet Yala was furious."

Saren shrugged one shoulder. "We all know I'm a liability on the battlefield, and without me around, she doesn't have to worry about me getting hurt."

"She does if you're planning to do anything risky while she's gone." Brenat tilted her head. "Are you?"

Viam's eyes narrowed. "This wasn't Nalen's idea, was it?"

"No," Saren said defensively. "I'm capable of screwing up on my own. If anything, I've made it an art."

"Stop deflecting." Viam's hands curled inward. "If you're staying, I want to know what you're up to. Has Nalen ever mentioned speaking to the Disciples of the Flame?"

341

"Except to talk about how shitting useless they are? No."

"What's that?" Brenat nudged her in the back. "Something I should know?"

"No." She'd refrained from mentioning her half-formed ideas even to Brenat, not wanting to further feed her notions of taking action in the king's absence. "They're the only people who came close to destroying the temple, that's all."

"They are." Saren hovered on the balls of his feet. "Nalen's been talking to some off-duty guards, but he'll be back by now. Want to talk to him?"

"Not in the open." The king's eyes might be on the captains for the time being—one reason she'd opted to wait outside for Yala's return—but now that she looked more closely at the palace, another source of her comparative lack of nerves presented itself. "Where did those void drakes go?"

"Oh, is that why it feels so much less like being crushed under the weight of terror in here?" Saren rocked on his heels. "I hope they don't come back."

"He didn't send them to Skytower, did he?"

"Better than him going with them," Brenat pointed out. "Anyway, *I'd* like to talk to Nalen."

Saren smirked at her and led the way to the barracks with Viam reluctantly trailing behind, unwilling to let Brenat out of her sight. They waited outside for Saren to return with Nalen. The burly, bearded man came striding into view with what looked suspiciously like a guard's uniform tucked under one arm.

"Did they give that to you?" Saren asked. "How many do you have?"

"A few." Nalen wore a satisfied smile. "The mission's set for All Gods' Day, and we talked the commander into letting us take the full day off like the rest of the palace staff. Helped that he was already in a good mood."

"Because you bribed him." Saren's voice was loud enough

that Viam trod on his foot in warning. "Or offered him a gift of Parvan wine by way of an anonymous donor. Do I have that right?"

Nalen grunted. "Cigars, actually, but close enough. Those two want to get out too?" He nodded at Viam and Brenat.

"Viam has a plan," Brenat ventured. "The Disciples of the Flame—"

"There is no plan." Viam's voice trembled under Nalen's questioning stare. "The last person to even go *near* that temple ended up dead at the king's feet."

"The Disciples of the Flame are the only people in the city who came close to destroying that temple the king opened," Brenat pointed out. "Is it true you have some city guards on your side, Nalen?"

"Yes, but not the ones who guard that place."

The Disciples of the Sea. Of all the city's guards, they were among the most loyal to their leader. They'd defied even their god to serve him. "This isn't going to work, Brenat. The Disciples of the Flame might not even *want* to leave their temple."

"If they do, they'll have to disguise themselves as regular people," Nalen said. "My allies can smuggle them out of the city but only if they don't cause a scene."

"If we did that, they wouldn't be able to come back."

"Maybe they won't want to." A shadow passed over Saren's face, a reminder that he hadn't forgotten that their refusal to leave the city had led to their deaths. "They're better off leaving. Fuck, so are we."

"But we're still here."

That, she realised, was the root of her nagging uncertainty. Practicalities aside, the point of Nalen's venture was to help anyone who wanted to escape the king's notice, to live their lives without becoming pawns in his war. Viam had followed that urge herself when she'd fled the city after the king's return, yet the weeks she'd spent in exile had only strengthened her certainty that there would be no true escape no matter how far she ran. Even if she found some distant corner of the world—turned her face away, closed her eyes—the king's conquest would continue. Mekan's reach would extend its grasping fingers until nowhere in Laria would escape from the god of death's wrath.

The Disciples of the Flame of all people would understand that... but they'd never been offered the choice.

"We are." Saren exhaled. "Fuck if I know why. Maybe the same reason those Disciples stayed. To save anyone left behind."

"Or to fight back." The Disciples had been defiant to the last. Viam didn't hold out hope that the others would be the same, but as long as they remained captives inside their own temple, they would remain estranged from Dalathik, stripped of any will to fight.

"You don't think we want to?" Nalen ground his teeth. "If we had more people, enough for a real uprising... you think those Disciples might help?"

"If nothing else, they'll regain access to their god when they're far enough from Mekan's influence," Viam said. "The king's war isn't here in Dalathar. It's out there. Against the Disciples."

Against the gods.

If another god joined the battlefield, the odds might not change, but even a small shift might make all the difference to the outcome.

———

The nightly attacks from the dead soon took their toll on Niema. There had been few injuries among the Disciples since the last time, but watching the tower from dusk until dawn left her exhausted, and each time she employed her abilities against the dead sapped a little more of her energy. It wasn't long before word of her talents had spread across Skytower, which only increased her anxiety that the king would find out too.

For all she knew, he might be behind the attacks himself. If his strategy was to wear them down over time, it was certainly working, at least on her. There came a night when she sat alone on the rooftop, tracing the stars speckling the sky for threats, and wondered if events might have turned out very differently if she'd made a different choice the first time she'd been up here, as a prisoner.

When she'd learned that Yala was a Disciple of Death, she'd been horrified. She'd never have guessed that a short while later, she would save that Disciple's life and bind herself to Mekan in the process, sealing her fate and that of so many others.

Knowing that, would she have chosen differently? If Yala had died, Melian would almost certainly have triumphed in her attempt to take the throne. Would the king have then hastened his return to Laria, deposed his son, and eliminated any chances of a rogue Disciple of Death rising to challenge his rule?

How could she know, any more than she knew the outcome of the upcoming battle?

She imagined the stars spiderwebbing across the sky as a series of possible futures, too distant to reach, while she hung adrift in a sea of blackness.

"I wouldn't sit that close to the edge." Kelan appeared at her shoulder, making her jump so violently she nearly tipped headfirst off the tower. Catching her balance, she shuffled backwards to safety. "Not getting any ideas about jumping off, I hope."

Niema huffed, drawing her knees up to her chin.

"Nothing of the sort. I'm here to keep an eye out for trouble. You can stay if you like, but I—"

"You can save us from the monsters. We get it," he finished. "The burden isn't yours alone, and it certainly won't help if you collapse from exhaustion before the king's army even shows up."

"He might not send the army at all," she murmured. "Why risk your life by attacking directly when there's a beacon for the dead sitting right here in the tower?"

"That would depend on whether he knows the dead are drawn to you, which, as far as we know, he does not."

"Yet." Her fingers tightened around her shins. "Your Superior was right. What if I *am* a potential weapon Mekan might use against the enclave?"

"Would Yalet have chosen you, knowing that?"

Niema had wondered the same countless times, but the certainty she'd experienced when she'd sworn her vows on the island seemed as vastly distant as the stars.

"There you have it," Kelan said. "Besides, I guarantee that hurling yourself off the roof won't achieve anything except ruining the nice scenery."

"Thanks, Kelan." She lifted her head and glared at him. "If that was supposed to be helpful, it wasn't."

"It's the best I could come up with." He sank down next to her. "I'll take over here. I won't let anything attack the tower."

Niema opened her mouth to argue and yawned instead. With a smug grin, Kelan reached out to take her arms. Resigned, she let him carry her down to the balcony near the guest rooms, where Hachim waited for her.

"There you are." Hachim peered at her face. "Are you all right?"

"She's trying to defend the tower single-handedly," Kelan told him. "I said we can spare her for one night, can't we? Who knows, you might even be able to distract her."

346

"What…?" Heat swept up her neck as his meaning sank in. "No!"

"Have fun." With a laugh, Kelan departed in a gust of air that carried him up the tower again.

Niema groaned, covering her face. "Ignore him."

Hachim's gaze lingered on the spot where Kelan had vanished. "Were you two alone up there? Together?"

"What?" Her thoughts stuttered to a halt. "No. For a minute, maybe, but it's not…"

"It doesn't matter," he said as his embarrassment flooded her and mingled with her own. "You're entitled to your privacy."

"No," she blurted. "Kelan is… no. That's not how it is."

"Isn't it?" His tone was carefully emotionless, but a twinge of relief travelled through their bond. "I understand if you want to pursue him. You deserve some fun."

"No," she said. "We're in the middle of a crisis."

"Responsibilities aren't the only thing that matter," he said. "If any good came of all this turmoil, I'm glad that you were able to see the world outside of the enclave. You got to live, really live, for the first time."

"At a cost." Tears burned her eyes. "How can you say that, even seeing all the suffering and loss there in the world?"

"Our Superior wanted to protect us, I know that, but she did us a disservice when she kept us from learning the truth of the world outside of Yalet's domain. However terrible it might be, I'm glad we can face it together."

Even if she hadn't been able to sense his emotions, she could read them on his face and knew that he meant every word. His face was flushed, his eyes wide, and some impulse made her reach impulsively through the bond that linked them, sensing the thrum of affection towards her—and yes, wanting.

He stiffened, and she hastily pulled back. "Sorry."

EMMA L. ADAMS

"It's all right." He looked away, fiddling with a loose thread on his sleeve. "I should have told you sooner."

That's what I get for prying. How long had he felt that way? More to the point, how had she overlooked something so obvious in a person with whom she shared a bond that went deeper than words?" "No. Your feelings are yours, and mine..."

"I never pried," he said, "but I always hoped you felt the same."

She lowered her gaze, trying to pry apart the confused threads of emotions roiling through her and travelling back and forth through their bond. Her feelings hadn't truly been her own until she'd left the enclave, and she'd been mired in so much doubt and conflict that her only thoughts for those she'd left behind had revolved around worry for them.

"It doesn't matter if you don't," he said. "Really."

"I don't know how I feel." An honest answer. "I can't see past the way things are now. The future... it's a black hole."

"Nobody can." He reached for her hand. "The future isn't set, but we can make it our own."

"How do you always know the right thing to say?"

"It helps that I generally know exactly how you're feeling."

A sob escaped, turning into a laugh. Niema couldn't have said that she returned his affection in kind, but Hachim was undeniably the most important person to her in the world.

And if she were to give herself to someone, she wanted it to be him.

Again, she followed the impulse and leaned into the thread connecting them until his warmth enveloped her too. Their lips collided before she'd fully regained conscious awareness of her own body. When they broke apart, a question lurked in his eyes.

In answer, she took his hand and pulled him towards her guest room. Their souls were already intertwined, always had been, and she didn't know if what she was experiencing was separable from the bond they'd always shared. She didn't know if this would outlast the coming war—but Hachim was right. She'd spent so long dwelling on the future that she'd forgotten what existed in the present and how very precious it was.

That looming darkness threatened again, the threat of the uncertain future, and she threw herself off the edge, trusting that Hachim would catch her.

34

The king led the flight division to Skytower on a clear morning, perfect for flight.

As her squad soared over the Larian country-side, Yala sought to lose herself in the sensation of the ground so far beneath her, the wind in her hair, and the calm brought by the knowledge that if this was the last thing she experienced, she would have been at peace.

The illusion shattered when Skytower appeared on the horizon as a tall shape jutting out of Laria's low mountains. The commander called the flight squads to assemble, and as with their last mission, they were separated into three groups, each focusing on a different part of Skytower. One would circle from the left and another from the right. The third would target the Superior.

Yala's squad had been assigned to the third. That meant she was all but certain to run into Kelan—and Niema.

The king addressed the squads this time, accompanied once more by the four identical void drakes that had been absent from the palace in the last couple of days.

"My orders have not changed," he told them. "My scouts

confirmed the Disciple of Life is present at the tower and that her abilities are indeed formidable. As a result, capturing her is to be your priority once you have occupied the tower."

He did not refer to the Void directly, but it was no big secret what he expected the captains to do. What he wanted Yala to do.

She was glad, she reluctantly admitted, that Saren had stayed behind.

Surel, her new squad member, stayed close behind her, his frightened eyes roving over the surrounding army of war beasts. Gorel had taken him under his wing—literally and metaphorically—but there hadn't been time to solidify their strategy even if Yala hadn't been distracted by the conflicting orders battering inside her skull.

Capture Niema alive. Corner the Superior, force a surrender… or kill her.

At the commander's order, Yala's squad flew towards the upper section of the tower. She could see the Disciples positioned around its edges, especially the topmost floor, forming a barrier between the Superior's office and the oncoming army. The Superior might be ensconced away, but her Disciples were as vulnerable as anyone else to a wound from a war drake's claws or teeth, and none wore protective armour.

It immediately became apparent why that was the case. The frontmost squad closed in on the upper floor, with Lisek at their head, but the Disciples of the Sky struck first. A prayer, shouted into the wind, brought a gust that slammed headlong into the war drakes. The squad in the lead was driven backwards, the momentum catching the squads behind and scattering them in all directions.

The Disciples, in their lightweight clothing and with command over the air currents, effortlessly regained their balance, while Yala clung to her war drake's back as they were tossed around like a ship in a storm. As the wind died down a little, she glimpsed Lisek shouting orders at her squad. Two of her fliers had been blown off their steeds outright, and the others converged below to catch the falling soldiers in midair.

Another shouted prayer from the lower level further scattered the soldiers' formation. War drakes veered in all directions, their riders helpless to do more than hold on for dear life, caught in the ferocious wind current conjured by the collective might of every Disciple in the tower. Several collided, their riders taking the brunt of the impact. The crunch of broken bones mingled with the cries of pain and the war drakes' disgruntled clamour as they lost control of their wings. One war drake did make it to a platform, only for its claws to fail to gain purchase as the Disciples stabbed and swiped at its exposed head and drove the beast away from the tower.

How did the king not see this coming? Either that or he had, and he'd sent the fliers ahead in the hopes that at least one person would manage to land, even if the others were blown off course in the process. It would only take one Disciple of Death to open the Void and unleash Mekan's army directly into Skytower.

Yala thought she spied Kelan among the mass of Disciples congregating in front of their Superior's office, but there was no sign of Niema either on a war drake's back or inside the tower itself. Perhaps she'd opted to lie low or to avoid taking flight so the Disciples' attempts to repel their invaders wouldn't hit her war drake too.

There was no doubt that their strategy had worked. The air currents drove back the war drakes with ruthless efficiency, and their blades were ready to slice at anyone who slipped through their defences. Within moments, the entire army was in disarray, while the Disciples had barely suffered a scratch.

Then came a cry that raised the hairs on her arms and caused a rumble of panic to travel through the already panicked war drakes. Yala's steed growled, its flight path veering sideways, and she twisted in her seat to look for the source.

The king's void drakes—all of them save for the steed that bore the monarch—cut through the scattered flight squads and flew towards Skytower at speed.

King Tharen, it seemed, had lost patience.

The Disciples of the Sky joined their voices in prayer, and Terethik's wrath met the void drakes in a wild gust that once again drove Yala's flight path sideways. War drakes and Disciples alike were thrown into chaos as the king's monstrous steeds fought to reach the tower. She dug her knees into the beast's back, eliciting a twinge of pain in her right leg, and saw that one of the void drakes had reached the Disciples converging on the tower's topmost floor. Steel flashed as the Disciples fended off their target, and Yala hastened to fly lower as another stray gust of wind buffeted her from above.

The king didn't seem to care that his monsters had thrown his forces into disarray. All four kept flying at the tower, aiming for the upper level, and each time they were repelled, more war drakes were knocked askew. Sooner or later, though, one would break through the defences.

Does he want a surrender, or has he changed his mind?

Yala wrenched her gaze away, her heart sinking when she saw that one of Lisek's squad had managed to land upon the lower level. Dark blood splattered the large platform at the base.

"This way!" she shouted to her squad. "Fly down!"

Their orders told them to attack the upper floor, but

between the void drakes and the Disciples, most had abandoned that command in favour of a strategy that wouldn't get them knocked out of the air.

A Disciple crumpled, Lisek's spear sticking out of her chest. The captain leaned forward, clutching the tooth she'd pulled from a void drake's mouth. Ready to open the Void.

No. Gods, no. Niema was nowhere to be seen, and as for Yala, striking down a fellow soldier in front of witnesses would all but seal her own demise. Moreover, there were more than thirty other captains present, each of whom carried a similar piece of Mekan's realm. Any of them might take her place.

Yala lifted her spear, and a whistle drifted from above, carried on the wind.

Niema.

———

Skytower trembled, each jolt rattling Niema's teeth. Superior Sietra dug her fingers into the sides of the armchair in which she sat, the sole admission of the anguish she felt for the Disciples risking their lives outside.

"We should be out there with them." Niema's nails bit into her palms. The safe room, concealed behind the large portrait of Terethik on the Superior's office wall, was big enough to accommodate both herself and Hachim as well as the Superior, but it contained only chairs, a table, and a small altar to the god of the sky. No windows nor doors save for the one they'd entered through. Listening to the assault on Skytower while unable to intervene left Niema's nerves ragged, and each hit to the tower shook her like a physical blow.

When the chorus of void drakes' cries broke through even the stone walls of their haven, she broke.

"I can't do this." Niema ran to the blank wall that had slid into place behind the portrait. "I can't stay hidden."

"They want you." The Superior sat rigid, her face lined with exhaustion. "You know that."

Niema's insides pitched downwards. The Disciples of the Sky sent to spy on the gathering soldiers had risked their lives in getting so close, but they'd come away with information that shook Niema to her very core. The king knew she was present. He wanted the soldiers to find her.

"You can't expose yourself," Hachim insisted. "I'll go—"

"I can control those beasts." Another tremor hit the tower; the walls shook with the sound of a heavy reptilian body slamming into the stone. "Nobody else can."

A grinding sound told her the Superior had activated the mechanism that moved the stone wall concealing them from sight. Heart in her mouth, Niema climbed out into the office, Hachim close on her heels.

The large window behind the Superior's desk offered a terrifying view of a void drake, its gore-slicked claws swiping and its teeth snapping at anyone who got into its path. She whistled, hoping the command carried through the glass, but the beast gave no reaction. She needed to get closer.

Like the hidden wall, the window didn't open without moving some complex mechanism. Hachim knocked on the glass, catching the attention of one of the Disciples on the other side. Kelan, his sword cloaked in dark blood, shook his head and continued to swipe at the advancing void drake.

Niema rapped her knuckles on the window, twice, three times. After the fourth, Kelan pulled back and let his fellow Disciples take over the fight, landing on the balcony with a long-suffering expression on his face.

"Don't leave this floor," he told Niema as the window slid open. "It's brutal out here."

EMMA L. ADAMS

Niema clambered out and staggered when a ferocious wind current rocked the tower. Kelan caught her arm to steady her, yelling, "Get back inside!"

Ignoring him, Niema let out a loud whistle, a command to the advancing void drake. *Leave.*

The void drake's attack ceased as it turned tail, veering sideways into a Disciple's sword. The blade glanced off its scaled skin, and its teeth snapped closed, narrowly avoiding the Disciple's foot.

"You know, it would help if you'd order them to fly into the path of our weapons," Kelan remarked as he flew over to swing his blade at the monster.

"I can't be that specific." She ducked when someone hurled a spear at the platform. Calling her own steed would make her into a target, but she had no hope of reaching her target with her feet on the ground. "Are there more?"

"Three." Kelan gestured to the balcony curving around the tower's edge. "Trying to get at the Superior, I assume."

"Where's Yala?"

"Haven't a clue. The war drakes aren't fans of those monsters."

Niema's heart plummeted. In sending the void drakes away, she'd also cleared a path for the flight squads to reach the tower without their steeds being frightened away. While the king's forces had long since lost their neat formation, the Disciples of the Sky had been driven in all directions by the airborne assault, and large portions of Skytower were now unguarded.

Niema whistled again, louder, directing her command at every void drake within range. Out of the corner of her eye, she saw another beast flee from the tower, taking a spear through the wing mid-retreat. Two more left her line of sight, but only four were accounted for. Where was the king?

A rush of cold nipped at her skin, flooded her veins,

356

turned her blood to ice. A decaying scent rose on the wind from somewhere below, and a familiar dread took root within her soul.

Someone had opened the Void.

———

Niema turned to Kelan, her eyes wide. "The Void. It's open."

"Shit." He glided to the balcony's edge, trying to see down to the lower floors. The platform below was slick with blood, and a large group of soldiers had converged on a patch of darkness spreading like spilled ink.

Niema drew her arms to her sides, a shiver racking her body. "I have to get down there."

"And expose yourself to the enemy?"

"Nobody else can close the Void. You know that."

True, but there was a very good reason the Superior had wanted her to stay hidden, and the odds of her being taken out by a stray spear were as high as being killed by intention. Before he could voice an argument, Hachim called through the window, "Niema, get back in here!"

"The Void, Hachim." Her voice cracked. "Fine, I'll call the war drake."

"You certainly won't." Kelan reached for her upper arms and lifted her into the air. Her brief struggle ceased when they dropped into a swift dive, parallel to the tower, clearing one floor, two, three.

At the lowest floor, the Void's presence hit him like the wind turned hostile, and he stilled, unable to look away. Bodies lay on the platform, soldiers and Disciples alike, soaked in the blood that had opened a path to Mekan's realm. A gaping slash knifed the air, darkness boiling within. A Disciple lay dead, his blood mingling with the shadows oozing from the Void—and then rose jerkily to his feet, his eyes glassy, the spear that had claimed his life still protruding from his throat.

"Kill them all!" shouted a voice.

Behind the pulsing darkness, Kelan's eyes picked out a soldier standing apart from the others, clothed in blood and holding a spear-sharp claw in her hand.

Yala was not the only Disciple of Death present on the battlefield.

The soldier—Veshan, the squad leader who'd led the last assault upon the tower—wore a wide grin as she watched the Disciple of the Sky whom she'd raised from death pull the spear out of his own neck and hurl it at the nearest soldier. The man collapsed with a gurgling cry, and the Disciple of Death's smile slipped.

"Stop that!" she shouted at the dead man. "Attack our enemies, not us!"

"I could have told you they can't tell the difference," Kelan muttered, wishing he'd followed his initial instinct and pitched her off the tower at their first meeting.

Niema squirmed in his arms, her forehead streaked with sweat. "Put me down."

"I'm not throwing you into the middle of that." He veered sideways as air buffeted him from behind, not from a Disciple but from an approaching war drake.

When he turned to the newcomer, he found himself faced with Yala. *Ah, shit.*

Yala didn't so much as blink. Turning on her fellow Disciple of Death, she shouted, "Fucking think for a minute. If you tell the dead to *kill them all*, they're not going to distinguish between our side and theirs, are they?"

Our side. Theirs. While he was glad that Yala was maintaining the act rather than getting beheaded by one of her allies, he felt Niema stiffen in his arms as if she wanted to call out to Yala.

Leaning down, he whispered, "Don't blow her cover. We're in enough trouble."

Though Veshan had retracted her command, the dead Disciple continued to lurch forwards, swinging his weapon at anyone living within range whether they were friend or foe. While holding Niema, Kelan couldn't draw his sword, and he'd have to fly directly into the dead man's path to reach the Void before more beasts emerged to join the void drakes circling the tower.

Too late. A dark shape stirred behind Veshan, extending a claw towards the nearest human prey.

Veshan tried to run, but she'd grounded herself when she'd sent her steed away, and her feet slipped on the blood-slick platform and sent her skidding onto her back. The claw latched onto her leg, and she screamed and scrabbled at the ground as the monster reeled her into the shadows.

Kelan seized his chance to fly over the platform, holding Niema above the Void's gaping mouth. "Not to pressure you, but I'd get a move on."

"I can't rush, you fool." Nevertheless, she launched into a breathless prayer. Green light bloomed around her hands as Yalet's power took hold, reaching bright tendrils to counter the encroaching darkness.

Her prayer cut off in a gasp when she and Kelan lurched sideways under the weight of something solid colliding with Kelan's leg. A bird-shaped beast clothed in scales hung from his cloak, its claws embedded in the material. He kicked out, trying to dislodge it, but the beast hung on. And there were more rising from the darkness to join their kin, all coated in the same dark scales that seemed to absorb light rather than reflecting it.

Kelan kicked again, and this time, the bird-like creature let go. A whistle from Niema sent it fleeing into the dark; as he flew higher, she resumed her prayer, her voice strained with panic. Below, the dead fell upon the platform, claws swiping at humans and soldiers alike, cruel beaks and sharp teeth biting into anything that moved. Any who fell dead immediately rose with their weapons still in hand, turning upon the living.

Green light rippled from Niema's hands as she raised her voice, her prayer ringing across the tower floor. The darkness began to flicker at the edges, shadows receding fingerspan by fingerspan. *Come on.*

"It's her!" someone shouted.

Kelan saw a group of soldiers descending, heedless of the monsters tearing their way out of the Void. One of the fliers leapt clean off her steed and landed, staggering, on the blood-drenched platform. Lifting a jagged claw in her hands like a sword, she shouted, "Move!"

The dead soldiers parted to either side, splitting the battle down the middle. Leaving the path clear to Niema.

Niema's prayer faltered on her tongue as the soldier closed in for the kill.

35

Silence hung over the palace grounds as Viam and Brenat crossed to the barracks. There, Viam found Saren lurking in the empty dormitory, dressed in a guard's uniform that had been pilfered from someone twice his size. At least the shirt's long sleeves concealed his bandaged wrist and hand.

"Don't tell me, I look woefully unstylish." He tugged on a sleeve. "Have these people never heard of colour?"

"The Disciples of the Sea have." Most of them wore necklaces of seashells and other adornments that would make them hard to imitate even if they hadn't known every one of their number by name. "Where's Nalen?"

"Bribing the guards at the gates. Are you ready?"

"No." Her heart fluttered with nerves. "What did you and Nalen plan to do to get us into the temple?"

The guards outside, being Disciples of the Sea, were impossible to replace with counterfeits, so it was on Nalen's allies to provide a convincing diversion. Or, failing that, convince the city's other guards to look the other way.

"We have it sorted." He strapped a shortsword to his belt
—also stolen, she assumed—and crossed the room. "Wait for
the tenth bell and then approach the temple from the back.
Good luck."

"Saren—" She swore under her breath as he marched out
of the room in a manner too unsteady to pass as a city guard.
"He's going to get himself killed."

"He might not, given that Nalen's people have turned half
the city guards to his side in the past few weeks," Brenat
murmured.

"Half of them?" Viam startled. "What has he even been
bribing them with?"

"Most of them didn't need bribery. Turns out that serving
the city under the leadership of someone with a habit of
hauling anyone who objects to his rule to be sacrificed on an
altar isn't all that popular."

Viam's stomach turned. "Don't they worry that collabo-
rating with Nalen will get them executed too?"

"A fair few plan to smuggle themselves out along with the
deserters." She lifted her head. "It's almost time."

Viam swallowed her nerves. She still didn't know if she'd
made the right choice in going to the Disciples. They might
not have long to talk, and the Disciples of the Flame might
prove impossible to reason with. So much hinged on them
finding the courage the king had stripped away when he'd
claimed their temple in Mekan's name.

Yala is risking her life out there, she told herself. *This is the
least I can do.*

When the tenth bell rang out across the barracks, Viam
and Brenat made for the back gate. The guards outside let
them pass without objection, having been placed here by
Nalen to give the illusion of normalcy. The pair then slipped
past the paddocks—eerily quiet without most of the war
drakes present—and emerged into the square.

At the front of the Temple of the Flame stood three guards dressed in standard raptor-skin uniforms but with hair braided with shells and other trinkets marking them as Disciples of the Sea. There wasn't much water here in the capital save for the river, but their presence projected a clear message both to the Disciples inside the temple and anyone else who might think of challenging the king's supremacy.

Two uniformed guards ambled towards them and casually engaged them in conversation. Viam didn't know what Nalen had told them to say, but the distraction was enough to offer them the chance to duck around the temple's side. As she did so, her hand crept to the sharpened claw she carried concealed in a leather pouch, her own grisly trophy from her most recent visit to the Temple of Death. She didn't want to use it unless she had to, but no guards stood atop the wall overlooking the temple's rear, nor did anyone guard the narrow passage leading to the back door.

"Nice job, Nalen," Brenat murmured, eyeing the empty passageway appreciatively. "Let's go."

Upon reaching the temple's rear entrance, Brenat darted up the steps, seized the door handle, and shoved it inward, sending a startled novice on the other side tripping over his own feet. Grabbing Viam's arm, she pulled them both into the temple and closed the door on their heels.

"Who are you?" hissed the terrified youth. "What are you doing in here?"

"We're here to save your lives," Brenat said. "We need to see your Superior."

"Superior Shralin is in his office," whimpered the novice, backing away. "I'll fetch him."

As he fled, more heads popped up from corners and from the balconies overlooking the wide chamber that dominated the lower floor. All of them wore the same pinched expressions, their faces drawn, their eyes haunted. They looked, in short, like a people under siege.

"The Superior will see you." The novice came scuttling into view, wringing his hands. "He's on his way downstairs."

"Who are you?" A middle-aged Disciple whose robe was adorned with golden embroidery that indicated a high rank stepped out from behind the rear of what Viam recognised as Dalathik's altar. "What do you want with us?"

"To save your ungrateful hides." Brenat flashed a grin towards Viam. "And to speak on behalf of Prince Daliel. He wants to forge an alliance if any of you are willing. If not, we'll gladly help you get out of the city."

The Disciple's eyes widened. "You overstep."

"You need our help," Brenat said. "Trust me."

"We certainly do not." Superior Shralin came stalking over, his headdress sliding back to reveal his balding scalp and his embroidered clothes askew. He all but shoved the other Disciple aside to glare at Viam and Brenat. "Who are you, exactly? You speak on behalf of the prince?"

Not exactly was the honest answer, as Daliel had made no efforts to contact her since their last visit to the temple. "He tried to send a messenger a few days ago…"

"This is not for your ears." The Superior waved an impatient hand at the other Disciples attempting to eavesdrop on them, including the man who'd initially confronted them. Upon their departure, he returned to scrutinising the pair of them. "Now, he sends you, while his father is absent."

"Good, you know about the mission," said Brenat. "That'll save time."

Superior Shralin gave her an incredulous look. "We also know that Skytower will fall today and that the king will then turn his sights to the forests where the Disciples of Life hide."

"Skytower won't fall," Brenat said. "It's as solid as this place, for a start, and the Disciples have the king's forces outnumbered."

"There is no need to demolish a temple when one can simply destroy it from within," the Superior said. "Allow me to demonstrate."

He beckoned to them to follow him into the hall proper, past Dalathik's vast serpentine statue. Despite the large number of prayer mats in front, nobody knelt there, nor did anyone occupy the alcoves that contained smaller altars to their god.

Viam's stomach turned over. The statue was intact, but the candles at the front were as cold as the grave. Shadows coiled in place of flames, creeping around the altar, and the claw in her pocket stirred at Mekan's presence.

"You see where we stand." The Superior's voice was as empty and cold as the candles in front of the altar. "Moreover, I suspect you're here on behalf of Yala Palathar, and my people will never ally with a Disciple of Death."

"If I was held captive in my own home, I'd make any temporary alliances I needed to save my people," said Brenat. "Also, Yala didn't send us. We're here on behalf of the prince, and *he's* willing to work with you despite your messy history with his father."

The Superior closed his eyes for an instant, exhaling a short breath. "Now, I suspect you understand why Superior Datriem acted as he did by exiling the king."

Viam's mouth parted. She'd hardly spared a thought for Superior Datriem in recent weeks save for wondering if, had he lived, he might have regretted sparing the king's life after all. Regardless of his motives for exiling the monarch, nothing excused the cruelty with which he'd treated his apprentices, to say nothing of his threats against Yala for speaking the truth about the events that had occurred on the island.

Viam pushed her own jumbled feelings aside. "I don't know how long we have before the flight division returns, but if anyone wants to leave the upper city, our allies are willing to help smuggle you out."

"I thought your purpose was to recruit us to help the prince," said the Superior. "Might I enquire as to how removing us from the city will help him challenge his father?"

"We're not removing you, we're offering the choice," Brenat corrected. "Not just to you either. Your Disciples deserve to have a say in their own fates, and if nothing else, getting away from Mekan will enable you to reach your god. It worked for the Disciples of the Earth, right, Viam?"

"And their temple swiftly fell to Mekan again, weeks ago," he retorted. "We're powerless against Him. So is every Disciple."

"The fuck you are," Brenat said. "Do you want your people to die out altogether?" I bet he's already killed a bunch of you on false charges, and you haven't been allowed to recruit anyone new since he had this place put under siege. Soon, there'll be no Disciples of the Flame left in Laria at all. Is that what you want?"

He returned his attention to the statue. "What I want has little relevance. I serve Dalathik, and He no longer speaks to me."

"And those candles?" Brenat cut in. "I didn't see for myself, but the candle you gave to those Disciples sentenced to execution nearly stopped the temple from ever awakening."

Superior Shralin closed his eyes and spoke in a low, tortured voice. "That is our only way out. If we don't choose to die on our own terms, Mekan will consume us, as He has so many of my people."

"Then, let the others decide for themselves," said Brenat. "Would they rather die kneeling at an altar to a god that isn't their own than on their feet in defence of Dalathik?"

Viam felt a brief stab of envy that swiftly gave way to pride. Brenat was better at this than she, and she had no doubt that appealing to the Disciples' bond to Dalathik would be far more effective than trying to convince them to help the prince. Their loyalty rested with their god, not with the Larian nation or the crown.

"That's right." The Disciple who'd challenged them earlier stepped into view, his face set with determination. "You no longer give us orders, Superior. You forfeited that right when you surrendered to the king."

The colour drained from the Superior's face. "You *dare* to challenge my authority?"

There came the distinct sound of someone knocking on the door. Alarm flooded Viam. *Shit. We've been found out.*

———

Niema's prayer died on her lips when the soldier came at her, swinging the void drake's claw like a sword. Readied to kill.

Then, Yala leapt, landing on her fellow Disciple of Death and tackling her to the ground.

"The king said to capture her alive." Yala's face was strained; tackling her fellow soldier had hurt her bad leg, but she held on, giving Niema the chance to scramble away.

The soldier shoved Yala off her, her face set in anger. "He never said she had to be in one piece."

The king ordered them to capture me alive. I can't stay here long.

As she opened her mouth to restart her prayer, someone grabbed Niema around the middle, dragging her across the blood-drenched platform. A hand clamped over her mouth, and its owner lifted her off the ground as she fought, kicking out in desperation.

In her palms, the last of the green light flickered and died.

A shout mingled with a chorus of war drakes' cries; Niema glimpsed winged beasts fleeing in all directions with riders helpless to regain control. Through the chaos flew a lone winged beast with someone seated upon its back.

The king. He's here.

King Tharen flew on, paying no heed to the chaos he'd inflicted on his own soldiers as the war drakes scattered to avoid getting too close to their monstrous counterpart.

The soldier holding Niema let go with a muffled cry; more beasts were emerging from the Void as if to answer their master's call to arms. Niema's feet skidded in a puddle of blood as she backed away, looking for Kelan.

He hovered with his back to the Void, his gaze fixed on the king's void drake. The beast's vast wings carried it closer, closer, angling towards Skytower's highest floor.

Shit. The king's going after the Superior. Not me.

Rising in flight, Kelan vanished from her line of sight. She hardly blamed him—if his Superior died, the Disciples would be finished regardless of whether the Void remained open— but without him, Niema had no way out of the path of the expanding darkness spreading across the lower floor.

The tower gave a mighty heave as though some great beast stirred beneath. Niema slid across the blood-drenched platform as more tremors rippled underfoot, rattling her teeth in her skull. The shadows closed in, creeping upon her as surely as a fast-acting poison.

"Niema!" The cry came from above, and Hachim

descended, seated upon a war drake, body aglow with Yalet's light.

His hand enveloped hers, helping her onto the war drake's back as another tremor rocked the tower, and the very stones quaked as if the great construction might shake itself apart from within.

Clinging to Hachim's back, Niema yelled, "What's going on?"

"The Superior is defending herself."

An air current ascended as if the very heavens themselves had drawn in a breath. The momentum caught their war drake's wings, too, carrying them upward along with the Disciples already rising to defend their leader.

The king hovered in front of the tower on his steed, holding a curved blade in one hand. Darkness trailed from his wrists, his arms, his entire body as if the Void itself had draped upon his skin like a cloak.

"You will not win, Superior," he said in a ringing voice. "Surrender, and no more of your people will die."

"That is a wrongheaded assumption, Tharen."

Her voice was clear, too much so to have come through a locked door. Niema peered over Hachim's head and saw Superior Sietra hovering *outside* her office, unprotected by the reinforced walls and armed Disciples ready to lay down their lives for her. The Superior floated in a seated position, her face impassive, her arms held out as if to embrace the god of the sky that served her will.

If her appearance had startled the king, it didn't show. "You will show me the proper deference, Superior."

"I will not cleave to any gods besides my own." She clapped, and thunder echoed, booming in the sky above the tower.

Lightning arced down, ploughing straight into the king.

The bright flash dazzled Niema's vision. She squeezed

her eyes shut and hung on to Hachim, the air trembling in response to the Superior's might.

When her sight cleared, she saw the king—untouched, unharmed, one hand upraised. The darkness itself had moved, forming a rippling shield between him and the Superior's attack and leaving him and his void drake without a scratch.

"You will expend yourself, Superior," he warned. "Give up."

"You lack the experience to make judgements, Tharen," was her impassive reply. "You're little more than a novice."

While she hadn't budged, her eyes, inexplicably, flickered towards Niema. One brow lifted subtly in an unspoken signal. With a jolt, she realised that the air current had carried her and Hachim directly behind the king's void drake, and with his attention entirely fixed on the tower, he hadn't noticed them at all.

"Then I will correct your misjudgement." Darkness surged from his outstretched palm as his shield was transformed into an attack.

The Superior countered with another bolt of lightning, its dazzling flash immediately swallowed by the dark. The collision sent her flying back into the tower wall with a bone-shaking crash.

"Stop!" Niema screamed the command at the king's void drake, at any monster within range. *"Leave!"*

The void drake obeyed and turned away from the tower with a beat of its vast wings. The king twisted in his seat, his face a mask of hate, his hands leaking darkness. Niema sucked in air—and agony erupted within her chest. She looked down, startled to see blood. So much blood. A curved claw protruded from her body, sharp and glistening with crimson.

Hachim screamed her name.

The soldier yanked out the claw in a rush of searing pain. Niema's legs lost their grip on the war drake's back, and she fell down, down, and into dark oblivion.

———

Kelan, seeing his Superior battling the king, shouted a prayer of his own. The wind rose, buffeting the void drake's vast wings, but the relentless darkness surging from his palms was unmatched.

When the Superior struck the tower wall, panic stole the breath from his lungs. As he flew upward, Niema screamed her command, a piercing whistle that sent the king's void drake into retreat.

Slowly, inexorably, the Superior began to fall.

Kelan flew faster. Another scream, quieter yet no less piercing, compelled him to turn his head in time to see a soldier yanking their weapon from Niema's back. She fell sideways, her fingers slipping through Hachim's desperate hands.

Kelan's gaze slid between her and his Superior, caught in a heartbeat of indecision.

Then, he flew to the tower, shouting a prayer to Terethik to slow the Superior's fall. Her weight slammed into his outstretched arms, pushing them both down towards the melee of soldiers and Disciples, of war drakes and darker creatures rising from the Void.

An air current caught them first; as a hand might catch a falling leaf, Terethik swept them onto an open balcony. Kelan sank to the ground, the Superior's head lolling against his arm.

"Superior!" A chorus of shouts came as the Disciples of the Sky rallied around their unconscious Superior. More hovered in front, readied to defend their tower—but King

Tharen was already turning away, shouting orders that Kelan didn't hear.

What's he doing?

Trusting the others to protect the Superior, Kelan lifted his blade and flew into the open. He rose upward on a current, taking aim at the king.

Sharp teeth met in his outstretched arm. A hoarse cry ripped out of his throat; he lost his grip on the blade as sensation dulled and blood fountained from the wound. As he yanked his arm free from the war drake's mouth, a spear's end collided with his skull and he, too, fell out of the sky.

————

Watching Niema and Hachim take flight, Yala raised her voice, shouting her squad-mates' names. "Bring me my fucking war drake!"

"Captain!" Gorel descended, his war drake refusing to land near the swathe of darkness enveloping the platform. Though the shadows left no impact on Yala, she was far from being able to call upon a beast from within to use as a steed. "Climb up here!"

She was in no position to be picky, so she took Gorel's outstretched hand and clambered up behind him. The rest of the squad had converged some distance from the lower floor, having taken Yala's command to avoid landing near the Void to heart.

Above flew the king, swathed in darkness that moved at his every command.

Yala dragged her gaze away, scanning the sky for a spare war drake. Sitting behind another person left her with no ability to control their steed's path even if they hadn't been at the mercy of the wind currents stirred up by the battling

Disciples and soldiers. The fight continued, but a large area had been cleared above. Around the king.

"Captain, it's your war drake!" The cry came from Yala's shoulder, prompting her to turn around. Yurel pointed eastward, her scarred face awed. "It's coming for you."

So it is. Now that they were away from the Void, the war drakes had ceased to panic but were slow to obey their riders, fighting only when a Disciple flew directly into their path and refusing to fly closer to the tower. As a result, it was easy to see the one war drake without a rider, soaring towards the battle with its eyes fixed on Yala.

"What power do you have over that beast?" asked Gorel in hushed tones. "Does it come with being a captain?"

Hardly. This was Superior Kralia's doing, and it seemed her commands had gone much further than making the beast easier for her to control. "Not exactly."

When the war drake neared, she readied herself to climb onto its back. Switching steeds in midair was awkward and required a lot of clambering that aggravated her bad leg, but within moments, she sat on the war drake's back, in control once more.

In time to see Niema fall out of her seat, trailing blood as she fell from the war drake's back.

"Shit."

Yala dug her heels into the war drake's sides and flew up, faster, angling towards the falling Disciple. Her squad members' shouts went unheard beneath the roaring in her ears.

Niema.

Yala braced herself, leaned back in her seat, but the impact of Niema's body slamming into the war drake's back sent a bolt of pain through her leg. Biting the inside of her cheek, Yala released her steed with one hand and dragged

Niema into a seated position with her legs splayed on either side of its neck.

"Niema. Niema."

No response. Niema's head hung limply, and a shocking amount of blood soaked her shirt.

A vast shadow blanketed them. The king, freed from any commands Niema might have uttered, descended together with his void drake. Shadows cloaked his body like a garment, and Yala's insides twisted with a mixture of hate and envy.

I have to kill him... but Niema was unconscious, maybe dying, unable to bend him or his monstrous steed to her will.

Yala lifted her chin. "You told us to bring her back alive. Not sure she'll stay that way for long."

"I did." He flew lower, studying the unconscious Disciple of Life. "We'll bring her back to the palace. The battle is over."

Where's the Superior? The shakes that had gripped the tower had petered out, and the air was free of the tremors she'd felt on the lower level. Did that mean Superior Sietra was dead? Getting close enough to see was impossible with Niema on the brink of sliding out of her seat and the king's watchful eye lingering on them both.

Soldiers peeled away from the tower as the order filtered through, attempting to reassemble themselves into their squads. Some war drakes carried two or more people, their steeds having fled or been blown off course, and her own squad was unique in that they'd escaped with no losses, even their newest member.

When they saw her passenger, Gorel gave her a questioning look. "Who's that?"

"King's prisoner," she said. "I have to take her directly to the palace. Stay with the others."

Yala owed them for helping her, she knew, but Niema's

dead weight continued to press against her injured leg, and her lack of responsiveness suggested that the wound was a challenge even for her healing powers.

As the army retreated, rain began to fall as if the sky itself was mourning the Superior. Droplets soaked into Yala's bloodied sleeves and trickled off Niema's limp arm draped over the war drake's side.

The king had not brought down Skytower, but he'd left with a far greater prize.

36

Kelan came back to consciousness with an unpleasant jolt, finding himself hanging upside-down from the tower's edge while raindrops slid across the edge of his nose and dripped into his eyes. He lifted his head and saw that Lakiel held him by the leg, having caught him on the way down.

"You?" He yelped when Lakiel let go; a quick breath of air caught his balance, and he righted himself, shedding droplets of water and blood. His arm hung limp at his side, and sensation was worryingly absent. "You saved me?"

"What possessed you to try to kill the *king?*" Lakiel demanded.

"Did I?" His memories of the battle were a jumbled mess, and the volume of blood drenching his sleeve did not help matters either. One thought cut through the haze. "Fuck. The Superior."

"She's alive." Lakiel's jaw tensed. "But the Void is still open, and one of the Disciples of Life has gone."

"Niema." Guilt speared him as sharply as those war drake's teeth. "Did she fall?"

"Someone caught her. Unfortunately." He didn't elaborate on his odd choice of wording. "The soldiers are retreating."

"They are?" He squinted through a curtain of rain, making out the winged outlines of war drakes flying away from the battlefield.

One hovered apart from the others: Hachim, watching the soldiers' retreat with his back to the tower.

"Don't you dare follow them!" Lakiel shouted. "We need you to deal with this."

Kelan followed his gaze to the floor below. The Void had spread to encompass the entire lower platform, and monstrosities continued to crawl out from within.

Hachim's head turned, his face a mask of pain. Tears glistened on his cheeks along with the rain.

Seeing the Void, he descended, whistling a prayer to Yalet. Green light spread from his palms towards the encroaching darkness.

Can he do it alone? Kelan moved to the platform's edge, his head spinning from blood loss, as Hachim closed in on the Void.

A raptor-like monster leapt forward, claws swiping at Hachim's heels. Kelan reached for his sword and found he'd dropped it during the fall. Spying a discarded spear, he grabbed the weapon and hurled it at the raptor. He missed, and spots dotted his vision as he fought to cling to consciousness.

With a curse, Lakiel glided off the platform, bringing down his blade in a slash that took off the monster's head. More Disciples closed in, encouraged by the brightening glow around Hachim's hands as the darkness began to recede. Together they repelled the dead, prevented them from striking at their saviour while the Void shrank, slither by slither.

As the Void vanished in a final green flash, Hachim fell to his knees. "No. Niema…"

"They took her." Kelan crouched beside him. "Did you see…?"

"Yala." Hachim's voice broke. "Yala took her."

His tenuous grip on consciousness faded, and he knew no more.

———

Saren was enjoying playing the part of a city guard more than he'd expected to. With everyone patrolling the city walls in Nalen's pocket, it was a simple matter to escort anyone who wanted to leave the upper city to the gate and let Nalen's allies handle the rest. More than once, the thought of joining them crossed his mind. Desertion carried a death sentence, but the punishment could hardly be worse than being forced to sacrifice one's life on the battlefield at the behest of the god of death.

He flashed Nalen a grin as they passed one another. "How'd you get so many people involved?"

Nalen wore the uniform considerably better than he did and carried a blunt club strapped to his waist. Like Saren, he refused on principle to use part of Mekan as a weapon, and even with the guards, he'd opted to distract or knock them out if necessary rather than leaving a trail of bodies behind him that might rise to join Mekan's army.

While Saren had no love for anyone who chose to serve the king, he didn't relish the thought of potentially giving Mekan even more weapons to wield either.

"You'd be surprised how many were willing," Nalen muttered back. "Some heard about the executions and got spooked, but plenty were happy to act while the king and his monsters are out of the city."

"How many are choosing to leave?"

Nalen's jaw tensed. "Fewer than I'd like. If the king *does* come back, the rest of us will take the punishment, make no mistake."

A shout rang out from near the temple. The Disciples of the Sea outside the door were engaged in a whispered argument; one of them pointed in the direction of the city wall.

Someone must have noticed the absence of the guards at the back gate, who Nalen had persuaded to leave their posts.

"What should we do?" he whispered to Nalen. "Viam and Brenat are stuck in there."

So were the Disciples of the Flame, who he didn't trust to lift a finger even to defend their own lives. *Ah, shit.*

Nalen muttered a curse. "I'll handle it."

He made for the market and wove through the stalls, approaching the temple from behind. Saren followed, one hand on the shortsword strapped to his waist. He'd refused to take the claw Yala had offered him, but he had to admit it would have been helpful in this situation. Two guards—or rather, Disciples of the Sea—stood in the deserted alleyway behind the temple, their voices raised in argument.

Nalen stepped behind the nearest guard, wrapping an arm around his neck and squeezing hard. The second man exclaimed, drawing his sword, and Saren moved in, parrying clumsily. He'd never been adept with a blade even when his hands had been steady, and his second swing missed, glancing off the temple wall. Nalen dropped the unconscious guard and moved to dispatch Saren's opponent too. Nodding thanks, Saren ran up the stone stairs and rapped a warning.

"Relax, we're on your side," Saren told the man—boy, really—who answered. "We've come to collect our friends, but if any of you also want to leave, I'd advise you to do so before these pricks outside wake up."

"What have you done?" Viam strode into view with

Brenat close behind, followed by several Disciples of the Flame. "Did the guards see you?"

"These two did, but we'll handle it." Saren nodded to Nalen, who stood at the foot of the stairs.

"I'll throw them into the river," Nalen spat. "See if their god'll take them back."

Viam's face fell. "I thought we weren't killing anyone."

"They saw our faces, Viam." Saren gestured. "Get the fuck out before more show up."

A commotion came from somewhere in the city square. Saren turned to Nalen and saw him staring at the alley's entrance. "What's going on?"

"The king's beasts are back." Nalen tensed, his gaze on the sky. "They're going to see that the city guards aren't where they're supposed to be."

"They're animals," Saren said, but the chill rising to his arms told him they needed to fucking move.

Animals or not, the void drakes' presence meant the king must be on his way back to the city.

———

Viam hurried down the stairs and craned her neck, trying to see if the void drakes had returned alone or with the king. A chill seized her in its grip, the claw strapped to her waist reacting to the presence of its kin.

Saren beckoned from the alley's entryway. "Get the Disciples out. The army's not here yet, and those monsters have scared every living creature in the market."

That accounted for the noise, a confusing clamour of human shouts and panicked animals. It would be an effective cover for the escaping Disciples, but the void drakes' return all but confirmed the battle was already won, and Skytower had fallen.

Her insides writhed. "Yala…"

"Never mind Yala." Brenat beckoned to the Disciples crowding behind her. "Follow Nalen. He'll get you out."

One Disciple hesitantly descended the stairs, followed by another. The void drakes' presence had cowed some, but others had accepted the risks when they'd chosen to leave, and twenty or thirty individuals opted to follow Nalen's lead. Viam could only assume he had a plan to move the guards' bodies, but such was the chaos that greeted them at the market that Viam suspected that nobody would give them a second glance. Hogs ran left and right, snorting in panic, while an entire crate of fowl had escaped their cages and ran amok in the square.

"That's got to be Nalen's doing," Brenat said out of the corner of her mouth. "He had people set up to let the animals out as a signal, I bet."

Viam didn't reply. By the time she and Brenat had reached the palace gates, the void drakes had returned to their usual posts above the palace, hovering expectantly. Waiting for their master.

Viam waited, too, sick with nerves. Several minutes later, a gong rang out from somewhere, heralding the monarch's return. The monstrous form of the void drake soared over the palace wall, and then a lone flier followed, far apart from the rest of the war drakes approaching the upper city. Viam squinted, making out two people seated on its back, though the person in front was slumped over as if unconscious.

A horrifying familiarity hit Viam like a slap.

"Yala." She reeled back. "She captured Niema."

Brenat's arm steadied her. "I bet His Majesty didn't give her a choice."

"She could have chosen death." Acid coated the back of her throat. The king had spilled enough blood on the altar for Yala to know he would not give a Disciple of Life a pleasant end, but Niema was more than an ordinary Disciple.

When Yala's steed had disappeared into the paddock, Viam ran for the back gates. The guards had moved aside to let the returning fliers pass through, some bearing gruesome injuries that looked more as if they'd been inflicted by a war drake than a blade. Two soldiers carried another who was missing part of their lower leg, while two more carried Niema's unconscious body into the palace grounds.

Fighting panic, Viam hurried after the soldiers. "Excuse me. Who is that?"

"King's prisoner," came the reply. "Don't think she'll last long."

Brenat snagged her arm and pulled her out of the path of more returning soldiers; within a heartbeat, she'd lost sight of Niema as she was carried into the barracks. *She's hurt. Really hurt.*

"For the gods' sakes, I'll clean this up." Yala's voice drifted over the fence. "Haven't there been enough injuries today?"

Taking the hint, Viam waited until the last of the soldiers departed, and the paddock quietened enough that she knew only Yala remained. Then, she pushed open the gate.

Yala leaned heavily against the fence, her face drawn and streaked with blood. She let out a prolonged breath when she saw Viam. "I know what you're going to say."

"I'd be surprised," Viam murmured. "I hardly know what to say myself."

"I don't need your recriminations." Yala lifted her head. "Niema's injured. She might die before she sets eyes on the king. Did Nalen's plan work?"

"We got some of the Disciples of the Flame out." She gave Yala a brief account of what she'd missed. "The void drakes came back sooner than we expected. What happened with you?"

Yala drove her fist into the fence with a thud that made the war drakes nearby growl in disapproval behind their muzzles. "I miscalculated. When the king took out the Superior, Niema almost had him, but—"

"The Superior is dead?" Viam's skin went cold, clammy. "Then Skytower is lost."

"She might have survived." Yala closed her eyes, her face taut with exhaustion. "I didn't see. As soon as I had Niema, he called off the attack."

Because he already had what he wanted.

"What will he do with her?" Panic fluttered inside her. "Will he torture her into betraying her Superior?"

"He won't." Yala's mouth pinched. "In her current state, she's hardly going to give away any of her fellow Disciples' secrets even under duress. Besides, he must know that she can destroy his temple, given the chance. He'll play it safe."

She can. Yala would never have brought Niema to the palace on purpose, but now she was here, Yala might be rethinking her plan to avoid striking the king inside his own domain. With his one weakness close at hand, who was to say what she'd do next?

"Aren't you scared for her?" she asked. "The king will try to use her abilities for his gain."

"Yes, I'm worried," Yala muttered. "But whether she wakes up or not, the king only has one group of Disciples left to subdue."

And then nobody left in Laria will challenge him.

———

Niema's awareness flickered in and out. She was vaguely aware of countryside soaring below, of someone's arm holding her against their chest to prevent her from toppling into emptiness. Her other senses told her of cold air

383

buffeting her, the sound of wings beating, the taste of blood on her tongue, the coppery taint in her nostrils.

Beyond all sensation was a burning pain in her chest and a chill deeper than any she'd experienced, as if the Void itself had penetrated her soul and obliterated all traces of Yalet's presence. Her breaths were shallow, her thoughts fractured.

I'm dying.

Yalet...

When she next came to awareness, she was being carried through a set of doors into a large room she recognised as the military's infirmary. The person carrying her laid her on a sleeping mat, waving away the curious onlookers with an impatient hand.

"Leave us." He turned to her then, eyes widening above his prominent grey moustache. "You're awake."

"Why am I here?" she rasped.

"The king wants you alive." The man studied her blood-soaked chest. "Assuming you don't die of your wound."

"I can heal," she murmured. "Yalet..."

The god of life's green light was absent, and no warmth soothed the cold, biting pain rippling through her body.

If she died here, which god would claim her soul?

The thought followed her into unconsciousness, where she dreamed of a dark place that no light had ever touched.

———

Yala waited for nightfall before she slipped out of the dormitory and headed for the infirmary. Niema was alive as far as she knew, but Yala hadn't realised that it was a void drake's claw that had pierced Niema through the chest until they'd landed, affording her the chance to look more closely at the wound. The bleeding had slowed to a trickle, but the sight of the pulsing dark splotch on Niema's skin had been burned into her brain. It was as if the Void itself had crept under her skin with its corruptive poison, and for all Yala knew, an injury inflicted by a piece of Mekan might be a wound that even Yalet couldn't heal.

Yala trod into the infirmary on careful feet, avoiding leaning too heavily on her cane despite the stabbing pain in her leg. The injured lay all around her, some as bad off as Niema, and nobody glanced at Yala as she crossed the room to the corner in which they'd placed the king's captive.

Two soldiers stood in front of her sleeping mat, keeping watch. One caught her eye, and Yala whispered, "Just checking that she's alive."

They accepted that—she'd been the one who'd captured Niema, after all—and neither intervened when she stepped closer to Niema's sleeping mat. Crouching awkwardly to avoid jostling her injured leg, she leaned over with the pretext of examining the wound. Niema's shirt had been cut back, revealing thick bandages swathing her torso.

A cough. Niema's eyes opened a fraction. "Yala."

"You're alive," Yala breathed. "Is your wound not healing?"

Niema groaned. "I think it is... slowly."

Conscious of the soldiers nearby, Yala scraped her cane on the floor to cover her voice. "If you get near that temple..."

Destroy it. The words died in her throat. Who was she to give demands to someone on the brink of death? To someone whose fate she might have sealed with her own hand? Yala swallowed, self-loathing writhing inside her like a nest of serpents. As Niema's eyes closed, she rose to her feet. Pain twinged up to her knee, and she let it wash over her, revelling in the punishment for entertaining the thought of using Niema in such a way.

As she'd expected, Yala spent a sleepless night contemplating the mistakes she'd made in the course of the battle.

Jumping on Lisek wasn't one of them, but her fellow captain had glared at her whenever their paths crossed since their return to the barracks. Likely, she'd been spared retribution only because the king *had* wanted Niema alive badly enough to abandon the battle when they had her in their hands.

The next morning, Lisek's rage had a different target.

"Why did nobody warn us that those monsters were going to fly right into the middle of our formation?" Lisek's voice drifted over from the table next to the one where Yala sat with her squad members. "Two of my people were knocked off their war drakes, and one nearly died."

"Who was supposed to warn you, the king?" Saren twisted in his seat. "That's what you get for playing games with Mekan—*ow.*"

Yala, who'd jabbed him in the back of the knee with her cane, gave Lisek an apologetic look that went unacknowledged.

"Fuck you." Lisek glared at them both. "At least nobody in *my* squad skipped out on the battle with a fake injury."

Saren adjusted the bandage, displaying the gouges in his wrist. "Does this look fake to you?"

Yala threw caution to the wind. "If you recall, *I* tried to warn everyone that Mekan's creatures don't distinguish between friend and foe on the battlefield."

Lisek's face flushed. "Don't think I've forgotten what else you did."

Yala bit back another retort; Lisek's growing doubt in the king's decisions was a wound to prod with careful hands. "The king told us to capture the Disciple of Life alive. If I'd let you kill her, he might have done worse than neglect to warn us about those monsters."

"The king *didn't* warn us," someone else muttered. "He knew, didn't he?"

"He did." Yala experienced a rush of satisfaction as a

ripple of anger travelled among the soldiers, including her own squad members. Gorel watched her in surprise, but Roven and Kithal exchanged dark looks, and Yurel dug her knife so deeply into her flatbread that the tip pierced the table beneath.

If their anger was directed at the right target, perhaps she could harness it. Even the king would have a hard job convincing the soldiers to mount an attack on another group of Disciples after the way he'd treated them the last time... or so she would have thought had he been an ordinary monarch and not Mekan's chosen.

For all he'd taught them in training, he'd held back from revealing what he was capable of. The truth had been stark when Yala had seen him wielding the Void as a weapon, wearing its darkness as a cloak that shielded him from harm. He'd bested even a Superior. Who was Yala to think she could surpass his faith in a god who had seemingly given him everything that He would ever offer a human?

Lisek spoke again, drawing her attention to the present. "When he asks us to come and report, I'll ask him for an explanation."

"I wouldn't," Yala said. "Can you imagine that ending any way other than terribly for you?"

A murmur travelled through the soldiers. Everyone who'd attended one of the ceremonies had known the danger they faced by mere proximity to the Void, let alone from the king himself, but the rest of the flight division had not witnessed the reality of the monster they fought behind until they'd seen him plough through his own soldiers to reach Skytower. Her squad had already been asking questions that she wouldn't be able to put off answering for much longer. She had never wanted to draw them into her schemes against the king, but with cracks forming in his control, now might be her chance to gain some new, crucial allies.

A cynical whisper in the back of her mind told her that the king might not even need the army now that he had not only the monsters of the Void at his command but a force that might prove even more formidable than Mekan's beasts in his possession.

A Disciple of Life with the power of death in her hands.

37

Green light nudged Kelan's eyes open. Hachim leaned over him, his hands aglow and outstretched over Kelan's injured arm. The numbness sharpened to pain, and he sat upright, gasping. "Superior Sietra."

"She's alive." Hachim bowed his head, his features lined with exhaustion.

As the light dimmed, the sharp pain faded to a dull throb. Kelan lifted his arm, the movement stiff. Painful twinges travelled up to his shoulder. "Ouch."

"Let me help with the pain." Hachim reached out a shaky hand.

"You can't heal everyone," said Kelan. "Gods, you're as bad as Niema."

Niema. They'd taken her. *Yala* had taken her, and he'd let it happen. He'd chosen the Superior.

Rising to his feet, he called upon Terethik to guide him to the upper level of the tower. The guards let him enter her office without argument; when he did so, a novice scurried past, whispering, "I think she's sleeping."

A door off the main room lay slightly ajar. Kelan nudged it open, careful not to make a sound. He'd never been into her private rooms before, and his insides pitched to see the Superior lying in bed, looking older and frailer than he ever would have expected.

Her eyes flickered open. Kelan opened his mouth, to apologise perhaps, but she gave him a minute shake of her head.

"It is lucky, in a way, that I already had no sensation from my lower back down to my legs," she murmured. "I'll survive."

Kelan would not have called anything about this situation *lucky*, but there was little doubt that Terethik's blessing was on their side. "Did the king assume you were dead?"

"Quite possibly." A smile flickered across her lips. "If not, he believes we are subdued. He is mistaken."

"I know, but we're hardly in a position to counterattack." They'd suffered fewer losses than they might have if the king hadn't aborted the mission immediately upon Niema's capture and the Superior's fall, but he doubted any Disciples of the Sky would be keen to mount a rescue mission. "And he has Niema now."

The Superior tilted her head up a fraction. "Where is the other Disciple of Life?"

"Hachim? He's healing the injured." He would all but certainly want to pursue Niema, but attempting a single-handed rescue mission would end only in his own demise. "I can help him send word of Niema's capture to the Superior."

"Do that." Her eyes slid closed again. "I'm told that Yala Palathar was the one who took her."

"I doubt she had a choice." His stomach turned. "The king won't kill her. He wanted her alive."

"To use for his own ends." Her eyelids flickered, and a faint breeze scraped against his skin. "This is as I feared. If

Niema should succumb to his pressure, her people will be the ones who will pay the price."

———

The king called in the captains to speak to him late that afternoon, when Yala had begun to wonder if he intended to acknowledge them at all after his return to the palace. Unlike their previous mission, this one had ended in a clear-cut victory, but the king's treatment of his own soldiers had not been forgotten, and there was a large amount of discontented muttering among the captains as they walked to the palace. Lisek in particular wore a sour expression that didn't fade when they entered the receiving room and assembled in front of the king.

"You fought well," King Tharen told them. "Mekan is pleased with you, as am I. Those who lost will be given a funeral in accordance with the highest honour."

Yala wondered if that would appease Lisek and the others. The number of injured or dead would prompt another reorganisation of the flight division, and the reserves were depleted. Moreover, Nalen's actions during the king's absence had shrunk the number of foot soldiers by a noticeable proportion too. Yala was surprised that nobody at the barracks had brought it up.

Yet. The king's eyes hardened, and dread pooled in her stomach. *He knows.*

"I heard," said the king, "that there was an unfortunate spate of desertions among the foot soldiers while we were occupied on our mission. A number of soldiers left the upper city, and some guards, too, have been reported missing. Rest assured that such a crime has not been unnoticed."

There it is. Yala gripped her cane in hands dampening with sweat. There was nothing whatsoever to connect her with those events, but if someone had recognised Saren or Viam or seen anyone entering the Temple of the Flame...

"These deserters are believed to still be present in Dalathar," the king went on. "All the city guards will search for them, but it is my belief that there may be dissenters both within the guard and within our own ranks. Because of that, the search will need to be supervised."

He scanned them, his gaze lingering on each captain. Yala's fingers loosened on her cane, and she schooled her face into neutrality.

"You have proven yourselves the most trustworthy among my ranks. As a result, you will seek out the deserters. Commander Sranak will set out the rota, and you'll begin tomorrow."

Lisek cleared her throat. "What of those of us who lost squad-mates? We'll need time to train them. We can't do that while we're hunting deserters."

"As I said." He spoke slowly, in a patient tone that did not convince Yala. "There will be a rota. You will have time to train, and you will also aid me in capturing those who sought to flee their responsibilities. Their lives will be forfeit, and their blood will clothe Mekan's altar."

Shadows rose around him as he spoke. Like in the battle, they started at his fingertips and spread outward until his body was outlined in darkness visible even with the bright lanterns adorning the walls.

"Then," he said, "we shall set our sights on conquering our final and most formidable enemy."

The shadows became more distinct, sharper, and Yala's hands tightened on her cane again as the longing to share in that power gripped her like a vice.

"We aren't flying to war right away, are we?" Lisek found her voice again. "We need to recover. There were losses, injuries, and even two captains were killed."

"They will be honoured," he said. "And you will need not fear for them in the oncoming battle, because most participants will be those brought directly from the realm of the one who serves me."

Did he truly believe Mekan served *him* and not the other way around? The Void might answer to his command, but with the god of death, there was always a price to be paid. The question revolved around who, exactly, would be the one to pay it.

The king's dismissal was swiftly followed by the words Yala had half expected: "I will speak with Captain Yala Palathar alone."

Lisek cut her a glance, but her expression held less envy than it might have, and worry creased her brow. While Yala wished she hadn't publicly challenged the king, someone had to, and if Lisek's eyes had begun to open to the truth, Yala was more than willing to contribute.

"I must compliment you on your swift action, Captain," he told Yala. "In capturing the Disciple of Life, you did me a significant favour."

"I followed your orders." *Against my better judgement.* "What do you intend to do with her?"

"She will offer me assistance in the oncoming war," he said. "After all, it is not against the Disciples whom we fight but against the scourge that infects Laria's core, wielded by those who call themselves Disciples of Life."

A faint echo followed his words, turned them into a whisper that raised the hairs on her arms. Had he and Mekan spoken in conjunction, or were their desires so intertwined that there was no distinguishing between them any longer?

"It won't be long now." The trace of a smile flickered across his mouth. "You will see the world that I intend to create, Yala Palathar, and it shall be a thing of beauty."

Not if I can help it. Niema might not be integral to his

plans, but if she survived her wound, the king would have her brought into the palace, and Yala would lose any chance of rescuing her from his grasp.

Yala had to act first.

————

When Niema next awakened, Yala was leaning over her. Her face was taut with pain, her mouth moving little, and she had to strain to catch the words. "I only have a minute. You aren't any better?"

Niema's chest burned with cold fire, and her skin was clammy, her breathing laboured. She'd been dreaming of the island, the peaceful calm that surrounded the Superior who'd died there and become one with Yalet. A calm she would never have for herself.

"The soldiers." Yala breathed the words. "You can take the life force from them. Right?"

While she'd been conscious of the other life forms around her, Niema had never thought to use her abilities that way. "I can."

"Do that, then *run*. Get out of here. Nalen will help."

"Nalen?" She lifted her head, spying a bearded man standing in front of her sleeping mat.

"He distracted the soldiers watching you, said he'd take over for them, but they'll be back soon." Yala adjusted her grip on her cane, her expression pained from crouching on the floor. At the sound of footsteps, she cursed. "I have to go."

She rose to her feet and was gone. Niema closed her eyes, marshalling her fractured thoughts. Yala wanted her to flee the city, but wasn't she alone capable of destroying the temple? If she fled into Dalathar, allowing what might be her only chance to rid the world of Mekan to slip through her fingers—no. She couldn't.

Niema held her breath as the footsteps became louder, and when she opened her eyes, King Tharen stood over her.

A gasp escaped. She tried to sit up, and pain ripped through her chest. Darkness crept at the corners of her vision.

The king's voice sounded muted, like an echo in a cave. "So the commander did not exaggerate the extent of your injury. I wondered."

He stepped aside, and an unfamiliar soldier leaned down, lifted her from the sleeping mat. The pain worsened, threatening to propel her into unconsciousness.

She reached for the nearest life form, and sudden warmth soothed the biting cold inside her. Energy flooded her limbs like a cork stoppering the pain leaking from her wound. The world tilted sideways as the soldier sank to the ground, and she twisted out of his arms, gritting her teeth against the lingering pain. The warmth soothed her, giving her strength to stand. To run.

Run. Now.

"Stop her!" The king's shout echoed as she broke into a sprint, out of the infirmary and down the corridor.

Adrenaline flooded her body, and she ran without stopping, without looking at where she was going—

Niema slammed into a solid form, hard enough to send a fresh wave of pain rippling through her body. Hands seized her again, rough and sharp. As she was lifted into the air, she reached for the warmth, for the flow of energy within her captor, and found none. He was dead.

The dead man lifted her over his shoulder. The world spun around her, and her attempts to wriggle free were to no avail. A dead man shouldn't have such strength.

A second newcomer flanked her as they left the barracks. The dark sky afforded little light to see by, but her view of the palace showed that the tiered floors were now decorated

EMMA L. ADAMS

not with flowers but with military banners. There would be no life in there through which to access Yalet's strength.

The dead man carried Niema through a side entrance and down a corridor lined with countless doors. Neither he nor his companion spoke, but the king walked close behind, and when he halted, they stopped too.

"Here will do." He opened the door to a small, modestly furnished room, or modest by the palace's standards, anyway. The carpet was plush red, the wooden furniture polished to a sheen, and silk curtains framed the wide bed upon which the dead men laid her.

Not men. Nor dead either but something much worse. Their faces were masked with dark scales, their bodies similarly encased, and while their form was humanoid in its shape, sharp claws protruded where hands should have been. No wonder she'd sensed no life force within them.

As for the king...

He studied her, eyes dark as pitch beneath a crown studded with gold. He wore a drakeskin coat topped with embroidered outerwear, and his hair had been neatly plaited out of his face. She'd never had cause to look closely at him for so long before, but though the shadows he'd wielded during the battle had retreated, cold licked at her bare arms.

"So you're the Disciple of Life," he said. "A Disciple of Life with some unusual talents. Please, allow me the courtesy of addressing you by your name."

"Niema," she whispered.

"Niema." The word came out as a hiss that echoed long after he'd fallen silent. "You were involved in the destruction of the island whereon I learned Mekan's secrets, were you not?"

Questions crowded her mind, but to what little he knew of her, she would give him no more.

"Your talents are impressive," he went on. "Draining the

396

life from someone until they breathe their last is a skill worthy of Mekan Himself, one might say."

Niema swallowed, her throat full of glass shards. *Did I kill that soldier?*

"But Yalet has never been as benevolent as She has led us to believe." He eyed her bandaged chest. "A wound inflicted by Mekan is poison to your kind, but you are no ordinary Disciple of Life, are you?"

No. Yes. Answering either way would condemn her and the others, and so she maintained her silence.

"I saw what you did when we fought the Disciples of the Sea," said the king. "Your actions at Skytower confirmed you are able to influence the creatures of Mekan as well as those of Yalet. This is a skill I wish to know more about. I will add that your cooperation might engender mercy towards your surviving Superiors."

He knows the Superiors are dead?

The ghost of a smile passed over his mouth. "I know that your people are suffering at Mekan's hands, but I can make it worse."

"You sent the monsters after them."

"Nothing so direct," he said. "Mekan's beasts are drawn to eliminate any traces of Yalet, and there is no halting the spread of Corruption despite the considerable talents your fellow Disciples hold. They have wrought their own extinction."

"You're blaming my people for what Mekan is doing to them?" Her voice became stronger. "We never started this war."

"The war began before either of us even drew breath." His eyes gleamed, black as night. "The gods' ancient conflict is beyond mortal comprehension, but through Mekan's eyes, I have glimpsed truths offered to no other human."

Liar. Niema's thoughts returned to the island, to the

vision Yalet imparted on her. She, too, had seen through the eyes of a god.

And two deities' power nestled inside her. She had to be able to use them against him.

"I'll ask you again," he said. "I have never heard of a Disciple of Life who was able to command one of Mekan's beasts. How did you come across this talent?"

At her silence, his mouth parted with a sigh. "Your stubbornness does you no favours. I'm sure I can devise some tests to tease out the limits of your talents, but I would prefer for you to tell me directly. I think you would find it less painful that way."

Niema's skin shrivelled with dread. *No. I can't give in.*

"Or perhaps I will inflict the punishment upon another," he said. "As I understand it, your people have an aversion to violence. A principle that I never understood. Why do you deny your nature?"

"You're wrong." She pushed herself upright, sweat beading on her forehead. "You don't understand us at all."

"Don't I?" Again, she heard the echo of another voice, a rasping whisper devoid of warmth. "I find your pacifism repellent, but it's all a matter of opinion, isn't it? At the least, you cannot pretend your people's hands have always been bloodless."

"No," she said, "but if my people hadn't destroyed Mekan's followers, your ancestors would never have made it to these shores."

"Perhaps." He offered her what might have been a pleasant smile if not for the flat darkness in his eyes. "If you survive that wound, you will witness the fall of your god. I promise you that, Niema."

He turned and left the room. Shadows lingered in his wake, pooling on the floor like spilled blood.

38

A chirruping noise woke Kelan the following morning, and a clawed foot prodded his shoulder.

"Molin," he said, smothering a yawn. "I thought you were with your Superior."

Superior. The cascade of memories prompted him to sit up, resulting in a thumping headache. Blearily, he took the note Molin held clutched in his clawed foot. It took several painful seconds for his brain to untangle the gist of the message Superior Kralia had sent, and he knew at once that it was meant for Niema.

Another Superior is dead.

A rapping on the door. Lakiel's voice. "Kelan?"

He rubbed his eyes with the back of his hand. "Yes?"

"Good, you're awake. The Superior is asking for you. She also wants you to bring the Disciple of Life."

"Nice of her to give me time to recover." His head pounded, his body ached with exhaustion, but he could hardly ask Hachim to heal such minor aches when he'd had more serious injuries to contend with the previous day. "Let me make myself presentable first."

He sent Molin to fly ahead of him while he pulled on fresh clothes and ran fingers through his tangled hair. His arm hurt a little when he stretched, but the teeth marks had faded to faint imprints on his skin.

He opened the door and found Hachim waiting outside his room. The young man looked more rested than he had the day before, but his face was drawn, his eyes shadowed.

"She'll want us to get Niema back," Hachim whispered. "She knows what's at stake."

"We just survived an attack," Kelan said. "And she also knows that you can't rescue Niema by yourself."

He carried Hachim to the topmost floor. Inside her office, the Superior sat dressed in her usual embroidered attire, but her hair lacked its elaborate styling, and her face was bare of paint. Her hand shook a little when she reached out to take the note Molin had given her.

"I think that was meant for Niema," Kelan ventured. "Hachim and I sent a bird last night, but our messengers must have missed each other."

"Yes." She placed the note on the desk and returned her trembling hand to her side.

"You should be resting." He half expected a reprimand, but the corner of her mouth lifted.

"I would tell you to take that advice yourself, Kelan, but I fear we have little time to spare. The king will all but certainly make use of his captive now that she's in his hands."

Hachim made a choked noise. "She was already injured. One of the soldiers stabbed her with a void drake's claw."

"Shit." Would she even survive a wound inflicted by Mekan? Even if she did, she'd be in no fit state to fight her way past the king and his monstrous allies to escape the palace.

"If she perishes, she will no longer be endangering her

fellow Disciples of Life," said the Superior. "That is a truth we cannot ignore."

"What?" Kelan's heart missed a beat. "She drove those void drakes away from the tower. She saved our lives."

"And the king saw her." She leaned against the back of her seat, her mouth pinching at the corners. "Her utility to him depends upon his knowledge of her abilities. It may be that she is able to resist for a time, but his status as a Disciple of Death is unmatched. He is a Superior in all but name."

No kidding. Kelan thought back to the way the darkness had moved at his command, as if he held power over the Void itself.

"Niema won't tell him anything, even under duress," he said with certainty. "She'd die first."

Hachim flinched. "We can't abandon her to death."

"Do you think the other Disciples of Life are likely to act now that one of their own has been taken?" Kelan asked him.

"Not unless they believe it's more dangerous for her to be held captive than the alternative," Hachim murmured. "Ragem and the others know that entering the capital will end in their deaths, but I can't leave her."

"I wouldn't advise you to risk your life, nor you either." Superior Sietra gave Kelan a pointed look. "Rather, if the worst happens and he *does* find a way to use Niema against Yalet, someone will need to oppose him."

Hachim made a choked noise. "You think that's his plan? He doesn't know anything about the Disciples of Life, and she won't betray us."

"Perhaps," she said, "but we know that her mere presence draws the dead. All the king would have to do is to take her to anywhere that is most sacred to Yalet. I would imagine they have certain places where Yalet's presence is particularly strong. Shrines or temples, if you will."

Hachim's spine stiffened. Kelan turned to him, compre-

EMMA L. ADAMS

hension dawning. *Of course.* If Mekan could have His own temple, why shouldn't the Disciples of Life have their own equivalent?

"This is speculation on my part," the Superior added, "but I thought I should warn you. I have no control over what you choose to do, Hachim, but I suspect your fellow Disciples will want to hear directly from you before they act."

"Yes." He sounded shaken. "I'll go. Right away."

"I'll come with you," said Kelan, who didn't entirely trust the young Disciple not to fly off and mount a single-handed rescue mission the instant he was out of their sight. "Unless you have another task for me, Superior?"

"No." A pause. "Yes, I think it's wise that you go to the Disciples of Life. However, I have my doubts that anyone will volunteer to accompany you."

"I didn't think so." Everyone was shaken after the battle, himself included, but he was more worried for Hachim, who'd worn himself ragged healing the injured immediately after closing the Void and banishing Mekan's beasts. "Are you sure the army won't come back, though?"

They'd be in real trouble if the king did attempt another attack while their Superior was injured and no more Disciples of Life were present in the tower, but that the king had departed without checking the Superior had survived suggested his priorities had shifted in favour of the valuable prisoner he now had in his hands.

"Not in the immediate future," the Superior replied. "He's already claimed his victory. As with the Disciples of the Sea who escaped, he will spare us, at least for the time being."

"Right." Such had been the turmoil of the past few weeks that the escaped Disciples had slid from his mind once Niema had confirmed they were safely away from harm. "He either can't mount an attack on several fronts at once or sees us as unworthy of bothering with. Like the Disciples of the Earth."

Come to think of it, the king had not unleashed Mekan inside the temple itself as he had with the Temple of the Flame, and from what he'd heard from Yala in their brief window of communication after she'd rejoined the army, he hadn't sent anyone to check on them either. The soldiers had more important tasks than checking no seeds of rebellion had sprouted among the temples the king had already subdued, with the possible exception of the Temple of the Flame.

"Both might be true," said the Superior. "As to the Disciples of the Earth, I have not heard from them since the occupation, but I imagined they would have cut off communications when the soldiers moved in."

"They didn't stay." He recalled Pehin's assertion that their home would not fall to Mekan twice. "And the king never went there in person. Right, Hachim?"

Hachim blinked. "No, but they're hardly in a position to help us."

"Aren't they?" He tilted his head. "Do they not owe your fellow Disciples a favour for getting rid of Mekan the first time around?"

Hachim wore a doubtful expression, but the Superior sat up a little straighter. "They do. It is no guarantee of cooperation, but you might want to remind them of that debt."

"I can certainly do that." Kelan knew she hadn't asked *him* to talk to the Disciples of the Earth, but Hachim had not been present when the Disciples of Life had flown into Setemar and obliterated the dead. Kelan had, and moreover, he did not share the Disciples of Life's aversion to conflict. He was more than happy to walk straight up to the new Superior's office if need be.

Superior Sietra watched him for a moment. "Go with Hachim. Send word to me when you reach Setemar."

Don't get distracted. She didn't add the last part, but Kelan could imagine her speaking it, followed by *Don't aggravate the king's soldiers.*

He could make no promises on either, but she must know that they hadn't a hope of defeating Mekan without cooperation. Without the help of the other Disciples.

Someone had to bring them together. Why not him?

———

Kelan, Hachim soon found, talked a *lot.* He refused to let the silence linger for longer than a few moments, and without anyone else to converse with, Hachim bore the brunt of the barrage of questions and comments. Maybe he was trying to distract Hachim from dwelling on Niema's capture, but for all his prattling, Kelan hadn't asked for the details of the place Superior Sietra had alluded to. Somewhere she shouldn't have known existed—but in hindsight, it was easy for someone of her stature and knowledge to have concluded that the Disciples of Life possessed a temple of their own.

And she'd implied the king intended to use Niema against it.

Hachim didn't want to believe it. Niema had been ridden with similar doubts until Yalet had accepted her into the highest rank of Disciple inside that very temple. Perhaps Superior Sietra was wrong, but if the king somehow learned of its existence, Hachim dreaded to think what he and Mekan would do.

Minutes turned into hours as they travelled over hills and fields, over farms and patches of forest. Niema's war drake flew beside his own, bereft of its rider, and he used its guidance to steer them in the right direction. The war drakes would know where their fellow elite Disciples were waiting, and the extra reminder of Niema's absence kept at bay the exhaustion that had sapped at Hachim's bones since he'd closed the Void. He'd expended too much of himself, both in that feat and in healing the Disciples, but resting was out of the question.

Kelan disagreed. When the sun began to sink beyond the horizon, he flew lower, scanning for a likely village or inn at which to spend the night.

"I'd have suggested we spend the night in Setemar." Kelan gestured at the shaded outline of cliffs to their southwest. "I can't say we'll face a warm welcome, though."

"You don't really think the Disciples of the Earth will want to help us, do you?"

"They do owe you a debt." Kelan frowned. "Where's that war drake going?"

Hachim's gaze went to Niema's steed, which had picked up its pace and dropped into a low glide. His own did likewise, while Kelan trailed behind with a bemused expression.

The war drakes skirted the cliffs marking Setemar's edge and carried on past the city to the river flowing south of its borders. When Hachim spied the war drakes crouched near the fast-flowing water, Kelan glided ahead for a closer look. "It's not the king, at least, but I don't think the Superior is with them."

"She wouldn't have left the forest."

They landed on marshy ground near where the Disciples of Life sat around a low-burning campfire. Several drew their weapons before they recognised Hachim approaching in the darkness.

"It is true, then?" Ragem spoke first, his face as devoid of emotion as ever. "Niema was taken?"

EMMA L. ADAMS

"It's true."

He told them of the battle at Skytower and the Superior's fall, followed by Niema's near-fatal wounding and subsequent capture. Aside from Bitra, few of the Disciples displayed distress; none had had time to grow close to Niema in the short time after she'd proven herself to Yalet. Nor did they seem to have arrived at the same conclusion that Superior Sietra had… that the king might try to use Niema against their home.

"So it has come to this," Ragem said. "There are no Disciples left to challenge Mekan except us."

Kelan cleared his throat. "Some of us are still here too. Also, the king didn't check Superior Sietra *was* dead, and there's no evidence he killed the leader of the Disciples of the Earth either."

Ragem took no note of the pointed hint in his voice. "There are two Superiors left. They need to be protected at all costs."

"Why are you here, then?" Kelan queried. "Seems a little far from the forest."

"Not at all." Ragem gave him a cold stare. "This river cuts directly into the heart of our territory. When the dead enter its waters, we are the ones who suffer. We are here to cut Corruption off at the root."

"The only way to do that is to destroy that temple." Hachim shrank a little from Ragem's cold stare but held firm. "This won't end until the temple—and the king—have gone."

"And conveniently, the temple is where your captured enclave member is held." Contempt dripped from Ragem's voice. "If you wish for us to mount a pointless attack on the palace that will certainly end in our deaths, all for the sake of your enclave member, then say so."

"Actually, since Niema's the only person who *can* stop the king, it's a valid question," Kelan interjected.

Hachim shot him a warning look, which he ignored. "We don't know if she's the only one, but she—"

"Didn't you see her control the king's void drake?" Kelan persisted. "I'm not going to try to change your minds, but don't condemn Hachim for stating the truth. She came within a heartbeat of ending his life there at Skytower."

That was a stretch, but had she not been stabbed, she would certainly have halted the army in its tracks for a second time.

"Entering the capital is out of the question," said Ragem. "We would be slaughtered. And you are mistaken if you can convince me to believe Niema is capable of taking anyone's life, even Mekan's chosen."

"I know who I'd bet on of the two of them."

How can he be so certain? Hachim trusted Niema, believed in her, but King Tharen was a Superior in all but name and bound to the deity that sought to obliterate every trace of Yalet's existence.

"Regardless of her capabilities," he said. "If the king tortures her, he might learn our temple's location. What then?"

Ragem's jaw tightened. "Niema will not betray us, even to her death. That I know."

True, no doubt, but if Superior Sietra was right, even the other Disciples didn't know the extent to which Niema might become bound to Mekan's will.

And Hachim knew, with sickening certainty, that if the king *did* try to use Niema to destroy her home, he would have to be the one to stop her.

***

The day after he brought her into the palace, the king took Niema to the Temple of Death.

While she was no longer on the brink of passing into Mekan's hands, the wound in her chest still ached, and her exhaustion crushed any thoughts of escape she might have harboured. She slept for hours, waking at dusk when she found herself being lifted off the bed. One of those faceless masked guards slung her over their shoulder, carrying her through opulent corridors lined with portraits and tapestries along a circuitous route that dimmed all thoughts that she might find her way out of this warren.

The guard placed her feet on the ground In a courtyard open to the night sky. Mekan's presence hit like a knife gouging at her wounded chest; she swayed, the guard's clawed hands gripping her shoulders, keeping her upright. In silence, her captor steered her into the temple proper. Tall pillars flanked a large altar. Old crimson stains marked the stone. The king stood at its side, moonlight flickering on his still face. In one hand, he held the sword he'd wielded at Skytower, a crude blade fashioned from a void drake's claw.

The guard shoved Niema to her knees. He watched her, not speaking. Then came the questions.

How are you able to control Mekan's kin?

What deal did you make with Him?

Are you truly allied with Yalet?

Niema didn't speak. Not when his pleasant manner lifted and his threats turned into wounds: gashes to her legs and arms, booted feet kicking her to the ground. The king let his masked guards take over the beating, looking on with that terrible sword of his held aloft. He did not use it on her, but that would have been a mercy.

Rather, he waited until his guards brought in a soldier—a deserter caught hiding somewhere in the city—and pushed him to his knees in front of the altar. After repeating his questions to Niema, the king pressed the blade against the trembling soldier's neck.

Niema's silence broke. "I don't *know* why I have these abilities. I just do."

"Really." The sword sliced deep into the man's throat, crimson rivulets flowing over its edges.

"It's true." She sobbed out the words. "There's nothing else I can tell you."

"Then we shall see if we can tease out the limits of your talent." He pointed to the soldier's body. "Command him to move."

Tears misted her vision. "I can't."

"Then I shall bring another." He beckoned a hand. "Give the command."

"I—" A realisation hit her like a bolt. He *wanted* her to use her powers—and he seemed to have forgotten that her abilities worked on him too.

She sucked in air, began to whistle—and a heavy blow struck the back of her head. She swayed, her vision wavering, a ringing in her ears through which the king's voice drifted as if spoken from the end of a dark tunnel.

"My guards will know if you intend to cause harm to me. If you try again, they will slaughter one of my captives."

Niema suppressed a whimper. Her head throbbed, and though she sensed Yalet's power trying to heal the wound, there was no life here to draw upon. Except the king, who was off limits and might not be truly alive regardless.

The king allowed her a few moments to catch her breath and then repeated the order. "Command this man to obey you."

Reasoning that she would betray nothing in revealing that her powers had no effect on the true dead, Niema whistled a simple command. As she'd expected, the dead man did not stir.

King Tharen's gaze flickered between the body and

Niema once, twice. "Interesting. Why, if not the dead, can you control the beasts of the Void?"

"I don't know." The words scraped against her dry throat. "I told you."

"Then we shall both find out." He nodded to the masked guard at her back. "It'll be less painful if you share what you know without resistance. I'll give you time to think on your options."

Then, she was swept away by hard, cruel arms and carried to her gold-drenched prison.

———

Three full days passed after Niema's capture before the king invited Yala into the palace again. Three days of combing the capital for deserters, or rather, taking increasingly elaborate detours to avoid venturing near actual safe houses. Nalen must have successfully got the Disciples of the Flame out of the city, at least, because none of the king's patrols found any sign of them. Any deserters they did find were hauled into the palace, and in the absence of any invitations to the temple, Yala could only assume the king wanted to offer them to Mekan himself.

Or else he'd forced the gruesome task on Niema. The idea of her enduring unbearable hardship ate away at Yala as the days wore on without any news of either Niema's fate or of the army's next mission.

When the summons came, it was directed at the whole army, not just the flight division. Yala walked at the head of her squad, her body tensed with anticipation that grew stronger when they passed by the receiving room and continued towards the temple. *He's ready to reveal it to the other soldiers, is he?*

Mekan was ready for something. His cold whisper lingered in the corridors, and thick shadows hovered in the air, swamping the lanterns flanking the courtyard's entrance. The temple itself was awash in darkness that became denser with each step and coalesced around the jagged opening of the Void above the altar. Fresh blood gleamed on the stone, but no bodies lay nearby, nor were there any prisoners to execute.

A few quiet gasps came from the other soldiers who hadn't been into the temple before, swiftly stifled when they set eyes on the king. King Tharen watched them enter with his expression as flat and cold as the darkness behind him. The prince stood on the altar's other side, his shoulders hunched inward as if he wished he could shrink to nothing and disappear.

"I've called you here," the king began, "to inform you that we are almost ready to begin our final assault upon our enemies. The hour draws close, and it is to that end that I will reveal to you the seat of my power. My temple and the instrument of my—*our*—victory."

Slip of the tongue? Yala thought. Few would be fooled; surely, word of his callousness towards his own soldiers had spread throughout the entire army by now.

Lisek spoke up. "Your Majesty, does that mean we're going back to Skytower?"

"No." He displayed no anger at her for speaking out of turn, but a chill prickled at the base of Yala's spine all the same. "The Disciples of the Sky are a minor inconvenience compared to the one who presents the greater threat to my rule. I speak, of course, of the Disciples of Life."

The cold whisper, always present, became louder, and the phrase *Disciples of Life* reverberated in the air as if the Void itself had echoed the king's words. Yala was seized with the overwhelming urge to run forward, to drive her blade into the man who claimed dominion over Mekan Himself.

As if he has the right to.

"During my exile, I learned much of Mekan and of those who once served him," he said. "There were many, whose history was concealed from us by Disciples past, who were driven to exile and brutally destroyed long before King Larial ever arrived on these shores."

Yala's resentment gave way to shock; a few soldiers gasped or muttered to one another in disbelief that their king was challenging the official story that had been taught to generations of Larians for centuries.

The noise dissipated when the king lifted a hand, shadows trailing from his fingertips and merging with the thickening darkness around the altar.

"Mekan has chosen me to reveal the truth to you and to avenge those who were cruelly destroyed," he said. "To that end, we shall enlist His service in our war."

The shadows thickened, extending cold tendrils throughout the room and eliciting a collective shiver amid the soldiers. Yala had spent long enough around the Void to have become wise to its effects, but a number of people shuffled out of line to avoid the shadows' cold touch, and the sound of uneasy mutters and whispers filled the background again.

"Then," said the king, ignoring the general discomfort he'd evoked amid his army, "we will have the strength to stand against the mightiest and most deceptive of the gods: Yalet."

"Yalet is the god of life, isn't She?" asked a wavering voice. "Is she not the one who created all of life itself, including us?"

"Yalet might have created all life, but She takes with equal impunity," said King Tharen. "Mekan alone ensured my survival after the followers of Dalathik cast me out of my own nation. All the other gods and their followers abetted them or looked the other way."

The soldier who'd spoken shivered but held his ground. "You said that Mekan's army attacked the city not two months ago. That you sent them away."

"That army was sent by Rafragoria." Ice dripped from the king's voice, as cold as the shadows creeping throughout the room. "Rafragoria has access to the same gods as we do, but rest assured that Mekan now serves me alone."

He's lying. The soldiers knew it too. Everyone had grown up with the same accepted story of Laria's founding; that the king casually pronounced this a lie was rivalled only by his casual dismissal of the stories anyone who'd spent any length of time in the capital would have heard concerning the gods. In fact, some would have joined the army to *avoid* being recruited into the Disciples of the Flame, like her former squad-mate, Dalem. That the king wanted them to pledge themselves to Mekan ran counter to every vow they'd sworn to serve their nation.

"I will listen to no more arguments." The king's voice rang out. "This country is suffering from a grave affliction. Yalet's lies have had us in a stranglehold for too long, and we will no longer tolerate this deception. This week, on All Gods' Day, we shall march south and begin our assault upon Yalet's last refuges in the forests of southern Laria."

As he spoke, the darkness behind the altar shifted subtly, and Yala glimpsed eyes glinting within. A reminder that he held utter control over the monsters on the other side silenced their complaints and ensured that nobody spoke another word of defiance.

"You are dismissed," he said. "You have time to prepare for the assault, and your commanders will give you further details. Rest assured that we shall stand victorious, and Yalet will fall."

The king had declared war on Yalet. Soon, they'd be on their way to the forest to destroy Her utterly.

But where does Niema fit into that plan? The question lodged in Yala's mind as she waited for the others to leave. The king had no reason to lash out at her, but the dangerous glint in his eyes prompted her to approach him with care.

"Your Majesty," she said when they were alone. "I wondered... what of your prisoner? What role does she play in this?"

"Why the interest?" he asked. "Did you wish to see her?"

"No, but I did bring her here," she said. "Given that she's a Disciple of Life, I expected you to have her sacrificed upon the altar."

"And you wished to perform the sacrifice." His gaze slid to the darkness clothing the altar. "In recent days, I have required the temple for my own purposes, but I have not forgotten my Disciples."

He'd thought *Yala* wanted to perform the sacrifice? Yala didn't know whether to laugh or vomit. Swallowing the taste of bile, she said, "I was curious, as you said that the culmination of our training will arrive when we enter the Void. Will we do that before we go to war with Yalet or beforehand?"

"That would depend on whether you are ready." Again, his dark eyes surveyed her, probing. "You are, I believe, but the consequences for failure are significant. Should Mekan find you unworthy, you will suffer. It is not a journey taken lightly."

"No." She'd seen the results of those who'd failed, whose bodies had rotted from the inside out. And those who'd succeeded had also lost their will—with one exception.

The king had talked Mekan into sparing him, and Yala's only conclusion was that the king had offered the god of death something that no human had ever given Him beforehand: the chance to destroy Yalet, His hated enemy.

"Very well," he said. "Tonight, you are invited to attend a private ceremony here at the ninth bell. Come alone."

"I am honoured, Your Majesty." The response came out without conscious input from her brain. Her heart kicked into a fast beat against her ribs. She hadn't expected such a concession, let alone a private invitation into the palace. Hadn't planned to have an opening—albeit a narrow one—to find Niema and get her out.

A short way down the corridor, someone stepped out in front of her. Daliel leaned in and whispered in a tortured voice, "Help me."

Yala tried to sidestep him. "Get out of my way."

"I'll help your friend," he said. "I know which room she's being held in. I can distract the guards, keep them busy while she runs."

"Even if I trusted your word, Niema might not *want* to run," Yala said. "She's the only person capable of destroying that temple."

"Let me at least try," he pressed. "I can't stay in here any longer. You have allies, don't you? People who can smuggle me out of the city."

Daliel's quiet words spoke of a pain of which Yala could barely conceive. She'd tried to avoid sparing any pity for the prince, but having to watch his father succumb to the god of death, to say nothing of the heinous acts he'd been forced to perform, would have wrought damage beyond her comprehension.

And what does it say of me that I was willing to perform the same acts with little hesitation?

Yala held the thought for a moment and then added, *If nothing else, it's proof that the king has no reason not to believe I'm worthy of ascending to Mekan's side.*

To the prince, she said, "I do. Tell me where he's keeping

Niema, and I'll let my allies know. Tell nobody, especially him."

"I won't," he murmured, his voice catching on a sob. "Thank you, Captain."

"Not sure you'll be using that title for much longer," Yala said in response. "Whichever way this goes, I believe my time in the flight division has come to an end."

39

"The Disciples of the Flame?" Kelan frowned at Ragem, who'd delivered the news to the other Disciples with his usual stoicism. "Did I hear that right?"

"That's what the scouts told me," answered Ragem. "They spied three wagons on the road south of the capital carrying Disciples of the Flame."

"That changes things," he murmured. "I never expected them to get out."

They must have had help, but from whom? Not Yala, and there hadn't been any other Disciples in the city either.

"It makes no difference to us," replied Ragem. "Our orders are to rid the area of Mekan's followers, but now that Hachim is back in our company, our Superior will expect to speak with him."

Kelan swivelled to Hachim. "Do you think she'll agree to let you meet me in Setemar afterwards?"

"She might." An apologetic note entered his voice. "I don't disagree that they might remember the debt they owe us, but

I don't see any of them being willing to aid us in rescuing Niema. Not while she's in the capital."

Would the Disciples of the Flame? Granted, they'd recently escaped the king's clutches themselves, but his curiosity as to how they'd pulled off such a feat eclipsed his desire to avoid the main road out of Dalathar in case there were soldiers roaming around.

"It is out of the question," Ragem said. "We shall speak with the Superior and see if her orders change. You may accompany us, Disciple of the Sky, if you so desire."

"I'll pass." Superior Kralia would be reeling both from the loss of yet another fellow Superior and from Niema's capture, and he had no desire to bear the impact of her wrath. "I'm going to look for the Disciples of the Flame. How close to Setemar are they?"

"A day at most," said Ragem. "Would your Superior approve of this detour?"

Probably not was the honest answer, but going into Setemar alone was hardly without risk, and he might as well find another task to occupy himself with while Hachim was speaking to his Superior. "She'll be pleased that I found more Disciples who might be willing to help us. They're also on their way to Setemar, so someone should tell them that the king's soldiers have occupied the city if they aren't already aware."

He wasn't clear on how much news had reached the Disciples trapped inside their temple, but they'd been under close enough watch that their escape attempt must have taken place during the assault on Skytower, when the defences around the capital had thinned.

Kelan glided upriver, cutting across fields to reach the main road linking Setemar with its northern neighbour. The villages and towns he glimpsed appeared deserted, and a stench hung in the humid air that he'd come to associate with Mekan. He passed one such village and held his breath as the acrid tang of smoke joined the putrid smell of the dead. Nearby, bodies lay in a crude heap where someone had tried to burn them, limbs twitching feebly as Mekan's power tried to move flesh too rotten to stand.

With other villages, the Disciples of Life's effort to slow Mekan's advance was evident in the greenery smothering the buildings and the smell of new life masking the dead. Yet the extent of Mekan's assault on Laria had not been apparent to him until now. The people out here had no defences, no way to prevent Corruption's maw from swallowing every trace of life in existence.

Kelan was shaken from his thoughts when he spied a group of individuals trudging north. Soldiers. Some carried heavy packs, their shoulders bowed under the weight, and their uniform was mud-stained and worn.

"Where are you going?" he called to them. "Dalathar? You might want to look in to finding transport. There are a lot of dead around here."

The soldier at the back whirled around, reaching for her weapon. This worried Kelan less than it might have, since she and her companions looked so exhausted that a slight breeze might have knocked them over. "What's it to you?"

He glided closer. "I thought the king provided better for his soldiers."

"Our wagon's gone." The soldier spoke through gritted teeth, one scarred hand on the shortsword at her belt. "Our raptors got spooked and ran when they saw the—"

"The dead," Kelan finished. "I imagine it's been hard to rest at night with all the screaming too."

The soldier's weary eyes narrowed. "What do you care?"

"I probably shouldn't." He didn't know where he was going with this, except there was a group of people loyal to the king in front of him who were clearly on the brink of losing their faith in the person giving them orders. If he gave them a firm push… "It seems that you've been ill-treated, and I can't say much for the odds of you being rewarded if you do somehow make it to the capital in one piece."

"We're on our way to meet the rest of the army, as a matter of fact," said the soldier. "They'll be on their way south in a few days."

"Will they now?" He raised a brow, but his heartbeat began to quicken. "Are they going to Setemar?"

"He doesn't care for Setemar," puffed out the man behind her, whose broad shoulders stooped under the weight of an enormous pack. "Our target—"

"Don't *tell* him that," the female soldier interjected. "He's a *Disciple*."

"So is the king." Kelan knew that would get a rise out of them and raised his voice over the collective noise of outrage and the scrape of weapons being drawn. "Now, it's no big secret. Everyone who witnessed the battle at Skytower saw him summon the dead."

Shouts rang out. This time, someone did throw a dagger at him, which he parried with a wave of his hand. A gust of air buffeted the soldiers and sent them staggering, a couple tripping over their own feet.

"I don't hold it against you," he added, ignoring the ripple of hostility that travelled amongst their group. "You clearly have no idea what the rest of your army is doing, but I'm sure someone will fill you in, assuming you survive to meet them."

He dodged another dagger, hardly able to summon up any fear of being hit when the odds were high that half of them would keel over before they reached the capital without him needing to draw a blade. Picking up speed, he overtook their group and spied the outline of an approaching wagon pulled by two raptors on the road ahead.

Given the general lack of other traffic, he could guess who sat inside.

Soon, two more wagons came into view. Kelan glided alongside the edge of the field bordering the road to avoid startling the raptors, making out several familiar faces among those seated inside the wagons. The Disciples wore civilian clothing, but their wide-eyed, wary expressions made it obvious that they'd never set foot outside their temple before. They huddled inside their wagons like a nest of baby birds hiding from a predator.

When they saw him, a couple of them leaned out of the wagon and pointed, exclaiming. "Disciple!"

"Not so loud." Kelan picked up speed, pointing over his shoulder. "You should know there's a group of soldiers ahead of you. They're not in the best condition, so you might be able to fight them off, but I thought I should warn you."

"Soldiers?" echoed the Disciple steering the frontmost wagon. He appeared older than the rest; his serious face was lined, and threads of grey speckled his neatly combed hair. "What is your purpose here, Disciple?"

"Right now? To stop you from getting killed." He gestured at the road. "The soldiers claimed to be on their way to join the rest of the army. It sounds as if the king's sending a large force from the capital."

The colour drained from the Disciple's face. "Did Skytower already fall?"

"Not exactly." He didn't have time to give them a full explanation, so he settled for saying, "Our Superior was incapacitated, which was enough for him to claim victory. His army can't fight on multiple fronts at once, and his true target has always been Yalet."

"The god of life," said the Disciple. "He answers to Mekan, does he?"

"I'm fairly sure he thinks Mekan answers to *him.*"

Whether the god of death agreed or not was another matter. "Both of them are completely focused on Yalet, so it makes no difference. The army's coming south, according to the soldiers I ran into."

"Then we'll kill them before they can meet."

"They didn't seem enthused by the king's current strategy," Kelan said. "Really, you should be on the same side."

That was what frustrated him. He'd seen the expressions of abject horror and betrayal on some of the soldiers' faces at Skytower when they'd realised their own king didn't care if he mowed them down to reach his targets and when he'd had them rip open the Void with full knowledge that they'd be directly in the path of any monsters that crawled out.

A shout cut through the Disciple's reply. Assuming that the soldiers had seen their approach, Kelan glided in front of the wagon and peered down the road, seeing that a commotion had broken out among the soldiers.

As he drew closer, Kelan saw one of them grappling with a skeletal man gripping a scythe in a hand that had rotted to the bone.

Ah, he thought. *That's a complication.*

———

When she left the palace, Yala felt lighter, as if a weight had been lifted from her shoulders. Soon, there would be no more need for deception. Tonight, one way or another, the king would know the truth of her.

Lisek waylaid her on the way to the barracks. "Were you talking to the king?"

"I was curious what he planned to do to his prisoner."

Lisek grimaced. "I wouldn't want to be her. He's fixated on obliterating her people. Why's he keeping her alive, as a hostage?"

"That, I'm not clear on." She allowed a little more truth to slip out. "But given that the god of death is using him as a mouthpiece, I doubt it's anything good."

Lisek's mouth parted. "Is that why he declared Yalet an enemy? It's not really him making the decisions?"

"It is and it isn't." Yala scowled. "I don't fully understand, and frankly, I don't want to, but we're not answering to a rational human being anymore. We haven't been for a long time."

"Guess that explains why he let us get killed at Skytower." She let out a dark laugh. "He expects us to be ready to march south within the week, as if we're in any shape to fight another battle. Our war drakes aren't going to be any use in a fucking forest."

Admittedly, Yala hadn't considered the practical implications of the king's sudden change of strategy. That was a problem for the commanders to worry about, and she suspected that the monarch's dead army would render any concerns around the living one irrelevant.

Lisek watched her as if she expected Yala to say something that might alleviate her scepticism or validate it or both. When neither came, her hand curled into a tight fist. "Can't the commanders talk him out of this farce?"

"Ask them, not me." Yala rubbed her forehead. "I'm not up to date on his military strategies."

"Then why does the king tolerate you challenging him but not me?" A note of resentment crept into her voice.

"That's what you think?" Sensing dangerous ground underfoot, Yala let her hand creep towards her weapon. "I never challenged him. That's probably why he invited me to a private ceremony tonight to take the next step in joining Mekan."

"Fuck me." Lisek let out a humourless laugh. "Or are you fucking *him*? Is that why he's playing favourites?"

"Don't be absurd." Yala's mouth flattened. "I'd prefer not to shed any blood before I enter that chamber, but I will if you turn out to be a problem."

Lisek's eyes rounded. "You think he'll let you get away with killing one of your allies?"

"Honestly? Yes." Yala allowed herself a humourless chuckle to match Lisek's own. "That's the truth of it. In the eyes of Mekan, taking your life would be the same as killing the enemy. That's why our deaths don't matter."

"Fuck that." The jealousy slid from her eyes like light bleeding from a setting sun. "I'm not playing this game any longer."

"Then don't." She'd tested the waters, and now, it was time to dive in. "I'm taking advantage of my private invitation to the palace to free that prisoner of his. You're welcome to help me do it."

Lisek lowered her voice to a hiss. "You're a traitor."

"We're all traitors." Yala offered a sweeping gesture at the palace grounds. "You haven't closed your ears to gossip, I'm sure. Nobody here wants to go to war at the behest of a monster."

"As if we have a choice." Her defiance faded. "What will freeing his prisoner achieve? Except death on an altar rather than on the battlefield?"

"You heard him," said Yala. "He intends to wipe the Disciples of Life off the map, and he'll use her to do it, either as a weapon or blackmail against the others, it doesn't matter which. If nothing else, setting her free will delay the start of a war which will end in our deaths."

"I doubt losing one prisoner will slow him down."

"She's valuable," Yala said. "The thing is, to get her out of the palace, I'll need a diversion, and I'll need everyone in the barracks to be looking the other way. If you're up for that, talk to anyone you trust. Then, come and find me after training."

She found her squad waiting for her, whispering among themselves. They'd been in the palace, too, and had heard the king's bold revelations. They'd witnessed his threats.

She hadn't wanted to bring them in on her treachery, but it would not be long before they, too, knew her true purpose here.

I swore to keep them alive. For that reason, it was Saren who she took aside while they were waiting for their turn with the war drakes and handed him the key to the paddock.

"What's this for?" He turned the key over in his hand. "Does that mean you're going to tell me what you were whispering to Lisek about? The others know, too, and let me tell you, I've heard some wild theories."

Yala ground her teeth. "Yes, I'll explain if you show a little patience. I need to talk to Nalen first."

"He's in the infirmary. Knocked someone unconscious on the way back from the palace and took a beating for it."

"What's he done that for?" Yala groaned. "Right, never mind. The short answer is, I need someone to *forget* to properly chain up the war drakes after training. Then, I need someone—possibly the same someone—to unlock the paddock gate just before the ninth bell."

"Meaning me." Saren clenched his hand over the key. "And what is getting myself decapitated going to achieve?"

"If you can stick your hand in a war drake's mouth and escape with a few puncture wounds, you can unlock a gate without suffering injury," Yala retorted. "It's you or one of the others, and you have more experience."

"This is how you think you'll stop the war, is it? Send all the war drakes away?"

"Not exactly, but that's the line I gave to Lisek."

"You recruited *her?*"

"Provisionally," she said. "We need to get Niema out of that palace, and if we can slow down the king's plan to invade the forest within a week, too, so much the better. I have a private invitation to the temple this evening. Should I fail to walk out of there, I want to at least leave enough chaos behind me to make a real problem for His Majesty's war efforts."

"That's fucked," he said in a hushed voice. "Yala, you can't throw yourself on his mercy. You'd die."

"Not my plan, believe me," she said. "Can you keep an eye on the others for half an hour or so while I talk to Viam?"

Viam was not a fan of Yala's strategy, but she and Brenat offered to keep watch outside the palace that evening. Yala didn't know what kind of shape Niema would be in, but if she escaped and Yala did not, she'd all but certainly need help getting out of the palace grounds.

Upon returning to the barracks, she was greeted by stares from her squad-mates, followed by a flurry of questions.

"Saren said you aren't going to let the king send us to our deaths," Gorel said. "Is that true?"

Roven nodded agreement. "He said you're freeing the war drakes."

"Not if you keep talking that loudly." She took in their eager faces and suppressed a sigh. "If you want in, all you need to do is leave the chains loosened so they can get out when Saren opens the gate."

"Why do you need them set free?" asked Yurel. "Saren mentioned a diversion."

"I can't tell you that." Guilt knotted inside her. "I'm sorry to all of you. I never wanted you to be a part of this."

"You expect us to risk our necks without knowing why?" asked Kithal. He hovered near the back with Surel, the newcomer, the only two of their number who hadn't immediately leapt in with questions.

"I don't expect anything," Yala retorted. "You can trust me, or you can trust the man who just announced his allegiance to the god of death."

"You knew," Kithal accused. "You knew what the king was doing, didn't you? You knew he was allied to Mekan from the start."

"Would you have told anyone in my place?" Yala challenged him. "The king's orders were to keep it quiet. I don't know about you, but I prefer to avoid antagonising monarchs with gods on their side."

"Nobody will stand for this," Gorel said. "I nearly joined the Temple of the Flame before all this. There are a few of us who swore the first vows here in the army. Serving another god is out of the question."

"If you can talk to any of those people, it'd be appreciated," Yala said. "I need all the help I can get, and the more people who are reminded of what we stand to lose by allying with Mekan, the better."

"I'll help," Gorel said, and the others nodded agreement. Even Kithal had no argument to add to that.

They were on her side. *Now, I just need to ensure none of them die for it.*

———

Three or four days after her capture, Niema woke to find herself tied to an altar.

She writhed, fought to escape the bonds tying her to the great slab of stone, but the ropes dug into her flesh, and the thick darkness rising from the altar pushed her downward like a solid block on her chest.

King Tharen watched her struggle, his eyes as dark as the Void that curtained the altar.

427

"I warned you that it would be easier if you cooperated," he said. "Are you ready to try again?"

"What do you want from me?" she rasped.

"I want you to answer my questions." His voice carried that whispering echo she knew without a doubt came from within the Void itself. "I want you to tell me what you are."

"I am a Disciple of Life."

"And yet." He reached down and pressed his fingertips into the wound. Niema stifled a gasp of pain as cold radiated outward, spiderwebbing across her skin and penetrating down to her core. "You were able to control Mekan's beasts before one of them wounded you. That suggests you carry the god of death's mark upon you. Certainly, such a feat cannot have come about as a natural occurrence."

"Neither is becoming a Disciple of Death." She gasped the words, squirming away from his icy touch. "Corruption is an abomination."

"The gods do not see in such terms," he said. "As Yalet chose you, then Mekan has chosen me as His representative in this world."

"Those two gods are not the same." She knew it was no use trying to convince him, but she couldn't help herself. "Mekan betrayed the other gods."

"He was betrayed by them." That cold whisper overlaid his voice again. "They will suffer for it, and none more so than Yalet."

"You're being manipulated." She addressed the man who must exist somewhere behind Mekan's influence if it were possible to reach him. "You think you're making the decisions, but it's Mekan."

"The god of death and I are in accord," said the king. "My decisions are my own."

He touched a fingertip to the wound again. She bit the inside of her mouth, her skin burning like cold fire.

"The wound still pains you," he mused. "Mekan's poison weaves through your veins even as Yalet's influence works to expel it."

Behind him, a pair of eyes blinked out of the darkness. The king stepped aside, allowing a monstrous creature that resembled a large raptor with black scales to loom over her, jaws agape, claws readied to kill.

The king spoke. "If you do not command this beast, Disciple of Life, you will die."

Then I'll die. With that acceptance came relief to return into Yalet's hands, to become one with her god.

Yet the cold burn inside her reminded her part of her was claimed by another god, one who would never let her rest peacefully, even in death. Should she fall into Mekan's clutches, she would never again know Yalet's warm embrace.

She would never find out why, despite everything she had done, Yalet had chosen her.

I trust Her, she thought. *I trust Yalet.*

She whistled, and the monster's jaws closed over empty air, its claw striking the altar instead of her neck. As her command took hold, the beast slunk away into the shadows, and the king stepped in to take its place.

"There," he said with satisfaction. "That wasn't so hard, was it?"

Niema's breaths came quickly, her chest throbbing with each heave. The Void caressed her with cold fingers.

"It's curious," King Tharen said. "To which god did you direct your prayer when you ordered that creature to leave?"

"I—" She didn't know. She'd mimicked the same prayer as she used to command Yalet's creatures, but the command did not invoke the god of life's name. All the times she'd used that power, she hadn't stopped to wonder who else might hear her request.

"You won't tell me, I'm sure," said the king, "but no

matter. It's clear that you bear Mekan's mark, that some of His power runs in your veins as surely as Yalet's does. I can see that I made the right choice in sparing your life."

Niema's breath caught.

"I am not as ignorant of the ways of your people as you may believe," he added. "I've gathered enough knowledge on the gods to know that Yalet is not so different from Mekan. She demands worship, sacrifice, even… but you don't like to use that term, do you?"

Niema gripped the altar with both hands, her skin slick with cold sweat.

"The gods of life and death might be bitter enemies, but their realms are estranged, and they are unable to harm one another directly. They, like all gods, rely on intermediaries to act within this world. Intermediaries like us. And you, Niema… I believe you are the direct line to Yalet that I have been looking for."

Mekan's cold whisper echoed his voice from within the shadows. A smile flickered onto the king's mouth as he said, "And you will help me wipe Yalet's followers from Laria altogether."

Niema found her voice. "I will *not.*"

She ended on a scream, a command that sent him reeling away from the altar. Rolling onto her left, she threw her weight against the bonds, again, again.

The king swung the claw-blade, sliced deep into her skin, and this time, the blood that splattered the altar was her own.

———

Superior Kralia met Hachim further down the river. She'd asked to see him alone, so he flew ahead of the other elite Disciples and found her near a village on the forest's outskirts. While verdant greenery cloaked their surroundings, the lingering smell of rot in the air told him that no living souls occupied the wooden huts he glimpsed through gaps in the swift-growing trees and vibrant flowers.

"Superior." He climbed down from his war drake to kneel in front of her. "I—was sorry to hear of the Superior's death."

"As was I to hear of Niema's capture."

Hearing her name pierced him as acutely as the wound her absence had left, like a blade's keen edge driven into his heart. "I know that rescuing her from the palace is out of the question, but I worry that the king will use her against the forest or else torture her to learn of our secrets."

Ragem's lack of interest in rescuing Niema was by no means a surprise, but the Superior of all people knew of the potential danger to the forest should the king discover the extent of Niema's capabilities.

"That is a valid concern." Her expression was as impassive as Ragem's. "All my spies suggest that the king does indeed intend to focus his efforts on Yalet now that he believes the other temples to be subdued."

"They aren't, though." He pressed on. "Kelan came with me from Skytower, and he planned to speak to the Disciples of the Earth. He thinks that the king has been paying little enough attention to them that he might be able to convince some of them to help us. They owe us a favour, don't they?"

"They will not risk themselves to save a lone Disciple of Life, Hachim."

The knife dug deeper into his heart. "That's not what I meant. The others saw some Disciples of the Flame on the road out of the capital too. They're a day from Setemar, maybe less."

A flicker of surprise crossed her face. "That would account for the rumours I heard from the Disciples of the Sea, that some disturbances took place in the capital while the king and his forces were assaulting Skytower."

431

"They've been back to the capital?" He'd forgotten how fast a Disciple of the Sea could move while in the water. "What did the rumours say?"

"According to Nanek, a number of soldiers left the army and were smuggled out of the city."

The knife didn't loosen, but a flicker of hope stirred all the same. "They're turning on him. At Skytower, the way he treated his soldiers... few would stand for it, however loyal they might be to the crown."

"That matters not when Mekan is the one giving the orders, not the king."

His hands curled into fists. "If anything, that makes it more urgent that we get Niema away from him."

"No," said the Superior. "Spare yourself the pain, Hachim, and accept that Niema is beyond help."

He sank to his knees. "Please," he whispered to the earth. "You *know* what's at stake. If he figures out that Niema can be used against the forest..."

"She will die before she submits to his demands."

"That's what I'm afraid of." Who was to say whether Niema's death would be the end? His worst nightmares had shown her blank-faced corpse rising from the ground, subject to Mekan's will even in death. "At Skytower, the king was strong enough to best a Superior, and the Void itself moved where he commanded. What if he's the one commanding Mekan, not the other way around?"

"That cannot be," said the Superior. "Perhaps the god of death sees an advantage to allowing the monarch to believe he is in control, but Mekan will certainly have plans independent of King Tharen."

"He'll also know what Niema can do." Even if the king hadn't figured it out yet, the god of death certainly would have.

The Superior surveyed him. "Hachim, this comes down to a simple question. Do you trust her?"

"Of course." Unlike the others, he'd never doubted her loyalties. Never doubted that she fought fiercely against Mekan's attempts to ensnare her and would do so until her last breath. And Superior Sietra's dire predictions might be unfounded. Yalet had chosen Niema regardless of any touch Mekan had left upon her—but it was undeniable that the dead were drawn to Niema. She was a weapon in the king's hands whether he knew it or not.

"Then you have a decision to make," the Superior said. "My orders to you and your fellow elite Disciples are simple: to protect our home. It may be that some will decide that an appeal to the other Disciples for aid will achieve that end. Others might desire to protect our temple above all else, while a few may choose to continue preventing Mekan's taint from spreading any deeper into the forest."

"We're going our separate ways." His heart sank. "Isn't that the opposite of what we should be doing?"

"On the contrary," she said. "Spreading our forces across Laria will decrease the odds of the king finding the spot where Yalet's heart truly lies. If the temple falls, there will be no returning."

Hachim's eyes burned with tears. He knew that he'd never convince her or anyone else that a sole Disciple's life was more important than their survival.

Except to him. Niema was his heart, and while he couldn't say for certain that she returned his affections in the same manner, their connection was soul deep. He couldn't give up on her.

And if nobody else would help, he would have to act alone.

ehind Kelan, the Disciples of the Flame had spotted the ruckus on the road. Raised voices bounced back and forth amid the wagons, arguing about whether to turn around and leave.

"You can't outrun them," he told the Disciples. "Not without leaving the road, and those soldiers are proof that you don't want to be stranded out here without transport."

"What do you suggest?" The older Disciple in front leaned over the wagon's side to watch one of the soldiers decapitate a man who already had half his intestines hanging out. "We can't run straight into them without putting our lives in peril."

"Haven't you tried to contact Dalathik yet?" he asked. "You're far enough away from Mekan's influence now, aren't you?"

"We haven't tried," said a young Disciple from the wagon behind. "We didn't want to draw attention. And—"

"Quiet," snapped the older Disciple. "We'll put it to a vote."

At a guess, the young Disciple had been about to give voice to the fear that Dalathik had forsaken them outright. Kelan hoped He hadn't, but the growing clamour from in front told him the soldiers were in a bad way. Several had fallen from exhaustion, while the relentless dead continued to rise to their feet no matter how many times they were put down.

Kelan drew his own weapon and flew towards the melee. The dead were already reduced to bone and sinew, and there was little he or the soldiers could do but sever limbs and slow them down.

The Disciples of the Flame were another matter... if their god listened to them.

The female soldier Kelan had spoken to earlier staggered across his path, swatting at a severed hand that had crawled up her arm and was attempting to reach her throat. "You!" She swiped at the hand and missed, narrowly avoiding hitting herself in the face instead. "Why didn't you run? Why are you helping us?"

"If I didn't, you'd be the next dead person to attack me." He lifted his blade and flicked the severed hand off her shoulder, where it flopped harmlessly on the ground. "It's in the interests of self-preservation."

That was when one of the wagons went up in flames.

Kelan spun around, shielding his eyes from the surge of white fire. The wagon's occupants leapt out, while the two raptors took off in a panic, dragging the burning remnants of their transport behind them.

The other Disciples climbed into the road with joyous shouts and ran towards the battlefield, voices raised in a chorus of "Dalathik lives!"

Kelan veered sideways to avoid being mowed down by the younger Disciple from earlier. His hands were ablaze, an expression of rapture on his face. "Dalathik lives!"

"You won't if you don't look where you're aiming that fire." *Shit. The soldiers.*

With a hasty glide, Kelan swept towards the ongoing battle and called out, "Watch out!"

The frontmost soldier threw himself flat as a torrent of flames shot over his head and set the skeletal attacker fighting him ablaze, while another was forced to let go of her weapon when the body she was stabbing caught fire.

Chaotic though the Disciples' approach might have been, they mowed through the dead with such efficiency that within minutes, all that remained was ashes, without so much as a twitching limb to be seen.

The soldiers' surprise was eclipsed only by the sheer wonderment of the Disciples of the Flame. Their faces were radiant, as if Dalathik had descended from the heavens to bless them.

A grin broke out on Kelan's face. "Nice teamwork, if I do say so myself."

The soldiers looked at one another, their excitement fading as it sank in who, exactly, had helped them. The female soldier Kelan had spoken to half-heartedly lifted a shortsword and pointed it at the Disciples.

"Steady on," Kelan said. "There's no need to kill your rescuers. I wouldn't have thought you'd want to avoid leaving more bodies for Mekan to claim either."

"They're traitors to the throne," said the soldier without enthusiasm.

"They saved your lives," said Kelan. "They're also capable of turning you to ashes if you provoke them, and there are rather more of them than there are of you. If I were in your position, I'd agree to a truce. You don't attack any Disciples, and we'll extend the same courtesy to you. How about that?"

The soldier opened her mouth to argue and then closed it. Nodded. "Fine."

Kelan gave the Disciples a questioning look. "And you?"

The older Disciple who'd led the front wagon cast a distrusting eye over the soldiers, but he nodded too. "It's a truce."

That went better than I expected, thought Kelan as the soldiers began to make their weary way north while the Disciples went in search of their abandoned wagons. Assuming the raptors hadn't been frightened into fleeing, they'd make it to Setemar within a couple of days, maybe less if he offered them help. Before he did that, it would be wise for him to make sure there were no unpleasant surprises waiting for them behind the city's walls.

With one crisis averted, it was time for him to check on the Disciples of the Earth.

———

The hours before Yala's final ceremony at the Temple of Death passed in a strange manner. Minutes crawled by, then hours passed in a lurch that left her wondering when the sun had set and if she had enough time to check that Nalen had given the right directions to the soldiers who'd volunteered to come into the palace to help smuggle Niema out. Daliel had claimed he'd be waiting to show them the way, but she'd convinced him to give her verbal directions to pass on in case he was delayed. Or, more likely, he was too scared to go through with the scheme after all.

Just before the ninth bell, Yala left the barracks. Several of Nalen's allies watched her leave, readied to enter the palace through the back door to meet Daliel, and she offered a nod she hoped was reassuring as she passed. On her left, the gleam of a lantern shone from outside the war drakes' paddock. Saren's signal. *Here we go.*

Yala was halfway to the palace when the first war drake's

cry shattered the night. Yala didn't look back, keeping her head low as she walked and the cries became louder, accompanied by the clamour of beating wings.

Yala held her breath as a void drake's shadow passed overhead. As she'd hoped, the monsters had noticed the disturbance first. Glad she'd told the others not to follow her, she continued, half trusting in the king's invitation to spare her from harm, half expecting to feel those claws embedded between her shoulder blades.

No attack came. Yala ascended the stairs, her leg burning with each step, her heart in her mouth. By the time she reached the doors, the void drakes had left the area above the palace in pursuit of the escaping war drakes, and the air rang with strident cries and vicious snarls. The guards on duty watched the spectacle with such absorption that neither of them noticed Yala until she cleared her throat. "I have an audience with the king."

"Yala Palathar, right?" One guard yelped as a pair of winged beasts flew overhead and hit the palace wall with a crunch that would have broken bones if either of them had carried humans on their backs.

The other guard pushed the door inward; taking that as permission, Yala ducked inside. The guard who met her in the entrance hall wasn't someone she recognised, but a nod confirmed him as one of Nalen's allies. Hoping the other guards didn't notice anything awry, she made her swift way down the corridor alongside her silent escort. No human sound stirred from elsewhere in the palace, but a faint whisper teased at her ears, faint enough to remind her that Mekan was always listening.

Yala halted when a breathless Viam appeared ahead of her. "Yala—she's not here."

"What the fuck are you doing?" Yala hissed. "I thought you were watching from the outside."

"It's him—Daliel." She lowered her head as if ashamed. "I had a bad feeling, and... he's gone. Niema isn't in the room he said she was imprisoned in."

"The king is also in here, in case you've forgotten," Yala growled through her teeth. "Get out. Now."

"Want me to go with her?" whispered the guard, who hadn't spoken to her until now.

Yala inclined her head. "Do it."

The sound of their retreating footsteps vanished beyond the whisper rising from the shadows like smoke from the walls, the floors, the ceiling, as if the Void itself lived within the stones.

If Niema wasn't in her room, the king must know there were intruders in the palace. Yala's nerves thrummed as she continued on her path, shadows trailing her into the court-yard and swathing her vision. She crossed the flagstones to the altar. And halted.

Niema lay tied to the great slab of stone. Her head lolled, her hands and arms hung limp within the ropes binding them, and shadows wreathed her unconscious body.

There was no sign of the king.

Heart in her mouth, Yala stepped closer and called out. "I'm here."

Was this part of the test somehow? Did he want her to kill Niema as proof that she was worthy of entering the Void? Yala was in no mood for games. When she stood directly over the altar, she whispered, "Where is he?"

Niema's eyes opened a fraction. "Yala? You shouldn't be here."

"I came to get you out." She reached for the void drake's claw and pulled it out, using the sharp edge to cut the bonds around Niema's wrists, trying not to look at the shadowy mass behind the altar urging her to take another step then another until she became one with the shadows herself.

"You shouldn't be here," Niema repeated. "It's too late for me."

"What?" Then she saw the gaping slash in Niema's body, far worse than the last wound. Her torso gaped open from chest to sternum, redness glistening within.

How is she still speaking? Still breathing? The faintest green glow told her Yalet was trying desperately to heal the wound, but there was no life to draw upon in this place of death and darkness.

"Take it from me. Take my life." If Yala died, at least Niema would have a slim chance of survival. "Go on."

Niema turned her head. "I... can't."

A voice whispered within the darkness. *"Are you not here to offer yourself to me, Yala Palathar?"*

Then, King Tharen stepped out of the Void.

————

Niema's flickering vision showed her the king emerge out of the darkness like one of the beasts he commanded, wielding the sword he'd used to slice her open. Not to kill her but to offer her as bait to someone he suspected was a traitor.

She'd die without telling him a thing. She had not broken, not even when he'd sliced her open and laid her bare, the life leaking out of her, the Void waiting to claim her.

I can't let Mekan take me when I die. I can't.

Yala hadn't moved. She'd offered her life, and Niema would not survive if she did not accept. She reached out and sensed the thrum of life pulsing within Yala, the fragile strength so easy to grasp, to drain from its source until nothing remained.

Niema resisted. Despite her fading vision and the sense of her own life leaking out, drawn into the endless Void, the vast presence at the edge of her awareness, almost a source of life all on its own...

Without meaning to, Niema cast her awareness into the Void as if to seek out any sliver of life that might exist within.

The breath returned to her lungs as the searing pain faded like a stone block lifted from her chest. Icy energy filled her veins, a sensation more like a gulp of refreshing water on a hot day than the biting cold that had been eating away at her, and her vision cleared, revealing shadows dancing around her in mesmerising patterns.

The Void... she'd healed using the *Void*.

With that realisation, Niema recoiled, pushing back the presence that had flooded her body with strength. At once, the pain returned, blurred her vision, stole her breath.

Yala's mouth brushed Niema's ear. "Do it again. Heal yourself, and we'll finish him."

Niema breathed in shadow, and then she screamed, her body lurching sideways off the altar as if a pair of invisible hands had seized her ankles. The king stood over her, shadows streaming from his palms and reeling her towards him.

But Niema was bound to the darkness too. She breathed in again, felt the bonds loosen and the pain lift as fresh energy surged through her blood.

Rising upward, she sucked in a breath and released it in a whistle, a command.

"Stop!"

King Tharen's body locked to the spot. The word held him suspended, frozen in time, shadows aloft in his hands.

Yala stared at him, then a grin came to her mouth. "Thank you, Niema. I knew I could count on you."

She lifted the void drake's claw and pressed it to the king's throat.

"No!" The cry came not from the guards but from a young, dishevelled man who could only be the prince.

Prince Daliel ran across the courtyard, and in their heart-beat of distraction, the king lunged at Yala. She fell sprawling, her cane rolling away across the floor.

The king shouted a command of his own. A monster leapt from the Void, cutting off Niema's whistle with a vicious strike across the face. Niema staggered, her mouth filling with blood. She spat out the copper taste, her fractured vision showing Yala rising to her feet, dragging her injured leg behind her.

With a wild lunge, Yala seized the prince by the scruff of his neck and pressed her knife to his throat.

"Don't touch Niema again," Yala said, her voice strained but clear. "Or your son dies. You don't want that, do you, Your Majesty?"

"Is that what you believe?" said King Tharen. "That I would not sacrifice my son for a greater cause?"

The prince uttered a faint whimper, his panicked eyes darting around the room.

Yala shook him. "I assume there was a reason you went to the trouble of forcing him to train as a Disciple of Death when he was so unwilling. You don't *entirely* have faith in Mekan not to take his life when you aren't watching, do you?"

This is a diversion. Niema breathed in the shadows again, and the sting of the wound on her face faded.

At the same time, Mekan's voice rasped against her ears. *"Thank you for allowing me to destroy my greatest foe."*

Sharp claws sliced into Niema's chest and tore her open once again.

41

The Disciples of the Flame had been a little too enthusiastic while demonstrating their newly rediscovered abilities. The wagon they'd set aflame had vanished outright, while another lay abandoned at the roadside. The remaining wagon still had its raptors harnessed to the front, but it took considerable coaxing for the beasts to get back onto the road, and there wasn't enough room in there for all the Disciples. Most would have to walk.

"I'll scout ahead," Kelan offered. "Make sure nothing ambushes you on the road."

Not that the Disciples of the Flame would have too much trouble dealing with any further encounters with the dead. He wanted to hear the full story of precisely how they'd escaped from under the king's nose, too, but he'd already taken one unplanned detour that day, and he wanted to at least have a closer look at Setemar before sunset.

He glided ahead of the Disciples' wagon, one eye on the cliffs that marked Setemar's boundaries. Within the hour, he spied the soldiers' overturned wagon, its raptors nowhere to be seen. Curiosity drove him to glide closer; a distinct rustling sound came from the bushes bordering the road beside the wagon, and he spied the outline of someone crouched beneath.

"Who's there?"

A head popped up, sporting a grin. Pehin, her clothes torn and her hair tangled, but her eyes shining with mischief. "If it isn't the troublemaker."

"What are you doing there?" He glimpsed several sacks behind her that he suspected she'd pilfered from the abandoned wagon. "Don't you have food in the city?"

"Not enough." A dark expression crossed her face. "Deliveries have slowed to a crawl. Too many farms and villages abandoned, and the best stuff goes to the rich fucks in the inner city."

"You aren't living in the temple?" He raised a brow. "Still fighting the occupation?"

She gave a wry laugh. "Not sure I'd call it an occupation. A half-hearted one at best even before those soldiers took off today. Nice of them to give us their supplies, though."

"I ran into them earlier," Kelan said. "They told me the king ordered them to head towards the capital. Most likely to bring reinforcements."

"Shit." She took a step back. "Thanks for the warning, I guess."

"Not for you," he clarified. "I'm not sure he cares about Setemar, not now that he has his eye on a larger prize."

"Does he now?" She glanced behind her at the sacks. "I need to get these supplies to the city, but we can talk later."

"Where're you hiding?" He lifted two of the sacks into the air and waited for her to pick up the others. "In the tunnels?"

"The tunnels are too far from any supplies. It's rough for anyone not in the inner city."

He glided after her down the dusty road to Setemar's outskirts. The city's outer region had grown like a patch of weeds, becoming wilder the farther one travelled from the well-built inner city. With the exception of the main road that most travellers used to get into the city, most of this area resembled farmland more than a suburban landscape, with houses interspersed with fields and gardens where the city's produce was grown.

Pehin approached a large farmhouse, waving a greeting to a couple of young boys playing in an overgrown vegetable plot. "This used to be a raptor farm, but the family moved out when their livestock bolted. There are too many dead roaming around to feel safe."

She pushed the door inward, revealing a dusty living room in which twelve or so Disciples of the Earth sat in varying states of dishevelment. They didn't wear their formal robes, and their ages ranged from their late teens to mid-thirties at Kelan's guess. All watched him with a mixture of curiosity and suspicion.

"So." Pehin dropped one of the sacks and turned to Kelan, propping a hand on her hip. "What have the Disciples of the Sky been up to while we've been dodging guards and fending off the dead?"

"Sorry we couldn't help," he said with a twinge of guilt. "Mekan attacked our temple a few days ago too. Now, he's got his sights fixed on the Disciples of Life."

"Shit." She cast a glance towards the others. "The Disciples of Life are the only reason Mekan hasn't infected our temple thanks to whatever they did to seal the Void last time."

"I think—and so does my Superior—that the king wants to destroy the Disciples of Life," said Kelan. "He and Mekan have an agreement, and the god of death's primary goal is to obliterate Yalet, so it sounds like they're on the same page."

Pehin's brows shot up. "King Tharen thinks he can kill a god?"

"He plans to destroy Her followers, at any rate," Kelan said. "He also opened a Temple of Death inside the palace and has Mekan's entire army at his disposal, so he's partway there."

"Oh, is that all?" Pehin said. "I can see why he wouldn't want to bother with the likes of us, then."

"That gives you an opening," Kelan said. "Would you like to reclaim your temple?"

"I wish," said Pehin. "There aren't enough of us. Thanks to half the city guards dancing to the king's beck and call, we're shut out of the inner city. We'd need outside help."

Kelan offered a smile. "Would a few Disciples of the Flame do the trick?"

———

Hands grabbed Yala, pulled her away from the prince. Hands that ended in claws, covered in black scales, gripped her shoulders, pushed her in front of the king.

"Yala Palathar," he murmured. "I am disappointed."

"Believe me, so am I." Gods, but it felt good to finally speak her mind. There was but one end to this, and she would seize every minor victory she could grasp on her way into the Void.

"I thought you loyal," he went on. "To me and to your nation. Yet you betrayed us both."

"I never betrayed Laria." She could almost believe, hearing him now, that he spoke as a king alone and not as an agent of the god of death. "This path you walk will lead to your ruin."

"I was led to believe you intended to walk the same path." He gestured at Niema, who lay broken and bleeding at the foot of the monster he'd called from the Void. "It's her, isn't it? She's corrupted you."

"Corruption." A bitter laugh escaped. "The clue's in the name, isn't it? Corruption will leave nothing for you to rule over but ashes."

"The Disciples of Life have poisoned you with lies." The king peered at Niema, at the shadows lapping at her body. "I saw her draw upon the Void itself to heal herself. Did you know she could do that?"

No, but it makes sense. Not that he'd believe her ignorance, and who knew, maybe throwing some answers at him would gain her some in return.

"I did," she said, "because I'm the one who gave her those abilities."

His gaze bored into her, seeking any trace of a lie. "You will tell me how you did this."

"She saved my life," said Yala. "Seems that a Disciple of Life saving a Disciple of Death has certain effects. I'm corrupting *her*, not the other way around. If you kill me, you'll do her a favour and weaken your own cause."

"Yala," Niema moaned.

Yala's heart contracted, but there was no time for guilt. Of the pair of them, Niema stood more of a chance of escaping this horror. Yala's fate was sealed, but if she made him think this was entirely her doing, she might spare Niema further grief.

"And what else is she capable of?" he asked. "Did she bestow any unusual talents upon you?"

Did she? The question had never crossed Yala's mind, but nothing in the time she'd spent in Yalet's realm suggested that she held any special affinity with the god of life. Mekan, she assumed, did not share His followers.

"Your guess is as good as mine," Yala said. "I suspect nobody other than Mekan knows the truth."

He leaned over Niema, peered at her ashen face. "We shall find out when she wakes."

While his attention was on Niema, Yala lunged, tore her way free from the monsters holding her. Pain ripped up her arms as she launched herself forward, not at the king but at the grasping shadows reaching from behind the altar.

The darkness's cold embrace swept her away, borne into the merciless Void.

———

Viam watched the scene unfolding inside the courtyard with mounting horror. She stood rigidly, Brenat's hand wrapped around her arm, tugging gently. "Come on, Viam. We need to go."

"Yala." If Viam's eyes weren't mistaken, Yala had dived past the king straight into the Void itself. Into Mekan's domain.

"She told you to run."

She had. Viam hadn't listened, even as Nalen's allies had left one by one. They'd known there would be no saving Niema from this prison nor Yala either.

Niema lay unconscious at the feet of one of Mekan's beasts, watched by the king's masked guards. Daliel watched, too, saying nothing, doing nothing.

In every way she might have imagined this going wrong, Viam had never expected that Daliel would be the one to sabotage Yala's efforts to stop the king.

When Brenat and Viam ran out into the night, Saren accosted them, dressed in his stolen guard uniform. "Where's Yala?"

"Daliel ruined everything," Viam said between breaths. "We need to leave."

"We can't." He pointed over at the barracks, where a large number of armed soldiers and guards ran amok beneath the winged shadows of escaping war drakes. "They've employed half the army to catch those beasts. The good news is that nobody suspects who was responsible for letting them out."

"If they figure out someone unlocked the gate, they'll blame Yala." Viam's stomach sank. "She took the fall for us."

"Tell me," Saren said, over his shoulder. "What in Mekan's rotting hell happened in there?"

"Daliel stopped Yala from killing the king." Tears sprang to her eyes. "I shouldn't have let him run after her. If I'd known..."

"None of that talk," said Brenat. "The prince is good-hearted to the point of ridiculousness, and you can hardly blame him for not wanting his father dead."

"I can," said Saren. "Is *he* still alive? Daliel?"

"Yes, despite Yala putting a knife to his throat."

"She didn't, did she?" Saren snorted. "And the king locked her up?"

"Worse." She couldn't look at him. "She ran into the Void."

"Shit." A long, tense pause stretched between them, filled with the clamour of fleeing war drakes, soldiers' shouts, and the occasional screech from one of the king's void drakes.

"She's as good as dead." Tears burned Viam's eyes, threatening to spill over. "And Niema's not much better off."

"If anyone can get out of the Void in one piece, it's Yala."

Viam looked at Brenat. "Do you believe that? Or are you just saying what you think I need to hear?"

"Why not both?" Brenat took her hand, squeezed it. "Come on. Let's help the guards recapture some war drakes. Win ourselves some goodwill. Then, we can figure out how to get Yala *and* Niema out of there."

———

Niema awakened in darkness so absolute she thought that she'd somehow pursued Yala into the Void. A soft bed cushioned her back, and the cold burn beneath her skin had faded, but the sense of subtle wrongness lingered even as the darkness faded enough to reveal the outline of the room in which she'd been imprisoned.

She lifted her hands and gasped aloud. The shadows were coming from her, trickling from her palms like blood.

Niema recoiled, rolled off the bed, shaking her hands to dislodge the darkness leaking from beneath her skin. She'd healed herself using the power of Mekan's domain. Now, she carried the Void within herself.

"Thank you for allowing me to destroy my greatest foe." Who had Mekan been addressing? Her or Yala? Or the king? Dizziness overcame her, and she lay back on the bed, scared to close her eyes in case the shadows kept pouring from her hands until the Void swallowed her whole.

She sat up again when footsteps sounded outside. The door opened, and the king's masked guards entered, followed by King Tharen. "You're awake."

Niema opened her mouth, and he lifted a hand. "If you make a sound, my followers will rip out your tongue."

Fear coiled inside her. She'd been intending to ask if Yala was alive, if she'd returned from that dark hole intact, but she had little doubt he meant his threat. She did not need her tongue to be of use to him.

"My army is preparing to march to war," said the king. "In a few days, you will accompany me to the forest that your people call their home. You will be there to see your fellow Disciples bleed, one by one, and to see Yalet's heart beat its last."

Niema shook her head, whispered, "No."

The king turned his back. "I shall see you when my army is ready."

He closed the door, and she was once again left in the dark.

42

Kelan retraced his flight path to meet the Disciples of the Flame. Despite being reduced to one wagon, they maintained a fast pace, no doubt buoyed by their euphoria at regaining access to their deity. Occasionally, they would stop to pray. Kelan bore this with patience, at least the first couple of times, but when they chose a spot entirely too close to one of the villages Mekan had destroyed for their third prayer, he put his foot down.

"You do want to reach Setemar by nightfall, don't you?" he said to the older man who seemed to have designated himself as their leader. The Disciple, named Liran, was ranked two tiers below the Superior in their perplexing hierarchy, and that was enough for him to claim authority. To his credit, he'd at least let the younger members of the contingent ride in the wagon while he walked. "Trust me, you don't want to camp out here."

"From what you told us, the outskirts of Setemar are no safer," he responded. "We'll take our chances."

"Pehin and the others plan to drive out the king's allies at nightfall," Kelan said. "You'd be able to enter the inner city then."

Assuming there was anywhere to stay. While they'd walked, Kelan had filled them in on his encounter with Pehin as well as the assault on Skytower and Niema's capture. They, in turn, explained how they'd escaped the capital with the aid of some of the king's soldiers. Kelan hadn't expected that level of rebellion, but in hindsight, it seemed obvious that ill temper had been brewing long before the king's actions at Skytower, and it wouldn't have surprised him if His Majesty faced a revolt from within the flight division next.

"Do these... *rebels* have a solid strategy?" Liran asked with all the distaste of someone who'd never broken a rule in his life.

"More solid than praying at the roadside next to a village full of walking corpses."

He was certain the Disciples of Life had taken care of the dead, but that was enough to convince the others to climb back into their wagon or resume their journey on foot.

As the cliffs of Setemar neared, Kelan glided ahead to check on the Disciples of the Earth again. Pehin had stationed herself near the soldiers' fallen wagon so that it would be easy for him to relay messages between them, and she was pleased to hear the Disciples of the Flame were open to helping with Setemar's liberation.

"You might need to convince them a little more," he said, "but I think the promise of a warm meal and a bed to sleep in in the upper city might be enticing enough. If the Disciples' Inn is still standing, that is."

"It is, I think," she said. "The soldiers haven't really *done* anything. They'd barely been in the city a week before half of them took off on some order or other. It sounds like the king is losing his grip on his army."

"Not the dead one, unfortunately."

The wagon soon came within sight, and he and Pehin led the way to the Disciples' safe house.

"With the soldiers gone, we have almost nobody in the outer city to worry about," she said as they walked. "We can use the tunnels and get in through the temple without anyone at the gates suspecting a thing."

"If we go in through the temple, those of us who aren't Disciples of the Earth won't be able to use our abilities," Kelan reminded her.

"True." Pehin's forehead wrinkled. "If some of us use the front gates, we can take them by surprise. I bet they'd never see us coming."

"I like the way you think."

When the last group of Disciples reached the safe house, he explained their strategy.

"Pehin thought we might enter via the tunnels and take the guards by surprise from behind," he told them. "But anyone who goes into the Temple of the Earth will lose access to their powers temporarily, so it's your choice."

"No." Liran lifted his chin. "We shall not be stripped of access to Dalathik again."

The others were in accord. Not everyone was thrilled at the notion of another fight, but Pehin was confident that it wouldn't take much pressure to drive out anyone who'd supported the king's half-hearted attempt to wrest control from the Disciples.

While most of the Disciples of the Earth opted to go in through the tunnels, Pehin accompanied Kelan and the others to the front gates. Both guards outside wore bored expressions and scarcely acknowledged the approaching group until one of them caught sight of Kelan's cloak.

"Who are you?" The guard's hand crept towards his sword. "Disciple of the Sky? You aren't welcome here."

In answer, Kelan blasted the gates open. Both guards reached for their weapons, too late; at a gesture from Pehin, the ground beneath their feet cracked open, and they sank to their ankles in mud.

"I'll take that." Pehin snatched a sword out of the guard's hand as she ran past, and Kelan swiped the second guard's weapon on his flight into the upper city.

They emerged into a street bisected by a deep scar that stretched all the way to the temple's doorstep, once ripped wide open by an entryway to the Void.

"Stop!" shouted one of the guards. "Stop them!"

A group of patrolling guards came running out of a side street, lifting their swords. Unluckily for them, that was when the Disciples of the Flame entered the inner city.

Flames sprang up, white fire leaping into the air and sending the guards scattering in a panic. A rooftop caught fire then another, the crackle of flames drowning out Liran's shouts of recrimination at the overenthusiastic novices in front.

"Stop that!" One of the guards at the gate had managed to free his feet from the ground.

Kelan sent a gust of air at him, sending him flying head over heels out of the gate.

Seizing the second guard by the scruff of his neck, Kelan threw him after and then conjured a breeze that swept the gates closed in front of their disbelieving faces. *Nicely done.*

The patrolling guards weren't having much luck either. The Disciples of the Flame had them on the retreat, and while Liran was fuming at the destruction some of his companions had caused in their wildly uncontrolled attacks, there was no doubt that they'd been effective. Kelan dodged a stream of white fire on his way to the temple. Pehin had already reached the stairs, and when he joined her, she threw the doors open.

"Hey there," Pehin called to the bewildered Disciples inside. "We're taking back the city. Want to help?"

————

The void welcomed Yala like an old friend. Its chilled touch caressed her skin, penetrating deep into her bones. Darkness cloaked her vision, yet she had the sense of being watched, as if a pair of unseen eyes was fixed upon her alone.

Some deep, animal instinct inside her yearned to flee, to turn her back on this presence and run until her legs collapsed beneath her, but she was in no more control of her body than if she were dreaming. All sensation fled save for the cold and the familiar harsh whisper brushing against her ear.

"You are mine, Disciple."

A shudder racked her from head to toe, yet she still could not move. Yala belonged to Mekan now, and there was nothing to prevent Him from infiltrating her physical body and remaking her into His image like the beastly creatures who served the king.

"What did you do to King Tharen?" Hearing her own voice startled her; she suppressed the urge to cringe away from its echo in the gloom. "How did he avoid transforming the way the others did?"

"He is mine too." The voice scratched her ears, the cold biting deeper. *"He will be mine truly when Yalet is dead."*

"He promised to help you destroy Yalet." It wasn't hard to guess. "What if he lied? He wants power for himself, not for you. I bet he said anything he thought you wanted to hear. He's sold out his nation, and he'll sell out you too."

"All mortals die in the end, no matter how they might try to run from their fate."

"You could be waiting years, decades," she said. "And I

455

wouldn't trust him even then. How do you know he won't give himself to Dalathik or another god? It's the sort of thing he'd do."

She didn't know if it was even possible for someone so deeply intertwined with Mekan to pledge their soul to another god, but the instant the words left her mouth, the cold brushing against her skin turned to a cold bite, as if an unseen creature sank its sharp teeth into her very soul. The god of death's wordless reply burned her eardrums, a sound half whisper and half screech slithering through her skull. She scarcely had the means to describe the sensation, but every fragment of her was certain that the being watching her from the darkness was readied to kill.

"I'll make sure he doesn't." Her voice sounded muffled to her ears. "I can make you a better deal. I'll give you him *and* Yalet. How about that?"

The whispering screech rose in volume, as did the cold bite sinking into her skin.

"No," Mekan said. *"You will not."*

He didn't believe her, but why had He trusted Tharen's word when He knew the king to be a liar? Or was it simply that he'd been the first human to offer to destroy Yalet's presence in Laria?

The whisper quietened, and the biting pain receded to a faint ache inside the centre of her chest. The darkness did not fade but somehow became less intense, and the oppressive sense of unseen eyes watching her lifted. Hard stone pressed against her back. Her leg gave a throb, and when she lifted her hand, it moved.

Does that mean I'm out of the Void?

A pair of clawed hands seized her and pulled her out of the altar's shadow. Her body protested in a series of aches that also brought back her desire to run. She twisted to the side, ripping herself free from the claws biting into her upper arms.

She ran, crashing straight into the second masked monster. The impact sent her sprawling onto the hard stone with a thud that sent a wave of pain up her injured leg. A strangled yell caught in her throat, and when she tried to rise, a clawed foot came down on her chest. Gasping, she lay on her side, waves of rippling white and red passing over her vision. Her mouth stretched open, her jaw aching with a silent scream she refused to release. She would not give them the satisfaction.

The boot lifted as the guards retreated, and King Tharen took their place. "You survived."

"That's right," she wheezed, her chest burning. "Seems Mekan thought I was worthy after all."

"It won't last," he said. "It's a pity. A horribly painful way to die, too, I'm told. Bring her to the east wing."

Yala once again found herself pulled to her feet, her injured leg a dead weight beneath her. The guards dragged her through a series of corridors and then threw her to the floor of a narrow, unfurnished room. A cell or the palace's equivalent.

The king dismissed the guards, and he and Yala were alone. "I would like to talk to you before you expire, Yala. Since you're never going to see daylight again, you might as well tell me why you betrayed me."

"I didn't betray you—at least not the King Tharen I knew." She coughed, her ribs aching. "If anything, you betrayed *me* when you sent my squad to that island to die."

Disbelief flickered across his features. "Do you believe I sought to be sent into exile by my own Disciples?"

Yala pushed herself into a sitting position, gritting her teeth when the motion wrenched her bad leg. "You also betrayed me when your followers—your *Successors*—killed two of my squad-mates and tried to destroy the city. And don't pretend that wasn't on your orders. Superior Datriem's death proves that."

"Wrong," said King Tharen. "I told them to ensure the Disciples of the Flame were no threat to my return, no more."

"You didn't think Melian had her own ambitions?" she said. "She tried to kill your son and steal his throne. I saved him, and he repaid me by having me locked in a cell because he didn't believe me when I told him the Disciples of the Flame were responsible for the attempt on your life."

"My son is not relevant to this conversation."

"Isn't he?" Daliel was the sole weak spot he possessed, the one route by which Yala might provoke him to end her quickly rather than by some heinous torture he and Mekan had concocted. "Mekan didn't make you immortal, did he? You still need an heir. I bet you wish you'd had more than one now. Gods, it must rankle you to have birthed a pacifist." The bitter words spilled out like poison as the last of her cares fled.

"You think to provoke me by attacking my son?" His tone was flat. "It ill becomes you, Yala. Your grievances with me, I understand, but my son has no involvement in this."

"Your son had me locked in jail for trying to stop an unnecessary war. Rafragoria never tried to have you assassinated, did they?"

"I needed to ensure they did not stand in my way," he said. "They are no longer a threat."

"And what now?" As some of the pain receded from her leg, she became aware of a peculiar ache in her chest, the sole remnant of the biting cold she'd felt inside the Void. "When all of Laria is yours, where will you turn next? The Parvan Empire? The world?"

Was this ambition his alone or Mekan's desire to destroy all life until only the dead remained?

"You will not be alive to see, so it matters not," King Tharen said. "If you are lucky, you will expire quickly. If not, your death will be a prolonged, painful affair that lasts long enough for you to feel every organ rotting inside your body. Either way, I will not waste any more time on you. Goodbye, Yala Palathar."

He retreated, the door closing with a soft snap. In the semidarkness, Yala took stock of her injuries. Bruises mottled her skin from her fall onto the stone floor, and when she lifted her shirt, the spot below her ribcage looked darker than it should. She pressed a finger to the dark patch, and her skin burned sharply cold.

She'd failed Mekan's test.

———

Hachim flew without ceasing until nightfall then got up the following day and did the same again. Rather than following the river north to Setemar, he headed east over the forest. Kelan would have to meet the Disciples of the Earth alone, but Hachim had the sense that they would be fine without him being present. If they did successfully escape the king's forces, Hachim had no expectation that any of them would volunteer to help him save Niema.

On the other hand, his encounter with Superior Kralia had told him that someone else had been in contact with Dalathar.

Hachim was startled out of his silence when someone called his name. A second war drake caught up to him, and Bitra waved from its back. Her friendly face had gained a few more lines in recent weeks in addition to a few scars, and her newly acquired elite Disciple's uniform was already worn and bloodstained.

"Bitra." He slowed to let her fly alongside him. "Why are you following me?"

"I don't know." She lifted a hand, pushed a strand of hair from her face that had escaped its braid. "I don't like this strategy. Splitting up. It seems to me that it just gives Mekan more chances to target us while we're isolated."

"I thought so too," he said, "but what I'm doing... it has to be done alone."

"You're rescuing Niema."

He turned his eyes forward. "I'm not sure how yet, but I am."

They flew for a little longer. He didn't have the heart to tell her to leave nor to reveal the grim truth gnawing at his insides: that he might have to kill Niema instead of rescuing her. It had been easier to deny Superior Sietra's claims when it had been Niema he needed to reassure, but convincing himself was another matter.

Bitra did not leave, and when they camped for the night, he pushed a little further. "You must know coming with me isn't going to lead anywhere good."

"Nowhere is." She tossed another stick into the campfire he'd lit. "I blamed Niema for what happened at first, but that wasn't fair. I guess I feel like I need to make it up to her."

"You haven't asked where we're actually going."

"The temple, I assumed," she said. "To ask for a favour from Yalet."

"Not a bad guess," he acknowledged, "but I'm not sure there's much Yalet can do for her now that she's inside a Temple of Death."

"That's where you want to rescue her from?" She jumped to her feet. "Shit. That's..."

"A death sentence, I know." He shuffled closer to the fire.

It was a humid night, but he couldn't seem to get warm, couldn't dispel the growing chill in the pit of his stomach. "There might be people inside the palace who are willing to help me get in."

"Oh, your friends." She sat again. "I forgot about them. Who're you going to meet all the way over here, then? The Disciples of the Sea?"

He inclined his head. "The Superior did say that they picked up on some rumours from Dalathar."

"You think they've heard what the king's up to."

Hachim didn't expect the Disciples of the Sea to be any keener to go into the capital than anyone else, but any fragment of news on Niema's state would be welcome.

They left their campsite early the next morning, and a short way into their flight, the shoreline came into view above the forest. Hachim angled north and was rewarded with the sight of the Disciples of the Sea's ship bobbing against the cliffs. As he and Bitra flew closer, he spied Nanek in the water, swimming alongside the coast.

When he saw them descending, Nanek swam towards the cliffs, where he pulled himself out of the water to wait for them. "I thought you'd be with your Superior, Hachim."

"The king took Niema," he said. "I expect you've heard if you've been getting news from the capital. How can that be?"

Nanek ran a hand through his sea-tangled hair. "I've been leading patrols to swim up and down the coast and watch for news. The other day, we spoke to some fishermen who regularly make the journey to Dalathar by boat. Or they used to. Bad stories are coming from there recently."

"What stories?" Hachim asked. "Did they mention Niema?"

"No, but they said that while the army was at Skytower, a large number of soldiers walked out."

"So did a few Disciples of the Flame," Hachim said. "Some

of my fellow Disciples were watching the road into Dalathar before our Superior sent us our separate ways."

"And you came here." Nanek gave him an assessing look. "You were not foolhardy enough to approach the city from the front, so you desire to follow the coast instead and to enter Dalathar that way."

A flicker of hope stirred. "That's right. I'm not going to ask anyone to come with me, but I know you're familiar with the route."

"Yes," Nanek growled. "It's my intention to use the docks to enter the city while His Majesty and his army are on their next mission. You're welcome to join me."

"I can't wait that long. Hachim's throat tightened. "When he next goes to war, the king will bring Niema with him."

"I thought she was a hostage." Nanek frowned. "Isn't she?"

"We're his next target. The Disciples of Life. He wants us *all* wiped out, including her." He couldn't tell Nanek that Niema served as worse than a hostage, that she was the means by which he might destroy his fellow Disciples. "Why do you want to go into the city, anyway?"

Nanek bared his teeth in a manner that made him want to back away. "There are some traitors to my kin who have a reckoning due."

43

Within a short time, billowing smoke filled the streets of the inner city and chased the remaining guards out into the main street. The Disciples of the Earth had wanted to avoid causing any damage to the city, but they hadn't entirely been able to prevent the Disciples of the Flame from setting a few more buildings ablaze, nor had Kelan been able to resist fanning those flames in the direction of the fleeing guards on their way out of the gates.

When the final pair of guards left, Kelan brought the gates closed on their heels.

Pehin sidled over with her hair singed, her face smudged with soot, and her eyes gleaming. "I'd call that a resounding success, wouldn't you?"

"I agree." He heard the distinct sound of guards pounding on the other side of the gates. "What should we do if they try to get back in?"

"I'm all for punishing the collaborators," she said, "but I should check with the Superior first."

"You'll be welcomed back into the temple, you think?"

While some of the temple's Disciples had come out to help chase off the intruders, the Superior had not deigned to show his face. Given his swift surrender to the king, Kelan suspected that he would not be pleased at his Disciples for upending the arrangement he'd made to ensure the safety of his people. Never mind that the king seemed to have forgotten Setemar altogether.

"Of course," Pehin said. "So will you, but I might have to work my powers of persuasion on the Superior. He'll want to talk to you in the morning, I expect."

"Does that mean I'm invited to stay?" He raised a brow.

"I'm sure the Disciples' Inn will offer a discount to the city's great saviours."

Kelan grinned. "At least some of the credit goes to you."

Now that he'd confirmed the Disciples' Inn was still standing, the Disciples of the Flame would have somewhere to stay once they'd put out the fires they'd inadvertently started. The inn's owner was taken aback at the influx of visitors, especially when Pehin brought a whole flock of Disciples to take over the inn's lower floor and ordered several bottles of rice wine.

The Disciples of the Flame, with their typical piousness, refused to partake. Kelan's attempts to coax them into joining the celebrations fell flat, and some feared retaliation if the guards returned with reinforcements from the army.

"They won't," Kelan told them. "Didn't you see the state of those soldiers we met on the road? I can guarantee a third of them will desert before they even reach the rest of the army."

"Exactly." Pehin pushed a full wine glass into his hand. "Also, it's obvious the king hasn't been sending orders for a while. If he keeps his eyes on the Disciples of Life instead, it's better for the rest of us."

Kelan drank from the glass, savouring the sweet taste. "Except the downside to that is that destroying the Disciples of Life will also probably mean obliterating every living thing on the continent."

"There is that." She poured herself a glass too. "Not that I wanted to ruin the celebrations by thinking of our imminent deaths."

"No, but since we're all here..." He took in the entire table, from the Disciples of the Flame seated in a huddle at one end to the more raucous presence of the Disciples of the Earth between. "I thought I'd ask who's willing to join the Disciples of Life in defending themselves against the king's army. They have an army of elite Disciples, but they'd appreciate any support from outside."

"An *army?*" Her brows shot up. "Doesn't their deity prevent them from taking lives?"

"I'm sure even Yalet is willing to make an exception if the alternative is their extinction."

"Right." She tipped back her glass. "How many people are in this army of hers, do you think?"

Kelan considered. "Less than a hundred. They're fierce fighters, though. They butchered two entire flight squads while defending the Disciples of the Sea."

"Disciples of the Sea?" Pehin studied him. "Is that what you're proposing? Setting up a force comprised of other Disciples to stand against Mekan?"

"That was on my mind." He let his gaze travel over the other Disciples, who wore expressions ranging from sceptical to curious. "We'd still be outnumbered, but don't forget that summoning Mekan's creatures is contingent on his ability to open the Void, which is significantly harder to do in Yalet's domain."

But not impossible if he found out the extent of Niema's entanglement with the god of death. Kelan had refrained from mentioning anything about her to the other Disciples except that she was a hostage. His Superior's fears about her utility to Mekan might not prove true, and it wouldn't do to cause unnecessary fear and confusion amid an already fragile alliance.

"We'd have Disciples of the Earth, Flame, Life…" Pehin counted on her fingers. "Sea, maybe, but I can't imagine they'd want to fight on land. And Sky, of course." She winked at him.

"I'll ask my Superior for reinforcements." He *hoped* she'd say yes. "We might even have help from other Disciples of Death if Yala can break away from the rest of the army or turn some of the other captains against the king."

"You haven't mentioned her so far," Pehin noted. "Is she fighting? Or in hiding?"

"She's trying to kill the king."

Pehin dropped her wine glass. Half the others gasped, too, and when another Disciple came running over to help clean up the mess, Pehin swatted her away. "I'll do it. Tell me everything, Kelan. Yala's trying to assassinate the king?"

"I don't know if she's succeeded yet," Kelan added. "The issue is that the army of the dead doesn't need the king to be alive to command it. It belongs to the god of death, and it's His war that the king is fighting."

A collective shudder followed. There was no avoiding that part of their predicament. Mekan was at war with the other gods, and as the gods' own mortal representatives, the Disciples stood in His path whether they wanted to or not.

"Opposing the king is challenge enough," said one of the Disciples of the Earth. "Opposing the god of death? We'll all but certainly be slaughtered."

"Is that any worse than being killed *after* watching Him lay waste to the entire Larian continent?" Kelan enquired. "If you fight alongside the Disciples of Life, you have a higher chance of survival. Also, don't forget they once came to your aid when you needed it. This will be your chance to return the favour."

"I'm in," Pehin said. "I'd say it'd be a waste for us to chase out the king's soldiers only to let them trample us again."

Several other Disciples of the Earth nodded in agreement, but none of the Disciples of the Flame ventured a word.

Kelan turned to Liran. "I'm not going to force the decision on you, but this war is going to hit the whole country soon enough. Nowhere will be safe."

"The Disciples of Life will never agree to fight beside us," said Liran. "Wouldn't they fear we'd burn down their forest?"

"No, but they'll appreciate you burning the dead."

"Exactly," said Pehin. "It's not conventional, all us Disciples fighting on the same side, but nothing about this fucking mess is conventional."

"That's my thinking." He caught her eye as he refilled his wine glass. "We'll revisit this after I talk to your Superior. Tonight is for celebrating our victory."

"That's right." She took the bottle from him next, letting their fingers bump against each other. It hadn't escaped his attention that her leg kept brushing against his under the table too. He suspected she was in as much need of a diversion as he was, and he was all too happy to oblige.

———

As All Gods' Day approached, Saren found himself resenting the rapidly healing bite marks on his arm and pondering the odds of a second injury getting him out of participating in the upcoming battle. Given the king's current mood, it wouldn't have surprised him if His Majesty would have forced him to march south with the rest of the army even if a war drake chewed off one of his legs.

It didn't help that he'd been put in charge of instructing

Yala's squad, since Commander Sranak was too busy meeting with the other commanders to coordinate transporting the entire army across the continent in a few days to appoint a replacement. Of course, the bright side of the commanders' distraction was that nobody had had time to find the culprits who'd freed the war drakes from their paddock the night of Yala's capture.

"They also know there was more than one of us," Nalen remarked when they met outside the barracks the day before All Gods' Day. "They can't assign all of us to clean the latrines at once."

"Not when we're short on captains already."

At this rate, Saren's squad would end up flying to war with no leader and without any hope of getting Yala out of the palace.

"No, but they're punishing us by ordering the foot soldiers to get up before sunrise to march ahead of the flight division," said Nalen. "Did the commander tell you that you get to sleep in?"

"What? No." He hadn't even *seen* Commander Sranak that day. "How much of a lead will you have?"

"Half a day."

Saren gave an incredulous snort. "Half a day? We'd overtake you within an hour."

"I doubt the king cares," said Nalen. "The point is, no foot soldiers will be in the palace grounds in the hours before you leave. We can't help rescue your friend until the king has gone."

"Wasn't that always the case?" He didn't hold out much hope that he'd be able to participate in the rescue himself, but the last time he'd seen Viam and Brenat, the latter had insisted that she and Viam could handle it themselves.

"Yes." A pause. "Are you sure Yala is alive?"

"I know she is." He didn't. She might be a rotting corpse

for all he knew. "I'll bet he's taking Niema with him but not her."

Not the prince either, but Saren didn't have any faith in Daliel not to hinder the rescue attempt.

"Anyway." Nalen reached into his pocket. "I got a weird message from one of my contacts outside the city, who claimed there's someone willing to come and help liberate the city from the king's control while he's gone. Didn't say who they were."

"Liberate us?" Who would have the audacity to make that claim? Saren cast his thoughts around and came up empty. "It's not the Disciples of the Flame who escaped, is it?"

"Doubt it. The note's too flammable." Nalen held out a rolled-up drond leaf on which someone had written in neat script.

Saren knew of only one group of Disciples who had a habit of writing their messages on leaves and pieces of bark. "A Disciple of Life?"

The note read: *Some of my people are coming to liberate the city while the king is at war. Anyone who wants to help can meet us at the docks at noon tomorrow.*

———

Viam and Brenat were talking behind the administration building during their lunch break when Saren came over with Nalen close behind him.

"Nalen got this note," Saren said. "From someone claiming they want to help liberate the city."

Viam took the note from him. "A leaf. It's the Disciples—"

"Of Life, I know, but it seems suspicious," said Saren. "We can't trust that it isn't a trap."

"From whom?" Viam asked. "The king doesn't need to come up with a scheme like this to lure out deserters. He's not going to waste his time on them when he has a war to fight."

"That's my thinking," Nalen said. "My gut says this is genuine. Who'd send a polite note announcing their intention to attack the palace?"

"See, that's why I thought it was the Disciples of the Flame," said Saren. "Question is, how're we supposed to send an answer?"

"We can't," Nalen said. "By noon tomorrow, we'll already be outside the city one way or another. You'll leave not long after."

"The king's sending the foot soldiers out first," Saren added for Viam and Brenat's benefit. "The flight division won't leave until later in the day. Doesn't make that much difference, given that we can fly, but the guards would think we were trying to desert if we left the grounds before then."

"Brenat and I have tomorrow off," Viam said. "We can go and meet whoever sent that message. We're not going to be able to get near the palace until after the flight division leaves."

"I'm on board," Brenat said. "A mysterious ally. I like it."

"Why would the Disciples care about liberating the capital?" Saren asked. "If it *is* the Disciples of Life, they'll want to destroy that temple, but I can't see why they wouldn't rescue Niema too."

"Whoever it is, it'll at least keep the guards distracted while we go after Yala," Viam said."

"You don't need a diversion," Saren said. "I thought that prince was happy to help. When he isn't being a spineless coward, that is."

"I haven't seen him." The king had not reinstated his habit of hosting ceremonies at the temple, and she hadn't heard from Daliel since his intervention in Yala's attempt on the king's life. Hadn't *wanted* to contact him. "We can get in there without his help. Are you certain the commander won't let you stay behind?"

"Unfortunately." Saren lifted his hand, baring the barely healed incisions from the war drake's teeth. "Looks like we're flying to our deaths with no captain."

Viam's chest tightened. Yala had claimed not to be attached to her new squad, but Viam knew her too well to believe her capable of not letting affection slip through her defences. Prior to her capture, it sounded as if her squad had been aware of at least some part of the truth, and they never would have wanted to abandon her to certain death.

"Not necessarily," Viam said. "I bet if you asked if they wanted to help get her out, they'd all say yes."

"Does it matter? The king would notice if an entire squad suffered a suspicious accident. "Unless you're implying that we should collectively turn around and fly straight back into the capital when we leave?" A scathing note entered his voice, but there was little venom left. Their old arguments had long since evaporated. They were united in a single cause, and that cause was getting Yala out of that palace.

"Maybe I am."

"What?" Saren squinted at her. "You're joking."

"It's not the worst idea," Brenat put in. "You fly at the back of the formation, persuade anyone else to look the other way…"

"And who is going to do the persuading, exactly?" Saren said. "Not me. And, as I just fucking told you, we don't have a captain."

"Now you do." Viam drew in a breath. "I'm taking command of Yala's squad."

44

The morning after Setemar's liberation, Kelan and Pehin walked to the Temple of the Earth.

"Fair warning," Pehin said as they climbed the narrow staircase to the Superior's office. "He's not pleased with any of us for our behaviour last night."

He raised a brow. "He isn't pleased that we saved his people from being trapped in their own temple?"

"He fears the king's wrath, I think, and who can blame him?"

"The king's wrath has a very specific target at the moment, and it's not him."

After the pleasant night he'd spent in her company, Kelan reasoned that he could tolerate another encounter with the Superior, angry or not.

The man who sat on the high-backed seat of the Superior was barely older than Kelan, with light-brown hair and a youthful face that did little to make him look authoritative despite the height he'd gained from being perched on the uncomfortable stone chair.

"I am Superior Geren," he said. "And you, I understand,

are the one responsible for rallying a group of rogue Disciples to fight against the king's army."

That makes me sound far more accomplished than I am, Kelan thought.

"I'm more of a bystander," he admitted. "I was travelling with the Disciple of Life, and they told me they saw some Disciples of the Flame on the road to Setemar. When I met them, they were happy to offer their assistance against the occupation."

"It was no occupation." His eye twitched. "We had an agreement with the king. One that you and your conspirators broke without my consent."

"The king would have seen your temple taken by Mekan if not for the protections given by the Disciples of Life the last time the dead attacked the city," Kelan pointed out. "He tried to do the same to my temple not three days ago and nearly succeeded."

Superior Geren gripped the sides of the stone seat. "Then you should know what we stand to lose by opposing him."

"You'd be in good company," Kelan told him. "His next target is the Disciples of Life. He's set on eradicating Yalet's followers from the continent, at the direct orders of the god of death."

"What?" The Superior frowned at him. "Mekan giving orders? What nonsense is that?"

"Absolutely true, I'm afraid. King Tharen turned the palace into a Temple of Death, and Mekan has convinced him that the god of life is the enemy to all of humanity, not Corruption."

"I am aware the king wants all Disciples to pledge themselves to the crown, but I cannot believe he wants to destroy every one of Yalet's followers."

"He certainly intends to try," Kelan said. "I would bring a Disciple of Life to back me up, but the dead have been assailing the forest for weeks, and they'd appreciate some help. The same kind of help they gave to you."

"I see." He drummed his fingers against the side of the stone seat. "Yalet's followers helped save my temple from destruction. It is undeniable that we owe them a debt."

Someone rapped on the door. Kelan tensed, his heart sinking. *The king's soldiers can't be back, can they?*

"Enter," called the Superior.

A breathless Disciple of the Earth ran into the room, shedding dirt everywhere. Mud smeared his face and covered his robes as if he'd been digging a tunnel, which was a distinct possibility.

"My apologies, Superior," he said. "I have an urgent message from our scouts. There's a rumour that the king plans to lead the army's next major mission on All Gods' Day this week. They didn't specify the target, but there's a strong indication that the foot soldiers will also be participating as well as the flight division. If they march on the main road, there's a good chance they'll come through Setemar even if we aren't their target."

Superior Geren leapt to his feet, jabbing a finger at Kelan. "See what you have brought upon us?"

"Don't blame Kelan." Pehin entered the office behind the other Disciple. "The king wants to go after the Disciples of Life. I doubt he cares what anyone in Setemar is doing."

"He'll probably fly right over it," Kelan added, thinking of the void drake. "As for his foot soldiers, it'd take at least two or three days for them to reach here on foot, and I doubt the flight division will hang around and wait for them."

"That's conjecture, not fact, and a few days certainly isn't enough time to smooth matters over." He paced to the door. "I will ask you to leave while I convene with my council."

"He's not best pleased with me," Kelan muttered to Pehin as they descended the stairs.

"I did warn you," said Pehin. "I'll leave him to cool off. Might join up with the scouts. Now that I'm not responsible for feeding all the Disciples trapped outside the upper city, I can travel outside."

"How are the scouts getting news so fast?"

"How d'you think?" She tapped a foot against the earth.

Comprehension sank in. "You're tunnelling all the way to the capital?"

"No, but there are shortcuts that don't exist above-ground," she said. "Handy for covering long distances in a short time as well as for spying."

An idea trickled into Kelan's mind. "I just thought of a way that you can slow down that army."

———

The commander stared at Viam. "What did you say?"

"I'd like to volunteer as squad leader," she said, louder, her voice wavering a little. "Yala's squad needs a new captain, and quickly. Since I have experience, it seems selfish not to step in."

A war of indecision waged on the commander's face. Exhaustion wore grooves into the skin beneath shadowed eyes. This was a man who expected to confront his own death too.

"I can't promise you'll have much time to establish yourself as leader," he finally said. "We're flying to war tomorrow, as you know."

"I understand." She wiped sweat-damp palms on her drakeskin trousers. "I'm ready."

"Then go," said the commander. "If you're sure."

If you're sure you want to die. Viam heard the unspoken words. She took in a few calming breaths, reminded herself of the plan.

If she couldn't save Yala, she would at least prevent her squad from giving their lives to Mekan's war.

Saren had the squad ready and waiting in a corner of the training grounds. The other squads had been given leave to train in whichever manner their captains deemed most urgent. Since only one or two squads were able to enter the paddock at the time, most had converged near the sparring grounds or were practising with weapons. Few paid much attention to Viam, though when she set eyes on Yala's squad, she became conscious of how pristine her uniform was compared to theirs, her skin unmarked by any recent injuries. Everyone else bore scraps and scratches and hastily mended sleeves, and they watched her approach with scepticism she felt was entirely deserved.

Viam summoned up her resolve. "I'm Viam," she told them. "I'm stepping in as interim captain in Yala's place."

You're supposed to establish authority, whispered a voice in her head, but she could barely muster the urge to look them in the eyes. How could *anyone* take Yala's place, really?

"I know we barely have a day to prepare." She spoke quickly, taking in their anxious faces. "And I don't expect you to trust me, but I hope we can help one another."

To start, they went through introductions, and she did her best to commit their names to memory. Aside from Saren, they were all in their early to mid-twenties at most, some younger than Yala had been when she'd taken the title of captain. All competent soldiers—most had survived at least two missions by now—but none trained as Disciples of Death like the captains were.

A young man named Gorel kicked off the inevitable questions. "You know Yala," he said. "You flew with her years ago, didn't you?"

"I did. She was my captain."

"Then you know she's innocent." He spoke urgently.

"Whatever the king claims he arrested her for, she's not a traitor."

The others nodded except for a twitchy youth named Surel, who'd been the last member to join as a last-minute replacement for Saren.

Yurel, a young woman with a scarred face, spoke up next. "She's innocent, and the king is a traitor to the whole nation."

"Quiet." Viam dropped her voice. "Not now. We'll talk later, but no, she's not a traitor."

That was enough to stifle their questions for the time being. She set them to practising with their spears and took Saren aside to ask for the latest update from Nalen.

"Nalen and a few others are planning to give the rest of the army the slip on their way out of the city," Saren said. "They'll go to the docks, wait there. I thought I'd go with them."

"To meet our mysterious ally?"

"That's right."

Viam's new squad leader status would make it more difficult for her to slip out of the palace grounds before the flight division was due to leave the capital, but she'd accepted that downside when she'd taken on the title. Saren was less likely to be missed.

"You'll come back and join us, right?"

"Yes, if you convince this lot to get in on the plan."

I think they're already on board.

When Viam had the squad alone in the paddock later that afternoon, she began with the question, "Did anyone tell you exactly why Yala was arrested?"

"She betrayed the king and the nation, supposedly," put in Vilat, who Viam had learned was the squad's most competent spear-thrower. "But we know she didn't. She wanted to rescue the king's prisoner and stop him from sending us to war."

"She told us not to come after her," added Roven, a brash young woman whose outrageous sense of humour would have won her a friend in Saren if he'd been of a mind to pay the rest of the squad the slightest attention. "Gorel and I tried, but Kithal dragged us back."

"To stop you from getting killed," said Kithal, a burly man who looked as if he'd be more at home in the docks than on a war drake's back. "I don't like her being locked up any more than you do, but the captain ordered us to stay behind. It was her last command."

"Yala tends to prioritise protecting the squad over her own safety," Viam murmured. "The thing is, she's not always right."

Hope gleamed in Gorel's eyes. "You want to rescue her?"

"Yes, but not now," she added as a ripple of excitement travelled through their group. "Nobody is getting into that palace until the king's long gone, and since we're supposed to be flying behind him, you'll have to make a choice."

"To do what?" Roven jerked her head towards Saren. "We all injure ourselves like he did?"

Saren cut her a glare. "One injury we can pass off as an accident. More than that and you'll be sent to war even if you cut off both your feet."

"No injuries!" Viam said. "Also, you can't breathe a word of this to anyone else."

"We want to help," said Yurel. "Yala saved our lives out there."

A murmur of agreement followed. Bringing this many people in on Nalen's plan worried her a little, but come tomorrow, they'd be on their way to their deaths one way or another.

"Yala told me—" Viam broke off. "Well, if we'd had time to talk to one another, she'd tell me to keep you alive. That means you need to avoid taking unnecessary risks. I don't want all of you breaking into the palace, but Yala might need some help getting out."

Kithal frowned. "How're we supposed to separate from the other flight squads without being seen?"

"We'll fly at the very back of the formation," Viam replied. "The king will be at the front, far ahead of the rest of us, with those beasts of his."

"We'll be out in the open, though," he said. "The guards on the city wall will have an easy job knocking us out of the sky."

Viam looked at Saren. "They'll be on our side. Right?"

"If Nalen has his way," he replied. "I'll try to get an update to you on what our mysterious new allies have to offer. Seems to me that they'd be an effective diversion."

"There'll be foot soldiers elsewhere in the city waiting to help," Viam added to the squad. "We haven't sorted out the details yet, but I wanted to give you time to consider the options. It's your choice."

"We're in," Gorel said.

"That's right." Yurel lifted her chin. "We're with our squad leader."

The others nodded, too, even Kithal and Surel. Viam took them in, this group of people who'd placed their faith in Yala's hands—and now, in hers too. "All right. This is what we'll do."

———

Saren paced along the seafront, scowling at the glittering water. "Nobody's here."

"It's not noon yet," said Brenat. "Have some patience."

"I'll have patience when I'm not waiting for my own death," he retorted. "Where the fuck are these so-called allies of ours?"

EMMA L. ADAMS

A few boats and ships bobbed against the shore, but the half-rebuilt naval division had been largely abandoned in recent weeks. There would be no seaborne fighting in this war, and the piers were deserted. As a result, they would have seen anyone approaching the shore within moments of their appearance.

Just before noon, Nalen came to join them together with a few of the foot soldiers who'd slipped away during the march out of the capital earlier that morning. He'd selected a small number to leave at first so as to avoid drawing too much attention from the commanders still loyal to the king.

"Anyone here yet?" asked Nalen.

"No." Saren scanned the water and then spied a shape bobbing above the water's surface some distance away. "Something's out there."

"One of those monsters?" One of the soldiers reached for their weapon.

"No… it's a person." Saren took a startled step back as several other heads broke the water's surface, and five or more figures began swimming towards them.

When a large man reached the pier and pulled himself out of the water, some of the soldiers drew their shortswords.

"Wait." Saren recognised that sparse clothing, the necklace of shells, the jewels woven into long hair. "I know you."

The Disciple of the Sea surveyed their group with serious eyes. "I am Nanek."

"You sent the note?" Saren looked at Nalen. "You want to liberate the city? Is that right?"

"Our companion is the one who sent you that note," Nanek said. "Two Disciples of Life travelled with us. It is their intent to pursue the king."

"And not you?" Granted, while the Disciples of the Sea owed her a debt several times over, Niema would all but certainly be flying with the king. Nobody had a hope of getting close to them.

"We are here to punish those traitors who turned on our people," Nanek said. "The scum who allied with Mekan."

Ah. He meant the Disciples of the Sea guarding the Temple of the Flame. The ones Nalen's allies hadn't killed and thrown into the river, at least.

"Some are already dead," said Nalen, who'd drawn the same conclusion. "I can help you with the rest but not in broad daylight. Too many guards still loyal to the king remain."

"And most of them are in the upper city," said Saren. "How'd you plan to get past the gates? You can't *swim* in. Also, there are what, five of you?"

"There are more," Nanek growled. "We did not come alone."

Brenat peered behind him, craning her neck. "There *are* monsters out there. Look."

Saren followed her gaze and glimpsed long shapes stirring at the water's surface. Reptilian heads crested the waves, serpentine bodies bearing human riders.

"Sea drakes." Saren stepped back. "Please tell me you didn't bring *Rafragorian* soldiers to help."

"What?" Nalen drew his shortsword, and two of the soldiers behind him aimed crossbows at the newcomers.

"I'd advise you not to strike against them," Nanek warned. "They will not hesitate to return the sentiment, and we are in need of their help."

"We aren't," Saren said. "You brought them to the capital to attack while the king's gone. That *is* treason. Also, the king's army will notice you hiding out here."

Except all the foot soldiers had already left the city, and the flight division would soon join them. The remnants of the city guard would be centred on the palace itself, he was willing to bet.

Still, if he let *Rafragorians* into the city, he'd be deservedly hanged.

"The Rafragorians have no intention of spending longer in the city than they have to," Nanek said. "They are here to aid us, no more."

"And you expect me to take their word for it?"

"Why not?" Brenat ventured. "They know the king has a Temple of Death in the palace, and he already used its monsters to devastate their country. They won't want to risk setting foot in there while the king is alive."

"This is fucked," said Saren. "This is incredibly fucked."

"It is," Nanek agreed. "The Rafragorians have no love for Larians, but the Disciples share no quarrel with them, and they will gladly aid us in freeing our temple from the tyranny of Mekan."

Gods. He's serious.

"I hope you're right," said Saren. "Because if you're not, you might have just dragged the whole country into another war."

———

Niema had long since lost track of time. The days bled into one another, distinguished by the thin ribbon of daylight streaming through the narrow window. The guards brought food and water to her cell intermittently but didn't commit to a regular enough schedule for her to get a good sense of what might be going on elsewhere in the palace.

Or whether Yala survived.

Her wound had healed enough for her to remove the bandages, but an ugly scar bisected her ribs, purpled at the edges like a bruise. If she breathed too deep, it burned cold.

When the king showed up again, he was in the company of his two masked guards. Without a word, one seized Niema's arms and dragged her to her feet while the other wrapped a cloth around Niema's mouth and pulled it into a tight knot behind her ears.

"Bring her," the king ordered. "Do not allow her to escape."

Where are we going? Niema tried to ask, but not a sound slipped past the gag biting into her face. The masked guards lifted her between them like a sack of grain and carried her out of the room.

They'd never brought her into the temple during the day before, and the courtyard was nearly unrecognisable with its pillars bathed in daylight. The king's void drake masked her view of the altar. The beast had been outfitted with new armour of gleaming black to match its pitch-dark scales, topped with a golden crown melded to its spiked head. The king wore a similar crown, his armoured clothing trimmed in gold and the claw-blade sword sheathed at his waist.

Dread sank its teeth into her. He wasn't going to sacrifice her. At least not yet.

The other four void drakes hovered above the courtyard with masked guards seated on their backs. She couldn't tell who they'd been before they'd ascended to Mekan's side. No traces of their human features had been left beneath a layer of solid scales around pitted dark eyes.

"Mekan will guide us to victory," the king proclaimed. "Today, we fly to war. Anyone in our path who dares to defend the god of life will be eradicated."

Clawed hands lifted Niema, seating her on the void drake's back. Chains were looped around the beast's heavy body and wrapped around her ankles, and cuffs snapped into place around her hands, allowing enough room for her to hold onto the void drake's back but not to free herself.

The king climbed up behind her. "If you somehow slip your chains, you might survive the fall, but I can promise any pain you feel will be magnified tenfold when I catch up to you."

I can handle it, she thought, but was that true? Pain and darkness had hollowed her out, had made her wonder how much a person could take before they broke. Her chest throbbed with the echo of her wound or perhaps a reminder that the Void lived within her, that she'd drawn it into herself willingly.

And now, the king intended to use that same power to destroy Yalet's followers.

Vertigo scattered her thoughts as the void drake took flight with a beat of its vast wings and the courtyard dropped away beneath them. They gained height, the palace shrinking to a blot amid a city rendered to a web of streets dotted with buildings scarcely bigger than her fingertip. The glimmering rim of the sea shone at their back, and the fields of southern Laria waited ahead. Beyond that lay the forest. Her home.

"It shall begin," said the king or Mekan. "At last, we shall end Yalet's rule and declare our victory."

45

Viam helped her squad saddle the war drakes, moving as slowly as she dared. She had yet to hear from Saren or Nalen either. She'd anticipated that the latter would have a hard time getting into the palace again after he'd sneaked away from the main army, but the former had no excuse, and while Viam had told the commander that Saren was held up in the latrines after a relapse involving rice wine the previous night, that excuse would last only until someone else went looking for him.

"Where the fuck is he?" Roven whispered.

A diversion came in the form of the terrifying sight of the king and his void drake ascending above the palace grounds, followed by four other steeds bearing dead riders. Everyone in the paddocks stopped to watch them leave, a chill breeze and a trail of shadow lingering in their wake.

"Back to it!" The commander recovered first. "Hurry up and get on your steeds."

The flight squads hurried to obey, albeit with little enthusiasm and with none of the pent-up excitement that usually preceded a mission. Nobody wanted to fight in this war. It wouldn't have surprised Viam if some of the others planned to flee or fake their deaths or otherwise choose their survival as a priority. Others would sooner die in an impossible fight than flee. The choice was theirs, if one might call it a choice at all.

When the last squad before theirs took flight from the paddock, the commander lost his patience. "I'm going to find him."

"Wait." Her feeble protest was lost in the sound of the paddock gate closing on his heels. "Saren, where *are* you?"

"Here." Saren himself shouldered his way past the startled commander and into the paddock. "Got held up," he gasped out by way of an apology. "Let's go."

The commander eyed him suspiciously but climbed onto his own war drake, while Viam moved behind Saren on the pretext of helping him climb onto his war drake.

"What were you doing?" she asked out of the corner of her mouth. "Is Nalen out there?"

"He is." He spoke louder when the commander's war drake took flight above theirs. "His diversion's coming, trust me."

"Why would we trust you?" Kithal voiced the question that no doubt the others were thinking. "You slithered out of the last mission and let us fly to our deaths."

"I'm not proud of it." He took his war drake's chain in hand. "You can choose not to trust me if you like, but trust Yala at least. We're doing this for her."

As Viam climbed onto her own war drake, a muffled thud like a large pair of gates slamming from a distance came from somewhere beyond the palace walls.

"That's Nalen," Saren said. "We'll take flight, follow the rest of the army out of the upper city, and then circle back."

"Who put you in charge?" Roven grumbled. "Viam,

remind me *why* we're putting our faith in someone who's out to save his own neck first?"

"Exactly," Yurel said. "Does *Yala* trust him?"

At one time, Viam might have replied, *I don't know.* Now, she said, "Yes, and so do I. Come on."

At her command, Viam's war drake rose with the rest. They left the paddock and followed the retreating outline of the commander's winged beast, craning their necks to see what was going on below. The source of the noise was unclear from this height, but her gaze snagged on a growing commotion on the other side of the upper city gates.

Gorel leaned over his war drake and pointed. "Look at the river."

The vast river cutting through Dalathar's centre had risen, overflowing its banks and sending a swathe of filthy water through the surrounding streets. People ran out of houses and shops, and guards left their posts as the clamour became impossible to ignore.

Abandoning all pretence at following the army, Viam veered eastward and led the squad alongside the upper city wall, keeping an eye on the chaos below. When she spied a group of soldiers making their way towards the back gate, her heart lifted to see a familiar face among them. "Brenat!"

"Viam." Brenat's face split into a grin. "I see you gave the army the slip."

"Not exactly." Viam flew lower, her war drake's claws skimming the rooftops. A couple of soldiers backed away warily. "What's going on down there? How'd Nalen...?"

"Flood the entire outer city?"

Nalen himself spoke from the back, not looking particularly pleased. "It wasn't my idea. I got out a warning to evacuate first, but a lot of people are going to lose their homes."

"Whose idea was it, then?"

A head crowned with seashells popped up behind him. *A Disciple of the Sea?*

"You sent the note," she concluded. "You're here to liberate the city… why?"

"We're here to avenge our god," the Disciple corrected, lifting a curved knife that looked to have been carved out of bone. "The scum who betrayed us will pay the price in blood."

"Yeah, he talks like that all the time," Brenat added. "As for us, it's time to take back the palace. What do you think?"

"The flight division's too close," she protested, though she'd long since lost sight of the commander's war drake over the rooftops. "If they turn around…"

"They won't," said Saren. "The commander's not going to risk a chewing-out from His Majesty for going after us miscreants instead of pursuing him on his all-important mission."

"The foot soldiers certainly didn't," Nalen added. "A good twenty or thirty of us walked off. Nobody gives a shit. If anything, they probably think we have the right idea."

"Come on." The Disciple of the Sea beckoned. "Let's move."

"Us too," Saren said. "We've given the army enough of a head start. Let's go back to the palace and get Yala out."

The guards at the back gate were still at their posts, but Saren flew straight at them with such speed that no weapon would have stood a chance of hitting him.

"Saren!" Viam closed in behind him, the rest of the squad on her heels.

As they swept over the gate, there were a few shouts of "Deserters!" quickly stifled when Nalen's team came running out of the side street and fell upon the startled guards.

Once they were inside the upper city, Viam and the others flew on until they came to the paddock. She dismounted and waited for the clamour that indicated Nalen's group had reached the palace gates. While Saren ran out to meet them, Viam spoke to the rest of the squad.

"Wait here for us to come back with Yala," she said. "We might need to make a fast escape."

While Viam was still concerned that the commander might turn around and come to investigate the chaos, the outer city flooded frequently enough that nobody would suspect the cause until long after the Disciples of the Sea had gone. She left the paddock and joined Saren and the others in their sprint towards the palace's back entrance.

"I didn't think you cared about rescuing Yala," Viam called to Nalen, joining him at the head of their group.

"I don't," he said. "I'm here to knock the shit out of any guards in there who are loyal to that scumbag on the throne."

Once he'd demonstrated on the guards outside the back door, Nalen let Viam and Saren enter the palace first.

Saren ran in behind Viam, snickering under his breath. "This is the most fun I've had in a while."

"Please take this seriously," Viam shot over her shoulder at him as she ran ahead. "We need to find—" She cut off, a gasp flying from her lungs as she rounded a corner and slammed into a solid figure. "Daliel."

He staggered against the wall, his mouth falling open. "Viam?"

"Don't even think about it," Saren broke in. "Get out of the way. Or better, tell us where Yala's being held prisoner."

"Please," Viam said. "Is Yala alive?"

"I think so." He looked positively ill, his eyes ringed in shadow and his hands trembling. "I can't... she tried to kill him. My father."

"Viam was far too nice to you," Saren said. "Your father is a monster, and it's your fault he's on his way to destroy the few people who can stop Mekan from conquering the whole country."

Viam started to object and thought better of it. To the prince, she said, "The king is gone. Please help us."

Daliel swallowed hard. "I'll see what I can do."

———

Yala was dying.

Dim light streamed through the narrow window, offering glimpses of her greying, dead skin. It had started with itching, a prickling sensation in her chest like insects crawling through her ribcage and nibbling on flesh and skin alike.

Now, the itch had turned hollow, as if she were a groundfruit devoured from the inside until naught remained but the shell. Each breath snagged in her lungs, brought the sense of Mekan's touch worming away like rot deep inside.

When she heard the unmistakeable sound of the flight squad departing in the form of countless pairs of beating wings from outside the palace, she couldn't summon up the energy to care. She might have endured long enough for the king to leave her behind, but the outcome would be the same: an eternity in Mekan's realm as retribution for daring to believe she could challenge the god of death.

Sometime later, Yala lifted her head at the sound of footsteps outside the door. The clink of a key in the lock followed, preceding a slight figure in an oversized guard uniform.

"Saren?" she said.

He threw a cane at her. "Thank Viam for remembering this. C'mon. We're getting you out of here."

"The king?" she rasped. "Niema?"

"They're gone," said Saren. "We came to get you out."

"He took Niema." She used the cane to push herself

upright, alarmed at the weakness in her limbs. "Weren't you supposed to go with the army?"

He grinned. "Luckily for you, His Majesty is more interested in the dead than the living. Also I'm hardly alone. That squad of yours turned out to be much more impressive than I expected."

"My squad?" Her thoughts moved sluggishly, her emotions equally slow to respond. "They weren't supposed to get involved."

"You know, it turns out if you ask people to help you, they're often willing to do it."

"But they had no leader."

"Viam," he said.

A cough rattled in her chest. "She's here?"

"She's around," he said. "Also the prince is here, but he promised not to screw up this time."

The prince. That triggered a reaction. A growl slipped through her teeth. "I want a word with him."

"I've had several already." He backed out into the corridor. "Come on."

Viam and Daliel waited outside the room, and the prince blanched upon seeing her. "You're alive."

"There's no need to sound so delighted," Yala said. "I'd say I'm sorry for putting a knife to your throat, but I'm not."

"Yala." Viam's objection lacked any force. "It's good to see you."

"Likewise." Yala coughed again. "I trust His Majesty has no intention of standing in our way?"

"No." Viam gave her a searching look, lingering on her hand and the greying fingers curled around her cane. "Are you all right?"

No. She wasn't. Her legs were like trembling stems, and the rattling in her chest worsened with each step. Her body was crumbling, corrupted from within, the bitter cost for failing Mekan's test.

I need to try again.

I need the Void. I can't live without it.

If Yala didn't go back to Mekan, and soon, she would die.

———

Saren had been mentally prepared to find Yala in a deteriorated state, but not like this. She looked ghastly, her skin grey and haggard, and her countenance showed the kind of grim resignation that he associated with missions in which she expected them all to die.

"King Tharen didn't take care of his prisoners," she muttered in explanation when he doubled back to wait for her to catch up. "Niema won't be in any fit state for battle either."

"Doesn't seem like she has a choice." He began walking again, with Viam and the prince slightly ahead of him. "I wish we could have helped, but the king had her personally chained to that monster of his."

Yala grunted. "So you came to let *me* out instead. Why?"

"Because you shouldn't have been locked up?" he said. "Because you're our captain? Take your pick."

"I'm not your captain," Yala retorted. "And there's nothing I can do if the army has already left the city, is there?"

"You're welcome." He dug his mud-stained heel irritably into the pristine carpet. "Did you know the Disciples of the Sea flooded the city as a diversion to help get you out?"

That got her attention. "What?"

"Well, it was also because they wanted to wipe out the traitors who betrayed their god," he amended. "Which have the bonus of leaving the Temple of the Flame unguarded. Not that they can do much with Mekan squatting inside their temple, but it's another blow against His Majesty, isn't it?"

"Against an army of the dead." Another rattling cough. "About as effective as a bloodfly facing off against a war drake."

"And we're the bloodflies now, are we?" What the hell was the matter with her? "You know, I reckon the army would happily follow your lead and turn on the king. They're loyal and willing to fight."

A soft snort escaped. "You expect me to galvanise everyone to march against him. Is that it?"

Saren frowned at her. "No. I realise none of this was in your plan, but you still want to kill the king, don't you?"

Yala coughed in answer, with a rattle that didn't sound healthy in the least. Was it just that she was weakened from her imprisonment or something more? Saren had seen her in worse states. Like when she'd had her throat cut, for instance.

"Your squad is waiting for you," he said. "So is your war drake."

Still, no reply came. Saren hadn't expected her to shower him in praise for his efforts—all right, maybe a small part of him had—but it would have been nice for her to show a little gratitude. He'd chosen to come back for her when he might have left the city with the deserters. Might have gone anywhere, hidden among the regular folk, and washed his hands of this war.

But he'd spent too many years mired in helplessness, believing that his actions would have no value or benefit at all, to run away any longer.

"Anyway." He slowed, seeing she'd fallen behind again. "I'll be around if you need me."

"I do." The voice was quiet enough that it hardly sounded like it belonged to Yala at all.

As he turned to her in surprise, someone else stepped out behind her. Or *something* human-shaped and covered in dark scales with claws in place of hands.

"Yala!"

At his warning, she pivoted, batting the claw aside with her cane. The monster recovered fast and went for Saren next. Its claws raked a fingerspan from his face as he stumbled over his feet, shouting a warning to the others.

Nalen came running into the corridor, lifting his short-sword. "What the hell is that?"

"Mekan's servant." Yala leaned on her cane, her face covered in a sheen of sweat. "I was starting to wonder if His Majesty left any security behind at all."

"I'd rather he hadn't." He had to admit it was a relief to see some of the fight come back into her eyes.

Saren lifted his dagger and tried to see if the monstrosity had any weak points to speak of. Its entire body was covered in thick, dark scales, but its pitted eyes were exposed, like a void drake's. He threw the weapon, but his dagger bounced off the hard scales covering its face.

As he dove to retrieve it, Nalen tackled the monster head-on. They crashed into the wall with a grunt of pain from Nalen but not so much as a gasp from the scaly beast that looked all the more monstrous for being so close to human. It shoved Nalen back with little effort and turned its pitted eyes onto Yala.

"What?" She glared back. "Let me guess, you're disappointed in me too."

The beast swiped at her, and she brought up her cane to sweep its claw away from her face. The action stole the little strength that kept her on her feet, and as she sank to her knees, Saren ran at the masked monster from behind.

The impact felt like tackling a tree, albeit one covered in spiky scales and equipped with claws worthy of a war drake. He landed flat on his back, looking up into the pitted depths of his eyes.

Saren saw his death reflected in plummeting darkness. The void swirled within, threatening to suck him into its midst. Mekan's voice rasped through the creature's throat. *"Come to me, Disciple."*

"Fuck that." He lunged upward, drove his dagger straight into one of those pitted eyes. The blade sank into shadow, and with one twist, the monster fell to the ground.

So did Yala.

———

Kelan flew to Skytower on the second morning after Setemar's liberation. It had taken some time to gain confirmation that the king did indeed plan to march south and that he'd declared open war on Yalet, the god of life.

"He's lost his mind," he said to his Superior when he conveyed the news. "Or rather, Mekan has taken over his mind and left nothing of him but an empty shell. The good news is that it's difficult for Superior Geren to dispute that his temple is unlikely to be the target."

"His concern is understandable, given his temple's previous occupation. He sent me a note earlier today saying as much." The Superior looked a lot better than she had a few days ago. She had colour back in her face, and her clothing was restored to its usual pristine state. Molin perched on top of a stack of papers on her desk.

"You heard from Superior Kralia too?" he asked.

"Briefly," she said. "It seems that Niema's companion has gone to rescue her."

Kelan's heart sank. "Hachim's gone to save Niema... alone?"

"So it would seem."

"That would explain why he didn't come back to Setemar." Kelan felt a twinge of guilt for not trying harder to convince Hachim to stay, but he shared her tendency towards self-sacrifice, and Kelan would have done the same had he been in Hachim's place. "Shit. I hope he's not going into the palace."

"You believe the king will bring Niema with the army?"

"Yes. Unfortunately." He'd been trying to avoid thinking of her trapped inside that palace, but he knew with certainty that she was alive, and she was suffering greatly. "There might be an opportunity to help her when the army reaches the ambush the Disciples of the Earth are setting."

"Yes. I'm glad to hear that Superior Geren has not dissuaded his Disciples from participating."

"He knows that they owe the Disciples of Life a debt," he said. "Not everyone will fight, but there'll be a sizeable number."

"And the Disciples of the Flame?"

"Uncommitted the last I heard, but since they're likely to be standing in the path of the army, too, they don't have a lot of options."

"That is true." A pause. "And you came here to ask if any of your fellow Disciples of the Sky are willing to help."

"It's that or wait for him to come here again, this time to finish us off." There was no point in underplaying the matter. "The Disciples of the Earth can slow down the foot soldiers, but they'll have a harder time with the flight division, and the Disciples of Life have scattered. They're no longer a unified force."

"I know." Her fingers drummed on the desk next to Superior Kralia's note. "It troubles me, but I believe you're right. I will let you make your proposal to the others, Kelan. We shall see how many you can convince."

All right, he thought, summoning all the charm he could muster. *Here's hoping I haven't lost my gift for spinning tall tales.*

46

The void drake's scales dug into Niema's legs. She fought to free herself from the chains binding her to its back, and the king let her, confident that her struggles would achieve nothing.

They'd long since left the capital behind, but she could already see the rest of the army marching ahead despite their half day's lead. She didn't notice anything awry until the void drake's flight path slowed so abruptly that she'd have been flung out of her seat if she hadn't been chained to its back.

The army had stalled, the soldiers spread across the road behind a winding trench that cut directly through their path and stranded them on the other side of a deep crevasse. Some were trying to climb over, while others had tried to take a shortcut through a nearby field. The latter had been similarly stymied, as a similar trench cut across the field as if some great beast had tunnelled beneath the surface.

Or someone has. Of course, blocking the road would have no effect on the soldiers in the air. The king swivelled in his seat and shouted at the masked riders on the other void drakes.

"Deal with this," he ordered. "Kill whoever is responsible."

The masked Disciples obeyed with their usual silent efficiency. As they descended over the wide trenches, a colossal wall reared up from nowhere, crashing into the void drakes with the force of a tidal wave. Niema closed her eyes against the spray of dirt that swamped all four void drakes and drenched the beleaguered soldiers in a hail of soil.

"Keep going!" the king shouted. "That's an order."

Niema blinked to clear her vision and saw the void drakes descending on the trench again, their riders oblivious to the thick layer of dirt clinging to their scales. One soldier didn't move out of the way fast enough. A void drake's claw caught him in the side of the leg, causing him to trip and fall into the trench. Niema winced, not needing to hear the impact to know that he was dead.

"More." The king raised his voice in command. "Open the Void."

Horror coursed through Niema. "No… you can't…"

The gag around her mouth muffled her protests, and the king paid her no more attention than he did the unfortunate soldiers below. Two more fell in a snap of teeth, and one of the masked soldiers leapt from their mount, driving their clawed hand into a soldier's spine.

A dark haze began to grow above the trench. Cold seared the inside of Niema's chest and brushed against her skin in cold tendrils. She didn't need to see the shadows coiling from the king's hands, a mirror of the dark crack splitting open below.

The Void had opened.

———

Hachim follow the coast to Dalathar. The Disciples of the Sea had left the water, but he'd declined to accompany them to the docks. A lone war drake would draw too much attention, so he'd timed his arrival in the city to coincide with the flight division's departure, thanks to information provided by Nalen's allies.

With Bitra at his side, at least he wasn't alone, but the worry fluttering in his chest became more pronounced the closer the city loomed. The cloudless day afforded him a clear view of the skies surrounding Dalathar, and he slowed his flight near the city's boundary to watch for the flight division departing. The king would be in the lead, together with the other void drakes, and if Niema wasn't inside the palace, she'd be with him.

A winged outline caught his eye then another. He picked up speed again, counting four, five dark blots high above the city, heading south.

As Hachim and Bitra drew closer, he spied a larger pack of winged beasts rising above Dalathar's centre. The flight division ascended in groups of ten and fifteen, angling southward after their leader. When the last departed, Hachim whistled to his steed to fly south, skirting the city's eastern edge.

"We'll be spotted," Bitra hissed at him. "They'll know we're not with the army."

"We can overtake them." Their close formation hindered their speed, and one war drake kept flying back to check everyone was keeping up. Their commander, perhaps. The king and his beastly companions would be far ahead of the rest.

As they left the city behind, he became aware that the fliers had slowed, their formation breaking apart in confusion.

"Hachim!" Bitra dropped in height, veering away from the spear someone had thrown in their direction.

A squad peeled away from the rest, their war drakes circling the pair of them.

"Who might you be?" asked a hard-faced woman who reminded him a little of Yala. "You're Disciples of Life."

"We're not here for you." Hachim tensed as she pulled out a weapon, not a spear or sword but a curved claw that could have only had one origin.

"Doesn't matter," she said. "My orders say that I'm supposed to cut you down, but I'd like to know *why* you're sneaking up on us from behind before I do that."

"We're here to save a friend."

Her brows lifted. "Yala? I thought she was dead."

"No, not Yala." Had they known one another? Her tone implied mild dislike but not outright malice.

"The other one." Her mouth twisted in a scowl. "There's no point in trying. The king has her chained to that monster of his."

Hachim's heart plummeted. "I still need to find her."

Did she know Yala? She must have if she was a captain, and he'd almost picked up on a hint of respect when she'd spoken Yala's name.

He weighed the odds—and the number of spears levelled at him and Bitra—and then asked, "*Is* Yala dead? Did the king leave her behind?"

"I don't have to answer your questions." She lifted the sharp claw. "Give me one good reason not to skewer you."

"This isn't what you joined the army to do." He was rewarded with an eye-roll on her part. "And you know the king is leading you all to your deaths. Killing us won't change that."

"I guess not." She watched him for a moment, and then she sheathed the claw at her belt. "Go and be a hero, then. Try not to make me regret helping you."

His heart pounded as they turned away, one of the other fliers saying, "Lisek, what are you doing?"

"Shut the hell up," was her response. "Those two are harmless. Now, come on. We have an army to catch up to."

The army hadn't gone far, though the fliers had begun to move again, following a road that appeared a lot bumpier than it should have. The route ahead was marred by trenches and walls of soil that had sprung up from nowhere. The flight division had scattered, and the void drakes stood out as dark blots diving at the earth-strewn fields.

One flew above the rest, two figures seated upon its back. Fear gripped his chest like a vice as his eyes locked with Niema's, seated in front of the king, her mouth covered with a gag and her hands cuffed to the void drake's back.

"Niema!" The hoarse cry escaped before he could stop himself.

The king saw him. He pointed, directing one of the void drakes to rise from the trench and fly at him with its claws and teeth outstretched, ready for the kill.

Bitra screamed. Hachim twisted to her, shouted, "Fly! Save yourself!"

Then, the monster was on him.

———

Viam was almost at the door when Saren came into view, supporting Yala on one side. Her forehead was slick with sweat, her eyes half closed, her feet stumbling at each step.

"She says she's dying," Saren said. "She wants to go back there."

"To the temple?" Viam's mouth went dry. "What did the king do to you?"

"I did it to myself." Yala opened her eyes and, with what seemed like a great effort, lifted her arm to expose her hand.

Her skin had turned greyish, her fingernails peeling off, and Viam was willing to bet that her clothing concealed worse. "I'm infected with Corruption. If I don't complete the transformation, I'm going to die."

"The transformation?" Viam gasped. "But doesn't that mean turning into one of—them?"

"Ideally not," she said. "But I'm already dying, and Mekan is the only one who can save me. That's the truth."

Daliel made a choked noise. "I—"

"Don't you start," Saren snapped. "I'm surprised you haven't become Mekan's servant too, but that's probably first on His Majesty's agenda when he's back from destroying all the god of life's representatives on this continent."

The prince's mouth hung open. Viam might have offered an apology on Saren's behalf if not for her worry for her captain. She took Yala's other arm and helped her upright, alarmed at how fragile her squad leader seemed, as if she might shatter at a touch.

"Was this always your plan?" Viam asked. "To go into the Void and ask Mekan to change you?"

"No, but since when have any of my recent plans worked out?" She coughed, gave a wry smile. "I told you I'm not capable of miracles. My squad should know that too. Keep them alive. That's my last order for the two of you. Understand?"

"Yes, Captain." Saren's voice was free of sarcasm. "It's not the last order. We won't let it be."

They reached the courtyard's entrance, and Viam and Saren helped Yala cross the threshold. There, she leaned on her cane and pulled herself free from their grip, taking stumbling steps forward. The message was clear. She had to do this alone.

As Viam watched, Daliel moved to her side. "Viam, I'm sorry."

She swallowed, her eyes burning. "So am I."

"It's too late for apologies." Saren glared at the prince. "If not for you, this wouldn't be happening."

"I want to fight my father," Daliel murmured.

"Do you?" Viam asked. "Because if you do, we're going to have to kill him. There's no other option."

His eyes glittered. "I know. I don't expect you to forgive me, but if there's anything I can do…"

"Get out of our way for a start," Saren cut in. "Otherwise, help us stop your father if he comes back."

Viam thought, considered what Yala might have said. With the soldiers left in the city now following Nalen's orders, it would be easy to maintain control in the capital, but the guards might be a source of trouble. "Daliel, if you want to help, you can order all the guards who remain in the city to obey your orders and not your father's. Then, set the Disciples of the Flame free. Tell them they're no longer under his orders."

The colour drained from the prince's face. "My father sent the Disciples of the Sea to guard the temple. They won't take orders from me."

"Oh, they won't be a problem." Saren gave a wicked smile. "They're preoccupied."

Daliel looked even more unsettled, but he gulped and nodded. "I can talk to the guards."

Whether they'd listen after his disastrous tenure as king was another matter, but he held more authority than anyone else while his father was absent. Someone had to give orders if not Yala.

Yala. Pain clamped around Viam's chest at the thought of her former captain entering the Void to plead for her life.

The lives of so many others might depend upon whether she survived her second visit to Mekan's domain with her mind and body intact.

Please, Yala, she thought. *Please survive.*

———

Yala entered the temple alone, taking slow, tortured steps. Her skin peeled off in grey flakes, her hands slipping on the cane. Soon, the flesh would give way to bone, and she'd crumble, the last of her awareness fleeing as Mekan welcomed her into His arms.

Her broken body responded to the Void's presence even in its current state of decay. The altar waited ahead, and the darkness beyond tugged at her chest like an invisible rope pulling her in.

Until she saw the second masked figure waiting, clawed hands raised to defend the temple.

I don't have time for this shit.

The masked monster came at her as strength rushed through her limbs. She straightened up and hit out with her cane, hard enough to make the creature stumble. Fingers grasped the dagger at her belt, pulled it free.

Dodging a swiping claw, she hurled the weapon point-first into one of its exposed eyes.

When the monster was down, she ran. Her leg screamed in protest, but energy flooding the rest of her body propelled her onward to the waiting dark.

"Mekan." She reached the altar, addressed the darkness. "I want to enter your realm. I'm back."

The temple disappeared. Once again, she found herself entombed in the realm of the god of death, disjointed from her physical senses save for the cold, the fear, and the fetid rot gnawing at her core.

Dark tendrils crept over her skin, soothing the pain, and her body responded, craving the reprieve.

Yala resisted. Given the chance, Mekan would replace her

skin with hard scales, turn flesh into armour, and meld her will with His until there was nothing left of herself. She couldn't allow that to happen.

A harsh whisper rose in her ear. *"I thought you would expire before you returned, Disciple."*

"Did you?" Yala murmured. "Too bad. We never got to complete our bargain."

"You will be mine, Disciple."

"I'm already yours." Her heart kicked against her ribs. "But I have someone I must kill. Someone whose life I must take with my own hands."

Surely, the god of death would understand. Mekan had only one drive, one interest, one goal. Death, Corruption, and the end of all who opposed Him. If that drive fell into alignment with Yala's, they might yet find common ground.

The whisper sliced her ear like the edge of a knife. *"He defied me. So do you."*

"He lied to you," she said. "He claimed that if he killed Yalet, he'd submit to you, but he never intended to do that. He'll defy you to his last breath."

"And then he will be mine."

"You're fine with waiting years? Decades?" She'd already given that argument and had ended with nothing but a decaying ruin of a body with a rapidly shrinking time limit on it. The king had thwarted her on every aspect... with one exception.

One card remained left to play, one that might ruin far more than her own life.

Aloud, she spoke the words that condemned her and so many others. "I have one advantage that Tharen does not. I'm bound to one of Yalet's followers myself."

"You lie."

The shadows slithered over her skin, passed through the surface to the rotting core beneath. Yala held her breath, grimacing at the cold prickling sensation creeping up her chest to her throat.

To the long-healed scar where Niema had healed her from Melian's fatal strike.

Biting pain searing her throat like she'd swallowed a live flame. The sensation spread down her chest, and the darkness muffled her cries as her body rocked and ached and burned with ice as hot as fire.

Then, it was gone. The darkness faded, the frigid air thawing, the numbness resolving into hard stone against her back and a familiar ache in her leg.

She opened her eyes, taking deep breaths that no longer rattled in her chest. Her body ached, but the sense of unbearable weakness had lifted too.

Sitting up, Yala reached for her cane with a hand that no longer resembled her own. Scales coated the skin, greyish black, extending up the wrist and disappearing beneath her sleeve. Her other hand was the same. She reached up to her face, huffing out a relieved breath when her scaled fingers scraped against the soft skin. The god of death hadn't claimed her yet.

Now, she thought, *to kill the king before Mekan figures out that I lied.*

———

The Disciples of the Earth had been busy. Kelan found their handiwork all over the route between Setemar and Dalathar in the form of towering walls of earth behind which Disciples of the Flame crouched, waiting to ambush them, deep trenches concealed beneath bushes, and other obstacles designed to make it nearly impossible for any army to traverse.

Of course, that didn't account for the flight division. That was his job, and that of the twenty or so Disciples of the Sky he'd rallied to accompany him. More than he'd expected, though Lakiel and Brikel were not among them.

In the distance, he could see a dusty cloud rising, blotting the sky, but it was too far off to make out who was winning that scuffle. He and the others had opted to wait for the army closer to Setemar, to ambush anyone who bypassed the Disciples' first layer of obstacles on the road. The cloud—or rather, a wave of solid earth—rose high enough that he suspected even a war drake would have trouble overtaking it, but the king's forces would doubtless grow wise to their trickery, and His Majesty himself wouldn't let anything like a few specks of dirt stand in his way.

Sure enough, within a few hours, they caught sight of the first winged beasts approaching the barricade where the Disciples of the Flame waited to ambush their unwary prey. Their disordered formation suggested that the Disciples of the Earth had had some luck in disrupting their forces despite being on the ground, and notably, he did not see the king among them.

He readied himself to attack, but the fliers did not follow the route to Setemar. Rather, they veered westward, over the fields and farms that stretched across Laria's west and north.

"Deserting, are they?" Kelan offered a smirk to Ranit, who hovered at his side. "No surprise. No promise of a medal of honour is worth dealing with this shit."

Ranit wasn't smiling. "What the fuck is that?" He pointed behind the fliers at what, at first glance, appeared to be a large storm cloud advancing at speed.

The mass of war drakes parted down the middle as the darkness closed in on them, and from within emerged beastly forms wielding sharp claws, leathery wings, razor-like teeth.

The soldiers began screaming.

"The king." Kelan looked around. "Where is he?"

"Coming this way." The voice came from below as Pehin emerged from the ground in a shower of dirt. She pulled a limp body out, and Kelan's mouth went dry when he recognised the features beneath the mud smearing his face.

"Hachim." He glided down, landed beside him. "Shit. Is he alive?"

"He *shouldn't* be, but those Disciples of Life are something else." She pushed a handful of dirt-strewn hair from her eyes. "Fool flew straight at one of the king's void drakes. Lucky I was there to catch him."

A green glow overlaid Hachim's skin, a sign of Yalet working Her magic. He coughed, spat out dirt. Opened his eyes.

"The king already opened the Void," he rasped. "He's heading for the forest."

"I don't see him." Unwise words. The soldiers' screams had petered out, but the monstrosities conjured by the Void had turned their attention upon the next target: the Disciples on the ground.

Dusty waves of soil rose as the Disciples of the Earth struck back, while a torrent of flame set three of them alight at once. The Disciples were more than a match for Mekan's lesser beasts, but in exposing themselves, they'd removed the element of surprise.

And the king was indeed coming towards them. Behind the rising clouds of dirt, Kelan spied a dark blot gaining speed and volume as it moved south. Within, he made out four or five winged beasts, each bearing a masked rider.

"It's them." Hachim tried to sit up, coughed, spat out more dirt. "Niema..."

"Stay down," Kelan warned. "Stay with the Disciples on the ground."

One jet-black steed overtook the rest, moving with speed

beyond any war drake he'd seen. Its wings were a blur, its head topped with a golden crown that drew Kelan's eye to the small figure chained to its back.

Niema, slumped over the void drake's head, her head lolling. *Is she hurt?*

Seated behind her was the king. He wore a crown to match his void drake's, his armour forged of jagged scales like his steed's armour, and rippling shadows coiled upward from the sword he held in one hand.

Anger rushed through his veins. Kelan drew his blade, weighing the odds of getting in a swipe before the king knocked him out of the sky. Not great, he admitted, given that armour.

"Kelan." Ranit sounded faint. "The plan?"

Right. He'd hashed out a few scenarios with the others while allowing for the fact that the chaos of battle would immediately scatter any detailed plan to the winds. "Down. Hit them from below."

He and the others descended behind the earthen wall the Disciples of the Earth had conjured in front of a deep trench. The intention was that any soldier who managed to breach the wall would immediately fall in, but it looked as though the king hadn't even pretended to give the foot soldiers any chance to catch up. He and his monstrous companions flew ahead, covering ground at a dizzying rate.

As they came at the earthen wall, Kelan called upon Terethik. His fellow Disciples raised their voices, too, and a gust of air rose, carrying the packed earth along with it.

The combined strength of both gods hit the void drakes with such force that even the king's steed veered into an uncontrolled dive. A blast of flame followed, vibrant white, and Kelan sent a gust of air to guide the Disciples' flames towards the attacking void drakes.

One caught fire, its wings igniting. An earsplitting

screech escaped, and its masked rider fell, toppling into the trench below.

Another flew at him, lifting its clawed hand. Air blasted from his palm, knocked the beast off balance. Kelan glided behind the masked figure and swung his blade. His first swipe bounced off its armoured skin, which was coated in the same dark scales as the beast it rode upon.

"I haven't seen you before," Kelan remarked, offering another swipe of his blade. The edge stuck in its scaled arm for a heartbeat before Kelan pulled it free, noting the thin trickle of dark blood staining the metal.

"Can you speak?" He ducked another spray of earth and fire from below. Several Disciples of the Flame had climbed out from their hiding place and stood on the earthen wall to better aim at their opponents. "Or does Mekan not permit that?"

The masked creature responded with a swipe that would have taken his head clean off if he hadn't darted out of range. He pivoted behind, aimed at its neck. The blade snagged, drawing blood. He tried again, and a stream of white fire caught the void drake from below. The beast let out a screech, its legs catching fire, flames licking at its lower body and rendering its rider powerless to escape.

"Now, you're just showing off," he called to Liran, who seemed to be the perpetrator. "Got a taste for destruction, have you?"

With the rider distracted, Kelan got in another swing, and this one sliced deep into the humanoid creature's throat, cut deep between scale and flesh. Blood bubbled to the surface, startlingly crimson. Human blood. Gods, had that creature once been a *Disciple?* Like Yala?

He looked again for the king, but the other void drakes were nowhere in sight. At least two had been killed, and he

EMMA L. ADAMS

spied the other Disciples of the Sky hacking at a third, which had no rider. No chains either. *Where is he?*

A hoarse shout drew him to the wall of earth. Hachim had climbed on top next to a bemused Liran, waving a hand to get Kelan's attention.

"Take me with you." Hachim held up his hands, insistent. "We need to catch up to him. To the king. I need to—"

"Get to Niema, I know." He lifted the Disciple into the air, his shoulder aching with the effort. "I can't see the king."

"He escaped," said one of the Disciples of the Flame. "Our flames… they didn't touch him."

Ah, shit. "I'll find him."

He and Hachim rose above the dispersing cloud of soil and flame, looking for their enemy. To the north, the sky was mostly clear save for a few bird-sized blots that might have been far-off war drakes. To the south…

Hachim gasped. "It's him."

A dark cloud swathed the area above the river south of Setemar, moving with unnatural speed. When Kelan squinted, he could see the monarch's great steed flying over the river.

Shadows swirled behind the king like a great pair of leathery wings, and from within that darkness poured the dead.

47

Niema's eyes flew open when the king gave her a shake. "Wake up. I need you conscious for this."

She groaned, her head pounding. Her mind sprang back to the last sight she'd seen before she'd passed out. The void splitting open. A monster, flying straight towards—

Hachim.

She reached out through their connection, and a gasp slipped from her mouth. He was alive. She could feel him, his heart beating alongside hers, but she no longer recognised the scene below. They'd left the maze of churned-up earth created by Setem's followers far behind, and when she turned her head, even Setemar's cliffs had faded into the distance. *How can that be?*

Near the city, a battle raged. Surges of earth struck like tidal waves, interspersed with blasts of white fire, while a group of individuals who must be Disciples of the Sky did battle with one of the other void drakes. Yet the king did not look back. Each beat of the void drake's wings covered more ground; her head spun with dizziness when she saw a village lurch past in a blink, leaving nothing but a blurred impression on her eyes and the stench of the dead lingering in her nostrils.

On the horizon, the forest's edge had appeared, a swathe of green that made her heart ache to see. Each beat of the void drake's wings brought them closer, closer to the place the king would see destroyed.

It had already started. A rotten scent swept towards them from a forest now more grey than green, with swathes of dead trees extending skeletal branches into the sky. Niema choked on bile behind her gag, her eyes burning with tears as they flew over the ruin that had once been her home.

"It won't be like this for long," the king said. "When we subdue Yalet, the destruction will cease."

Niema's insides pitched. "You can't destroy Yalet without ending life itself. You can't rule over the dead."

The gag muffled her voice, but her meaning must have gone through, because the king replied softly, "Can't I?"

They began their descent, following the river's curve, the void drake's wings casting a wide shadow over their surroundings. No landmarks painted the way to the Disciples of Life. The king, if he wanted to find them, would need help.

As if he'd sensed her thoughts, the king leaned forward and whispered in her ear. "I know your people are in hiding, and you are going to take me to them. Or else I will have you watch your beloved forest consumed piece by piece."

She fought, feet clanking against the chains, eyes watering from the rotting stench of the advancing decay.

Then grey became green, and verdant light shone from below, a beacon of hope and despair in the same instant. They'd reached the part of the forest that Mekan had yet to penetrate.

"It's your choice, Niema," the king said as they descended.

The world tilted sideways with a lurch. Niema grabbed the chain in front, but her hands were cuffed so securely that she barely moved a fingerspan as the void drake tipped onto its side and then righted itself.

Another jolt brought a volley of curses from the king; the chains scraped painfully against her back as he grabbed hold of them to keep his balance when the void drake tilted the other way. Niema fell against the chains, her head spinning with vertigo. The green glow intensified, drawing her gaze to the forest, to the green mass miraculously untouched by the dead.

A vine had risen to ensnare the void drake's clawed feet, thick as the chains that bound Niema. More vines ascended, beating at the dead creatures attempting to advance, and a patch of dead trees returned to life like a breath inhaled after a life of suffocation.

The forest. It's fighting back.

Trunks twisted, branches turning to spears and sharp thorns biting deep. As she watched, another void drake tumbled out of the sky, impaled through the neck and spine. A vine wrapped around its rider's throat, squeezing hard. The forest had turned brutally upon its invaders and defended itself with all the might of nature.

Once, the violence might have repulsed her, but now, she felt naught but relief. The dead were an abomination, an affront to Yalet's existence.

I'm an abomination too. The thought lodged in her mind, clung like a bloodfly feasting on an exposed limb. As someone marked by Mekan, Niema was a blight on the forest, and if she didn't get away from the king, he would use that grim fact to destroy the forest and its people.

Niema's hands and feet strained as she fought the bindings. A green glow shone from her own skin, a response to the presence of her god, but even Yalet couldn't shatter the chains binding her to the void drake's back. The material binding her mouth muffled her prayer as she pushed her hands against the cuffs, pleading with Yalet.

Set me free. Break the chains.

Or break me first.

Niema screamed as the bones in her thumbs snapped, twisted at unnatural angles. Her stomach churned with nausea, and her vision wavered as she forced her hands free, Yalet's healing power soothing the pain.

With a shout, the king reached for her hands, and she flung herself sideways, over the void drake's side.

Chains scraped her body, snagged her legs, held her upside-down. She wriggled, kicked, felt herself slip free.

Lightheaded relief washed over her as she fell down into the forest and into Yalet's open arms.

———

Saren watched Yala emerge from the temple: intact, upright, *alive*—yet undeniably changed. Scales cloaked her hands; greyish smoke coiled from her fingertips and wrapped around her cane. Her face, however, displayed all the stubborn will to live that he'd come to expect from his captain.

"Thank the gods," Saren breathed. "Fuck. What did you promise Mekan in return for sparing you?"

"Never mind that."

"I do mind, thank you."

His words went unheard; Viam pushed past him and hugged Yala, her shoulders trembling with sobs.

"You're alive." Viam let go, wiped her eyes on her sleeve. "It's good to see you, Yala."

"Likewise." Gods, she spoke so casually, as if nothing had changed. As if she hadn't gone into the fucking *Void*.

Fighting a shudder, Saren turned his back. "Can we get *out* of here now?"

Yala took a step forward and scowled, spying the prince lurking behind Saren. "You're still here?"

Daliel flinched. Saren smirked. "Yes, and he knows you'll get out that knife of yours again if he does anything we don't like."

"Saren!" Viam tutted. "Yala, he's going to help us. Let's go."

Saren led the way to the exit, stepping over the body of the masked creature he'd stabbed. He trod on its face for good measure, laughing to himself.

Outside the palace, Nalen's rebellion was in full swing. The back gates lay wide open while soldiers ran in and out of the barracks, seizing weapons with impunity and dealing beatings to any guard unlucky enough to get in their way.

The front gates were unguarded, too, and the sound of weapons clashing rang out from the square. Saren hoped Nanek and the other Disciples of the Sea hadn't caused too much damage, if only because it would be a lot harder for the prince to convince the guards to take their side if the Disciples of the Sea had killed more than their own kin during their revenge on the guards at the Temple of the Flame. To say nothing of the Rafragorians.

"I'm going to check on the temple," Saren told the others. "See what those Disciples are up to. Anyone with me?"

"Daliel?" Viam gave the prince a questioning look.

"I'll speak to them later," he said in tones that one might use if asked to recapture an escaped raptor. "I need to talk to the guards first."

"Tell them to stop beating on our people," Saren said. "This'll go a lot easier when we've established that we all want the same thing."

Do we, though? he couldn't help thinking. Ostensibly, everyone involved in the uprising wanted to oppose King

Tharen and his divine advisor, but they doubtless had very different ideas about how to go about establishing order in his place. That was someone else's problem, not his, and after being hemmed in the palace for weeks like a wild drake in a pen, being able to walk straight through the open gates into Ceremonial Square was a welcome improvement.

At the Temple of the Flame, several bodies lay on the temple's front steps. Nearby stood a bloodied but triumphant Nanek, his bone-knife now stained crimson.

"Nanek." He walked up to the temple stairs, sidestepping the twisted body of a Disciple of the Sea. "Any trouble?"

"No," he replied. "It is done. My people are avenged."

Fuck me, those Disciples are dramatic. Shaking his head, he climbed the stairs and reached for the temple's front door.

"What are you doing?" Nalen came jogging up the stairs behind him.

"Recruiting them, what else?" Saren pulled the door wide open on a group of Disciples who looked no more ready to fight a war than to sprout wings and fly. Half of them were hiding behind pillars or crouched under the stairs. Of course, he should have expected as much from the Disciples who'd been too cowardly to leave their temple during his last rescue attempt.

"Come on." Saren stepped into the entryway. "You could stand to crack a smile or two. We're here to set you free."

"We will not leave our temple," said an individual wearing an elaborate headdress who Saren identified as the Superior. "You will not condemn more of my people to certain death."

"The king is gone," Saren told him. "He's flying to declare war on Yalet as we speak."

"Then your endeavour is pointless," said the Superior. "When Yalet falls, the rest of us will follow, and it is not worth gambling our lives for a breath of freedom."

"Oh, for fuck's sake." Saren sighed. "Do you not understand? Mekan's guiding the king's actions so thoroughly that he probably doesn't even remember you exist."

"His city guards certainly do," said Superior Shralin. "And I might remind you that our deity remains beyond reach. We will not endanger our lives in your rebellion."

"You can't tell me not a single one of you knows how to fight," said Saren. "Weren't you trained in combat like the rest of us were?"

Compared to Superior Datriem, this man was about as threatening as a flowering plant. Saren had hated his predecessor with such passion that it was a surprise to find himself feeling more pity for the fool than anything else.

"The army has left the city," Nalen added from behind Saren. "Those of us who stayed behind are no threat to you, and the prince is convincing the guards to step aside as we speak. You won't face opposition if you choose to leave."

"Exactly," Saren said. "You can either cower in here and wait for death, or you can come outside and defend the deity you claim to have pledged your lives to."

"You understand nothing," said the Superior. "Without our temple, we are not Disciples."

"Why're you still wearing the uniform, then?" He looked for support among the others and saw that a fair few of the Disciples had apparently had enough of their leader's attitude problem too. Several had made a move towards the open door, unable to resist the taste of freedom. "Like I said, it's your choice."

"If you want to make amends with the Disciples of the Sea, there's one waiting outside," Nalen added. "I think he wants to come in."

"Correct," Nanek said from the doorstep. "I will not enter without permission, but it would be a pleasure to meet you, Superior."

Superior Shralin looked as if he'd thought of a great many words, none of which was in the vicinity of "pleasure."

"Go on," Saren said to him. "Make it a historical first and meet your counterpart without drawing a weapon. He can't use his powers in here, right?" He was pretty sure that was a rule, though there wasn't so much as a drop of water for a Disciple of the Sea to draw upon regardless.

"He cannot." The Superior's lips compressed. "Very well. You may enter."

Nanek came in, and Saren sidestepped him on the way out, raising a brow at Nalen. "Didn't see that one coming."

"Their people have an unpleasant history," said Nalen. "I bet Nanek wants to make amends while he can."

"Before Mekan kills us, I know." He shook his head. "And where are the Rafragorians?"

The burly soldier scowled. "Nanek claims they left the city as soon as it became obvious we had the upper hand. He said they're waiting at the docks, but I don't trust those fuckers."

Neither did Saren, but he had trouble conjuring any real hatred for the Rafragorians when too many others deserved his ire.

"Forget them. Let's go and see if the prince needs help shaking some sense into the city guards."

———

Yala walked away from the palace, each step bringing a jolt of pain to her leg. Mekan might have healed her rotting body, but the bruises from the fight in the temple and the pain of her old wound had not faded. She savoured every twinge and ache as proof that Mekan hadn't claimed her yet.

Though from the terror on Daliel's face, He might as well have. Likely the prince didn't trust her not to put a knife to his throat again. She had no intention of doing so... provided he behaved.

"Are you sure it's a good idea, freeing the Disciples of the Flame?" she heard him ask Viam. "We don't know how many might be loyal to my father."

"They have no access to their god," said Viam. "They can't cause any harm."

"Seems like there's little point in setting them free, then," Yala muttered, but their circumstances seemed a lot less like a lost cause now that her body was no longer falling apart with each step.

Regardless, her fate was postponed, not averted. At some point in the near future, she'd have to answer for the lies she'd told to win Mekan's favour. The knowledge that she'd betrayed Niema so deeply weighed in her chest like the rot that had once eaten away at her body and will.

Whatever ended up happening to her, Yala would not let Niema share that fate.

"Your squad is waiting in the paddock," Viam said to her. "If you want to fly."

"I do." She'd guessed, then, that Yala's priority would be pursuing the king. "And you?"

"I'm more use here." She looked guiltily at the prince. "Daliel needs my help, and we need to ensure the city is secure in case the king's forces come back."

"Then, I suppose this is goodbye." For what might be the final time. As she'd learned long ago, it was impossible to know except in hindsight if a goodbye would end up being the last.

Yala's squad waited outside the paddock. Upon seeing her, all six of them exclaimed in relief and joy. Roven and Yurel actually hugged each other, and Yala was alarmed to feel the sting of tears prickle her eyes. *Gods.*

EMMA L. ADAMS

"I don't know what Viam said to convince you to stay, but thank you."

"You're our leader," said Gorel. "We couldn't betray you."

The simple words went straight to her treacherous heart. "I need you to stay here and help Saren and Viam. Help the prince."

"You're going after the flight division, aren't you?" said Roven. "We're coming with you."

Yala shook her head. "I can't ask that of you."

"You don't have to ask." Yurel opened the paddock gate, where their war drakes were saddled and ready for battle. "We've already made up our minds."

"All of you?" She took them in, saw her own determination reflected in six pairs of eyes. "Then let's go."

She approached her war drake and climbed onto its back, wondering how far she would have to fly to catch up to the king. If she had to guess, he and the flight division would have left the foot soldiers in the dust, but there was no telling how many other advantages Mekan might have bestowed on him to quicken the journey to the forest.

When everyone was seated on their war drakes, she commanded them to fly.

She squeezed her knees around the war drake's neck as they rose into the sky above the palace grounds and the square. She spied Saren near the gates, and when he saw her, Saren lifted a hand in a salute usually reserved to bid farewell to soldiers flying into battle from which they might never return.

Yala returned the gesture and then turned south, away from the city she'd called home for a time. She might have spent longer in Dalathar, but Yala's true home had always been here, in the sky, with the wind in her hair and a war drake ready to fight at her command.

Yala flew towards the world beyond Dalathar's walls and

the battleground where Yalet would wage war with Mekan and only one victor would emerge intact.

———

Kelan and Hachim flew over the forest as the trees came back to life to fight the dead. Rotting branches became fresh boughs, and vines lashed at the two surviving void drakes. One had no rider, while the other wore a golden crown. *There he is.*

Hachim gasped. "She's not there."

"Niema?" Kelan looked more closely at the void drake. Chains dangled from its back in front of the king, but Niema herself was nowhere to be seen.

"Put me down." Hachim squirmed in his arms. "I have to find her."

"I don't think the forest is open to outsiders." Kelan dodged a stray vine as he descended, trying to see through the thick canopy. Healing abilities aside, Kelan was less than enthused at the idea of dropping Hachim into a net of hostile trees baring sharp branches at anyone who flew near them.

"I can sense her," Hachim insisted. "Let me go."

Hachim whistled, and the web of branches parted, allowing Kelan to descend to a spot where Hachim could climb down into a tree. As little as he wanted to leave him and Niema to the king's mercy, even the monarch would have trouble finding two small humans in the chaotic snarl of greenery.

Kelan hastily ducked below the tree line when a dangling chain brushed his cloak. The king had managed to free his steed from the vines and now flew higher, out of the forest's reach. His voice echoed, drifting over the trees. "You can't hide from me, Disciple."

Can't I? Kelan knew full well he was addressing Niema,

not him, and it would have been comical that the king seemed to believe someone on the forest floor could hear him all the way up there... if not for the echo that caught his words and amplified them, turned them to a cold whisper that froze the marrow in Kelan's bones.

Fighting the fear, he flew higher, but any hopes of sneaking up on the king vanished when he saw the same dark cloud shadowed the monarch's path, as though he carried the Void itself upon his shoulders. As Mekan's beasts began to pour out of the darkness again, the king held out his arms as if to embrace the new world of Corruption he'd unleashed.

A swathe of darkness rose from his palms and surged over the treetops. Vines withered, newly regrown branches died, and green turned to grey once more.

The true invasion of the forest had begun.

48

Niema landed in a web of vines that caught her, slowed her fall. Soothing light caressed her limbs, healing the broken bones, and the vines lifted her gently down into a bed of soft greenery. Branches curved overhead, forming a shield between her and the world above.

"Yalet," she breathed against the gag around her mouth. With her newly healed hands, she pulled the material free, shuddering with relief. "Thank you, Yalet."

"Niema!" Hachim came running, clambering over fallen branches and vines, and reached for her hand. "You're alive. I thought—"

She took his hand, wrapped her arms around him. "I'm alive."

They ran through the miracle Yalet had created. Trees once felled bloomed with new life, and fresh energy coursed through her body as the sheer relief at being back in Yalet's domain bolstered her, banished the lingering chill left from her time as the king's captive.

When a dark shape passed overhead, casting a cold shadow over the trees, she slowed.

"I can't stay in the forest," she gasped between puffs of air. "It's too dangerous."

"If you expose yourself, the king will find you." He tugged at her hand, and she reluctantly picked up speed again. "We can't let him."

"I know." She swallowed around a lump in her throat. "I didn't tell him anything, I promise."

His breath hitched. "I know."

They continued to run, swerving between the tall trees. The shadow persisted, giving her the sense of being pursued like an animal fleeing a predator. Yet at Hachim's side, she felt stronger, their bond restored now that they were both back where they belonged.

No matter what kind of bond she shared with Mekan, she was Yalet's hand and had always been Her devoted follower. As they ran, Niema marvelled at the sight of the trees rising to strike at their attackers, to repel the wave of claws and teeth.

"Who is doing that?" she asked.

"I'm not sure," Hachim admitted. "It's like a whole group of Disciples of Life putting their collective faith together to repel Mekan's forces."

"Or the Superior." Where was she? The forest was unrecognisable in its current state, and she hadn't the faintest idea which way the enclave lay or even if the Superior was there at all. "Gods. I can't go back."

The king was somewhere above, and he would not stop until he found her. She could never lead him to the enclave.

"It'll be all right." He squeezed her hand again. "Yalet is with us."

Not just Yalet. Fear locked around her chest when she glimpsed the dark cloud above, as if the Void itself hovered above the forest, searching for her.

"It's not going away," she murmured. "I don't know how he's doing that, but he must have bargained with Mekan. Perhaps when he opened the Void on the road near the capital."

"I saw that too." Hachim clambered over a fallen trunk. "Oh, gods. I left Bitra there."

"Bitra?" she asked. "She was with you?"

"She came with me to find you." His expression was distraught. "I lost sight of her when I saw the king—and you."

"I hope she escaped." If she had to guess, Bitra would have tried to dissuade him from his foolish rescue attempt, and she'd have been right to.

"I told her to warn the Superior," Hachim said. "We were outnumbered by those monsters. The ones who look almost human."

"They *were* humans. Once." A shudder travelled through her body and through their bond, too, a bone-deep disgust at such an affront to Yalet's nature. "They're what Disciples of Death turn into if they're particularly favoured by Mekan."

"That's horrible," he choked. "Who would choose that fate?"

"People willing to take the risk to win Mekan's favour," she said. "Or people who had no choice."

Like Yala. Niema might never know which fate had claimed her, but she knew Yala would have chosen death over becoming Mekan's servant in this world, a weapon to be wielded against His enemies.

"Not the king," Hachim said after a short pause. "He didn't change. Why?"

"I don't know." She hunched her shoulders. "He still has his own mind, but he's being heavily influenced by the god of death's wishes. He just thinks he isn't."

For that reason alone, Yalet's own command dictated that

he had to die. Yala, too, had told Niema to perform the act if she was incapable of it, and with her gone...

A sharp pain seized her chest, piercing cold and centred on the area where the void drake's claw had stabbed her. Hachim released her arm as if her skin burned to the touch. "Did you feel that?"

She gasped, the pain lifting as swiftly as it had arrived, but the cold lingered together with a foul stench that made her gag. All around, the green glow dimmed like a cloud had passed over the sun, blocking any light.

The wave of shadow rippled throughout the forest, creeping into every crevice and infecting the air with the smell of rot. The newly formed vines crumbled. Trees decayed, branches shrivelled, and leaves fell as desiccated fragments. Niema held onto Hachim tight, horror coursing through her as she watched the forest fall apart around them.

"No." Her voice rose to a scream. "No!"

"No." Hachim's disbelief and horror collided with hers, made her stagger as a wave of weakness washed over her. "What has he done?"

"I don't—" Niema staggered again, hit not by weakness but by strength, a rush of energy akin to when she'd drawn upon Mekan's power. The pain disappeared altogether, but Hachim fell to his knees, his weakness reverberating back to her even as her own strength grew. Around him lingered a layer of shadow, the same dark haze that now permeated the forest.

"Niema." His head hit the ground, wide eyes fixating on Niema's hands. "Gods."

Thick shadows circled her too, but they weren't draining her as they were Hachim. She shuddered, trying to push them away. It's Mekan. I can't make it stop."

"Then run," he croaked. "You're strong enough to run."

"I'm not leaving you." Her heart pulsed with his pain, and

she clung onto that pain, ignored the invigorating energy coursing through her veins. Losing him would tear her apart. "Take my life force."

Green light sprang to her palms, pulsing into him. He protested feebly, lifting a hand to push her away. She seized the chance to push more of her life force into him until the strength returned to his limbs and he was able to let her pull him to his feet.

"I'll keep you alive," she said. "I promise."

Hachim leaned on her as they continued to walk around fallen branches and rotting trunks, through shadows thick as fog. How far did the devastation spread? Had it reached the enclave? She couldn't see an end to it, not from here.

A faint green glow caught her eye. They came to an opening amid the decay that had once been a clearing, now overgrown with greenery that rotted even as it grew, stems sprouting and then dying, flowers blooming only to wither.

Bodies lay beneath. Disciples, perhaps those who'd given the forest their strength to fight off Mekan. All were reduced to skeletons as their flesh rotted as swiftly as the surrounding forest, yet the faint green pulse of life tried to deliver their remains to Yalet's hands.

Hachim sank to his knees again. "They're dead."

"Not the Superior." She forced herself to look at the bodies, to seek any traces of familiarity on their rotting features.

"No," he murmured. "She'll be with the enclave."

Niema spoke a prayer to Yalet, reaching for the pulsing life she knew lurked beneath the outward decay. The green light brightened, only to be extinguished by a shadow cast from above.

Through the gap in the canopy, she glimpsed the king's monsters descending, drawn to the sole patch of life amid the death and decay. She whispered a prayer to Yalet, but the god of life was silent.

"There will be no help for you, Disciple," Mekan whispered, *"except from me."*

————

Hachim flung himself flat as the king's beasts descended. Claws tore, seeking exposed flesh, and teeth snapped viciously at his heels.

Niema let out a shrill whistle that sent their attackers into an instant retreat, but the darkness lingered despite the faint glow around the bodies of the fallen Disciples.

We need a stronger Disciple. We need the Superior. The two of them alone couldn't hold back the god of death's advancement through the forest.

"You have to find the others," Niema said as if a similar thought had occurred to her. "Without me."

"No." He sensed her pain through their bond, but with it came a strange calmness, as if she'd accepted the inevitable.

She whistled again. Branches rustled as a void drake descended, this time not baring its teeth or exposing its claws. Rather, its reptilian head bowed as it landed, its spine flattening as if to let her climb onto its back.

"I wish I could take you there." Tears glistened on Niema's cheeks. "I wish…"

"Don't." Her plea drew tears to his own eyes; he drew her into his arms, held her tight. "You're worth more than any mark Mekan might have left on you. Yalet will prevail."

He had to believe those words, had to believe that their true god would triumph over the one whose shadows followed Niema herself, clung to her back like a spectral presence. No wonder the dead were drawn to her. While the thought sickened him to admit, he knew in the shards of his breaking heart that the enclave would not survive if she set foot inside its borders as she was now.

Niema tore herself from his embrace and clambered onto the void drake's back. Her knees settled into place on either side of its head. One beat of its leathery wings carried her up, above the canopy, taking half of Hachim's heart with her.

He wrenched his gaze away, turned instead to the bodies entombed within their forested home. The faint green glow bolstered him, gave him strength enough to continue, in search of the last people who might heal the wounds Mekan had inflicted.

───────

Yala's squad departed with a sweep of wings, the breeze lifting Viam's hair and bringing the sting of tears to her eyes. Across the square, she caught Saren's eye, and they exchanged a look of understanding. No hostility existed between them now. Its last remnants had burned away, as if scourged by Dalathik's fire.

Speaking of the Disciples of the Flame. Two had gained the confidence to approach the palace gates, near which the prince stood conversing with a small group of guards.

"I know you have good reason not to trust them," he was saying, "but my father's imprisonment of the Disciples of the Flame was unjust and cruel, and it is not something I can condone."

"And when he comes back?" One of the guards waved a hand at the Temple of the Flame. "What's he going to do when he sees those traitors walking free?"

Viam stepped in. "The king isn't himself. He's following the will of the god of death."

The guard snorted. "I'll not deny that temple of his is no

natural creation, but the man is human, no matter how many arcane gifts he might possess. He's also our king."

"Does that make him right?" Saren asked. "He could call you a traitor tomorrow if he wanted. He's killed enough of you on that altar of his."

"Yes, and I'd rather not be one of them," he said. "He'll execute the lot of us if the palace is in this state when he returns."

"And if he doesn't?" Daliel asked. "Didn't you once answer to me, not so long ago? In my father's stead, I am the higher authority."

Viam was taken aback at his assertive tone, but the guards didn't blink. Of course, they'd been taking orders from the prince instead of his father until a few weeks ago and would be accustomed to deferring to him.

Viam turned to Saren. "Did you speak to Superior Shralin? Is he still in the temple?"

"He refuses to leave." Saren rolled his eyes. "His temple is corrupted. You'd think that'd be an incentive to get the hell out."

"A Superior cannot so easily leave their domain." Nanek came over, holding a carved bone-knife dripping in blood. "Not without forfeiting the right to their title and risking punishment from their deity."

"Is Dalathik even capable of inflicting punishment on anyone with the temple in that state?" An image entered Viam's mind of a candle igniting in a Disciple's hands and devouring him alive. "If the Disciples aren't able to access their connection to the god of the flame until they're far away from Mekan, the same should apply to the Superior."

"No." Nanek's mouth flattened into a grim line. "The Superior is bound to the temple. They can restore its strength, if they offer a sufficient tribute to please their deity."

"He's been able to set the temple free from Mekan all along?" Saren made a soft disbelieving noise. "That's what you're implying?"

"What tribute?" Viam's thoughts turned again to the candle, to the white fire burning out as the last Disciple died at Mekan's altar. "Their life?"

"It is the greatest honour," Nanek said. "No temple can be created or revived without sacrifice. It is my intention to perform such a tribute for my own temple when I return home."

"Shit." Saren gaped at him. "You're going to die? And you're fine with that?"

"I would gladly offer my life to rid my temple of Mekan's taint and to set my fellow Disciples free," he said. "Superior Shralin, I suspect, will need to make a similar choice."

"Oh, that prick would never sacrifice himself," Saren said. "He surrendered to Mekan to save his skin."

"To save his people," Nanek corrected. "He may yet change his mind."

"Well, shit," said Saren. "Either he lets his temple be eternally infected by Mekan or he sets himself on fire as tribute to his god? Hell of a choice."

"I suppose most Superiors don't usually have to make that choice." The implications were staggering. "Since it's so rare for a temple to fall to Mekan."

This couldn't be common knowledge. In fact, it wouldn't have surprised Viam if this was a secret typically held for Disciples alone, and if she'd had the luxury of indulging her scholarly interest, she might have asked more questions.

"And *that* temple?" Saren pointed at the palace. "Those guards had a point. What if the king *does* come back? Or—gods, what if someone else gets ideas?"

"Like Melian did?" Viam said. "You're right. She and her Successors took orders from the king, but they fed on the public's dissatisfaction with his son when they recruited allies. We need to stop the cycle outright."

"We can start by destroying that temple." Saren took a decisive step through the gates, tilting his head up to the palace. "Oh, *shit*."

The sky above the palace had darkened as though a storm was about to break over its roof alone. A rumble came from within, accompanied by a shuddering tremor that conjured a memory of the island, of the ground tearing itself apart as if the very earth had split to its core.

When a dark, winged shape rose above the palace roof, Viam's blood iced over. "The temple."

The king had no intention of losing his grip on the capital while he was absent.

————

Kelan watched the tree line, reluctant to leave Hachim and Niema to be hunted like animals. Even when he flew right out into the open, the king paid him no more attention than he might an overly persistent tree-raptor, which Kelan found rather insulting. *Maybe those shadows are impeding his vision.*

He was certainly going *somewhere*, though, and with purpose. Behind him trailed Mekan's beasts, clawed monstrosities that dove at the forest with the enthusiasm of carrion birds feasting on a corpse. Kelan pursued at a distance and slowed his pace when another dark blot rose from within the trees, resolving itself into the highly improbable sight of Niema seated on a void drake's back.

"Niema?" He flew to meet her, wary of those sharp claws. "What are you doing? Hachim was looking for you."

"I can't stay with him." Her voice cracked.

"So you're going after the person who you recently escaped from?" Flying on a void drake? "I'm not sure I've ever met someone so prone to foolish and self-destructive activities in my life."

"What else am I supposed to do?" She shifted on the void drake's back, her expression mingling revulsion and despair. "My bond with Mekan is stronger than it ever was. Just by being here, I help Him invade and destroy my home. I—healed myself using the *Void*, Kelan. There's no returning from that."

Kelan's mouth parted in surprise. *She healed using the Void?* "That doesn't mean you need to make the king's job easier. And you know, you could always turn that power against the king."

"And kill him." Her expression was as bleak as the Void itself. "Kelan, think. What use would that be? Mekan would still win. This is all His scheme, not King Tharen's."

"I think it would matter to all the people he and his army are killing." Though she'd raised a good point. If the king meant as little to Mekan as any of His followers, the god of death would simply find another mouthpiece to take his place. The war with Yalet would continue to its inevitable end. "If you're going after him for the sake of sacrificing your own life, I'm afraid I can't let you do that."

Kelan cast a glance over the forest. The darkness continued to advance without ceasing, leaving no tree or plant untouched. Kelan couldn't see Hachim below the rotting canopy, but he might well be the only living thing left in there.

"I abandoned him." Niema followed Kelan's line of sight. "Hachim. I didn't have a choice. The dead were drawn to us because of me."

"And he's more likely to survive alone in there?"

"He'll find our Superior." Her eyes glistened. "She's the only one who might be able to defend the forest from—that."

"And where is she?" At a guess, she'd be at the enclave,

protecting her surviving allies. "Gods, how is he moving so fast?"

"Mekan." Niema turned north, then her void drake's head swung around so abruptly that if not for her remarkable control over her steed, he might have lost a limb.

Shuddering at the close call, he asked, "What is it?"

"That…" She pointed with a trembling hand. "That's not coming from the forest."

On the other side of the mass of thickening shadow, a glow gilded the horizon, tinted green like the life that had once imbued the forest. *Is that the Disciples of Life?*

Niema launched into flight, her void drake's wings sending billowing gusts of air that knocked him off-balance. Recovering, he flew alongside her, his eyes fixed on the line of gilded green. He couldn't see any individual figures among them, but while distance impeded his vision, he could make out the king's golden crown amid the shadows as he flew to meet the oncoming glow.

———

Yala and her squad flew south of the capital, cutting across fields and farms and passing over villages and towns scoured to ruin by Mekan. The destruction was rampant, entire communities rendered to empty shells, abandoned and piled with rotting bodies.

The main road between Dalathar and Setemar was all but impassable courtesy of an impressive expanse of churned-up earth. Bodies were strewn over the mud, mostly soldiers, though some wore the robes of Disciples of the Earth.

"Impressive," she murmured. The sheer scale of the destruction suggested that they'd fought the flight division all the way down the road to Setemar, crossing a distance that would otherwise have taken days in a matter of hours or minutes.

She flew lower to check if anyone was still alive. A twitching limb caught her eye, but its owner was missing her head, and her hands swung blindly at the air. *Mekan's been here, has He?*

In fact, those wounds had not been inflicted by human weapons alone. Some of the soldiers' bodies bore the marks of sharp teeth ripping off limbs and tearing open chests to expose glistening organs. The king's void drakes had spared nobody, and amid the spread of human bodies lay those of scaled beasts too.

"Captain?" Yurel called to her. "Should we keep going?"

"Yes." Yala dragged her gaze from the dead. "The flight division will be somewhere ahead of us."

They might well have already reached Setemar, depending on the extent of the obstacles they'd faced. From there, accessing the forest would take a matter of hours at most. Despite the trail of destruction Mekan's creatures had left in their path, the Void itself was silent, and no traces of its presence nudged at Yala's awareness. Mekan had been present here but was no more. They'd arrived too late.

They'd be more likely to catch up to the foot soldiers first, the ones who'd survived the Disciples' ambush, but the carnage below seemed endless, torn-up roads bordered by fields and farms in an equally brutalised state. It was hard to say how much of the destruction had been wrought by the army and how much had already been destroyed by Mekan's assault on Laria's people.

Any soldiers who still follow him after this deserve naught but death.

"Captain!" shouted Gorel. "Below!"

A visible tremor ran through the churned-up earth, and then, a robed figure emerged in an explosion of soil.

Shielding her face with both hands, she dodged the earthen spray and caught sight of a second Disciple of the Earth rising to join the first, taking aim at her.

"Stop that!" she shouted at them. "I'm on your side."

"Yala *Palathar?*" shouted one of the Disciples, who was covered in so much dirt and blood that it took a moment for Yala to recognise her face.

"Pehin, right?" Yala called back. "What the hell is happening?"

"What else? We're losing." She spat out a mouthful of earth. "The king and his dead army are destroying the forest as we speak."

Her heart gave an unpleasant jolt. "The Disciples of Life won't let that happen."

"I don't see them defending their home." She pointed up at the sky to a mass of dark clouds gathering on the horizon.

Not clouds. The forest was hours away even if she pushed her war drake to its limits, and the king hadn't had *that* much of a head start.

"I wouldn't fly too close," Pehin added. "I think the Disciples of Life and Death are doing battle in there, and it's obvious who's winning."

Niema. Shit. "Then I'll have to even the odds."

How had the king moved that fast? Had Mekan gifted him with some unnatural way to travel at far beyond a human speed? She wouldn't have put anything past either of them at this point. From here, the darkness ahead might have been mistaken for a distant storm, but soon, she came upon the first remnants of the king's surviving foot soldiers. They'd split into a disorganised shambles of pairs and groups trying to navigate their way around the various obstacles on the road, often running up against walls or disappearing into sudden holes. They were such a miserable lot that Yala hadn't the heart to do more than pity them as they flew.

It wasn't until the cliffs of Setemar appeared that Yala spied the first war drakes. Their formation was as chaotic as the foot soldiers', with some having left the road altogether and others doing battle with robed figures in mid-air. Disciples of the Sky.

She was too far away to see if Kelan was among them, but if she flew any closer, they'd take her for the enemy.

Or will they? Yala swivelled in her seat and addressed her squad. "Go and help the Disciples of the Sky fight off those soldiers. Better, see if you can convince some of them to quit or switch sides. I'm sure it's on some of their minds."

Gorel made a noise of protest. "What will you do?"

"I'm going after the king. Don't follow me."

She wasn't surprised when nobody listened to her. All six stayed in formation as they flew past Setemar's cliffs and dodged the scattered remains of the king's flight division. No squads were intact, and instead, lone fliers grappled with Disciples of the Sky or dove at Disciples of the Earth when their heads emerged from the ground. She even glimpsed a few blazing-white flashes that might have belonged to Disciples of the Flame, but she didn't allow herself to look back. She'd long since lost track of how long they'd spent in the air, but it would take several hours more to reach the forest, and the dark cloud showed no signs of slowing down.

"I meant it," she told the squad when they flew over a village consisting entirely of piled-up corpses. "I don't know how the king is doing that, but I doubt anyone other than a Disciple of Death can get near him."

Or a Disciple of Life. As the shadow over the forest became distinct, a faint glow caught her eye somewhere beyond. The horizon shimmered with the vibrant golden-green haze she associated with Niema's fellow Disciples.

For the second time, her squad ignored her orders and continued to fly. While the shadow continued to expand, so

539

too did the light gilding the horizon until Yala had little doubt that the shadow—the king—was in retreat. The sheer speed at which the light spread overcame the dark suggested the Disciples of Life must be flying towards the enemy, driving him back.

Yala kept both eyes on the light as they flew onward, with the result that she saw the exact moment the glow went out and the darkness returned in a wide sweep as the Void cracked wide open.

49

Niema flew, keeping one eye on the horizon's brightening glow and the other on the darker blot that comprised the king's forces. The darkness might have seemed never-ending, but the green-gold glow extended beyond her vision and advanced upon the king with speed to rival Mekan's assault upon the forest. Within minutes, it became clear to her that the shadows were shrinking while the vibrant green only expanded further, bathing everything it touched in radiant light.

Niema's heart lifted as the darkness retreated before her eyes. Fresh greenery replaced rotting trunks, plants and flowers bloomed brighter than ever, and the smell of the dead was buried beneath the aroma of new life as the darkness receded like night fleeing from the coming dawn.

They can't have disappeared. Can they?

As they flew closer, Niema's steed shied away from the green glow, a whine escaping its throat. It feared the light as much as a regular war drake feared the dark, and each wingbeat brought more resistance to her control.

Kelan overtook her, peering into the green haze above the forest. "I can't see the king."

"He'll still be there." Niema cringed when the void drake let out an earsplitting screech. "I need a new steed. A living one."

"Looks like there are a few over there." Kelan pointed at the advancing wave of green light, in which she could make out the distinct shapes of winged beasts. "Or behind us, with the army. One's got to be missing a rider."

A whistle expelled from her mouth, calling to any war drake within range. Sooner than she'd expected, the sound of wingbeats came from somewhere to her left. A war drake approached, its clawed feet skimming the newly restored treetops. At another whistle, it flew below her as she lost her grip on the void drake altogether. The beast lurched as if to throw her off, and she let herself fall from its back, tumbling to land neatly upon her new steed's back.

Kelan glided down to her level, offering an approving look. "See? You're still a Disciple of Life. Also, I wish Yala had seen that move. She'd have been impressed."

Niema shook her head at him, a smile stirring despite herself. The decay below faded, new life bloomed, and the king's destruction might never have touched the forest.

With her renewed hope came determination, and Niema resumed her flight towards her target. She didn't believe for a moment that Mekan would be so easily vanquished.

The king had vanished from sight, but the winged shapes within the light were now close enough to distinguish, and she recognised several faces among the fliers, including Bitra. She must have found her way to the others after all.

Her gaze snagged on Ragem, who was shouting an order from his war drake with a bloodied blade in his outstretched hand, pointing at someone's neck.

The king. Disciples surrounded him, the light masking the dark so thoroughly that even the shadows that had extended like wings behind his back had shrunk to almost nothing. He might have been an ordinary man, helpless to resist as Ragem brought the blade across his throat.

Darkness rose, formed a shield that hit back with such force that the weapon flew from Ragem's hand. More shadows extended like tentacles from the king's palms and wrapped around Ragem's throat.

"No," Niema whispered. "Ragem."

The light died with him like a candle had been snuffed out, and the forest began to decay as quickly as it had recovered. The Disciples screamed, a collective howl of grief that caught Niema too. She bit back the cry threatening to escape, to give her presence away to the king.

The king, seated on his void drake, was wreathed in shadow like the god of death Himself made flesh. Dark tendrils unfurled from his fingertips and extended in all directions, wrapping around the other Disciples. Bitra screamed as she was dragged free of her war drake's back, while Kelan swore, beckoning to Niema to fly lower.

Too late. The king had seen them, and the shadows streaming from his fingers reached her too.

"Come, Niema," the king called to her. "Return to me, and no more of your people need to die."

Dark tentacles wrapped around her legs and dragged her off the war drake's back, holding her suspended in the air. She fought to free herself as the darkness spread up her legs and climbed up her body like a forest spider entombing its prey.

"I will offer you one chance to surrender, Niema."

"I won't." The shadowy ropes had reached her shoulders, and as she inhaled, ready to whistle a command, they

EMMA L. ADAMS

wrapped around her face, mimicking the gag he'd made her wear. "Mekan is capable of nothing but inflicting destruction and suffering."

"There will be no suffering," he said. "Once Yalet is gone and the Disciples of Life are no more, there will be no need for anyone to live in fear."

"People don't fear us." She raised her voice, fought to be heard behind the layer of shadows pressing against her mouth. "They fear *you.*"

"Because years of indoctrination have taught them to believe that your people are saviours, not destroyers."

"Do you really believe that?" The words were muffled, but it didn't matter if the king heard or not. He was too far gone. As far as she knew, King Tharen had never even *met* a Disciple of Life before Mekan had whispered lies in his ear. And while he professed to be in control of his own will, in the end, there would be only one victor in the struggle between mortal and god.

"Now," said the king, "I will ask you to cease resisting and tell me where your surviving Superiors are hiding."

Do both Superiors live? She couldn't have given him an honest answer even if she knew, but she could hazard a guess that at least one of them would be on the island with Yalet's temple.

Clutching the dark ropes in his fingers, the king dragged her towards him like a fish caught on a line, helpless against the darkness he wielded.

But isn't the darkness part of me too? Did she not carry part of the god of death's power inside herself?

"Take me to the heart of your forest," he ordered. "Take me to the place where the surviving Disciples of Life are hiding."

"I won't." As the shadows dragged her in front of him, readied to place her upon the void drake's back, she sucked

544

in air, drew power from the shadows themselves until their grip loosened. "I *won't*."

As she tumbled into the heart of the Void, the darkness swallowed her scream.

———

When Viam began climbing the palace stairs, Saren groaned. "You can't go in there. The palace is probably crawling with monsters."

As if to prove his point, the void drake descended, its claw reaching for Viam. Saren grabbed her arm and pulled her downstairs as someone else overtook them and thrust a spear upward. The weapon tangled with the void drake's foot but spared them from being gored to death.

"Brenat!" Viam gasped her name. "Get away from there!"

"Bit late for that," Brenat wrenched the spear to the side, drawing blood from between the beast's sharp claws, and a second thrust of the spear caught its oncoming mouth. Blood fountained; Saren threw his arms over his head to block the spray from getting into his eyes.

Several guards came running up to the palace stairs, weapons in hand, looking at the dark cloud hovering above its roof. When more dark shapes rose from the darkness, forming winged creatures with sharp teeth and claws, they began to back away.

"Don't you even think about it," Saren snarled at them. "This is your fucking job. Protect the prince."

Daliel was out in the open, exposed. One guard ignored Saren and ran out into the square, shouting for help, but the others converged around Daliel. Viam joined Brenat in fighting the void drake with a claw taken from one of those very same beasts. It made Saren shudder to see her wielding a piece of Mekan as a weapon despite his rational mind telling him no weapon was better equipped to tear apart one of those monsters than its own claws.

Saren ducked another spray of blood as Viam drove her weapon up to the hilt into its gaping mouth. The beast collapsed, its tail lashing in its final throes. A spear-sharp spike brushed against his leg, and a faint whisper sounded, a quiet voice urging him to grab the spike and turn it into a weapon himself.

You won't get me that easily, Mekan.

The palace doors crashed open under the weight of a beast that somewhat resembled a raptor, albeit twice the size it should be. It leapt and half slid downstairs in a way that might have struck him as comical if not for its size and those sharp teeth protruding from its jaw. Mekan had warped the creatures into dangerous predators, turned them into twisted reflections of their living selves with one purpose: to spread Corruption. To destroy the living.

When nobody ran to confront it, he spun around and saw the prince stood frozen behind his guards, useless.

"For fuck's sake." Saren jogged over to him. "Have you forgotten you can give orders now? Tell them to fight."

Daliel turned haunted eyes upon him. "The last time I did that, too many people got killed."

"They're going to die anyway." A second void drake rose above the palace, uttering a blood-chilling cry. "At this rate, so are you. You can't hide in the palace this time."

Thanks to his father, the palace was no safer than the rest of the city. The rest of the army had long gone, and he doubted the king would care in the least if his monsters tore the capital to pieces in his absence.

As the raptor-like beast continued to slide downstairs, Nalen came running over, a dripping sword in his hand. "What the fuck is that?"

"Mekan," Saren answered. "Someone in there must have called for backup."

The raptor-like monster left the stairs in a leap, impaling a fleeing guard on its talon. The guard's intestines spilled out in a greyish mess. Saren's gorge rose, not so much at the violence but at the sheer fucking inhumanity of Mekan's creatures. They didn't care whose side anyone was on.

Tossing the guard aside, the beast turned on Nalen next. He blocked with the flat of his shortsword, and more soldiers came in to help, their blades making quick work of the monster. Two more had already emerged to take its place, and a flurry of snarls and growls erupted from behind the palace's open door.

"That temple." Nalen lifted his blade. "How're we supposed to stop this?"

"Good fucking question." Saren glanced at the square and spied a group of fleeing Disciples of the Flame. "*They* might be able to help if their Superior makes a decent choice for once in his worthless life."

Otherwise, nobody could. Not even Yala, but he'd already accepted that she wasn't coming back to save them. That thought brought more comfort than he'd expected. Not because he enjoyed seeing his own nightmares wrought in flesh but because now, everyone else could see them too. His shame and fear were no longer his to shoulder alone, and if he admitted it to himself, losing his squad had hit as hard as it had because they were the only proof he had that he'd not imagined the horrors they'd seen on the island. That had always been a wedge between him and anyone he grew close to. Giran was a prime example.

He wondered where Giran was now and if he'd left the city or had stayed. He was surprised to find he didn't mind either way.

A second raptor came barrelling downstairs, breaking

him from his brief distraction. If nothing else, he was at home in chaos, and the weapon in his hand brought a sense of purpose and the knowledge that he might just get that heroic death after all.

———

As the dead fell upon the city of Dalathar, Viam fought at Brenat's side, which also meant staying next to the prince. While his guards were ready to defend him, none were keen to run into the palace and deal with the threat more directly.

The front doors lay wide open, and an array of beastly creatures descended the palace stairs, while huge bird-like monsters swept down from the palace to grab their fleeing prey. Anyone they slaughtered rose at once to join Mekan's ranks, turning their weapons upon their former allies.

As Saren and Nalen brought down one of the monstrous raptors, Daliel cringed away from the spray of blood. "How do we stop this?"

"We can't." Saren dug his blade into the dying beast's throat, his arms caked in gore. "Unless you have a Disciple of Life hidden somewhere that I don't know about?"

"No." The prince cringed behind his guards, face ashen. "The temple has been there for weeks. Why is this happening now?"

"Because your father's pissed off at us for going behind his back," said Saren. "If you'd like to go in there and yell at the Void to stop throwing monsters at us, feel free."

Someone might have to go in there. The prince was as much a target as the rest of them, and as a rising shadow from the palace warned her of another void drake's approach, Viam heard one of the guards saying to the prince, "We have to leave the city. It's not safe for you."

"I can't," he insisted. "My place is here. I cannot abandon my people."

"If you want to live—" The guard cut off in a gasp as a blade pierced her through the back, emerging from her chest in a torrent of gore.

Nalen cut down the source—a dead soldier turned Mekan's servant—and watched both bodies fall with a grim expression on his face. He saw the same defeat reflected in the eyes of the other guards, too, even if they wouldn't admit so aloud.

The void drake descended, and Nalen and the others ran in to meet it with their weapons raised. The guards pulled the prince out of the way of its slashing claws, shielding him with their bodies, and a shower of blood and viscera sprayed them all.

Saren shouted, voice hoarse, "Nalen!"

Viam lifted her head. The burly soldier had fallen to the ground, his shortsword clutched in a limp hand. His head followed a moment later, missing its right ear, landing in a puddle of gore.

"Hey!" Saren shouted, hurling a dagger at the monster's face. The throw missed but caught the monster's eye. As its claw swiped at Saren, Viam drove her blade into its spine.

The sword sank in, wedged between scales, and the momentum wrenched the weapon from her hand and sent her sprawling to the ground. She landed hard on her right-hand side, gasping at the shooting pain in her right hip and leg. Nearby, the prince crouched behind two of his guards, his fine clothes soaked in blood.

Out of the corner of her eye, Viam saw a flash of light somewhere on the other side of the palace wall.

Not light. Fire.

Fire.

The beast lifted its head, its attention captured by the

flash too. Brenat leapt in, stabbing with her two-pronged claw weapon. One side sank deeply into its pitted eye, and Saren finished it off, screaming Nalen's name.

That fire...

Viam tried to push upright, but her leg folded, her hip burning with pain. Seeing, Brenat came to help her. Leaning on Brenat, she stumbled towards Ceremonial Square and the pillar of light that now shone on its right-hand side.

"Shit," Brenat breathed. "That's the Temple of the Flame."

If Nanek's claims had been accurate, those flames could have only one source. "Superior Shralin. He must have…"

He'd sacrificed himself to destroy Mekan's influence. Saren hadn't thought he had it in him.

Viam limped out of the gates and saw an audience of Disciples similarly entranced by the display at their temple. As she watched, one lifted a palm alight with white fire, turning it upon one of the winged monsters diving upon the square. Flames spiraled up, engulfing the bird-like beast and turning its decaying feathers to ashes. A second Disciple gasped as his hands ignited too.

"This way!" Viam shouted at them. "Come and help us!"

Brenat jabbed a finger at the palace. "Come and protect the prince. Make amends."

"Stop those monsters." Viam raised her own voice. "Help us!"

Since the monsters were already on them, the Disciples had little choice but to fend them off with blasts of fire that set dead skin alight and broke through even a void drake's tough scales. Gradually, the Disciples began to move towards the palace gates, encouraged by Brenat's shouts, and unleashed Dalathik's flames upon their monstrous attackers.

Laria's capital was not defeated yet.

———

Yala followed the trail of destruction the king had left in place of what had once been pristine forest. Dead trees formed a ruined expanse that stretched as far as the eye could see, while any settlements they passed were abandoned ruins. Likely the same was true of the village near the cabin in which she'd once lived in exile, now reduced to nothing but a small part of Mekan's endless destruction.

They flew for more than an hour before she saw him, hovering above the ruins of Yalet's domain, a dark slash opened in the air at his back. The king's golden crown was the sole colour amid the dark, and the sight brought a rush of hatred so potent that she had a spear readied without being conscious of moving. Her squad was ready, too, spears in hand as they approached their foe.

None of them saw the other enemy below until a gust of air scattered their formation and a void drake rose in a wide sweep of its leathery wings. The masked humanoid seated upon its back lifted a clawed hand, sharp as a void drake's claw.

Two spears flew from her squad but left no mark on the armour-like scales covering both beast and rider. Yala hurled her spear, and the weapon pierced straight through the void drake's eye.

As her squad-mates closed in, spears and daggers striking at the wounded beast, the rider gave a sudden leap, clearing the trees in an elegant glide and landing heavily in front of Yala. Her war drake snarled, its head tipping downward under the added weight, and Yala swore explosively as she fought to keep her balance. "What the hell are you doing?"

She jabbed her spear at the Disciple's masked face, the pointed end glancing off hard scales. As the Disciple brought up a clawed hand to counter her spear, the momentum pushed down on the war drake's head and caused them to drop. Together, they fell through the canopy, into the mass of rotting trees that had once been thriving forest not long ago. The fall slowed as the war drake's wings were caught between branches that then gave way, sending them crashing to the ground.

As the war drake's clawed feet hit the forest floor, Yala threw herself forward and landed on top of the Disciple. The momentum jarred her injured leg and brought the sting of a hundred cuts where the scales dug into her still-human flesh, but her knees pinned the soldier down for the moment she needed to pull the void drake's claw free of its pouch.

She aimed the claw at one of those inhumanly dark eyes and felt an inexplicable jolt of recognition. Somehow, she *knew* this person. She knew whose face lay beneath the scales even before the Disciple spoke in a voice distorted to a guttural groan. "You shouldn't be here."

"Lisek," she breathed. "Is there anything of you left in there?"

No response. Lisek had travelled into the Void—voluntarily or otherwise, Yala would likely never know—and her will was no longer her own.

Someone screamed above. *Gorel.* With a curse, Yala squeezed her war drake's neck, but the tangled branches ensnaring its wings and the combined weight of two riders prevented it from taking flight.

Lisek swung a clawed hand. The sharp edge bounced off the scales now coating Yala's chest, and the slight widening of her eyes indicated that Lisek knew what fate Yala had chosen.

Lisek's mangled voice rattled in her throat. "Kill ..."

"Kill the king?" Yala jolted when the war drake shook itself in a motion that threatened to send the pair of them tumbling from its back. A hail of branches and leaves showered her face as it shook itself again, this time breaking her grip on its back.

As Yala began to fall, Lisek's claw-like hand locked around her arm, hard enough that the claws would have pierced the skin had there not been scales in the way. The other hand swung her weapon jerkily as she emitted another strangled noise. "Kill... me."

Kill me. Lisek didn't want to harm Yala, but Mekan had total control of her body. The only way out was death.

Another scream from her squad-mates urged Yala to action. Rebalancing herself, she swung the void drake's claw and drove the point into the depths of one of those deep, dark eyes. As Lisek's grip loosened on her arm, Yala stabbed the other eye for good measure and shoved the body off the war drake's back.

It's done. Heart heavy, she left Lisek's body on the forest floor and flew up, in search of her squad-mates.

A body fell past. One of her squad-mates—Surel, the new scout—tumbled into the forest, his body riven in two. Shadowy tendrils crept overhead, crossing Yala's line of sight like creeping vines, and lashed at her squad-mates, tightening around their necks and tearing at their flesh. Vilat fell next, limbs sprawling as his broken body crashed through the canopy. Gorel followed, his mouth stretched wide with terror, the upper half of his body preceding the rest. Kithal writhed and struggled against the shadowy vines, uttering gurgling cries, before he too succumbed. Roven swore and kicked; her cries were stifled as the life bled out of a gaping hole in her chest.

Yurel was the last to die. She gasped Yala's name as the shadows tightened around her neck and her head snapped to the side with a crack.

Numb, Yala watched the shadows retract into the hands of their owner. The king sat on his void drake's back, cloaked in the shadows that had so swiftly eliminated her allies.

"Such a pity," he said. "A waste of fine soldiers."

"As if they wanted to fight for you." Her words were as cold as the icy feeling in the pit of her stomach. *He killed them. He killed my squad.*

The cries of fleeing war drakes resounded as the beasts abandoned their dead riders. Yala gripped her own war drake's neck firmly to prevent it from doing the same, her gaze panning over the king's armoured steed. Chains hung loose from its front, but Niema was not there. Had she escaped, or had he killed her too?

"And you…" He looked her over, lingering on her scaled hands. "I expected the Void would have destroyed you by now. I should have known better."

"You aren't the only one who knows how to bargain with Mekan."

A fine job she'd done. Delivering the king's life would be near impossible without Niema's help, to say nothing of the second part of her promise. That she would offer Him Yalet too.

Despite the shadows roiling around her, she felt none of the energy that had coursed through her veins inside the temple. Here, the Void obeyed only the king.

"Keep your word, Mekan," she murmured. "And I'll keep mine."

Her fingers tingled, grasping shadows, raising them like a shield.

The king lifted a palm and sent a wave of rippling darkness at her. Shadow clashed with shadow, the momentum threatening to pull her off her steed.

Her grip broke first, and her war drake let out a piercing cry as the void drake closed its jaws around its neck.

She sensed the beast die, and Mekan claimed its body almost at once. Shadows coiled around the war drake's carcass, seeping beneath its skin, as she struggled to regain control, to wield those shadows in her own hands.

"Come on," she snarled. "Obey me."

As the dead war drake stirred, the monster released its prey and went for Yala herself instead. Teeth clamped around her waist, biting through skin, through flesh, through bone.

Mekan's voice bore her down into the darkness. *"Now, you are mine, Disciple."*

50

Niema fell into a place of darkness so profound that no speck of light might have ever disturbed its gloom. A wave of crushing terror pressed upon her from all directions as every thread of connection to Yalet was cut off and awareness of any living creature obliterated.

The Void. The name suited the place. The sheer magnitude of its emptiness was beyond imagining. A place life had never touched except to be snuffed out. It was anathema to her being. And yet...

Undeniably, part of her felt *alive* here, the part that burned with curiosity, the desire to know more about this terrible place.

"Mekan." She spoke the name almost unwillingly, as if another mind had taken control of her mouth.

"You carry Yalet's taint, Disciple."

Mekan's reply made her heart jangle against her ribcage. She twisted in search of the speaker, unable to see even her own hands in front of her face. Not a speck of light offered her any clue as to the dimensions of the room or hole or whatever kind of place this was. No ground cushioned her feet, no roof existed above her head. She hung suspended in nothingness, in a yawning pit without end.

"You are no use to me," the voice went on. *"Yalet's creatures are an abomination."*

He knew she belonged to Yalet. One wrong word, and the darkness would crush her, stamp her from existence, yet even that was preferable to making any kind of bargain with this creature of the dark like the king had. Like *Yala* had, she was sure.

Yala came here. She got out. But even if she'd survived the experience, Yala was beyond reach.

"If I'm no use to you," she said, her heart fluttering, "let me go."

Could Mekan understand a word she spoke? She wasn't clear on how she understood *Him,* given that a deity who had predated humanity would surely have no reason to speak modern Larian, but nothing about this experience obeyed the rules of the physical world she was accustomed to. Though there was no air here, she had not suffocated, and her body had not frozen to death despite the lack of any warmth within the dark.

The god of death's response rippled through her body, resounding like an echo in a dark tunnel. *"Will you bargain with me, Disciple?"*

"You want to bargain?" Disbelief bled into her voice. What did He think she had to offer? *Best not think about that.*

"Do you want to bargain with me, Disciple?" Mekan repeated.

No. A louder, ravenous voice echoed from the depths of her mind: *Yes.*

This, she was sure, was how it started. With a bargain. Nobody travelled to this realm and emerged in the same state in which they'd entered. Like those Disciples of Death who no longer followed their own will, Mekan seized any creature that entered His domain, infecting them with Corruption. But He'd inexplicably offered her the choice. Perhaps that was how it worked. A sacrifice had to be offered willingly.

"What will you do if I refuse?" she asked. "Kill me?"

"It is not I who takes life. That is Yalet's role, not mine."

"Yalet isn't a killer." Her voice wavered, but she held firm. "She gives life to all."

"She takes life away too," said Mekan. *"Is it not She who claims your mortal remains when your existence comes to an end?"*

"That's how nature works," she said. "We live, and we die. What *you* do... isn't that."

A horrible, chilling laugh sounded, one that raised every hair on her arms and made her heart give a great leap as if to lunge out of her chest.

"Nature is death," Mekan whispered. *"All life comes to an end, and I am what awaits after. Or I was, if not for the other gods and their treachery."*

What did he mean by that? Part of her was hardly able to believe she was *talking* to a god, and now, she was certain they were communicating using a means other than words, in the same way that her body was both physically present and yet cut off from its natural senses.

Another, smaller part of her wondered if He was talking to her out of loneliness. No other life existed here, nothing but his monstrous creations. If this punishment had been inflicted upon anyone else—but she'd seen the way Mekan's followers had obliterated any other Disciple who stood against them. She'd witnessed the effects of His unending wrath. Deserved or not, she couldn't afford to offer any pity to the god of death.

"You were exiled for betraying the other gods."

"Human lies, spread by the treacherous gods they worship."

"Then what's the truth?" Her thumping heart urged her

towards caution, to avoid provoking the one whose realm she was trapped inside, yet Mekan had not attacked her yet.

Perhaps He can't.

The thought slid through her mind; she cast it aside as if even holding that notion would invite retribution upon her.

"Betrayal is in our nature. They betrayed me as they betrayed their human followers."

"That's no answer." She spoke carelessly, distracted by the voice in the back of her mind whispering that if the god of death could have killed her, He would surely have done so by now.

"They accused me of treachery. I was no more guilty than they."

"And what does 'treachery' mean in that sense?"

Cold tendrils brushed her skin, drawing a shudder as they caressed her face, crept over her chest to the wound the void drake's claw had inflicted. *"Corrupting their followers. Like you, Disciple. Choose now. Will you bargain with me?"*

"You tried to steal their followers?" Like all gods, Mekan's existence in the material world depended upon His followers; it was through humans that the gods were able to act at all. Infecting other temples and turning their inhabitants upon their deities, though... it was no wonder the other gods had objected.

"They convinced their followers to destroy my temples. I returned the treachery in kind."

Now, I get it. His position almost made sense if not for the glaring reality of the rampant destruction consuming Laria as a result of His uncontrolled wrath.

"You have a temple now," she said. "In Dalathar. Is that not enough? You don't need to destroy Yalet to claim a place in Laria."

"Yalet will never permit my existence," He replied. *"Yalet claims I am an abomination, yet every root She has planted in that*

559

country of yours is dripping in the blood of those whose lives were taken in Her name. You cannot deny that, Disciple."

Niema opened her mouth and closed it. While most of the modern enclaves swore vows against taking life, the elite Disciples continued to do so, and their bloody history was woven into that of Laria itself. The entire country had styled itself upon a legacy of conquest and might.

Moreover, Yalet *was* directly fuelled by the lives of Her followers. Niema had seen for herself that Yalet's temple had been born out of the sacrifices offered by past Superiors. But that was in no way similar to Mekan's rampant greed and desire to consume all life.

"I ask again, Disciple, will you bargain with me?"

"I won't." Letting herself succumb to Mekan would never be a solution. All He knew how to do was destroy, to strangle all life until any hope of change or growth was extinguished.

"Pity."

No other words followed.

"Is that all?" she asked tentatively. "I can… leave?"

There had to be a catch. The god of death did not permit humans to come and go as they would. She shuddered as the cold tendrils brushed over her again, lingering on the spot on her chest where she'd been stabbed. The bruise-like scar was a physical sign of her bond with Mekan, and perhaps that alone had spared her from harm inside His realm. She felt the cold within her, imagined the shadows swirling around her skin, and spoke with all the force she could muster. "Let me out."

The Void parted like curtains folding to either side. All her senses returned in a dizzying rush, dominated by the sight of countless sharp branches rising up to meet her as she fell.

———

As he watched Yala die, Kelan's hopes withered like the forest that lay dead beneath the gaping hole the king had torn open in the sky. He brought up his blade to repel an oncoming void drake's claw, wincing when one of the spikes on its wing clipped his face. The few surviving Disciples of Life fought the dead as best they could while ensnared in shadowy ropes, but some who tore themselves free fled outright, the loss of their leader having had a similar effect on their resolve as seeing Yala's death had had on Kelan.

And Niema had fallen—no, *jumped*—into the Void.

With Yala gone, the king would turn back to his captives, the few who were still alive. He had to move. Bringing the blade up to its hilt in the void drake's eye, he twisted until he heard a sickening pop. As the flailing beast fell, he let himself drop into a glide that carried him through the canopy and into the forest. Husks of dead trees formed a graveyard choked in the smell of rotting leaves and dead animals—but he saw only one human, lying in a bed of desiccated plants. Alive.

"Niema!" He flew to her side, noting the torn clothes and fresh blood staining her limbs. "Niema. Are you all right?"

She lifted her head. "I think so."

"Mekan let you go?" If she'd fallen, her powers must have healed her on the way down, but how in the gods' names had she got out of the Void to begin with?

"He couldn't harm me." Niema sat up, looked wonderingly at her own outstretched hands. "I'm immune. I don't know why, except that it might be through my bond to Yala."

"She's dead." He hadn't meant to be so blunt, but it was impossible to conjure more than the barest words to encompass something that he still couldn't accept as truth.

"No." Niema drew her arms to her chest. "She can't be. I'd know."

"Would you?" A rustling above reminded him of the

enemies close at hand. "Have you strength enough to close the Void?"

"I don't know." She sounded lost, dazed from far more than the news of Yala's death. No surprise. Hadn't she just travelled to another world entirely, to a place held only for the god of death and His most twisted servants?

He crouched beside her, tried to look into her eyes. "Did you *speak* to the god of death?"

"In a way," she murmured. "I don't know how to describe the Void. You can't see anything—can't really hear anything either—but we communicated, and I'm sure that if He could have killed me, He would have."

"He didn't by any chance let anything slip about how to put a stop to this destruction?"

"No." Her pale lips turned down at the corners. "He just emphasised how much He resents Yalet and the other gods for banishing Him into the Void and said that they all deserve to suffer for it."

"I bet Mekan thinks He's the victim, not them," Kelan surmised. "At least you survived the experience."

Dead branches creaked with a warning as something small and scaly came crashing into the back of his head and dug sharp claws into his back. He stumbled, batting at the creature with his hands. Its grip broke, and it flew into a tree, shrieking as it did so. The small monster wasn't one he'd seen before, scaled like all Mekan's beasts but with a long tail that lashed the forest floor, stirring up rotting leaves.

Niema whistled a prayer. Green light sprang to her palms and swept over the beast, quietening its shrieks and stilling its thrashing tail.

"Was that a kekin?" He grimaced, rubbed the back of his neck. "There's nothing Mekan won't corrupt."

She rose to her feet. "I'll close the Void."

Niema murmured a prayer, uncertain at first but gaining

strength and volume with each moment until the green light grew wide enough to reach the dark haze above their heads.

When the Void winked out, Kelan flew a little higher to see if the king was still nearby. Even Niema's prayer hadn't touched the thick layers of decay around them, but with Mekan's creatures gone, he risked peering above the branches.

The king was on the move again, the wave of darkness in his wake cutting through the forest like a scythe. He must have believed both Yala and Niema to have perished, but if he turned around, he'd realise someone had closed the Void.

"Is he going somewhere in particular?" He glided back down to her level. "Or is the goal to destroy the whole forest?"

"He's looking for the enclave," Niema said. "The king thinks that's where the heart of the forest is."

"And it isn't there?" He recalled his Superior's suggestion that the heart of Yalet's power rested inside a temple or the equivalent and Hachim's horrified reaction to her words.

"No." She closed her eyes. "That's why I can't let him find me."

Kelan might have pointed out that given the rate at which he was destroying the forest, the king's path would take him to the centre of Yalet's power one way or another, but he held his tongue, waited for her to offer the information by choice.

Niema glanced at him. "It's an island off Laria's eastern shore. I didn't know it existed until I was taken there to swear my vows as an elite Disciple."

"The king has no idea?"

"No." Her mouth pinched. "I didn't give anything away, but all it takes is one slip."

"Not if we stop him first." He reached for her arms, and she let him lift her off the ground.

563

As they flew above the forest, he found his gaze drifting to the spot where Yala had fallen, her body pierced by the void drake's teeth. It didn't feel real, but nobody could survive a wound like that, not even her.

Niema followed his eye. "I can't believe she's really gone."

"Yala wouldn't want us to dwell on her." He knew the words were true even as he struggled to accept her fate. "She'd want us to—"

"To finish the job, I know." Niema spoke with quiet resignation. "It has to be me."

———

Hachim walked for over an hour before he sensed another living creature within the forest. A golden-green light brought hope that he'd reached the end of the darkness eating away at the forest's heart, guiding him through the maze of dead trunks to the enclave.

His home was a bright haven in the darkness, but while the wooden huts were intact and the trees as vibrant as ever, not a soul was outside save for one individual in her clearing, seated upon a rock. The Superior's face was drawn, and her war drake lay curled at her feet.

"Hachim." She watched him enter with weary eyes. "I thought you were searching for Niema."

"She—" His voice broke. "She and I went our separate ways. I came to find you. The king... he's destroying the forest."

"I know." She pushed to her feet, the faint green glow shining from her skin the sole indicator of the strength she was feeding into this part of the forest to keep it alive. "I advised those who cannot fight to evacuate the enclave. I fear I condemned them to death, but as Superior, I am the primary target."

"And Niema." He swallowed, his throat dry. "The king will want to recapture her. She betrayed none of our secrets while he held her captive. He has no idea the island exists."

"I am glad of that." A pregnant pause ensued. "I do not know why Yalet blessed her so."

"What?" His heart pitched downward. "When Yalet let Niema join the elite Disciples, you mean? But that—that's a sign that Niema's bond with Yalet is stronger than any hold Mekan might have over her, isn't it?"

"Yalet was mistaken, perhaps," said the Superior. "I can think of no other reason why She would hasten Her own demise."

She can't mean that. "Or She has a plan."

"We can no longer gamble with that." Her eyes hardened. "You may stay here if you will, but it is time for me to return to Yalet's side."

For a heart-dropping moment, he thought she meant offering her own life. Then, he remembered. "The island?"

"We must keep Corruption from entering Yalet's heart," she said. "The temple is our last haven, our last hope. I am the sole Superior remaining."

"No." What had happened to the others? Had they been among the bodies he and Niema had discovered, the ones whose strength had temporarily enabled the forest to fight back against its invaders?

"I'm afraid so." She exhaled in a weary breath. "I know that gathering in one place condemns us to perish with our temple, but it is also where we are at our strongest."

That was true, but her tone suggested she'd already accepted defeat. She was grieving a battle that hadn't been lost yet and mourning someone who still drew breath, still lived.

His spine straightened. "I won't be coming with you."

———

Saren jumped back as flames leapt past him, devouring the body of the monster bearing down on him. A torrent of white flames roared past his face, singeing his hair and devouring the beast's tough scales as though they were nothing but wood. The Disciples of the Flame followed, hands ablaze, following Viam's lead.

About fucking time.

"Ready to destroy that temple?" he asked.

"You want us to go *inside* the palace?" said one of the Disciples, staring up at the seething cloud spewing monsters into the sky.

"That was implied, yes," he said. "I'll drag you in there myself if necessary."

Nalen's loss was raw, but it had also stripped away much of his fear. Anything that lurked on the other side of death couldn't be worse than what they faced here and now.

The Disciples all looked to the prince. Daliel crouched behind his guards, splattered with blood, staring at the pile of ashes that had once been a ravenous monster. He had not thanked the Disciples for saving his life, but then again, neither had Saren. He'd been too startled to, and frankly, he didn't even know how to feel about it.

"They want your permission to go in," Brenat called to the prince. "Go on."

"I…" Daliel hesitated, no doubt recalling their unpleasant shared history and weighing that against their current dilemma.

"Come on," Saren said. "The longer we wait, the more of those monsters will come out."

"We can't use our abilities inside a Temple of Death," one of the Disciples ventured.

"No, but you can stop those monsters," said Saren. "Like

the island, the first time. Remember?" He addressed Viam, who nodded, her expression torn. She, too, remembered Dalem, engulfed in flames, offering his own life to Dalathik to close the Void and win the rest of the squad the chance to escape. "I don't see too many options here. Personally, I don't trust any of you, but I don't want giant monsters rampaging all over the city either."

Viam gave him a poke in the arm. "Saren, really. Isn't this our chance to rebuild trust with the Disciples?"

"We might as well make peace with Rafragoria." Though they at least seemed to have kept their word and hadn't come into the upper city that he'd seen.

"Is that a bad thing?" she said, a plea in her voice. "Can't we *stop* fighting one another?"

"I don't know." Even if they survived this, they might well learn nothing as a nation. Laria might continue the endless cycle of war and violence and act in service to Mekan even as they denied doing so—but if the country didn't make it through the war, nobody would ever have the chance to try.

"Yes." The prince addressed the Disciples. "Close the Void. Destroy the temple if you can. It does not matter if anything else is destroyed in the process."

The Disciples gathered at the foot of the stairs and fell to their knees as one. Their collective prayer merged with the crackle of flames as white fire surged up, consuming the dead and everything else that stood before them.

With a grin on his face, Saren watched the palace burn.

———

Pain sank its teeth into Yala. As the jaws of the Void closed over her head, she struggled to resurface, to reach the king.

"Damn you, Mekan," she growled through the blinding pain. "We had a deal."

A false promise, to be sure, and one that seemed infinitely more impossible to fulfil with the life bleeding out of her. As the strength drained from her limbs, the renewed power Mekan had gifted her with waned, threatening to revert her body into its decaying ruin.

Yala's mind filled with the faces of those she'd lost. Her newest squad-mates first then the old ones: Dalem and Temik, Machit and Vanat. Before that, Hothen, her first captain, and the other brief companions she'd flown with who hadn't lived to see her become leader. Finally, in the haze of distant memory, her parents, killed in a fire on their farm that had spared her alone. As someone whose life had been steeped in death from its inception, Yala had always been the ideal instrument for the god of death.

"You are mine, Disciple," Mekan said.

"Not yet," she breathed. "I made a promise. I want strength enough to kill Tharen. I want him dead. Then I'll help you destroy Yalet."

No response came. Shadows continued to creep over her failing body, extending cold tendrils to probe beneath her skin. She gritted her teeth as they reached her neck, brushing over the spot where Melian had once slashed open her throat.

"Yalet's mark is on you."

Yala stiffened. "I told you that already."

Had she? Yes and no. She'd told Mekan that she was bound to Yalet but nothing of how that feat had come about nor the nature of their bond. A bond neither she nor Niema understood, but that the god of death had accepted the bargain at all should have been a warning sign on its own.

The cold tendrils pressed against her neck, penetrating the skin. Yala tried to squirm away, but there was no hiding from the god of death. Nor from the growing fear that she'd offered far more than a false promise when she'd confessed to being bound to Yalet.

When Niema had saved her life, she'd been marked by Mekan through the bond they'd forged. Had something in the reverse also occurred to Yala? She'd never had cause to ask. After all, unlike Niema, she'd never denied or fought her connection to Mekan, at least not since she'd been forced out of exile.

Her mind raced. She'd made the promise under the assumption that the king was the sole driving force behind Corruption's spread through the forest and that when Yala killed him, it would give Niema and the others the chance to banish Mekan's influence from their home.

But if part of her was bound to the gods of Corruption *and* life, Tharen's death might not be the end of it.

And if so, Niema had never been the key to Yalet's destruction. The king had taken the wrong hostage. It had always been her, Yala, in whose hands the choice rested that would spare one god and condemn the other.

The cold tendrils brushed her throat again. *"Your mortal body is already broken. Soon, you will expire."*

"Not before I take Tharen's life," Yala gritted. "I will offer him to you, and then, you can have us both. We had a fucking deal."

"You promised to offer me Yalet too." The cold pressure on her throat bit deeper. *"If I spare you, you will take me to Yalet's heart and help me destroy Her."*

"Yalet's heart?" She hadn't the faintest idea what He meant, but the king did, and if Mekan brought her to him, she could do the rest. "Fine. Just give me strength enough to kill him, and I'll take you there."

The pressure on her throat lifted, the cold sensation instead spreading down her chest to the place where the monster's teeth had sunk into her skin. The pain numbed, and she felt the skin heal, her flesh harden to scales.

Mekan did not stop there. The spreading cold extended up her torso and down her legs. Sensation dulled; even the old wound on her right shin ceased to ache as shadows replaced the wounded flesh.

When the prickling chills reached her face, she shouted aloud. "Stop! This wasn't part of the deal."

Shadows flooded over her face like water, sealing her mouth, folding around the back of her head and hardening to a mask of scales.

Her transformation was complete, and her body was no longer her own.

Yala belonged to Mekan now.

51

K elan carried Niema over the forest in search of allies, but the other Disciples of Life had, perhaps wisely, gone into hiding. She had no way of knowing if Hachim had reached the enclave nor if the Superior was there or somewhere else.

For a mercy, the king had continued his advance over the forest without looking back, but she had trouble being glad to have evaded him when he destroyed more of her home with each sweep of his void drake's wings.

But not all. She sensed the occasional pulse of life, either a surviving Disciple or someone else who'd escaped the king's rampage, and a whistled command brought her a war drake to ride upon. Having a steed again made their journey faster, but they'd flown for more than an hour before she sensed a spot that Mekan hadn't touched, where Yalet's heartbeat pulsed under the surface.

"The enclave." A gasp escaped her. "It's safe somehow. Untouched."

Did she dare to look for herself? No. She'd left Hachim

for a reason. She resisted, turned away, but that thrumming heartbeat pursued her, lingered at the edge of her awareness.

And she felt the moment that heartbeat stopped like her own heart breaking. In the same instant, pain pierced her chest below her ribcage, as acute as a knife thrust into her by an expert hand.

Niema gasped, clutching her chest. Kelan flew to her side, caught her arm to prevent her from falling from her war drake. "What's going on?"

"It's Hachim. He's dying."

"What?" Kelan stared down at the forest then at her. "Are you sure?"

"Of course I'm sure, Kelan." The words snapped out, her body trembling as the pain reverberated through her in a way that she'd only ever experienced when one of her enclave members was suffering terrible pain.

The king must have found him. But how?

There was only one possibility: the enclave was already lost.

Her gaze travelled to that bright spot she'd sensed, the sole remnant of Yalet's beating heart amid Mekan's destruction.

Kelan swore under his breath. "You want to go down there?"

"He's there." Nothing else mattered. "I have to go to him."

She descended in a beat of her war drake's wings over trees no longer pulsing with life. The Superior's clearing lay open to the sky, and within, a lone figure sat on a tree stump. A gasp tore from her mouth. *Hachim.*

He lifted his head as they descended, his eyes glassy, pleading. Her chest pulsed with pain, her eyes watering, but Hachim was upright and appeared unharmed. Why was she in so much pain? She slid from her war drake's back, her knees buckling, her hand reaching for his.

"Niema," he whispered. "He's... here..."

Niema's war drake took flight with a shriek of terror as a wave of shadows passed over the clearing, leaving wilting grass and dead trees beneath. The king stepped out from behind the Hachim sat upon and offered a faint smile. "I thought that would draw you to me."

"I don't understand." How could he make her feel pain that should have only been possible if he'd inflicted terrible suffering upon one of her enclave members? Unless Hachim was hiding an injury she couldn't see?

"Niema," Kelan murmured. "We need to get out."

"You should," she whispered back. "I'm staying here."

He gave a faint groan but stayed put.

When the king reached the tree trunk on which Hachim sat, a masked Disciple of Death stepped out of the trees behind him, coated in scales like all of them, hands transformed to curved claws like a void drake in miniature.

The king's smile widened. "How about an incentive?"

The Disciple lifted a clawed hand and seized Hachim's arm, pulling him to his feet. Pain ripped through Niema's chest again, and she fell to her knees with a moan.

"That worked far better than I expected, I admit," said King Tharen. "Don't you recognise my new companion, Niema? You can certainly feel her pain."

Niema forced her head up, her blurred vision revealing that the Disciple who stood behind Hachim had been stabbed too. A knife protruded from their chest, below the ribcage, and Niema's chest throbbed in the same spot.

Gods. No, please no.

Niema met the Disciple's eyes, now turned to dark pits that did not quite hide the pain within, the same agony that reverberated into Niema through their bond.

Yala.

She no longer resembled herself. Her skin was encased in

dark scales, her face a mask without features or expression. Despite the dagger jutting out of her chest, Yala showed no outward indication that she felt anything at all.

"She answers to Mekan now," said the king. "She answers to me. And if you refuse to take me to Yalet's heart, *she* will."

———

Yala stood with her weapon pressed to Hachim's throat, her body a tool in itself and no more subject to her will than the knife the king had stuck in her chest. He'd cut deep, wanting to see if the pain of the injury would pass to Niema through their bond, as would have been the case for a Disciple of Life. Yala had hoped, prayed that he'd be wrong.

Her hopes had faded the moment she'd returned from the Void and found herself lying on the forest floor beside the stirring body of her dead war drake. Or rather, void drake. The beast had been transformed, the same as she had, and she had been unable to stop herself from climbing onto its back and taking flight.

When she'd reached the tree line, the king had spotted her. He'd turned his void drake around, flown to her side, examining her newly transformed body with approval.

"I'm glad to see you come into your own, Yala," he'd said. "I trust you won't be a problem for me in the future?"

"No." She'd spoken—gods, she'd spoken like *Him*—and she'd wished she could cut out her own tongue.

"Excellent," he said. "Did you see your friend? The one bound to Mekan and Yalet both?"

"I did not." Again, her tongue had betrayed her. "If she entered the Void, I doubt anything in there can harm her."

"Interesting." He'd studied her then as if wondering what a treasure trove he'd stumbled upon by finding her like this, with her will entirely removed. "Of course, you told me yourself. A Disciple of Life saving a Disciple of Death created something that's both and neither, you said, but were you talking about her or yourself?"

"Both." She tried, unsuccessfully, to bite her tongue. A cold, rasping laugh resounded in her ear as Mekan took pleasure from her struggles to resist the force moving her body against her will.

"Then we shall find her, you and me. Take me to her home."

And she had. Her void drake had carried her over the forest while she fought an unseen battle with every beat of its wings. Mekan didn't need her mind, not when He held total command over her flesh, and all she could do was watch like a spectator through her own eyes as she led him to the enclave.

Now, Niema looked at Yala, searching her eyes for any traces of her real self behind that scaled mask. "No. Please, Yala, fight back."

I am. Yala wanted to speak, but her mouth refused to move. Knowing that she'd played into the king's hands made her rage burn brighter. He'd always intended for her to become this. Always. And she'd let herself succumb, because she'd been fool enough to believe the god of death would let her take Tharen's life before He ensured she held up the other part of their bargain.

Yala's clawed hand gripped Hachim, pulled him in front of her. Her other hand rested at the base of his throat, the sharp edge nicking the skin.

"She knows the way to the enclave," the king went on. "She will lead me there. And you will comply, or you will watch your friend die."

"This *is* the enclave." Her voice was guttural, a strangled mockery of her own.

"Is it?" He looked at Niema and Hachim. "Then this is not

575

Yalet's heart."

No, Yala thought with a twinge of cautious triumph. She *didn't* know where the others had gone, or if Yalet's heart, whatever that meant, was a real place at all. She couldn't betray Niema with knowledge she didn't possess.

"There's somewhere else." The king looked between them, disappointment flickering in his eyes. "Niema, you didn't tell her, did you? You trust your friends so little?"

Niema said nothing. Her eyes were round with horror.

"Very well," he went on. "You will tell me the location, or your friend will die, and Yala will be the one to deal the killing blow. It's your choice."

———

Kelan watched the standoff, helpless to intervene. He could hardly believe *Yala* was the person behind that mask, standing statue-like with her weapon pointed at Hachim's throat and ready to strike at King Tharen's command. Unless Niema led the king to the surviving Disciples.

Kelan himself was of no interest to the monarch, but he was also hardly a match for two powerful Disciples of Death, one of whom had someone's life in her hands.

Yala, fight back. She *was* fighting, he was sure. She knew what her body was doing and was fighting with every breath, but it wasn't enough.

"Go on," said King Tharen. "Make your decision, Niema. I will give you this one chance. Tell me your answer."

Niema's hand pressed to her chest, her mouth taut with pain. Kelan's gaze went to Yala, to the knife protruding beneath her ribs, and realisation dawned. Niema had assumed it had been Hachim whose pain she'd felt, but she must have a similar bond to Yala as she did to her enclave members. The king had laid his trap well.

But he couldn't read her mind. He needed her to offer the information willingly.

"I will take you there," Niema gasped. "It's impossible to find without my help."

Is that true? He would hardly have blamed her for lying, given the circumstances, but she would never gamble with Hachim's safety.

"I do hope you're not lying, Niema." The king reached for the dagger in Yala's chest and yanked it out in a spray of blood.

Yala gave no outward reaction, but Niema folded in on herself, whimpering with pain. The hole in Yala's chest remained open, droplets of blood glistening on the scales. Shadows moved in, lapping at the blood like a wild drake's tongue. *Delightful, Mekan.*

Gods, Kelan had to do something. His hand crept to his blade, pulled it from its sheath.

A shadow lashed at him, fast as a whip, and yanked the blade from his hand. He stared, bemused, as the shadows tossed his sword away as though they possessed a will of their own. It seemed His Majesty—and Mekan—had not forgotten Kelan after all.

"You should have left while you had the option, Disciple." The shadowy whip reformed into a rope wrapped around Kelan's throat. "I think I'll kill you first."

"No," said a loud, ringing voice. "You won't."

Superior Kralia stepped out of the darkness, a halo of golden light circling her body. The light extended like the sun's rays, breaking the shadows' hold on Kelan and restoring life to the wilting trees around the clearing. Her eyes simmered golden-green, but the king did not appear cowed in the least by her appearance.

"You're the last surviving Superior, are you not?" he said. "If you die, your people will have no leader."

"Perhaps not," she said to the king, "but I have already chosen my successor."

The king lifted his hand. The shadows moved as he willed them, forming a solid force that clashed with the light streaming from the Superior's palms.

Gods. What's she doing? Why is she exposing herself?

He knew why. The rest of the enclave must have evacuated, and she'd stayed behind to win them time to run and to keep the king's eyes off the true source of Yalet's power. Kelan's own Superior would have made the same choice.

The light grew, blinding even as the darkness rose to swamp the golden glow, and the Void opened wider to expose monsters baring sharp teeth and claws. The Superior staggered beneath the onslaught, weaker in this dying forest than she would have been if they'd fought near the source of her strength. But she'd made her choice to fight on uneven footing rather than expose Yalet's heart to the enemy.

"Superior!" Hachim screamed, unable to move with Yala's claw pressed to his throat.

But Kelan could. He whistled a prayer to Terethik and took flight, air blasting from his hands and sweeping the rotting trees into a torrent.

The Void swallowed Kelan's attack, and the king did not deign to offer him so much as a glance. He had the Superior on the defensive, swamped in shadows, the golden light dimming like the sinking sun.

"Stop!" Niema echoed Hachim's cry. "Superior, stop, *please*!"

"I trust Yalet." She smiled inexplicably. "And I trust you."

Fresh golden light bloomed, pushing back the darkness. The king let out a snarl of fury, then threw his hands over his head as an explosion of greenish gold erupted over the forest.

The Superior's body ignited like a flame.

52

Niema screamed, a raw sound torn from the depths of her very soul, as the Superior vanished in a pillar of light so blinding that even the Void vanished beneath its glow.

A pulse of green-gold followed, rippling through the forest and through Niema too. Her vision blurred to a white haze.

When her eyes cleared, she was no longer in the forest. Rather, she soared above the ocean, over the island and the Temple of Life. She saw the trees inside the temple ignite with gold, their radiance shining bright enough to reach the heavens.

That same light poured into her, and all her senses ignited. Including the nameless force that kept her entwined with her enclave members, the part that shared in their sensations, their emotions. An invisible thread connected her to them, dividing into four separate branches. Hachim, Diamen, Threl...

And Yala.

Unlike the others, the thread connecting her to Yala

pulsed cold, not warm. As it did so, darkness crept in at the edges of her vision, and she had the sudden, chilling sense of someone else watching the vision through her eyes.

"I see it now," said Mekan. *"You cannot hide from me, Yalet."*

"No!"

Niema was yanked out of the vision with the force of a stone loosed from a catapult. She stumbled, catching her balance against a tree with a hand aglow with golden light. Her body pulsed with renewed energy, but she stooped under the weight of a sudden heaviness in her chest. She'd felt a similar burden when her Superior had loaned her strength to destroy Mekan's temple, but now, the Superior stood rigid as a tree, her eyes open but sightless, her expression at peace. That strength now existed in Niema alone.

"Superior," Hachim whispered. "My Superior."

No. Horror washed over her. *It can't be me.*

Niema was bound to Mekan. She was corrupted. Mekan had *been* there, in the vision. He'd seen...

"You?" The king eyed Niema. "Your Superior chose *you* as her successor?"

Images flickered through her mind, showing her figures walking between trees rotted to the roots and others standing in daylight on a shore. *I can sense the others. The other Disciples of Life. That's how the Superior always knew where we were...*

She shook away the images, unable to afford the distraction.

"No matter." The king swivelled back to Yala, whose claw still pressed against Hachim's throat. "Superior or not, you have a choice to make, Niema. His life or the location of your god's heart. You know where Yalet truly resides, do you not?"

"Yes."

Mekan's voice came from Yala's mouth. The king's gaze snapped to her, disbelief flickering across his face. "What?"

"I know." Yala's mouth moved beneath the scaly mask even as her eyes darted around, panicking, her mind locked in an invisible struggle to escape.

The king smiled at her. "You know where Yalet is hiding?"

"Yala," Niema whispered. "Please."

She reached for the pulsing thread that she could now sense between them in the hopes of finding some way of reaching the real Yala beyond Mekan's control. The thread was still there, its cold burn resonating with the lingering chill around the spot on her chest where she'd been stabbed. Even taking on Yalet's power had not removed that scar, had not erased her bond with Mekan.

Maybe through that bond, she could reach the real Yala. She held the thread, focused on the cold until shadows rose to her palms and dimmed the glow around her skin, but Yala showed no signs of having felt anything. Even if she had, it didn't matter when Mekan commanded her body.

Niema pulled away, seeking out the new weight upon her soul, the power her Superior had passed on to her. The shadows vanished under gold light once more, and the power thrumming in her veins sought to escape, to destroy Mekan's creatures—and to destroy Yala too.

Hadn't this started because Niema had saved Yala's life? When she'd acted against her better judgement and spared a Disciple of Death? If she was a true Superior—if she ever deserved Yalet's legacy—then she had to finish this in the only way possible.

"I wouldn't, Niema." The king scarcely needed to glance her way to guess the direction of her thoughts. "You don't need to let anyone else die."

Hachim. Yala's claw bit deeper into his throat, drawing a thin stream of blood.

"Ignore him," Hachim rasped. "I'll gladly give my life for Yalet. It would be my honour."

"Pitiful." The king beckoned to Yala. "Bring him with you. We shall destroy Yalet's heart together."

The Void rose around him, and from within stepped two reptilian beasts. Each void drake bowed its head to its master. The king climbed on one, and Yala guided Hachim to the other, her claw still pressed to his throat. His eyes met Niema's, and she shook her head, urging him not to fight back. Yalet would never want him to sacrifice his life unnecessarily.

Or did She? Had Niema ever really known what her deity wanted? This was as close as she'd come to understanding, but despite having seen directly through Yalet's eyes herself, she'd never heard Her voice. Otherwise, everything she'd been told of her deity had come from Superior Kralia. Maybe even the decision to allow Niema to become the next Superior had been hers alone.

Why had Superior Kralia allowed her to absorb the images of the island when she must have known the god of death might be watching through Niema's eyes? Why had she let that information fall into the king's hands?

Tears fell, thick and fast, as the two void drakes took flight, leaving her behind. The king didn't need her any longer, and if she dared to unleash any of Yalet's strength upon him, Hachim would be the one to bear the consequences, not her.

It looked as though her only act as Superior would be to watch her people die and to witness the final demise of Yalet in this realm.

"Niema." Kelan reached out an uncertain hand as if he wanted to comfort her but wasn't sure how. "Should we follow?"

"What would be the point?" she choked out. "I can't *do* anything. Yalet will lead him to the island, and Mekan will—"

"Are you certain about that?"

"Don't start." Her hands clenched. "There's no loophole in this situation, Kelan. Yala saw what I did. She saw through Yalet's eyes."

"You don't think the god of life was capable of stopping Yala from watching if She'd been willing to?"

"What?" Niema's mouth dropped open. "I don't know."

She did. She knew, deep down, that it hadn't been Superior Kralia who'd made the final choice to select Niema as her successor. Yalet could have rejected her, could have stopped Niema from seeing that vision, but She hadn't, even if it meant betraying Her temple's location to the enemy.

Kelan's mouth tilted up at the corner. "See? You follow them. I'll see if I can gather anyone else to come and fight with us."

They'll get there too late. Niema knew that, and likely so did Kelan, but if it got him out of harm's way, she was glad to let him leave.

Niema would follow Yala and the king alone, carried by Yalet's blessing. She would see this through, whether it ended in triumph or ruin.

———

Yala flew without stopping, her newly transformed steed clearing ground at a rate that went far beyond even a war drake's capabilities. The king followed her lead, though she had nothing to guide her but instinct and the images she'd seen through Niema's eyes.

Why had Yalet permitted her—permitted *Mekan*—to see those images? It had been Superior Kralia who'd named Niema as her successor, so the blame lay more with her than with the god of life, but both shared in the culpability for allowing Mekan to access something that should have been between god and Superior alone. And so did Yala herself, for the sheer hubris of daring to believe Mekan would ever fall for her human trickery.

Hachim sat hunched in front of her, not speaking or moving. A glow in the corner of her eye appeared after a short while, a sign that Niema was following them, but either the king did not believe her to be a threat or he thought Hachim's presence alone would ensure she didn't lift a finger against either of them. Kelan was not with her, but if he had any sense, he'd have gone back to his fellow Disciples to wait for the end.

When the ocean's glittering curve appeared, she caught her first glimpse of the island. Though smaller than she might have expected, it was likely around the same size of its northerly companion and similarly attired in thick jungle. Disciples of Life crouched within the trees, not knowing their doom descended upon them with every beat of the void drakes' wings. In the island's centre lay a clearing surrounded by tall trees arranged to resemble pillars.

The king made a soft noise of understanding. "I see. Clever of them to hide their temple upon an island, just as Mekan's followers once did. I wonder which came first: this one or the other."

"Yala." Niema closed in behind them as Yala's void drake began to descend over the island. "Please."

A flash of golden light pierced her eyes; Yala's steed was flung sideways as a green-gold barrier appeared, shimmering above the island's surface.

"Yalet will not permit us to land." The king gestured to Hachim, seated in front of her, his eyes fixed on the island. "Drop him."

"Niema!" He cried out her name.

Yala's hands lifted of their own accord and shoved Hachim off the void drake's back.

"Hachim!" Niema flew below, hands outstretched, but too

late to catch him. He tumbled past her, straight through that golden shield.

Niema's war drake dropped into a dive. A glow shone from her skin, mirroring that of the island itself as she picked up speed and came out of the dive beneath her falling companion.

This time, she caught him. He landed in her arms, the momentum pushing the war drake down until its feet brushed the treetops and the golden light embraced them both.

"I thought so." The king sounded satisfied. "Only a Disciple of Life can land upon these shores, but you are permitted to enter despite the mark Mekan left on you. That should mean…"

I can enter the temple too. Niema's bond to Mekan had not prevented her from landing, because she was bound to Yalet as well.

And through her, so was Yala.

"Go on." He gestured to Yala. "You jump next."

"No!" Niema shouted.

Yala's body was already moving, leaping from the void drake's back into a graceful dive. She hoped, for a brief, desperate instant, that the golden shield would repel her and fling her into the open sea—but no such luck.

Instead, the golden light embraced her, slowing her fall. The trees moved, their branches rising upward to catch Yala, to guide her downward.

"No!" Niema, too, leapt off her war drake.

Hachim screamed as she plummeted down, but the golden light caught her too, guiding her down into Yalet's domain.

"That's better," said the king from above the golden barrier. "Go on, Yala. Destroy Yalet's heart."

Yala's hand moved. She fought—*gods*, she fought—but the

585

resistance that had repelled the void drake from landing on the island was there no longer. In some twisted way, Yalet recognised her as a Disciple of Life.

"Do it," said King Tharen. "Now."

Yala might not know how to destroy a temple, but Mekan did. Niema uttered a cry of despair as Yala thrust her hand deep into the golden light rising from the island's core. The glow spread up her arm, above the scales Mekan had wrapped around her body, and she felt its pulse beneath her skin, thrumming in tandem with the island itself. Yalet's beating heart, open to her.

Mekan's shadows came to her fingertips, and dark tendrils spilled out of her hands, dampening the golden glow, slowing that pulse of vibrant life. At once, the island began to die. Grass withered underfoot, flowers decayed on the spot, and Mekan's triumphant laughter resounded in the air as Yalet's domain fell apart.

I win, Yalet.

Yala was dying, yet Her golden glow still lingered over Yala's skin, and she felt an inexplicable warmth centred somewhere in the region of her throat, on the spot where Yalet had marked her.

Yala welcomed that warmth, drew it into herself. The numbness beneath her skin began to thaw, and sensations returned, starting with pain. Her right leg burned, threatening to give way, and the agony under her ribs where she'd been stabbed reasserted itself with such force that she fought to cling to consciousness. But it was she who moved her own legs, took one step back, then two.

"Yala." Niema spoke in a hushed voice. "Are you—?"

The island gave a great shudder as the king landed, his void drake no longer repelled now that Yalet's strength was fading. The shadows cloaking his body further dimmed the golden glow until the only source left was the clearing where

Yala and Niema stood, face to face. Reflections of one another in every way. Yala could see that clearly, the pulsing shadow beneath Niema's skin mirroring the golden light beneath her own. Yet the shadows held the upper hand, and Mekan's laughter greeted the king's arrival.

"This will become a Temple of Death." He stepped into the clearing, no fear upon his face even as Yalet's fading light washed over him. "Marked by the death of the last Superior. Yala, kill her."

Yala's hand jerked to the pouch at her waist. Her own hands were weapon enough on their own, but Mekan did not prevent her from pulling out the void drake's claw. She swivelled, her body an instrument beyond her control, but she managed to meet Niema's eyes.

She forced her lips to move. To mouth the words, *Trust me.*

Then Yala lifted the claw and threw it, point first, at King Tharen.

The king's eyes widened as the void drake's claw speared him through the neck. He stood, incomprehension stark on his face, suspended for an infinite heartbeat before his body began to topple.

The king hit the ground, his blood spilling onto the ruin of Yalet's heart. Mekan cried out, not in rage but in delight. The god of death cared not whose blood He was given, and He had not protected Tharen in the end.

Niema gasped. "Yala. You're... you."

"No." Her voice was mangled but sounded more like her than before. She held out a hand in warning, conscious of the shadows streaming from her skin. "Don't come any closer."

Despite Tharen's death, the island's golden glow had not returned. The opposite, if anything; the blood spilled on Yalet's heart mingled with the shadows spilling from Yala's hand. Ice frosted the air, a warning that the Void would soon open, obliterating any vestiges of Yalet upon the island.

Niema let out a moan of despair. "Gods. He's already won, hasn't He? That's why He let you kill—"

I know. "The god of death isn't known for being particularly attached to His Disciples."

As for Yalet? Yala hardly counted as one of Her Disciples, but it was Her golden heat that pulsed beneath Yala's skin, under the long-healed wound on her neck where Niema had saved her from death and sealed their fates.

Yalet has marked me too. Mekan Himself told me that.

And His mark lay on Niema. Yala could see His shadows rising from her skin, joining with the darkness Mekan had inflicted upon the island. They were bound by an invisible thread, an image so vivid that she almost fancied she could see it taking form as a thread of light and darkness intertwined.

"Gods." Niema stared down at the thread that now pulsed in the air as if Yala had somehow conjured it into being. The stream of light and darkness travelled between the pair of them, golden light swirling around shadow as both gods fought for dominance within their human vessels. "You can see it too?"

"Yes." It was almost two separate threads, the light and dark scarcely touching one another, and while the shadows were more potent on Niema's side, on Yala's, the light dominated.

Yala focused on the golden glow and on the cord linking the pair of them and *pushed.* The golden light hovering above her skin moved as she willed it, travelling down the thread towards Niema.

Yala's body began to numb again, the shadows growing more distinct, but on Niema, the effect was the opposite. She brightened, her skin aglow, and life began to return to the island. Tendrils of gold spread outward, reviving dying trees and withered grass.

Niema stared in wonder. "What did you do?"

"Gave some of Yalet's strength back to you." Not all of it. Most of the god of life's power lingered beneath Yala's skin, enabling her to speak, to move without Mekan guiding her limbs.

"You can't!" Niema said. "It doesn't matter how much you give to me. Mekan will still be here, in both of us."

She was right. Even being chosen as Superior had not removed Mekan's mark from Niema. The thread linking the two of them kept their fates intertwined and ensured that even if Yala perished here and now, Mekan would be waiting to claim her upon death. And He would try to claim Niema, too, given the chance.

Yala would not allow him that luxury.

She focused on the golden glow again, on the current of warmth travelling along their link—and this time, she pulled that warmth towards her as one might tug sharply on a war drake's chain.

Niema screamed. So did Yala as a sudden rush of sensation flooded her bones, her blood, every part of her igniting in agony. Yala felt her flesh softening, the scales receding, old wound returning with a vengeance.

Mekan's grip on her loosened, unable to bear being so close to Yalet's life-giving strength.

Yala took that strength into herself, and Niema began to fade. Her heartbeat slowed, the glowing thread linking the pair of them dimming. The shadows shrouding Niema's body remained, but she and Mekan had made no bargain. He had no hold over her.

Mekan screamed in Yala's ear, but He could do nothing as Yala sent that golden light back along the fading bond, offering the life that Niema had given to her.

589

Mekan screamed again as Yalet's power returned to its wielder. Shadows faded, obliterated in an instant by a blinding pulse of light from within the island's beating heart.

As Yalet accepted the sacrifice She had been offered, Yala's last thought was, *we're free.*

————

Kelan felt the moment everything changed.

He'd flown as fast as he could, back to the battlefield where the Disciples fought the remains of the king's army. Few were left in the sky; the army's already fragile strength was depleted, and the king's departure had not helped morale in the least. Kelan rounded up a few Disciples of the Sky, including Ranit, and they took flight for Laria's eastern coast.

With their slower speed, they wouldn't have a hope of catching up to the king before he and Yala reached the island, but something in Kelan told him that he needed to at least try. However this battle ended, his Superior would want him to witness history being made.

As a result, he was among the first to see the surge of golden light rising into the sky, gilding the horizon like sunrise.

Was that Niema? He picked up speed and whistled a prayer to Terethik to guide the winds in his favour.

As he flew closer to its source, the golden light spread further. The effect rippled over the forest, shadows receding from the ruined trees, fresh greenery springing up in their place.

Does that mean they won?

With Terethik guiding his path, Kelan tracked the source of the glow to an island that lay just off Laria's shore. Vibrant gold spiralled up from its surface, and a breath of wind carried him close enough to see a lone figure standing in a clearing amid the dense jungle, bathed in golden light.

Niema lifted her head, tears streaming down her face, as he touched down next to her.

Flowers bloomed around her feet and around a body that lay on the grass, face upturned, at peace. Yala, but no longer as he was used to seeing her, cloaked in dark scales and her face a mask of shadow. Now, she was untouched by the darkness, smiling as radiantly as the light streaming from Niema's skin.

"Niema." His feet knocked against a second body. This one wore armour overgrown with moss, and weeds sprouted from a face rotted to the bone. An equally overgrown claw protruded from its neck. "Is the king... dead?"

"Yala." She sobbed the name. "She—"

"Saved us all." That much was clear. "Am I right?"

Niema fell to her knees, pressed her forehead to the grass. "Yalet. Save her. Please."

"She wanted this." Yala had never wanted to become subject to Mekan's will, to lose control over her own fate. She'd chosen death on her own terms, and Kelan didn't need to know the specifics to guess that it was Yala's bond to Niema that had saved Yalet and saved Laria.

Niema continued to sob into the grass. Kelan crouched, awkwardly putting his arms around her. "Come on. You're Superior now, remember?"

"No." She lifted her head, her voice thick with grief. "I can't be. It shouldn't have been me."

"Shouldn't it?" he said. "I can think of worse. I think you'll be less prone to inflicting punishment on your followers for associating with Mekan than your predecessor, don't you?"

Niema glared at him through the tears. "Fuck you, Kelan."

"Now is hardly the time or the place..." He ducked as she swiped half-heartedly at him, relieved to see some of the

EMMA L. ADAMS

spark return to her eyes. Her grief was immense, and no wonder, but her people needed a leader, someone to repair the damage Mekan had caused.

As for Kelan, he couldn't quite believe Yala was truly dead. Death was too mundane a term to apply to someone like her.

The rustle of branches told him they had company. More Disciples of Life emerged tentatively from the jungle, and with Hachim leading the way, they trickled into the clearing.

One by one, they knelt before Niema and murmured, "Superior."

Niema stiffened. Then, slowly, she rose to her feet and walked out to face her Disciples.

"Today," she said, "Yalet has offered us a miracle."

EPILOGUE

Three days passed before Niema could bring herself to return home.

She'd been prepared to return to the mainland the morning after her ascension to Superior, but instead, the Disciples had come to her. The large group who'd taken refuge on the island had included a number of elite Disciples who'd survived the battle and who needed someone to give them orders in the wake of Ragem's death.

Niema was hardly qualified to choose their new leader, so she let them vote on it, with Hachim and Bitra as impartial observers. Once they'd selected a leader, she'd ordered them to fly back to the mainland to spread the news across the other enclaves that the battle had been won and that Mekan had been vanquished.

All the Disciples of Life had sensed the impact of Superior Kralia's death and had known what it meant. Few had anticipated that Niema would be the one chosen to take her place, but they all knew they'd come within a breath of being destroyed, and their lingering shock might account for the lack of any objections to Niema taking the title of Superior. She'd expected some to be reluctant to take orders from her initially, but whatever doubts they held had vanished in the wake of Mekan's defeat. When she addressed them, Niema let Yalet guide her and saved her misgivings for when she was alone with her god. There was too much damage to repair for her to be assailed by doubt.

Yalet's power had restored the forest, but most of the Disciples had been displaced from their homes, to say nothing of the missing and the dead. Hachim had taken command of the group dispatched to help the Disciples who'd evacuated find their way back to the enclave. Niema had wanted to join him, but her sense of obligation extended to all the Disciples, not just her former enclave, and so did her dizzying new awareness of every Disciple within Yalet's domain. If she wasn't careful, that awareness overwhelmed her, flooding her with sights and sensations that weren't hers.

As a result, she spent those first days gaining control over her newfound abilities, letting Yalet guide her progress. While the people within her immediate orbit were easier to locate, she could track a Disciple of Life on the other side of the forest if need be. It was no wonder Superior Kralia had always known when it was safe to leave the enclave and when to return home to protect the Disciples.

Niema couldn't govern alone, and in the long term, there'd need to be more Superiors appointed. The decision would be Yalet's, but She had imparted no new visions on Niema since her ascension. She'd waited for hours, surrounded by the monuments of past Superiors, praying for guidance, and it was there that Hachim found her. His war drake landed at the clearing's edge, and upon dismounting, he knelt before her.

"You don't need to do that." A familiar ache stirred inside her. Though she sensed the beating hearts of every Disciple on the island, the threads that had once bound her to her enclave members had joined hundreds more, and she was no longer more attuned to Hachim than she was anyone else. "I don't want things to be different between us."

"They will be," he said. "It's unavoidable. Will you ever come home? Kralia made sure that we were able to rebuild the enclave."

Her heart gave a dull throb at the reminder that Superior Kralia's body was there too. Would she want Niema to bring her back to the island, to join the other Superiors? She might, and her sacrifice had been as instrumental as Yala's.

"I will."

She called her war drake and joined him in flight. For a short time, they shared in the calm joy of companionship, of being alone save for each other. That much hadn't changed, and when combined with the expansive view of Yalet's domain offered from the sky, she hardly believed she'd once hated the very notion of flying on a war drake.

In the enclave, new life already bloomed in place of old, and the wooden huts below the trees were occupied once more. If anything, this part of the forest was more vibrant than ever, with bright flowers lining shady paths, kekins clambering in the trees, and the heady smell of nature in the air.

In her clearing, Superior Kralia's body stood as strong as a tree. Niema walked to her and knelt before her former Superior. Golden light embraced them both as Niema whispered her thanks. Though she'd come here intending to remove her body, there was something undeniably peaceful and fitting about the way the Superior stood, as if she'd taken root in the place she'd called home.

EMMA L. ADAMS

A thud came from behind her. "Ouch."

"Kelan?" She climbed to her feet and looked at Hachim. "Did you bring him here first?"

"He just showed up," Hachim protested. "And I told him *not* to come into the temple."

"The... temple?" She turned back to the Superior, her mouth parting. "No."

"Yes." Kelan flashed her a grin. "Your Superior played a long game."

"A Superior can create a temple if they sacrifice their own life." Niema's heart leapt. "She knew that when she died."

And now that the enclave was a new temple, Mekan would not so easily gain a foothold here again.

Fresh tears burned her eyes as she faced the Superior's monument, now an eternal part of the enclave. Niema hadn't agreed with all her choices, and in the end, they'd been reconciled only out of necessity, without any of their initial trust.

Niema might not know how to be a Superior yet, but she knew that she would not repeat the same mistakes.

A chirping sounded, and a small reptilian head poked out from behind the Superior. *Molin.* As the tree-raptor hopped onto Niema's outstretched hand, a smile nudged her lips. "Molin. I hoped you were just hiding."

"I bet he's been waiting here for you too," said Kelan. "You're his master now."

"Maybe." She sniffed, turned away. "Why else are you here, Kelan? You can't possibly have known I'd come back today."

"No, but I was prepared to wait." He shrugged. "I'm here because there are rather a lot of people who would like some help permanently removing a certain Temple of Death."

"Have you been back since the battle?"

Did you tell Yala's friends?

Guilt flickered in Kelan's eyes. "No. I was needed at Skytower, and to be honest, there was quite enough cleaning up to do. The flight division—or what's left of it—has gone back to the capital, but the rest of the army is scattered everywhere between Dalathar and Setemar and further afield."

"And Mekan's creatures?" She'd told the elite Disciples to keep an eye out for any openings to the Void the king had left behind, but they wouldn't have vanquished all of the monsters that Mekan had unleashed on the continent in only a few days.

"Your people helped take care of the worst parts," he said.

At least there's that. The scale of the damage was overwhelming, and perhaps ridding Laria of Corruption entirely would prove an impossible task even for her elite Disciples. But removing the temple would at least ensure nobody would be able to take the king's place as Mekan's chosen.

Kelan tailed her to the island, although she hadn't asked him to. He called upon Terethik to speed up their journey, and when they touched down on the island, her breath caught as she laid eyes upon Yala's body. She looked so peaceful that Niema didn't want to move her, but she knew in her heart that Yala would not want this to be her final resting place.

"I doubt she wants to stay here," Kelan commented. "No offence to Yalet, but being buried in *any* temple isn't her style."

"She wouldn't want the Disciples of the Flame to burn her either."

"Give her to her friends," Kelan ventured. "Let her former squad-mates decide."

"And him?" She pointed in the general direction of Tharen's body.

"Throw him into the sea?" he suggested. "The Disciples of the Sea would object to that, I'm betting."

"Have you seen them? Since the battle?"

"That's my next stop." He offered a smile. "I have some good news for them. According to recent communication from the capital, their temple has been purged of Mekan's presence. They can go home."

Good. She smiled back, her heart lighter, though it gave a twinge when she saw Hachim's war drake descending nearby, landing at the edge of the clearing.

"I thought you were planning to stay in the enclave for a while," she said.

"I was, but I'm not letting you try to destroy the Temple of Death single-handedly."

He knew her too well, and her heart ached to know there was a distance between them that hadn't been there before. Their bond hadn't shattered, but it had been absorbed into the myriad threads now connecting Niema to the rest of the Disciples of Life.

Perhaps that was as it should be. It was fairer to Hachim that he now had the chance to find out what he wanted for himself without her.

"And someone needs to help you with him." He gestured at the king's body. "You don't want to leave him here, do you?"

"No." He was harmless in that state, but Yalet's heart didn't deserve to be tainted with the reminder of how close it had come to destruction. "The Disciples of the Flame can have him."

"You'll be pleased to know that they have their temple back," said Kelan. "Superior Shralin finally made a sensible choice. As a bonus, they did some damage to the Temple of Death. Destroying it will be no bother for you."

"Good." She whistled, calling to her war drake. When the

beast dipped its head to let her climb on its back, Kelan watched with a curious expression she couldn't read.

"What?" she said.

"I was just thinking," he said. "I have to wonder if old King Larial made up that story of bringing an army of winged beasts from the northern continent when he settled here in Laria. I bet they were already here, with your people."

"That's probably true." The island contained countless carvings from Disciples past, going back hundreds if not thousands of years. She'd delve into those waters someday, but for the time being, her primary concern was with the future and not the past.

With the two bodies secured to the war drakes' backs, she and Hachim rose into the air, side by side, as if nothing had changed. The resulting ache in her chest prompted her to murmur, "You know I think you should have been chosen instead, don't you? You were always better than I was. A better Disciple."

"Drakeshit," Hachim said, surprising her with his vehemence. "You're the one who was chosen, and you'll be a better Superior than our last one. Kelan was right."

"Don't tell him that. He'll be insufferable."

"Don't tell me what?" Kelan enquired.

"Nothing." She sniffed. "It's time to take Yala home."

———

Dalathar rang with the sound of celebration, bells echoing over the rooftops and military songs spontaneously erupting on street corners. The vibrant blue-and-gold Larian flags draping every building were garish enough that even the soldiers rolled their eyes at them, but the city had been in mourning for so long that a little levity was sorely needed.

Two weeks had passed since the battle. Two weeks of

soldiers returning home either alive or in coffins, of bodies being pulled out of jail cells and the smell of funeral pyres a permanent fixture in the upper city. Of course, some of that was due to the lingering fumes from the palace, now reduced to a skeletal husk in which the Disciples of Life had obliterated any last traces of Mekan's temple. Otherwise, nobody had set foot in there since the battle, not even Daliel, who Kelan suspected had had to be talked into holding a proper ceremony for his second coronation.

Kelan and his fellow Disciples found a spot at the edge of Ceremonial Square near a contingent of Disciples of the Sea. They were clad in as little clothing as ever, though admittedly, the warm weather and the dense crowds made him wish he'd forsaken his cloak. Across the square, more cloaked figures assembled outside the Temple of the Flame, but Dalathik's followers seemed as unconcerned with the heat as ever. They did look impressive in their orange-and-red attire, though Kelan didn't see the white robe of a Superior among them. He hadn't confirmed if they'd chosen a new leader yet.

The Disciples of the Earth stood next to them, having arrived the previous night. Pehin flashed him a wink across the square, which he returned, anticipating a chance to enjoy her company later in the newly reopened Disciples' Inn, following the first meeting of every group of Disciples in Larian history.

At least, Superior Sietra claimed it would be the first such meeting, and he was content to take her word for it. It had been his idea, in fact, though he hadn't expected the Disciples to agree to assemble in the same place. Not everyone had, of course. Lakiel, the main objector from among his own people, wore his customary scowl as they watched the proceedings, though some of his annoyance might have been because Brikel had talked her way into accompanying them to the ceremony with her foot still in a brace, refusing to miss out on a historical occasion.

On that point everyone agreed: It *was* historic. Even the Larians who'd founded the nation had been divided from the start, and while the Disciples of Life undeniably laid claim on the continent first, they all had the chance to rebuild this world anew, upon a foundation of trust.

Speaking of whom, the Disciples of Life had yet to show up, even as the ceremony was starting. When the procession began to walk out of the palace, cheers rang across the square, and Larian flags flew high. As the first rows of uniformed soldiers marched out, he spied a couple of familiar faces making their way through the crowd. Brenat looked odd in her fine clothing, as if she'd be more at home on a construction site than at a party, and it was Saren who walked at her side and not Viam.

"She's with that useless prince," Saren said in explanation. "King, I mean."

"What, as his bodyguard?"

"Or official advisor, as I understand it." He gestured at a raised platform amid the soldiers, supported by guards on either side. "I don't understand what she sees in him, but he's managed not to summon the god of death in the past two weeks, which is a blessing after what we've been through."

A gust of wind swept overhead as a procession of war drakes flew out of the palace above the marching soldiers, also draped in Larian flags.

"I'm surprised the flight division is taking part in the ceremony," he remarked.

"I'm not," said Saren. "They can't resist the opportunity to make this as over-the-top as possible. As if we've forgotten who here is a collaborator. Or just a coward."

"Hmm." Kelan's attention panned over the crowd,

lingering on the Temple of the Flame. "That includes everyone in there too."

Saren scoffed. "Yes, but since the Superior gave his life to save their temple, the others are hailing him as a hero. As if he didn't kneel before the king and get half his people killed before he did the right thing."

The sound of beating wings interrupted his tirade, heralding the arrival of a second group of war drakes, this one from the opposite direction. Niema led the Disciples of Life, and they skirted the square so as not to fly straight into the king's procession. Kelan saw a few people duck or run for cover, though the Disciples of Life held impeccable control over their mounts as they descended over the paddocks. He smiled, recalling Niema's discomfort the first time she'd flown on a war drake. Now, she was as comfortable in the sky as he was. As Yala had been.

Kelan caught Niema's eye as she made her way around the square with her fellow Disciples and settled near their group. She'd lost the golden glow that she'd possessed inside the Temple of Life, but she held an undeniable air of power and authority that drew attention. Whispers pursued her, some from Disciples surprised that the Superior had shown up in person. Since she was supposed to preside over the upcoming meeting, Kelan had expected no less.

Saren sidled over to her. "I can't believe you're the new Superior. That means you aren't coming back here to help me attract customers who want to be healed by a Disciple of Life, I take it?"

"You won't have any trouble finding people," she said. "Healers are in high demand."

"True," he said. "Oh, there's Viam. I thought the king would never let her leave his side."

Kelan spied Viam making her way through the crowd to Brenat, who embraced her before they came to join Saren and the others. Viam now walked with a slight limp courtesy of injuries she'd suffered in the battle, but she'd reacted with horror to Saren's suggestion that she claim Yala's cane.

"Aren't you supposed to be with the king?" Saren asked. "You know, advising him not to trip over his own feet or whatever it is you do?"

"He doesn't need advice at the moment." Viam's lips pursed with mild annoyance, but she didn't snap at him as she once might have. "Anyway, he told me to talk to Niema and ask if you'd be willing to come and speak with him after the ceremony."

"Oh." Niema blinked in surprise, her expression more like her old self. "Of course. What's this about?"

"He's trying to foster friendships between all the Disciples and the crown," Saren interjected. "Do I have that right?"

"Is that a bad thing?" Viam said. "He doesn't want to make his father's mistakes."

Saren groaned. "Please tell me he hasn't invited Rafragoria too."

She hesitated. "He did ask them to attend the ceremony, but they said no."

"Does he *want* to get assassinated?" Saren looked incredulously at the others.

"Keep it down," hissed Viam. "No, they're going to sign a peace agreement. The Rafragorians helped us during the battle for Dalathar, you know that."

"Yes, but there were extenuating circumstances." He rubbed a hand over his forehead. "I know it's for the best, but Yala would be pissed off."

Viam sucked in a breath at the mention of Yala's name. A brief silence followed, an anomaly amid the general noise of raucous singing and cheering from the rest of the crowd.

"She'd be pissed off at this revelry," Kelan ventured with a sweeping gesture at the crowd. "She'd say the king shouldn't be wasting his money on a second ceremony when there are more important things for the army to be doing."

"Then she'd agree with the king himself." Viam half smiled, her eyes shining. "*That* would piss her off, no doubt."

"Yes." Niema's own eyes glittered with unshed tears. "She'd understand. I'm sorry I couldn't come to the funeral."

"Yala wouldn't care." Viam sniffed. "She always hated military funerals. And they only added her name to the list of the dead as an afterthought."

Kelan, too, hadn't been able to stay long enough in the capital for the military's collective funeral for the lives lost in the battle, and neither would have been welcome there regardless. That the military had chosen to recognise Yala's sacrifice was a welcome development, but her friends would have to grieve for her in their own way.

"We buried her at her family's old farm," Saren added. "Told the commander her body was lost. She wouldn't have been wanted to be handed to the Disciples of the Flame."

"I know." Viam stifled a sob, and Brenat put an arm around her. "She's the one who held us all together, even after everything we went through. I don't know how to live in a world without her in it."

"I know." Kelan might not have been her squad-mate, but he couldn't entirely wrap his head around the idea of Yala being gone. She might as well have left temporarily, and it was easier to picture her in some distant place, seated on a war drake's back with a weapon in her hand, than it was to imagine her no longer around. "But it's because of her that we can live in this world at all."

"I know." Saren rubbed his eyes, glaring at the Temple of the Flame. "I still don't think she'd want us befriending the likes of them."

"You don't have to," Kelan ventured. "Leave that to

Niema. She has a remarkable knack for doing the precise opposite of pissing people off. Even the king likes her."

"Only because she evicted his unwanted visitor from the palace without burning anything down," Saren said. "Where's he staying now, anyway?"

"In a temporary residence," Viam answered. "He doesn't want to rebuild the palace, but I don't know if he'll win that argument. Everyone thinks we need as much stability as possible, and the palace is a symbol of that."

"Yes, there's nothing more stable than being ruled by a man who let his palace get taken over by Mekan and then burned down," Saren said.

"Saren!" Viam threw up her hands, exasperated. "You know he didn't *want* to take the title back, especially after the last time, but we need someone in charge who isn't…"

"Allied with Mekan, I know," Saren said. "Sorry. Just, you know. Old habits."

Viam nodded, accepting the apology. "I've talked to him. When the country is more stable, we can look at other options. There are certainly other people inside the palace with opinions on his fitness to rule, but nobody has been able to provide a viable alternative."

Kelan had no liking for the monarch either, but he'd have been the first to admit that there were few other contenders here who knew how to run a country. Certainly none of the Disciples qualified.

"And maybe an independent entity isn't who we want in charge either," added Saren. "All this started because Melian tried to start a coup, didn't it?"

"Actually, it started because King Tharen found that island and decided he needed to claim Mekan's power for his own," said Viam. "And we can safely say Daliel isn't going to repeat that mistake."

Kelan had to agree, and seeing the Disciples mingling

with the regular people of the city was an undeniable sign that the balance of power in Laria had shifted beyond recognition.

While there was no guarantee this attempt at cooperation would end any better than Tharen's bid to bring all Disciples under his rule, there was a palpable sense of hope in the air. The sound of laughter and song reverberating through the city carried the sense of having left unspeakable horrors in the past and of facing the bright promise of a new future.

ACKNOWLEDGMENTS

I can't believe we've come this far. When I started writing the Death's Disciple series back in 2021, I never would have believed that this series would reach as many readers as it has. I'm continually blown away and grateful that so many readers, bloggers and reviewers have supported each new release up until the final instalment. Thank you to you all for keeping me going through the long and often gruelling process of writing such a complex and twisty adventure.

I also wanted to offer my eternal thanks to my editor, Sarah Chorn, for championing this series from the start, and to everyone else involved in the process, including my cover artists at Deranged Doctor Design. And I also want to thank my dedicated assistant Mary Fields for keeping my social media functional while I've been grappling with this book.

As always, I owe my thanks to my Patrons over at my Patreon and to everyone who backed the Kickstarter campaigns for all four books in the series, whether you're new to the series or have been there since the start. You made this happen, and I'll never forget that. Thank you all.

ABOUT THE AUTHOR

Emma spent her childhood creating imaginary worlds to compensate for a disappointingly average reality, so it was probably inevitable that she ended up writing fantasy novels. She has a BA in English Literature with Creative Writing from Lancaster University, where she spent three years exploring the Lake District and penning strange fantastical adventures.

Now, Emma lives in the middle of England and is the international bestselling author of over 30 novels including the Changeling Chronicles and the Order of the Elements series. When she's not immersed in her own fictional universes, Emma can be found with her head in a book or wandering around the world in search of adventure.

Find out more about Emma's books at www.emmaladams.com.